A Ch

Mary Mackie is an English writer of over 70 fiction and non-fiction books since 1971. Work of hers has been translated into 20 languages. She is known especially for light-hearted accounts of life looking after a country house for the National Trust.

Also by Mary Mackie

Sandringham Rose
The Clouded Land
A Child of Secrets

MARY MACKIE
A Child of Secrets

🔟 CANELO

First published in the United Kingdom in 1993 by Headline Book Publishing, UK

This edition published in the United Kingdom in 2022 by

Canelo
Unit 9, 5th Floor
Cargo Works, 1-2 Hatfields
London, SE1 9PG
United Kingdom

Print ISBN 978 1 80032 810 5
Ebook ISBN 978 1 80032 498 5

Look for more great books at www.canelo.co

Printed and bound in Great Britain by Clays Ltd, Elcograf S.p.A.

1

For Pat Midgley and all Friends of True's Yard Museum, in appreciation for friendships formed and for allowing me access to the gold mine of information regarding the fisherfolk of King's Lynn. In the event, I was able to use only a little of the material I researched, but it's good to know you're there for future reference.

June, 1919

She found herself walking slowly, deliberately, her hands spread on the perambulator handle while her mind rehearsed the things she would say. She wasn't afraid of him, now. A little nervous, perhaps, but not afraid. No, not any more. Too much had happened. Too many years between.

'Soon be there, my man.' She smiled at the baby in the pram, who was watching the sky and the passing trees with fascination. Such eyes he had. Great big eyes, blue like forget-me-nots, in a merry face given to smiles and dimples. Blessed little man! she thought with a fierce surge of affection. But, even as she smiled at him, her eyes misted and grief cloaked her throat.

She took a quick breath and lifted her chin, looking ahead to the confrontation she had planned. Once, she'd never have dared to do it. But it was a different world now, after the Great War. There'd been Zeppelins in the skies, even here in West Norfolk, and bombs dropped, killing and injuring folk in Lynn – folk she knew. Now, in the aftermath, everything was changed, the old order swept away and new rules applying. So she was coming back to get things straight. Once and for all. For Lily's sake. Maybe both of them would sleep easier after this day.

With the June sun beating down on fields where haymaking was in full swing, she felt hot and over-dressed in her town clothes. She'd wanted to make a good impression, so she'd put on her new 'utility' suit, with a fox fur round her shoulders, and a little black straw cloche with two long feathers. Now she wished she'd at least had the sense to wear her older shoes, for the new, cloth-topped boots, elegant though they were with their waisted heel, were beginning to pinch. She had forgotten just how far it was from the station to the big house. Nor was she as young as she had been when first she walked this road.

Nearly thirty years ago. Lord, but she hadn't realised it was so long. It made you feel old thinking of it. Not that she felt any different. In her head she was still the same Jess Henefer. Still taking it upon herself to set everyone else to rights, as her mother would have said.

Beyond a squat cottage built of the local sandstone, the Lion Gates of Hewinghall stood open. Made of wrought iron, they were in need of a fresh coat of paint – the black was faded, with patches of rust showing. Jess half expected someone to come out from the lodge and challenge her, but despite the drift of smoke from its chimney the place appeared deserted, dreaming among its roses and its tall pink hollyhocks. She walked on, making down the long driveway that tunnelled through a tangle of oaks, their trunks lost in rhododendrons thick with huge purple flowers.

Her keen eyes made out more signs of neglect. The drive beneath her feet was badly rutted and the bushes on either side had run riot, choking other growth and filling the rides. Once upon a time it would never have been allowed to get into such a state, but then a lot of things had been let go during four long years when all the young men had been occupied elsewhere.

The baby jumped and threw up his hands as a shotgun went off in the woods. There was a clatter of wings, another blast of shot. 'That's all right, my little man,' Jess crooned. 'Never you fret. That's on'y somebody as'll be eating pigeon pie for supper. Reuben used to bring me pigeons. Blasted fiddly things they are, too.'

As she started off again, she became aware of the silence in the wake of the shots. It made her think how much more quiet it must have seemed on the battlefields when at last the great guns stopped. Jabez had said how the noise of it got into a man's gut, and into his dreams; the booming and the reverberation, the smoke and the stench. And the fear. Yes, he'd talked about the fear. He'd known it was only fools who claimed not to be afraid. Well, for him the fear was over, and the pounding, and the noise...

They'd printed a nice piece about him in the paper – a piece that named all the boys from West Norfolk reported lost and missing in the final weeks of the war last November. She'd read every word, still feeling numb, still not believing it – Corporal Jabez Henefer, killed in action. And then, reading on, she'd seen another familiar name. It had seemed to leap out at her, trying to tell her something, under the heading 'Tragic death of Baronet's heir'. The few lines of print told of the sudden death, from influenza, of four-year-old Hammond Fyncham Stroud, only grandson of Sir Richard Fyncham of Hewinghall.

That was when she'd written the letter – written it and posted it off before she could change her mind. Reuben hadn't been pleased about it, but she'd managed to convince him that they couldn't deny the baby his rights.

For months, all through the winter and into spring, she'd believed the old man was ignoring her letter; then at last had come the summons, naming time and date. 'Come alone,' he had written. 'Just you and the child.'

And so she had come back...

The view opened out across a field where beet tops showed green, beyond which a small flint church nestled in a hollow of the park. The drive began to climb between pairs of elms, so that the effort of pushing the heavy pram made Jess sweat. She hardly noticed. She was watching twisted chimneys peer over the top of the rise, pushed up by long slated roofs and gable ends, as if the house were rising out of the landscape. Its languid red brick nestled against a backdrop of woods, like an old woman comfortably settled with a shawl at her back to protect her from draughts. The pasture was dotted with oaks and sweet chestnuts, drifted with peaceful sheep. Just as she remembered it.

Behind that stately façade there had always been bustle and noise: family and visitors, servants and horses and dogs and carriages; maids hurrying up and down the bare back stairs; Mrs Roberts red-faced as she pored over her receipts in the kitchen's heat; Bella chasing in the garden after the cat, with petticoats flying, and Lily... Lily in so many moods.

Memories came crowding, each one clamouring for attention, becoming a blur. For a moment she simply stood and let it wash over her, all the different things that Hewinghall had brought her: sorrows and joys, bitter fears and bounding happiness. And puzzles... That was another reason she'd come back – to fit that last piece into the picture. After so long, surely he'd have no reason to refuse to tell her the whole truth?

Today, Hewinghall looked deserted. No smoke twined from its barley-sugar chimneys and most of its windows were blinded by grey shutters, closed behind the glass. Rough pasture grew up to the wrought-iron fence which guarded a gravelled courtyard where, someone having left the gate open, a couple of sheep wandered, chewing at the grass around the bases of two cannon brought back by some Fyncham ancestor from some forgotten war. Dandelions grew at the foot of the fence and the gravel was patchy, worn to bare earth in some places, puddled with dark moss. The whole place wore a sad, seedy air, as if no one cared for it now, as if its master had given up. Perhaps he had.

The front door was made of oak, bleached by the slaked lime with which it had been preserved. It was a solid old door, three inches thick and patterned with wooden knobs to simulate the iron studding of an earlier time. Some of the knobs were missing. There was dirt ingrained on the stone step, and tendrils of weed growing in the cracks. Jess's hands longed to be at those weeds, but instead she reached and pulled the brass bell-pull, noting how badly it needed polish.

You couldn't hear the bell from outside the front door. It rang deep in the house, in the corridors and the butler's pantry – assuming it still worked, Jess thought as she stepped back and looked up at the house towering above her. Big white clouds, gleaming in the sun like fresh sheets on a line, framed the parapets. The place looked to be shut up, except that, on the first floor, the library shutters had been folded back and one of those windows was open to let in the air. She sensed that the old man was in the library – it had always been his favourite room. Perhaps he had watched her approach.

'Maybe he's as windy as we are,' she murmured to the child, but saw that he had settled to sleep. Tucking his cover more closely round him, she stepped up to the door again and pulled the bell with a longer, more determined action.

Standing there, she felt the old house like a physical presence, its brooding silence making her nerves thrum. She wasn't as confident as she'd made believe; underneath her outer composure a pulse beat hectically in her throat and her palms were damp with nerves inside her best kid gloves.

There came a sound from inside, the bang of a door, the shuffle of feet on stone flags and an impatient muttering. Jess heard bolts being drawn, and then a key grating as if it had not been turned in many a long day. Finally, the door opened a few inches and an old man peered out at her, bald, unshaven, wearing a faded tailcoat and a collarless shirt open at the throat.

Longman! She was shocked to see how old and unkempt the butler had grown. She hardly recognised him and, to judge by his suspicious frown, he certainly did not remember her. As he peered at her she decided not to complicate matters by trying to remind him.

'I'm here to see the squire,' she informed him.

The butler drew himself up. For all his untidiness he could still assume a disdainful air. 'The master does not see anyone, except by prior appointment – in writing. Besides, he's already expecting a visitor.'

'That's me!'

Longman looked her up and down. 'Not unless you're Mr Sanders of Truelove, Sanders and Truelove, it isn't. Good day to you, madam.'

As he began to close the door, Jess stepped forward, placing a hand on the smooth, lime-bleached oak. 'I have a letter here in my bag, written by his own hand. I won't be turned away, even if he *have* changed his mind. You now go and tell him I'm here.' She raised her voice, aiming it at the open window of the library above. 'Tell him Jess Henefer is here. Tell him Jess Henefer has come to see him, as arranged.'

The butler's eyes narrowed to a squint. 'You'd better wait. I'll see what he says.' The door closed in her face: manners at Hewinghall had evidently gone to pot along with everything else.

She became aware of the high, piping call of dozens of house martins, darting and swooping through the air above the courtyard, teaching their young ones how to dive after flies. The birds came every year to build their nests in the eaves of the great house, to rear their young and see them fledged. Their departure signalled the end of summer, but you always knew they'd be back. Always, always would. Some things didn't change...

If only it were that simple with people. People changed all the time. As well as you thought you knew folk, they could still surprise you and leave you with riddles.

Ah, there you had the nub of it. It was the not-knowing that niggled, the last questions that needed answers.

Though she'd loved Lily like a sister, she hadn't understood her. No, never. She'd watched, and listened, and wondered, but she'd been an onlooker most of the time, helpless to prevent the onrush of fate. Perhaps, today, she'd finally find the key. Perhaps, at last, she'd solve the enigma that had been Lily Victoria Clare.

She found herself looking back across chasms of time, past memories both bright and baleful, to a winter day when, distant in time but not far from this spot where she was now standing, she and Lily had first met.

How young they had both been, that December day in 1891…

One

Jess hadn't eaten in four days, except for some brambles cocooned in cobwebs. As the cold red sun went down she knew she was near the end of her strength. She forced her feet to move, one in front of the other, heedless of the briers that tore at her tattered skirts and shawl. Branches reached out under cover of the uncertain light, clawing at her eyes and hair. She stopped, startled, as a pheasant flew up and battered away through the wood giving its loud 'cock-uck, cock-uck, cock-uck' of alarm. The panicked beat of her heart in her throat made her feel sick.

Now that she had stopped, her muscles seemed to have seized up; she wanted to move but couldn't. She stood there, shivering with cold, her mouth so dry she couldn't raise a spit, her stomach so empty it was gnawing itself. And then she heard the voice, singing.

It was a woman's voice, a mellow contralto, rich notes floating warm and unearthly on the cold air. Jess thought she was probably dying and angels were coming to meet her – except that she was quite sure her destination would not be heaven. Murderesses did not go to heaven.

The singing went on, coming nearer.

Straining her eyes in the fading light, Jess saw a figure moving behind a network of branches. A dark shape, cloaked and hooded, its arms gestured to emphasise the yearning music of the song. Plaintive words spoke of unrequited love and longing. But they stopped abruptly. The figure threw out its arms in theatrical appeal to the lowering crimson sun and began to declaim aloud:

Gallop apace, you fiery-footed steeds,
Towards Phoebus' lodging; such a waggoner
As Phaeton would whip you to the west,
And bring in cloudy night immediately.
Spread thy close curtain…

7

The apparition was coming closer, her path bringing her round towards an inevitable confrontation. Run! Jess ordered her legs, but they were too weak. They could scarcely bear her weight, let alone move her on.

...love-performing night!
That runaway eyes—

The words broke off as the speaker realised she was not alone. The little dog pattering ahead of her had stopped, with a questioning bark, looking at Jess with its ears pricked. 'Gracious goodness!' the young woman said half to herself. 'Whatever...'

Jess didn't blame her for being startled. She too might have baulked if she had been walking alone in the woods and come suddenly upon a slight, thin figure up to her knees in tangled undergrowth, shaking with cold, ragged as a scarecrow, her hair wild, her face smeared with dirt and old tears. She wanted to run away, as she'd been running for four days, but her feet were rooted to the frozen earth. It looked as though her flight was over, one way or another.

'Are you real?' the gentle, husky voice asked. 'I almost took you for a phantom.'

Jess only stared back dumbly.

Cautiously, holding her heavy skirts bunched away from trailing briers, the young woman stepped nearer. With the light behind her, her face was a pale blur in the shadow of the cloak's wide hood, backed by a network of bare branches with the cold sky above and the red sun hanging low. 'Whatever's wrong?' she asked in concern. 'Who are you? Are you ill?'

Jess hadn't the strength for coherent thought. All she wanted to do was lie down and let exhaustion have its way. She couldn't seem to speak, so she shook her head.

'Oh, but you are!' the other argued. 'You must be. Why... you poor thing, you're frozen!'

The stranger was no more than a girl, younger than Jess herself. Seventeen, perhaps. Her face was a perfect pale oval, framed by the wide hood and by dark hair dressed in curls above her brow. But her eyes... Jess felt the shock like a physical blow.

For, in that pale, pretty face, blessed with a pink mouth and straight dark brows, the eyes that stared back at Jess were not a matched pair:

one was blue like the speedwells that grew by the banks of the Ouse, the other was brown as the moleskin cape that Jess's mother had guarded so jealously from moth. Jess's shaking knees buckled and she sank down among the crackling undergrowth, into a white mist. She fought it, struggling to stay conscious, fearing that if she let go she might never wake up.

The dog barked again, a short, gruff warning. Faintly, as if from far distances, Jess heard another voice, a man's voice. Was it her dad, come to fetch her away to eternal damnation? But no, 'Hardlines' Henefer had had a great loud voice and this man was soft-spoken, with a strange inflection that wasn't Norfolk. He sounded annoyed, demanding to know what they thought they were doing. Then evidently he recognised the girl in the cloak for his voice changed, becoming respectful.

'Oh, it's you, Miss Clare.'

'Yes, Mr Rudd. Only me.'

'You're out late, miss. It'll soon be dark.'

'Yes, I know. I forgot the time. Dreaming, I'm afraid.' Her tone mocked her own frailty, begging his indulgence. 'And I know you've asked me not to bring Gyp into the woods, but he's on his lead, as you can see, and he's really very good – he doesn't bother your birds at all. And look... I found this girl. I think she's ill.'

Jess heard the undergrowth crack and swish as the man forded through it. He bent beside her, examining her with swift efficiency, his hands warm, strong and sure. 'She's not feverish. Just weak. Exhausted, poor lass. What the heck's she doing in my woods?'

'Who knows?' The girl's voice turned gently dry. 'But don't concern yourself unduly, Mr Rudd. She doesn't look as if she's hiding any illicit pheasants.'

'Maybe not. Not yet.'

'You don't seriously suspect her of poaching, surely?'

'I suspect anybody who's in my woods and shouldn't be,' was the response. 'Who is she, any road? She's not from round here. D'you know her, Miss Clare?'

'I've never seen her before. You're right, Mr Rudd, she isn't from any of the local villages. I believe I know most of the people in the parish – even those who don't come to church.'

After a pause, the man said stiffly, 'I'm a chapel man, myself.'

'Oh... Mr Rudd, I didn't mean...' She laughed, a low, melodic sound. 'Forgive me, I had no intention of taking you to task. Gracious goodness, where you worship is between you and your conscience. My only thought was for this poor child. Whoever she is, we can't leave her here. She isn't very big. Can you carry her to the rectory, do you think?'

'You intending to take her in, then?'

'What else should a Christian do, Mr Rudd?' was the grave reply and, after a moment, 'I was a foundling once myself, you know.'

Jess felt herself being lifted, tossed up in strong arms that held her safe and conveyed her along at a steady pace. Her head rested on the man's shoulder and from his coat came a scent of tobacco smoke and open air, perhaps a hint of dog. The smell was alien to a girl more used to the tang of salt and fish, but the man was blessedly warm. His presence surrounded her with a feeling of security so strong that she let go her senses and sank down into darkness.

—

Lily Clare found herself tingling with elation as she led the way along the woodland path. This was real adventure, rescuing a lost girl. The sun dipped behind the horizon, leaving an angry glow on the under-side of a dark wedge of cloud that was sliding across the sky like a shutter. Out of that cloud came the first icy flakes of snow, spitting down through the tracery of branches in the wood.

'Dash!' Rudd said severely. 'Heel!'

His dog, a young, black, curly-coated retriever, obediently left his investigations of the smaller King Charles Cavalier spaniel, only to have Lily's pet follow him, wanting to play. Shivering a little, Lily bent and scooped Gyp into her arms, careless of the mud that got on to her cloak – one of the servants would brush it off when she got home; it wasn't important. 'How is she?' she asked the gamekeeper.

'Passed out. She's near frozen. Who do you think she is, Miss Clare? Some gypsy?'

'Perhaps.' The thought was heady, and at the same time alarming. 'Let's go this way, it's quicker.' Reaching a fork in the path, she held aside a branch while the gamekeeper passed and then she hurried after him, hugging Gyp and trying to keep her cloak from snagging in the undergrowth.

Through thickening twilight they came to a great escallonia hedge whose green branches had been clipped back around a wicker gate which led into the rectory grounds. Beyond the gate a gravel walk ran through an orchard and crossed a plank bridge over a stream before descending through a dense shrubbery to where the house could be seen, its ivy-clad walls half hidden behind clumps of laurel, the whole surrounded by a palisade of towering elms. Rooks circled, cawing, in the last of the daylight, and a ragged skein of geese moved against the flow of slatey cloud as Lily hurried to the front door and threw it open.

'Lily, is that you?' a voice cried, and a grey-haired woman came waddling from the drawing room. 'I've been growing anxious. It's so late I...' The sentence trailed off as she stared through oval *pince-nez* at the spectacle of Sir Richard Fyncham's gamekeeper entering the house – through the *front* door – burdened with a limp body dressed in filthy rags.

'I found her in the woods,' Lily said, setting the spaniel on the parquet floor where he immediately pattered towards the open door of the drawing room.

Oriana Peartree cut him off, using her foot to stop him as she hurriedly closed the door. 'How many times must I ask you to bring Gyp in by the side door when you've been out walking? Look at the mud—'

'Someone will clean it up!' Lily was impatient with such trivial matters. 'Where's Eliza? Tell her I want her to make up the bed in the guest room. And get Dolly to light the fire, and bring some hot water. Come, Mr Rudd. This way.' Realising that Miss Peartree was still standing there, watching her reproachfully, Lily remembered her manners, saying somewhat impatiently, '*Please*, Cousin Oriana.'

'That's better,' Miss Peartree grudged.

The maids were summoned. The guest room bustled with activity. Lily sat on the window seat supporting Jess, helping her drink some water, while Eliza put fresh sheets on the bed and young Dolly built a fire. Leaving the women to tend their charge, Rudd took his leave and headed back to his game preserves.

Miss Peartree stood blinking unhappily at Lily. 'But who is she, my dear? Where does she come from?'

'Does it matter? Cousin Oriana, she's a child in need of help. Isn't that enough? Eliza... fetch one of my warmest nightgowns. Then give the poor girl a good wash. That will make her feel better.'

Miss Peartree still looked worried, but she too was swept up in the need to care for the unfortunate. She went to prepare a hot drink that would soothe and settle an empty stomach.

'Your father wants to see you,' she said when she returned. 'You'd better go at once, Lily Victoria. I'll take over here.'

Reluctantly, but feeling she ought to explain to her father what was happening, Lily returned downstairs.

The Reverend Hugh Clare was in his lamplit study, seated behind a big mahogany desk strewn with books and papers. Quill pen poised in his hand, he had been working on a manuscript which was set out before him. As he gazed at his daughter the expression on his pink face, topped with wispy white hair, was of studied, condescending patience. 'What is the cause of all the commotion, Lily Victoria? You know I'm trying to work. How can I concentrate with—' He winced and glanced at the ceiling as something thumped on the floor above. His study was directly below the guest room, and near to the stairs which had seen a good deal of coming and going on Jess's account.

Knowing better than to argue, Lily said meekly, 'I'm sorry, Papa. It will all settle down very soon, I promise you. I… I discovered a poor child, lost and frozen in the woods.'

'Frozen?' His mouth pursed, bushy white eyebrows lifting as he questioned the exaggeration. 'Then she must be dead. One cannot remain alive and be frozen.'

'Half frozen,' Lily amended dully. Taking her words literally was his way of reprimanding her habit of embroidering some truths with the colours of fancy. 'She was shivering with cold, wearing nothing but rags, and near starved.' There, that was cold fact. 'What was I to do, Papa? I *had* to bring her home.'

In a fleshy face which fell by nature into a misleadingly mild expression, his eyes were pale blue. Frosted blue, Lily always felt. They conveyed permanent disapproval of her. 'I cannot help but wonder where this will end,' he said. 'Birds with broken wings… a sick squirrel… stray cats… and now a lost urchin. The rectory is becoming a home for waifs and strays, Lily Victoria. How can I work amid such cacophony?'

'I'm sorry, Papa.' She shrivelled with misery, feeling as if she had been whipped. Nothing she did was ever right, not as far as the Reverend Hugh Clare was concerned. His work was his all, teaching in the school, or sitting as a magistrate; he spent his spare time writing, another volume of his *Words of Wisdom for the Worthy Poor* or *Sermons for the Good Servant* or whatever it might be. Lily often thought he would have been happier as a single gentleman, living alone in a house where he could demand permanent quiet and solitude. A wife he had tolerated, barely. A daughter was an intrusion.

Except that I'm *not* his daughter! she thought fiercely. Hoorah, hoorah, I am *not* his daughter. And when my real father comes…

When her real father returned, *everything* was going to be different!

'Very well, you may go.' He waved a hand at her, dismissing her with fat pink fingers, his gaze already returned to the manuscript in front of him as he reached his pen to the ink well.

Lily went out quietly. She drew the door behind her, until it was open only an inch or two. Then she closed it sharply, making it bang. A shocked 'Oh, no!' came from the study, and 'Lily Victoria!'

'Papa, I'm so sorry,' Lily apologised, looking round the door. 'It slipped out of my hand. I'm so sorry.' He had, she saw, made a great blot on the page. The pen must have jumped in his fingers, shedding its load of fresh ink. Oh dear… 'I hope you haven't spoiled the page.'

'I shall have to write it out again. Oh, really, it's too bad…'

Retreating, Lily closed the door with extreme care, so that barely a click could be heard. She stood holding the shiny round knob, its brass polished daily to a high golden sheen, while she laid her forehead against the hard, cool wood of the door and closed her eyes, sighing. She hadn't meant to cause him extra work, but she was reduced to playing tricks in order to win his attention. Not that it made any difference. He had never loved her. He never would.

But it didn't matter, she assured herself, straightening her shoulders with a little toss of her head. Her own father – her real, true father – would love her even though she had a wayward spirit and funny, odd eyes. Even though everybody else stared at her, or laughed at her, or feared her. They would learn not to be so unkind when her real father came. He would make them treat her with the respect that was due to his daughter.

'Lily Victoria…' Cousin Oriana was coming down the stairs. 'I thought you said you'd found a child.'

'So I did.'

Oriana Peartree tutted impatiently. 'She's not a child at all – she's a young woman. And she's in a terrible state. Heaven only knows how she came to be in the woods, or what drove her there. No…' As Lily would have rushed past, Oriana grasped her arm. 'No, don't go up now. Let her rest – which is more than I shall do until I know exactly who she is and what she's doing here. I declare, when I came to nurse your poor mama I never dreamed what a legacy she was leaving me. You never stop to think, that's your worst fault. You rush in on impulse and...' But seeing Lily's face she stopped herself and sighed, reaching a mittened hand to pat the soft cheek. 'But there. It's the way you are. And it's caused by kindness, I know. But really... you will have to learn to curb your impulses, my love, or one day something will rebound on you. Badly.'

—

Jess came slowly back to life, disturbed by the sound of someone making up a fire. When she stirred and lifted her head, a small aproned figure went flying away in a panic, shouting for someone named Miss Peartree.

A pale glow came from the fire, where yellow tongues were starting to lap round fresh coals. Otherwise the room was dim, its window shaded by heavy curtains, but a wash of grey daylight crept in through the left-open door. Jess was lying in a bed – a big, soft, warm bed such as she had never slept in before. Even her mother's prized feather mattress had never felt as soft as this, nor the covers so thick and cosy. And the room around her seemed cavernous. She was used to the cramped quarters of the cottage in Salt's Yard, two up and two down – and that was roomy, compared to other homes around the Fisher Fleet. This house must be huge. A mansion. Someone had, she recalled, mentioned a rectory.

Now she remembered being carried here, brought to this room, people coming and going, curious but kindly. Most of them, anyway. The person who had helped her out of her clothes and into a flannel nightdress had not been very kind, or gentle. She recalled a drink of some kind, hot and sweet, fed to her in sips that had trickled all the way down and made her stomach feel warm.

But that had been last night. Now it was morning. Now, she'd be expected to give some sort of account of herself.

Oh, whatever was going to become of her? She didn't ought to be here. She struggled to sit up, planning to leap off the bed and run for it, but her body wouldn't obey her. When she got half up her head went all fuzzy and she felt sick. So she lay down again, sinking into sweet-smelling pillows. Lavender, she thought. It was lavender, that scent. It took her back to the apartment over the butcher's shop in Lynn, where she'd been maid-of-all-work. Mrs Bone, the butcher's wife, a notoriously fussy-particular woman, had had little sachets of dried lavender flowers in her underwear drawers. The memory made Jess's chilblained fingers ache with echoes of soda and endless scrubbing.

Other memories wanted to come crowding on the heels of that first one. Darker memories. Frightful memories. But she blocked them out. She didn't want to remember. Not yet.

Someone was coming, stumping unevenly up the stairs and along the passage, breathing hard as if the climb had tired her. Cowering under the blankets with just her nose showing, Jess peered through her lashes as the woman came into the room and went to the window, to throw back the curtain with a noisy rattling of brass rings. Sharp white light bit at Jess's eyes, making her pull the blankets over her head.

'Well, now,' the woman said, stumping back to the bed. She took hold of the covers and pulled them down. 'Come along, none of that nonsense. I know you're awake. Well, well. So how are we feeling this morning?'

Blinking against bright daylight, Jess peered up into a lined face with oval spectacles perched on a sharp nose. Grey hair was tortured into a frizz of curls on her forehead and near her ears, the rest covered by an old-fashioned lace cap.

'H'm.' A cool, dry hand settled on Jess's forehead, testing her temperature. 'You're a tad feverish. You'll do better with something inside you. Could you drink some tea? I'll send Dolly up with some. Then perhaps a little arrowroot and a soft-boiled egg. Best things for a delicate stomach.'

The young maid, Dolly, brought a cup of sweet tea which helped to restore Jess's spirits. Dolly was no older than Jess's brother Sam, who was twelve years old, but there was another, grown-up maid, with a sniffy looking-down-her-nose sort of sneer on her face. Wearing a more amiable expression she might have been handsome, for she had a good figure and thick brown hair, swept up in a bun. She it was who had so roughly undressed Jess last night.

Sent to assist now with washing the patient's hands and face, the older maid wielded the flannel with a hard hand, evidently furious at being expected to play nursemaid to such a scrawny mawkin.

'Help the girl sit up, Eliza,' Miss Peartree instructed as she returned, accompanied by the younger maid with a breakfast tray. 'Well, plump the pillows properly. Really, do you have to be told everything?'

Eliza's hands bit into Jess's arms, yanking her upright; then the maid bent behind her, pummelling the pillows with unnecessary force, breathing angrily through her nose.

'That will do, Eliza.' Miss Peartree dismissed her with a sharp glance. 'Go back to your duties.'

'Not much wrong with her as I can see,' the maid muttered.

'I don't recall enquiring for your opinion,' said Miss Peartree. 'And I want that drawing room properly cleaned today, not just whisked over. My eyes may not be what they were, but even I could see you hardly touched it last week. I could write my name in the dust under the dresser.'

'I got called away last week!' Eliza protested. 'I never had no chance to go back to it. Do this, do that. I can't do everything.'

'You're bone idle, that's your trouble. I've had maids who could do twice the work in half the time. You're not setting a good example for young Dolly. Unless you mend your ways I may have to speak to Reverend Clare again, and next time he might not be so forgiving.'

There was a silence that tingled, then, 'Yes, Miss Peartree,' but her voice was flat and her expression truculent as she went out.

Miss Peartree sighed, coming to straighten the bedcovers. Light slanted across her spectacles as she looked at Jess with faded blue eyes and forced a smile. 'Well, well. You've a little more colour in your cheeks, I see. Are you ready for breakfast?'

Jess never forgot lounging there in luxury, being waited on and given food like she'd never had before. First came the arrowroot, which tasted strange – 'It's flavoured with sherry wine,' Miss Peartree said as Jess spooned the mixture from a tumbler. Sherry wine! Jess thought in amazement; she wasn't sure she liked the taste. And then there was the soft-boiled egg and the thin bread and butter. Lord, this *was* a dream, but she was determined to enjoy it while it lasted. Sooner or later the questions would start, and then she'd be out on her ear, if not carted off to jail in chains, on her way to the gallows. But for now... for now it was wondersome.

Sitting up, she could see trees beyond the window. Every branch bore a thick layer of snow. That explained the whiteness of the light. There must have been a heavy fall in the night, and from the leaden glower of the sky there was more to come. Were the lanes impassable? Did it mean that any pursuit would be halted?

Did it mean that her escape was cut off?

There was a commotion somewhere below, a dog's excited yipping, and then footsteps on the stairs, someone coming in a hurry. In a whirl of velvet and lace, the girl Jess had encountered in the woods erupted into the room, pink-cheeked and breathless.

'Gracious goodness, why didn't someone call and tell me she'd woken up? I told you I wanted to know.'

'But you didn't say where you were going,' Miss Peartree replied. 'If you go out without saying—'

'I was only in the garden. Building a snowman. The snow's so deep! There's a great curl of it, taller than I am, along near the wall. Like a frozen wave.' She flung herself on to the window seat to peer out. 'Look, you can see the end of it from here. It's wonderful!'

'Yes, dear, I'm sure, but...' Miss Peartree sighed, shaking her head so that the ribbons on her cap shook like wattles on a cockerel. 'Lily Victoria, how many times do I have to ask you *please* not to come upstairs in your outdoor shoes unless they're perfectly clean and dry? And your skirts are all wet. You're dripping everywhere.'

'Oh, what does it matter?' Lily cried. 'Eliza can clean it up. At least I made Gyp stay downstairs.'

'Then I suppose I must be grateful for small mercies. I despair of you, Lily. When will you learn that you're a young lady and not a hoyden?'

'I was in a hurry to see how my foundling was. When I saw the curtains open I—'

'She's hardly a foundling,' Miss Peartree objected.

'I found her, didn't I?' The pert retort was tempered by a smile so sweet that Miss Peartree only shook her head indulgently and removed her spectacles to polish them on a handkerchief.

Lily swirled back towards the bed, pausing midway to stare at Jess. By daylight Lily was even prettier than she had looked in the dusk, a girl on the verge of womanhood, skin white and fine on a heart-shaped face blessed with dark brows and curving pink mouth; hair black and glossy, rioting with a curl that owed nothing to heated tongs. Even so, her beauty was fatally flawed. Jess hadn't imagined those extraordinary eyes, one blue and one brown. It wasn't natural to have such eyes.

Jess had once seen another creature so afflicted – a stray cat that had come scavenging in Salt's Yard. Its fur had been part black and part white, and its eyes had been odd, one tawny and one milky blue. The boys had cornered it and beaten it to death with sticks and stones, calling it a devil's creature. Nobody had tried to stop the killing – there'd been only relief when the thing was dead and thrown in the Fleet for the tide to take.

But, strangely, it wasn't fear that Jess felt now. It was pity. For what she read in Lily's sadly mismatched eyes was uncertainty – a lonely soul crying out for help: despite all her privileges of birth and upbringing, something deep and dreadful gnawed at Lily Victoria Clare. Jess sensed it as surely as she sensed when the wind changed, or the temperature dropped below freezing. It made her want to reach out and offer comfort.

But the moment darted away as Lily tilted her head and smiled a gay smile. 'Welcome to Hewing rectory, my foundling.'

'Lily...' Miss Peartree objected.

'Oh, stuff. Cousin Oriana! I'm only teasing. She doesn't mind. Do you?' Taking the answer as spoken, she went on, eyes sparkling, 'But we can't go on calling you "Mysterious Stranger". What's your name?'

'That—' Her voice cracked on the word and she cleared her throat, trying again. 'That's Jess, miss. Jessamy.'

'Jessamy!' The strange eyes widened, brimming with delight, though she wasn't poking fun, she was more excited and intrigued. 'That's unusual. Most unusual. Did you hear that, Cousin Oriana? Her name is Jessamy. Isn't that pretty?' She turned again to the bed, saying eagerly, 'It's a gypsy name, isn't it? I guessed that—'

'Gypsy? Lord, no, miss!' The notion horrified and insulted Jess. 'Not as I know of, altogether.'

Lily seemed disappointed. Her pink underlip thrust out in a pout. 'Are you sure? I was sure I'd seen you last summer, at the camp on the beach lane. Wasn't it you?'

'No, miss.' Jess shook her head. 'That weren't me. I've never been this way afore.'

'The gypsies come here every few years,' Lily said, unwilling to let go of her theory. 'Don't they, Cousin Oriana?'

'So I believe, my dear,' Miss Peartree said, taking her arm, gently easing her towards the door. 'Now come, we both have things to do, and our guest must have her rest.'

'But I wanted to know—' Lily began.

'I'm sure. And I'm sure she will tell us, all in good time.'

Did Jess imagine it, or was there a hint of warning in the mild look behind the spectacles? Warning, and suspicion? Well, she couldn't blame Miss Peartree, who knew nothing about her save that she was a ragged, starving urchin found wandering the woods. They'd already been uncommonly kind, taking her in, giving her this lovely room and bed, and feeding her. Out of Christian charity, no doubt – this was a rectory, after all.

But, as Jess had reason to know, an outward show of religious belief didn't always guarantee an inner glow of Christian charity. Preacher Merrywest had taught her that.

A cold finger of memory made her shiver and cower down into the warmth of the bed, while the tasty breakfast turned to bile in her stomach. She was thankful that neither Lily nor Miss Peartree knew the truth about her. She must keep it that way, until she found a means of leaving.

Two

Sitting by the fire in the drawing room, with Gyp's weight warm across her lap, Lily tried to read, but the light had grown so poor that she could no longer make out the words. More snow was falling, the clouds closing down to bring an early twilight. With a sigh, Lily put aside her book.

The rectory was a gloomy place, surrounded by towering elms and great laurel hedges which blocked out much of the light even on the brightest day. Sometimes Lily felt the need to hide amid the house's shadows; at other times, when she was plagued with restless longings, she was driven to escape, to go walking for miles through the woods to work off her feelings. Yesterday had been one of those 'other times'. She had needed to be occupied, to give her mind something other to do than brood. That was why she'd been singing, and acting out Shakespeare, though, her mood being what it was, she'd found herself reciting a speech put into the mouth of the lovelorn Juliet. All on account of...

Oh, why couldn't she stop thinking about him?

Grabbing Gyp up in her arms, she wrenched herself to her feet, thinking that she would go mad if the thoughts didn't stop. What could provide a distraction? Then she remembered the girl who lay upstairs. Poor lost Jess.

Lonely and vulnerable herself, Lily empathised with all God's weakest creatures. She had tended birds with broken wings, rescued an injured hedgehog, made pets of farmyard cats. She adored her darling Gyp, a gift from a parishioner whom Reverend Clare had not liked to offend by refusing to take the puppy. And now there was Jessamy.

She glanced across the room to where Miss Peartree was resting on the chaise longue, feet up and a shawl draped across her. Her eyes were closed and she was snoring loudly, sound asleep.

'Hush, Gyp,' Lily breathed. 'Hush. Good boy.' Setting him down on the rug, she straightened, holding her breath as her petticoats rustled.

But Cousin Oriana remained oblivious, even when Lily crept from the room and quietly closed the door.

As she climbed the stairs, moving softly on slippered feet, she heard a sound from above. Gaining the upper hall, she stopped in surprise as she saw Eliza Potts by the door of the guest room. Lily had the distinct impression that the maid had just stealthily closed the door behind her.

'What are you doing?' she hissed, and the maid jumped visibly, turning a startled face. Caught out in something, Lily felt sure. 'Didn't Miss Peartree tell you to leave our visitor to sleep?'

'I was... I was a-goin' to light the lamp, Miss Lily. Thought as how the poor soul might be frit if she woke up all alone in the dark.'

As she moved closer, Lily saw how the maid shrank away, her right hand going behind her back as if to hide something. Lily's suspicions bristled – she'd never trusted Eliza. 'What have you there? What are you hiding?'

'Nothin', miss. Nothin' at all.' Wide-eyed, the maid displayed her hand, spreading her fingers to show she was concealing nothing.

Feeling uncomfortable and foolish, Lily dismissed her and watched as Eliza dipped the merest of curtseys and backed away, keeping her eyes on Lily's face until she reached the door to the back stairs.

Lily shook herself, shrugging off her feelings of disquiet. She simply could not bring herself to like Eliza; that was all it was.

The guest room was lit by dim daylight, huge goose-feathers of snow brushing silently past the window. The lamps had not been lit, so perhaps Eliza had not been in the room – unless she had had another purpose than lighting the lamp. Jess was asleep, twitching restlessly. As Lily watched, she turned over, dislodging the covers from one shoulder and muttering something incoherent. Softly, Lily pulled the blankets up and tucked them round again, as she might have done for a child.

In a jar on the mantel reposed some long spills, one of which Lily lit from the fire and used it to light a lamp. The green glass shade shed a sickly light over the sleeper. Lily had at first taken her for a child of about fourteen, though now it was clear she was at least Lily's age, perhaps older. But she was all skin and bone. Her long, straggly hair was still matted with mud, thanks to Eliza Potts's carelessness, and her hands and face were badly scratched...

Who was she? Where had she come from?

'No!' The denial was spoken so loudly that Lily stepped back, startled. Was the sleeper about to awake? But no, she was soundly asleep, moving her head from side to side, her face contorted as if she were in pain. 'Oh, no...' This time it was a moan. 'Oh, dear Lord. Please. No!' Agitated, Jess thrashed her head, tossed off the covers, turned over. 'No. Oh, no. Don't!' Then, 'Mother!' the desolate cry wailed out. She threw herself on to her back, opening her eyes to stare in confusion at Lily.

Lily's pulses were jumping, mimicking the fear she had sensed in the sleeper. Heart thumping wildly in her throat, she said, 'It's all right. It's only me – Lily Clare. You were dreaming. Bad dreams?'

Jess licked her lips, croaking, 'Yes.'

'What were they about?'

But Jess shook her head. 'Can't remember. Gone now.'

The dreams had been terrible bad and the terror of them lingered. Nor was it all dream. Some of it had been memory. Now, woken by sheer fright, she was confused, trembling and sweating, her mind filled with visions of blood.

As the images faded, she realised she was all wrung out, weak as watered gruel. She didn't know where she was, except that it was a place she didn't know, and standing over her was a beautiful girl holding a green-shaded lamp. Jess had seen her somewhere before. Something about those eyes...

Seeking comfort, her fingers crept to find the thread she'd tied around her neck, with the wedding band on it. It was her talisman, her lucky piece. But she couldn't feel its small weight anywhere, and when she felt further she realised the thread itself wasn't there any more.

The ring was gone!

She half sat up, her head swimming as she patted frantically about her throat and chest, not believing that she could have lost her only treasure, her only means of support, all she had left in the world...

'What is it?' Lily asked.

'My ring. The wedding ring that was round my neck.'

'Hush. Don't distress yourself.'

'But it's gone! Oh, no... oh, no!'

Lily set down her lamp and poured water from the carafe on the night table. 'Here, take some of this.' She sat beside Jess, helping her sip the water, remembering Eliza Potts skulking on the landing. 'We'll find your ring, don't worry. I believe I know where it might be.'

The liquid slid down, cool and quenching, sending bad memories further away. But Jess couldn't think clearly. She was burning up. Her whole body felt slippery and the flannel nightgown was damp with her sweat.

Lily felt the heat radiating at her. Putting aside the tumbler, she laid a cool hand to the dewed forehead and caught her breath. 'You're ill! Lie down, now. I shall send for the doctor.'

'No!' Jess clawed weakly at her arm, protesting. 'No, don't get nobody. I'm all right. That's nothin'.' She didn't want a doctor. Doctors might ask too many questions. Doctors might lead to enquiries, police visits, arrests…

'Don't argue with me,' Lily answered. 'If I say you shall have the doctor then you shall have the doctor. I'll send for him at once.'

In the days that followed Lily was seldom far from the sick room. She tended Jess herself, helping her take sips of water, easing spoonsful of slop into her, sitting with her half the night and even sponging the patient down. She didn't trust the maid to do the job properly. Eliza seemed to resent the cuckoo that had flown into her nest and lodged there, causing all manner of extra work. Besides which, Lily suspected that it had been Eliza who took Jess's ring. But when Lily asked about it Eliza denied ever having seen any ring.

Lily was horrified to discover bruising on Jess's body, which Eliza had failed to tell her about. When Dr Michaels came again, she drew his attention to the marks and he sent her to fetch Cousin Oriana, with whom he had a long, serious conversation that Lily was not allowed to hear. Afterwards, they told Lily that Jess had been badly beaten, more than once, over months. It made her feel all the more protective.

'Don't know why you're botherin', Miss Lily,' Eliza remarked one day as they changed the patient's nightgown yet again. 'You'll get no thanks for it.'

'I don't expect thanks,' Lily said quellingly.

'Just as well.'

'Why, what do you know about it?'

Eliza shrugged. 'I know her sort. Born to badness, this mawther. She're a runaway. Might as well let her die. What've she got to live for?'

'I shall give her something to live for,' Lily replied. 'Oh… be more gentle! You're hurting her. Here, let me.' She pushed the maid aside, feeling her flinch away from the contact. 'Go and… go and make a pot of tea. I'm thirsty.' Sensing the maid's hesitation, she flung round to glare at her in sudden temper. 'Now, Eliza!'

The maid paled visibly, staring at Lily's face, her glance darting uneasily from blue eye to brown and back again, as if afraid their bright regard might bewitch her. 'Don't you lay your spells on me!' she choked, backing away towards the door. She flung up her hand, making a strange sign as if to ward Lily off while she backed towards the door, her free hand fumbling behind her for the door knob.

When she had gone, Lily remained where she was, trembling. Something welled up inside her, escaping in a sound between a sob and a snort. That stupid woman! Stupid, superstitious…

All her life, Lily had been the victim of ignorance and prejudice. Name-calling was the least of the assaults she had borne from other children. Few people were able to look into her eyes without displaying some flicker of revulsion, or fear, or distaste. Even the bishop, meeting her for the first time, had gone pale and covertly crossed himself.

In company she made herself put on a bold face, smiling in order to disguise the pain. But it didn't help. Rejection still hurt. Every time. She had learned to seek solace in her own company, in secret places where she could hide away and dream her dreams, building a make-believe life where miracles might happen and no one would ever dare be cruel to her again. But she couldn't hide away all the time.

'Please, miss.' Behind her, Jess shivered. 'I'm cold.'

Instantly, Lily forgot her own troubles. 'Oh, I'm sorry. How thoughtless of me. Of course…' She made haste to pull down the nightgown over Jess's feet and replace the covers, tucking them round the shivering body. Then she sat beside Jess, looking into a face grown frighteningly thin and wan, shadowed with violet. But for the first time in days the great whisky-brown eyes were lucid.

'Why… you have lovely eyes,' Lily said softly.

Jess stared at her, so weak that tears welled up and dripped down her temples even as she tried an unsteady smile.

'It's true,' Lily said, stroking back the damp, tumbled hair, feeling a brow that was cool at last, the fever gone.

For a moment she had envied Jess her lovely eyes, but only for a moment. Everything else about the girl was nondescript. Her hair was lank and rat-coloured, her hands calloused and hardened by menial work. And yet, contrarily, it was Jess who was regarding Lily with compassion.

Compassion. Not fear or loathing, not superstitious awe, just a soft, friendly sympathy.

'Don't mind that warmint Eliza,' she croaked.

Lily felt something give inside her, a long-locked door springing open as if forced. Hardly able to breathe for fear of dispersing the moment of empathy, she managed, 'You heard?'

'Some on it,' Jess admitted. 'That seem as how I bin driftin', in an' out. Like scum on the tide.'

Lily's tears blinded her. 'You're safely ashore now. You're back with us. Thank God.' She dashed her tears away and got to her feet, going to stir up the fire and add more coal, building it into a blaze. 'I sent Eliza to make some tea. Do you feel well enough to drink a cup of tea, if we make it very weak, with lots of milk and sugar? Cousin Oriana says sugar's good for restoring energy. Oh...' Feeling elated and ready for anything, she flung out her arms and whirled round, letting her skirts fly. 'And then we'll talk, Jessamy. We're going to be friends, you and I. Aren't we? Oh, do say we shall be friends!' She rushed back to the bed, looking down anxiously into the pale face and bewildered brown eyes. 'Jessamy?'

'Yes, Miss Lily,' came the faint answer at last, 'we'll be friends. Long as we can.'

'For ever, Jessamy,' Lily vowed, overcome with emotion. She had found a kindred spirit. A soulmate. Lily would bind her close with silken ties of love and mutual affection, much as she had done with Gyp. For the first time in her life Lily would have a real, true, human friend.

–

Lying staring at the fire, late into the night, Jess wondered if real friendship was possible between two girls as different as herself and Lily. It was a wholly wondersome idea, but surely too many things stood between them – their difference in station, in education… and there was Jess's history. She was a wrong 'un, altogether. How could she ever be a friend to someone as sweet and good as Lily Clare?

Her memory of the last few days was a confused blur, drifting between horrors imagined and horrors remembered, sometimes aware of the people around her, sometimes not. But instinct had told her when Lily was nearby – she had sensed the tender undertow of her concern, and her gentle hands had felt very different from the rough treatment meted out by Eliza Potts. From the maid, Jess sensed only hostility; Eliza was all blank walls and bristles. But what flowed from Lily was warmth and a genuine, unselfish kindness. It had reached even through Jess's worst nightmares and calmed her; she'd always been aware when Lily came into the room.

–

At last there came a morning when Jess was strong enough to protest at Eliza Potts's brusque attentions. When the maid came at her with a flannel, to wash her face, Jess fended off the stubby-fingered hands.

'Hold you hard, Eliza. Give that here cloth to me. I'll do it.'

Eliza relinquished the flannel and stepped back, arms folded. 'Feelin' better, are we? Not afore time, neither.'

'How d'you mean?'

'I mean you've already hung too long on folks' charity. Reverend Clare don't care to have his house turned into a 'firmary. He say so. I heard him. Trouble is, Miss Lily's spoiled. She bring in all sorts o' mangy strays what ought to be left to fend for theirselves. She do just as soon get tired on 'em, howsomever.'

The feeling Jess got from the maid was like a fence of that new barbed wire stuff, all prickly, cold and purple: *Keep off, don't come close.* It puzzled her.

'What now make you so unhappy, Eliza?' she asked.

Eliza stared at her narrowly, suspiciously. 'What?'

'You must be terrible unhappy, to be in such a passion all the time.'

The maid twitched, her fine features twisting into a scowl. She snatched back the wash-cloth, tossed a towel at Jess, took up the bowl of water and emptied it into the slop-pail. 'Sooner you're gone away, Jessamy No-Name, the better I'll like it. Blasted diddicoy.'

'I'm no more a diddicoy than you are!'

26

Flaring her nostrils, narrowing her green eyes, Eliza said, 'Well, I have more to do than tend to a titty-totty mawther what's no better'n she ought to be. I know about you, even if Miss Lily don't.' Going to the door, she looked back to toss her handsome head and add ominously, 'And what I don't know I'll soon fy out.'

Jess stared at the door as it closed, her hand vainly seeking the thread that had held the gold wedding band. It was not her nature to let herself be stepped on. '*Sharp, that's you, maw*,' her dad had observed when she was a little 'un, all elbows and knees, full of whys and what-fors. '*Sharp of bone, mind and tongue. Little Miss Jessie Sharp.*' Sooner or later, she knew, she'd be obliged to sort things out with Eliza Potts.

Eliza must have reported the patient to be recovering, for young Dolly brought up a tray laden with gruel, bread and tea. In Salt's Yard the gruel had been watered to make it go round the whole family; the bread had been hard and usually plain, unless there'd been a scrape of lard to be had, and the tea had been weak, second or third time brewed – when it hadn't been nothing but boiling water poured over burned crusts. Here the gruel was thick enough to chew, sweetened with honey; the bread was fresh, spread with real butter, and the tea came hot and strong, with milk in it. Jess couldn't help but think that she didn't deserve such fortune, and that it couldn't possibly last.

Dolly had just taken away the empty tray when Lily came dashing in to enquire after her protégée's health. Close behind her came Miss Peartree, pale eyes watchful behind glinting spectacles.

'Eliza tells me you're feeling better,' she remarked, folding her hands over her apron.

'Much better, m'm,' Jess said.

'It's "miss". You should call me "miss", not ma'am. My name is Miss Peartree.'

'Yes'm–miss.'

'And what do we call you – apart from "Jessamy"?'

Jess felt her belly turn cold with apprehension. Here it came. She'd known it was too good to last. 'They call me Jessie Sharp, miss.' It was true, after all – her dad had called her 'Miss Jessie Sharp' and because he thought it such a joke other folk had used the nickname, 'times.

Even so, she had a feeling Miss Peartree knew she wasn't being honest. 'Do they, indeed?' the old lady said.

Lily had been hovering, listening anxiously, looking from one to the other, seemingly under instruction not to interrupt the interview. Unable to contain herself, she said, 'Don't you have a family?'

'Not any more.' That was the truth, Jess reasoned. She'd cut herself off from everybody and everything; she couldn't imagine them wanting her back. She was a runaway now, an outcast. Jess No-Name, as Eliza had said.

'No one?' Lily was all sympathy, her strange eyes wide and soft. 'Oh, Cousin Oriana, what did I tell you? The poor thing—'

'It doesn't explain what she was doing in our woods,' Miss Peartree said worriedly. 'Do you have a situation, girl? You haven't the hands of a field-worker. Where do you come from?'

Jess sank further into her pillows. 'I can't say.'

'Why not?'

''Cos you'll send me back. And I en't never goin' back. Never ever!'

'Why not?' Miss Peartree asked again.

'Oh, Cousin Oriana!' Lily cried. 'Don't make her tell you if she doesn't want to.'

'But we must know! Don't you understand? To have a stranger under our roof... You know what your father said. The least she can do is account for herself.'

'Then at least promise that you won't force her to go back if she has a good reason not to.'

Miss Peartree considered that, regarding Jess askance.

To her own surprise, Jess found answers waiting at the tip of her tongue. The truth. Well, some of it. 'I was a maid-of-all-work,' she said, and spread thin hands which still bore scars and calluses and itching red chilblains. 'The missus treated me like a skivvy. She despised me. She said bad things about my family. And... there was a man. He... He...'

A man... Memory came flooding in sickening detail, catching her unprepared. Her skull felt as if it might burst with hate and rage and self-loathing. She threw her hands to her head, as if to hold it together.

'Don't!' Lily cried, her white face mirroring the horror she saw in Jess's eyes. 'Don't say any more. Of course you can't go back. You shall never go back. You shall stay here with us. Shan't she, Cousin Oriana?'

Miss Peartree didn't know where to look. Her spinster's soul was shocked by thoughts of atrocities her imagination was unable to conjure. The doctor had hinted at it, but she'd had to make sure. She took off her spectacles and began to polish them on a corner of her apron. 'We shall see. For now, at least... We shall speak with your father, Lily Victoria. I'm sure he will… when he knows what… oh, dear me, how very unpleasant.'

Covering her mouth with her hand, as if feeling sick, she escaped from a room which was suddenly crowded with unspeakable horrors.

In her wake, Lily and Jess stared at each other wordlessly. Then, unable to face what she read in those wide, questioning, mismatched eyes, Jess turned her head and sank deeper in the bed, taking refuge in weakness.

Lily, too, turned away, her half-skipping step taking her to the window. 'Sir Richard's men have cleared a way through the snow. I think I shall go for a walk later.'

Jess lay silent, her eyes aching behind closed lids, her heart beating breathlessly. The sickness remained, a stagnant pool inside her. She'd never be free of the taint of evil. Never.

'Mr Rudd came earlier,' Lily chatted. 'Do you remember Mr Rudd – the gamekeeper? He brought us a brace of partridge, from Sir Richard. He was asking after you. He's a nice man.'

Impressions came wafting like a cooling breeze on a baking August day, overlaying memories of horror. Mr Rudd. Yes, Jess remembered his soft northern voice; she'd sensed a self-conscious stiffness mingled with innate kindness. Her nostrils recalled the scent of tobacco smoke, and hints of dog, and a musky, elusive odour that was his alone. She knew she would like him, if ever they met. Whether he would like her was another matter. With so many sins blackening her soul, she doubted it.

She looked up, seeing the other girl watching her, her strange eyes troubled. Lily leaned over her, saying earnestly, 'You're safe here, Jess. I shan't let them make you go back, or do anything to betray you. We're friends. There's sanctuary here for as long as you need it.'

'Whatever I've done?' Jess asked.

'Whatever you've done!' Lily declared, then, 'Oh, what do you mean? It wasn't your fault. If your master and mistress mistreated you…'

'Mebbe I've misbehaved, too.'

'I don't care! None of us can claim to be spotless as snow. Even if you have made mistakes, they can't have been all that bad. I simply won't believe it of you.'

Lily's innocence made Jess feel about a hundred years old. 'That's good on you, Miss Lily,' she managed. 'But I 'on't put on your kindness longer'n I have to. Soon's I can get about—'

'We'll discuss that when the time comes,' Lily interrupted. 'You must indulge me, dear Jess. You owe it to me. If I hadn't found you, you might be out there now, lying frozen dead under a mound of snow.' Tossing her skirts, she settled side-saddle on the edge of the bed, giving Jess one of her bright looks. 'Now, tell me… Do you remember anything about our meeting in the woods?'

'I remember you singin'. I thought it was angels comin' for me. You sing beautiful, Miss Lily. Wholly beautiful.'

'I know.' But a shadow veiled her eyes as she said it. She almost turned away, saying no more, but bitter words burst from her: 'It's my "compensation", God's special gift, so Mama always told me. It's supposed to make amends for the curse he put on me, but—' Her eyes filled with helpless tears and she whirled away and ran to twitch the curtain back and stare out at the snow-covered garden and the leaden sky. Her hand on the curtain, clutching the velvet, told of the struggle she was having to contain herself.

Then all at once she spun back to face Jess with a brilliant smile that was pure fakery. 'Gracious goodness, you must have thought me quite alarming. Singing to myself, and quoting poetry. I do that when I'm melancholy. Did you recognise the speech? It was Shakespeare. Juliet's soliloquy in the orchard. "Gallop apace, you fiery-footed steeds…"'

As Jess wondered what Shakespeare might be – and who was Juliet? – the trundle of wheels and the muted clop of hooves on thin snow announced the approach of a conveyance. Exclaiming, 'It's Cousin Oliver's carriage!' Lily flew from the room, apparently to have another view from the front of the house. She returned moments later to announce, 'It's Clemency, and her mother.' Her emotion veered between pleasure and panic. 'The snow can't be as bad as I feared if they've come all the way from Syderford. Oh… I must go down. I'll bring Clemency to meet you.' In the act of rushing away, she paused, her face bright, to add, 'She's my second cousin. I know you and she will like each other.'

The moment Jess laid eyes on Clemency Clare, however, she knew that Lily was wrong. Beautiful though she was, with a fur-trimmed bonnet framing a china-doll face, there was a brittle emptiness behind the façade. Clemency was about the same age as Lily, seventeen or maybe eighteen, young enough still to wear her golden hair loose in waves down her back, but old enough to look at the world through cynical eyes.

She stared at Jess disdainfully, her nostrils flaring with distaste, much as the fishermen of Lynn looked at some ugly specimen of marine life caught in their nets. She directed her conversation at Lily, as if Jess were indeed an animal, or deaf and dumb. Certainly beneath her notice.

'I thought she was a gypsy,' Clemency remarked in her high, clipped voice. 'She doesn't look like a gypsy to me. She's not dark enough.'

Too quickly, Lily said, 'That was a mistake. I only thought—'

'You mean you *hoped* she was a gypsy. You're obsessed with gypsies, Lily. But since she evidently is not a gypsy, then where did she come from?'

'She ran away. Her employers were cruel to her, so...' Lily was twisting her hands together in an agony of confusion. She had forgotten how easily Clemency could reduce her to jelly and make her feel unutterably stupid, but now that they met again the reality was as distressing as ever.

Clemency's cool blue eyes flickered across Jess. 'How can you be sure she's telling the truth? Mama says one can never be too careful with beggars – helpless as they look, they can still steal, or take account of what you have and where it is, for their confederates.'

'Why...' Lily's flailing hands told of her floundering thoughts. It had never occurred to her to doubt Jess's story.

'Oh, really, Lily,' Clemency drawled with weary condescension and the faintest of smiles. 'You are so naive, my dear.' Abruptly tiring of the subject, she turned away, her glance weighing and pricing everything in the room while she contrived to exchange small-talk with Lily.

News of the lost waif had reached the Manor some days ago, it seemed. The Clares had asked among their servants and workers for anyone who had old clothes to spare, and had now brought with them a bundle of garments which, with a little alteration and repair, would provide Jess with a good wardrobe. Most of the clothes were better than she had ever owned, despite their need of a good scrub and a stitch or several.

Even so, grateful as she was for the charity, Jess didn't take to Clemency Clare. Not one bit. Her presence had reduced Lily to stammering uncertainty, so that Jess sensed the years of insecurity which had gone before, with Lily wanting so much to be loved but finding herself barely tolerated. Jess, the onlooker, could clearly see that the uppish Miss Clemency Clare would hardly be happy to have such an oddity tacked on to her family.

The girl was like Granny Henefer's pin-cushion, which the infant Jess had thought the prettiest thing she'd ever seen. But when she'd grabbed it in her small squeezing hands she'd discovered the hidden sharp points. How she had wailed: 'That bit me!' It had been a family joke for years; every time a Henefer dropped something, someone would say, 'Did that bite you, then?' and everyone would laugh.

Now, suddenly, she saw that Lily was looking as if her beautiful cousin had bitten her, colour ebbing and flowing in her face and her unmatched eyes bright with both hurt and panic.

'Staying at the Manor? Is he? You didn't tell me he was expected.'

'I didn't know myself until yesterday,' Clemency replied. 'And really, I can't imagine why it should matter to you if we invite a friend to stay with us for a few days. Just because you happen to be mashed on him—'

'I'm not!' Lily's flush deepened to scarlet.

'Oh, of course you are. The way you blush at his very name... It's quite a joke at the Manor. Dickon can be very amusing on the subject.'

'Dickon's hateful!' Lily muttered.

Clemency regarded her with cool blue eyes. 'When you behave like a lovesick calf you must expect to be teased for it.'

Lily was miserable, her mouth shapeless with distress. As if to cover her lips' trembling she nibbled at the skin around her bitten nails.

'You really are a silly goose,' Clemency told her. 'Ash Haverleigh will never look twice at you. He's looking for a wife with a fortune of her own – and he has an eye for beauty. I doubt he even knows *you* exist.'

Lily chewed at her thumb unhappily, finding no answer.

'Anyway,' Clemency shrugged with a tilt of her fair head, 'I thought it only kindly to warn you that, since we shall be coming to service at Hewinghall until Syderford church tower is made safe again, Mr Haverleigh may be in church with us on Sunday. I trust you will not be so ill-mannered as to stare and embarrass him.'

Watching Lily's face, where every ripple of emotion was written clear, Jess wanted to rear up in her defence. But since it was not her place to interfere she kept quiet, sensing the tug of puzzling undercurrents. Why did Clemency enjoy hurting the vulnerable Lily? Was it jealousy that Jess's intuition scented?

In a small, shaking voice, Lily said, 'I don't do that. I don't stare at him.'

'But, my dear, you do!' Clemency Clare exclaimed. 'You wear your heart on your sleeve. It's so gauche.' Without further ado, she made for the door. 'I must go. Mama and I have to visit old Mrs Witt. She's dying, so they say. A bore, but, well, *noblesse oblige.*'

'I'll come down with you,' Lily offered, anxious to please – anxious to make amends, as if she had been the one to cause offence.

'Just as you like.'

Some while later Jess heard the carriage departing and when Lily returned to the guest room she had rediscovered her smile and was pretending the visit had gone well.

'Clemency's beautiful, isn't she?' she chattered. 'She takes after her father. Cousin Oliver was the handsomest man, in his youth, so they say. But Dickon…' Mention of Clemency's brother made her look a little desperate, her smile straining to stay bright. 'He's more like his mother. The Clares are all such wonderful, clever people. Unlike me.' Pulling a comically mournful face, she tugged an end of her lustrous hair, drawing it out straight before letting it spring back into its natural ringlet. 'Cousin Oliver is Papa's nephew, you know. His father was Papa's older brother.'

'Ah,' said Jess.

'Papa grew up at the Manor,' Lily added. 'He was curate at Syderford in his youth. Then he worked at the cathedral for a while – that's where he met Mama, in Norwich; then later, when the living here at Hewing fell vacant, Sir Gerald Fyncham invited him to take it. After he adopted me I became a Clare, too. We're not really related, not by blood, but they think of me as their cousin, because of Papa.'

It was as if, by repeating that she was accepted by her adoptive family, Lily mesmerised herself into believing it.

'And this Mr Haverleigh?' Jess asked. 'Who might he be?'

'Oh…' Lily coloured, tossing her hair, giving a little laugh. 'No one, not really. Just a friend of Dickon's. No one of any consequence.'

Despite her attempts at self-deception some unhappy thought laid a shadow over her eyes as she turned away, going to stare out of the window.

When she remained silent, Jess said, 'Somethin' wrong, Miss Lily?'

Lily looked round, smoothing the front of her skirt with the palms of her hands. 'It's just... Oh, perhaps I am a silly goose, just as Clemency says. But Mr Ashton Haverleigh...' Misery made her fold her arms round herself as she began to talk of the young man, speaking half to herself as she described him. 'He's the third son of the Earl of Morne. They keep a country house near Fakenham, twenty miles from here, though Lord Morne stays mainly in London. I believe Cousin Oliver acts as his lawyer locally. Mr Haverleigh is a close friend of Dickon's. He comes sometimes to stay at the Manor with the family and...'

Ash... so tall and slender, hair like spun gold, eyes, in contrast, so dark, with the profile of a Greek god, like the statue she had seen on a visit to one of the London museums. She imagined his body to be like the statue's, too – strong and muscled, glorious in its nakedness, but made of warm flesh and blood, not cold stone. The image came to her in dreams and made her wake sweating, restless for something she could not name.

'He *does* notice me!' she cried. 'Oh...' She threw out her arms before wrapping them about her own shoulders. 'No woman with any sense should ever fall in love. Only an idiot would allow herself to come under the spell of one of those cruel creatures we call men. Don't you agree?'

Jess shook her head. 'I dunno, Miss Lily.'

'Haven't you ever been in love?'

To Jess, the question seemed ridiculous. Women like her didn't have time for fancy notions like 'in love'. At Fisher's End you got wed when it was time, to whichever man your family chose for you. 'In love' wasn't part of the bargain, though loving might come later if you were lucky – so Mother had said.

'Never thought about it much,' she said.

Lily seemed surprised, her odd eyes widening with a little pucker between the dark brows. 'How old are you, Jess?'

She had to think a moment to remember. 'Nineteen. Twenty, come February.'

'Two years older than I am,' Lily said. 'Two years and a few months. My birthday's in May. At least... that's what Mama decided.'

'Didn't she remember?'

'No.' Lily looked at her without expression, her eyes – the blue and the brown – hiding all her thoughts as she said slowly, 'The man who

34

hurt you… What did he do? How did he… Can you tell me about it?'

She wasn't prying, Jess understood. She wanted to know because she was seventeen years old, a child becoming a woman. Even so, Jess was not the one to enlighten her. Just thinking about it made her want to scream. Her insides seemed to shrivel, curling up into a tight ball. 'No. No, I can't. I'm sorry, Miss Lily, but you shouldn't ax me such things. Don't let's talk about it, if you please.'

'Very well.' Lily moved away, petticoats whispering under her bustle as she walked across the room and paused a while in silence, then said brightly, 'I know what we'll do – I'll read to you. Would you like that, Jess? We'll have some of Mr Dickens, shall we? I'll go and fetch my book.'

Three

When Lily returned with her copy of *David Copperfield* she settled herself in the window seat, summarising the early part of the story so that she could get to where David met Dora and the ill-fated love story began. That was Lily's favourite part. She acted out the story, using different voices, amusing Jess no end.

After a while, when the story paused between chapters, Jess said, 'Did you name your Gyp after the dog in the book?'

Lily looked up slowly. 'Yes, I suppose I did. Except... Except that I spell it differently.'

'Ah,' said Jess, to whom spelling was a mystery.

Making a little dismissive gesture, Lily said, 'It's foolishness, but... it's short for gypsy.'

'Ah,' Jess said again. 'Diddicoys, we call 'em. You fond of gypsies, Miss Lily?'

'I?' Lily flushed and shrugged. 'Why... no, not especially. What makes you ask?'

'I recall you wonderin' if *my* name come from the diddicoys, and then Miss Clemency say...'

'Oh, that!' She shook back her curls, moving her shoulders as if she felt a draught from the window. 'Gracious goodness, it's getting colder. If it snows any more there'll be *no one* at the service on Sunday.' Getting up, she went to hold her hands to the fire, her back turned to Jess.

As silence stretched, Jess sensed her companion's turmoil. It swirled in the air around her like clouds building for a storm.

Lily looked round, seeing Jess lying against white pillows, looking small and frail – only two years her senior but much older in experience. Lily couldn't match her knowledge of life's mysteries, but she did have secrets she could share. Wanted to share.

Not knowing where to begin, she blurted, 'I do know how it must be for you, because... because I was once a foundling, too.'

Jess's eyes grew round. 'Oh, Miss Lily...'

'It's true!' Lily cried. 'I was found on the doorstep – here, at the rectory. Mama and Papa took me in, and looked after me, but they're only my adoptive parents, not my real parents. You see, Jess... I was stolen away from my real home. I was stolen by the gypsies.'

Pale and intent, Lily came to sit on the bed. Her slender fingers, the nails bitten below the quick, traced patterns on the coverlet while her luminous, mismatched eyes glowed into Jess's. In a compelling, story-telling voice, she began, 'It was late in October, a wild, stormy night, with the wind blowing and rain beating across the windows. When Mama first heard the sound she thought it must be a cat, caught outside in the downpour. She sent Papa to look and... there on the doorstep was a rush basket – such as the gypsies sell – and cradled in it, wrapped in a knitted blanket, was a baby. Me.'

'Oh!' Jess breathed.

'Yes!' Lily responded, her eyes glowing with an inner fire that betrayed her excitement. 'And that's not all. There were other things in the basket – things that prove who I really am.'

'What things?' Jess asked, caught.

Lily jumped from the bed and made for the door. 'I'll show you.'

Jess waited expectantly. She loved stories. Her grandmother had had a talent for telling the most fantastical tales and Jess had loved to be amazed, or terrified, safe on Granny Henefer's knee.

When Lily returned, she brought a small bag made of blue linen, fastened at the neck with black ribbon. Using great care, as if the objects inside were infinitely precious, she pulled open the neck of the bag and let the contents slide out on to the coverlet. There was a gold bangle, and a string of strange, orange-coloured beads.

'I still have the basket, too,' Lily said. 'I'll show it to you one day. The mice got at it, so Papa made me put it away, but I wouldn't part with it for anything. And look...' Sliding her hand inside the bag, she removed a tattered piece of paper with some writing on it. 'This was pinned to the blanket in which I was swaddled. It says...' The tip of a pink tongue came out to moisten her lips before she went on in a hushed voice, 'It says, "Her name is Lilith".'

Jess's eyes widened. Was it possible that it was not just a made-up story? 'Lilith? That's a queer sort o' name.'

'See for yourself.' Lily thrust the crumpled paper into Jess's hands.

37

Jess looked at the scratchy marks on the page, shaking her head. 'I – I can't read, Miss Lily.'

'What?' Lily stared her astonishment. 'Didn't you go to school?'

'Oh, I had some schoolin',' Jess said. 'Learned a lot of hymns, and some Bible stories, and how to mind my manners in front of my betters.'

In the North End of Lynn, the schoolteachers hadn't bothered much with educating girls, except in ways that fitted them for their future as workers and wives. And Jess had often been kept away from lessons because Mother had needed her help with the little 'uns. Fanny ought to have done it, being the oldest, but Fanny had a hasty temper and a way of lashing out, so the gentler Jess had been preferred as a baby-minder.

Truth to tell, Jess didn't understand why folk laid so much store by reading. What you needed to know you could learn by watching and listening, surely? That was the way it had always been done in the North End. And, as her mother had always said, what did a mawther from Fisher's End want with book-learnin'? Books didn't teach you how to crack mussels for bait, or feed a family on a tail-piece of salt herring.

Pushing back her hair with a gesture that also pushed aside painful memories, she said, 'Go you on, Miss Lily. When did you find out, about your bein' stolen by gypsies?'

'Oh, not until I was ten years old. Mama... Mama fell very ill. Lung fever. Cousin Oriana came to nurse her, but we all knew the end was coming. I prayed and prayed for her to recover, but God didn't hear me – he never does answer when I *really* want something.

'Then, one day when her mind was clear, Mama sent for me. She told me then, about my being found on the doorstep. She said she loved me just as much as if I were her own, but since I wasn't really her daughter she felt I ought to know...' Her voice trailed off as her eyes filled with tears and it was a moment before she shook herself and went on, 'So you see... My name isn't really Lily Victoria Clare. I don't belong here. My own father – my *real* father – is a very important man.'

Jess, caught up in her new friend's distress, felt her heart beat slow and heavy, making it hard to breathe. 'Your... *real* father?'

'Yes. My real true father is a great lord, perhaps. Even a prince.'

Lord! Jess thought. Miss Lily was a princess? Lord!

38

'Of course, I can't be sure,' Lily went on earnestly, 'until he actually comes for me. But I know he will come, some day. He's been searching for me all this time – that's why the gypsies abandoned me, because he was after them. But he's still looking for me, and one day he'll find me and take me home where I really belong.'

Jess's brain was beginning to work again. The sensible part of her – the practical, down-to-earth, commonsensical Jess – wanted to dismiss the tale as squit. There were holes in it that a seal might swim through. But it was apparent that Lily believed every word. Her lovely face was alight with faith, her strange eyes intent, holding Jess in a spell.

'And your real name is… Lilith, did you say?'

'That's what it says on the note – I think my real mother may have been of foreign blood. But Mama Clare preferred to call me Lily, and Papa added "Victoria" – he had me baptised to make sure it was done properly, and he always calls me "Lily Victoria". He doesn't like Lilith because… because it has bad associations.'

'How come?'

Lily's brow wrinkled. 'One of the girls, at the school I attend in Cambridge, said that Lilith was Adam's first wife, who turned into a demon!'

'Adam who?' said Jess.

'Adam… Adam and Eve!'

'What?' Jess was astounded. 'Why, whoever say he have another wife? That's a load of old squit. That's not in no Bible story *I* ever heard.'

'No, nor I,' Lily agreed. 'I looked, but I couldn't find any reference to it, and when I asked Cousin Oriana she told me not to talk such nonsense – but you know how obtuse adults can be. Anyway, the gypsies left me other clues to my identity, so my father will know me. This necklace… It's made of amber beads – look, there's a fly caught in one, can you see?'

Peering, Jess could just make out the small black shape transfixed inside what looked like a blob of orange glass. It gave her the strangest feeling, like an icy wind passing over her scalp.

'Amber's a powerful charm to ward off danger,' Lily said. 'It was meant to protect me. And the gold bracelet is inscribed with letters. Look…' She displayed the inside of the bangle. 'An "R" and an "S", all twined together. Those are my real parents' initials, I'm sure of it. I think she was probably called Rosalinda, and my father was Simon, or

39

Stephen. It's solid gold, worth a lot of money. I expect my real father had it made specially for my mother. And here it says "MIZPAH". That's a special love word my parents had between them.'

Jess had heard that word before. '"The Lord watch atween me and thee when we be apart from each other",' she quoted under her breath.

Lily's head came up, her eyes narrow as they focused almost accusingly on Jess's face. 'What?'

'That's what Granny say that mean. She have a brooch with that word on it. Grandad Henefer won it on the coconut shy at the Lynn Mart, when they was walkin' out, so she say.'

'Say it again, what it means,' Lily ordered.

Jess did so, her tone as reverent as her grandmother's had been. Even though Granny Henefer had been a very old lady, widowed for twenty years before she died, she'd never stopped treasuring that brooch.

It was odd that Lily hadn't known what the word meant, and her so educated. Unless… was it possible that, because she hadn't known the word, she'd made up an answer to fit her story?

Jess began to wonder what else Lily had made up.

'You see!' Lily's eyes were round with delight. 'It *is* a special message. A message for me from my real father. It's a promise that he *will* come for me, one day. Oh, Jess… *Now* do you believe you were sent here to be my friend? It was fated – I know it. The moment I saw you there in the wood, I had a feeling our meeting meant something special.'

Though she would have liked to deny it, Jess too had had the strange feeling of being in fate's hands.

'You will stay with me, won't you?' Lily begged. 'And then, when my real father comes, you can come home with me. We'll be sisters. You'll never be cold, or hungry, or ill-treated, not ever again.'

With loving hands, not waiting for an answer, she returned her treasures to their bag and took it back to her room.

Behind her, Jess lay staring at the painting above the hearth – a scene of a mountainside with a great stag poised on a rock. To Jess's eyes the animal, with branches growing out of its head, looked as unlikely as Lily's story had sounded. She thought of her youngest brother, Joe, who'd had an imaginary friend he trailed around with him. Lily's fantasy about her 'real father' seemed similar. But Joe had been four, and he'd grown out of it; Lily was seventeen, nearly adult.

Thinking of it, Jess shivered and huddled closer into her blankets, touched by a chill that was more than physical. She felt as though a great black raven had swooped over the rectory, blurring the daylight and leaving behind it a feeling of menace.

—

On Sunday morning, Miss Peartree decreed Jess well enough to be allowed out of bed to sit by the bedroom fire, well wrapped up in a dressing gown, with a blanket round her knees. The morning being grey and dreary, Lily elected to sit with her; she lingered by the window, staring out, her mind on Ashton Haverleigh.

'This awful mist...' she mourned. 'I can't even see the church tower this morning. Surely the Clares won't come all the way from Syderford?'

Curious to see more of her surroundings, Jess eased herself to her feet and made her unsteady way across to the window seat. She could see part of the garden now, snow-covered humps of shrubs massed around a curve of driveway that someone had roughly cleared. Tall elms loomed black through freezing fog. Off to the left was part of a garden wall, with beside it the great frozen wave of wind-blown snow that Lily had described days before. It was marked by the faint tracks of birds and animals.

'The church is over there,' said Lily, pointing into grey distance. 'It lies beyond a hill, so you can only see the tower from here. In between, the footpath from Hewing village leads across the park.'

The rectory and its garden stood inside the grounds of Hewinghall House, its drive connecting with one of the main driveways. It had been built in a hollow, well out of sight of the big house and thus well away from the church, which now stood isolated in the park.

'The old village was torn down after the Black Death killed all the inhabitants,' Lily said. 'But sometimes, in very dry weather, you can see the humps where the houses used to be, all around the church.'

'Black Death?' It sounded horrible to Jess.

'It was a disease. It wiped out thousands of people in... Oh, ages ago. Whole villages were left empty. Old Hewing was one of them. At least, that's what they say. My cousin Clemency says it's more likely that one of Sir Richard's ancestors had it moved because it spoiled his view. After all, they did build the rectory where they couldn't see it, so—'

'Lily Victoria…' Miss Peartree put her head round the door. 'I shall be leaving for church in five minutes. Be ready.'

Lily was torn in two. To go to church and perhaps see Ash – though he might not come at all, they might none of them come – or to plead a headache, stay away and… Her desire to see him proved strongest.

Cousin Oriana liked to be in church half an hour before the service began, to sit within the confines of the wooden box pew allotted to the rector's family and prepare herself with silent prayer. Lily spent the time trying not to fidget, practising the waltz with tiny movements of her toes, or playing music with her fingertips inside her muff and watching her breath turn to steam as it met the freezing air. The oak-carved pulpit loomed over her like the prow of a ship, carved with a pair of remarkably ugly, squint-eyed angels at whom she pulled faces to while away the time.

As the pews behind her gradually filled it took all her willpower not to keep glancing round to see exactly who was arriving. She was desperate to know whether Ashton Haverleigh would attend the service. Every step and rustle of movement caused her flesh to eddy in flurries of alternate hope and horror.

'Be still!' Oriana Peartree admonished more than once.

But what if he comes? Lily wanted to cry. *And what if he doesn't?* her heart replied. *Oh, let him come. Just to see him…* Not that it would make any difference. Even if he did come, he wouldn't notice her as a person. He never did. To him, she was like a shrub in a hedgerow, part of the scene but not important enough for special regard. Oh, Ash…

In came the tall, slender, slightly drooping figure of Sir Richard Fyncham – alone today; his wife was not a keen church-goer and today had the excuse that her daughter was ill with a feverish cold, though young Bella could safely have been left to the care of her nanny and her nurserymaid. Still, Lily's papa wouldn't dare say anything about it, except to applaud Lady Fyncham for being a caring mother. Which would be sheer hypocrisy when everyone knew Lady Fyncham was more interested in horses than in her sickly daughter.

When the church door opened again, Lily could hardly contain her wildly beating heart as she saw the Clares come in – first the lawyer Oliver Clare, with his wife Letitia, he stocky and handsome with greying fair hair, she tiny, her full figure held in place by corsets. Clemency looked stunning in sherry-gold trimmed with dark fur, and behind her… Nerves made Lily shake so much she dropped her hymnal and had to bend and fumble for it, drawing everyone's attention, or so it seemed: her face burned and the back of her neck crawled with awareness of eyes on her. She dare not turn round again, but from the corner of her eye she watched the family, and a few of their guests, make their way down the aisle.

Ashton Haverleigh was not among them.

After the service, Clemency found time to murmur, 'Ash and Dickon had other things to do. You didn't really expect him, did you? Silly Lily!' Her smirk said she knew exactly what terrors Lily had been under.

How they must have laughed about it, Lily thought bleakly. Clemency, and Dickon, and – yes, probably Ash, too. Once again, she had made a total fool of herself. But this was the last time. The very last time.

–

While she completed her recovery to health, Jess passed her time with needle and thread, making alterations to the clothes folk had kindly sent for her. She hung them in a mahogany wardrobe which had a real mirror – full length! – on its door. Trouble was, the mirror served to show her how gaunt she'd grown, with sunken eyes and lank, nondescript hair.

At night the bad dreams came strong: many times she woke in a sweat after reliving, in awful, twisted unreality, some detail from her life in Salt's Yard. Even by daylight, when she let herself relax the memories were waiting to pounce. Memories, and regrets, and great black gulfs of grief. But she tried not to think about the past, or the future. Each new day, an hour at a time, was enough.

In the week before Christmas she was invited downstairs to help Lily and the two maids put up decorations, with interruptions and interferences from a playful Gyp. How big the house was, how dismal and cold with its polished wooden floors, its dark panelling, and its tall what-nots holding heavy, ugly ornaments and spiky, dark-leaved plants. Supervised by Lily, the maids hung baubles and ribbons, pinned candles on the tree, and draped holly and ivy on most available surfaces.

Finding herself with a few last swags of greenery, Lily decided she would deck her father's study, too.

'He 'on't like that,' said Eliza darkly.

'You mind your own business!' Lily snapped. 'Get back to your duties, Eliza. You too, Dolly. Come, Jess, we can manage alone.'

Jess was awed by the study. It smelled of cigar smoke and was full of books, crammed floor to ceiling on every available wall. Reverend Clare must be a very learned man, she thought. There were books on his desk, too, and pages of close handwriting whose neatness she admired though she couldn't understand a word.

'Sermons,' Lily said. 'They go into books. Like these.'

Reverend Clare wrote books! Lord, what a clever man he must be.

Beyond a broad bay window trees loomed, giants moving in the wind against a darkening sky. To counter the advancing evening a fire flared bright in a marble hearth. It was here that Lily decided to hang a swathe of ivy, but she had barely secured the first frond when the door opened and her papa walked in, startling her so much that she dropped the loose end of the branch as she whirled to face him.

Jess, still by the window and now transfixed by apprehension, was surprised to see how short Lily's papa was, his legs disproportionate to his long, heavy body.

'Lily Victoria?' he began, questioning her presence in his study. Then he caught his breath, his horrified gaze going to the fire. The ivy was smouldering among the coals! Lily grabbed at the swathe, trying to break it off above the burning part, but it only bent and twisted in her hands, sending up smoke that made her cough.

Crying, 'Are you trying to burn the house down, child?' the Reverend Hugh pushed her aside and removed all the ivy from his mantel, bundling it on to the fire and placing the guard across as sparks spat. Brushing his hands together, he afforded Lily a reproving stare. 'I don't doubt you mean well, Lily Victoria. But that is no virtue when your well-meaning actions lead to chaos. If I had not entered when I did the whole house might have gone up in flames.'

Lily looked at the hands she was twisting at her waist. 'Yes, Papa.'

'If only you would *think* first.' He sighed again, and glanced to where Jess was standing. 'Very well, you may go. Both of you.'

Lily trailed away, making for the door. Jess hurried to catch her, but as she passed the rector, he added, 'By the by...'

Jess stopped, not daring to look at him, hardly daring to breathe. Lily had stopped too, and looked round.

'Yes?'

'It would appear that Miss Sharp is recovering well,' he said. 'That being so, I cannot allow her to continue to take up the best guest room.'

Lily gazed at him in dismay. 'You're not going to send her away now? Not at *Christmas*? Papa...?'

He let the silence lengthen, while the last of the ivy spat itself to twisted blackness, then he said, 'I had hoped that you knew better than to raise your voice to me, Lily Victoria. Shouting at your father will not get you your way. Nor does it flatter me to know that you think me so heartless as to turn away someone in need, especially at this season.'

He paused, waiting for an answer, and she, eventually, muttered, 'I'm sorry, Papa.'

Again he let the silence stretch, dominating the room by the force of his presence. Jess could hear her heart like thunder in her ears. What was he going to say? He was as cold as the east wind off the Wash and she began to understand why Lily had had to dream for herself another kind of father.

'Since I'm not insensible of your concern for this girl,' he said, 'I have instructed Eliza to prepare the attic room. Miss Peartree and I have decided that she should be allowed to stay at least until Twelfth Night.'

'Twelfth Night?' Lily was dismayed. 'But Papa... she has nowhere to go! Would you turn her out in midwinter? She has no family to go to. No friends. Oh...' In a passion of pleading, she fell to her knees and would have grasped his hand had he not drawn it out of reach. 'Papa, please... You've often said we need another pair of hands. Eliza's lazy, and slovenly – Cousin Oriana is always saying so. She's sly, too – I don't trust her. And she's always burning the food. If you let Jess stay, she could be our cook. Oh, you can't send her away! It would be too cruel.'

The Reverend Clare looked down at his adopted daughter with faint distaste. 'After Twelfth Night... I shall give the matter further consideration.'

'Oh... thank you, Papa.' She leapt up, and to her own surprise – and his – threw her arms about his neck and kissed his cheek, only to draw back, hotly confused. His expression of astonishment made her laugh even as she blushed crimson. 'I need no more Christmas present than that, Papa. Thank you. Thank you! Come, Jess.'

Reverend Clare stood for a moment with a hand to his cheek, where her lips had rested. Jess darted past him, but turned at the door to see him wipe away Lily's caress with impatient fingers as he went to stir up the fire, destroying every trace of the ivy.

Four

Jess liked her new room. Somehow it felt more homely than the great open spaces of the guest room, though it was cold up there under the eaves, with one little window half covered in ivy. But the bed felt familiar, a wheeled truckle with a hard pallet; there was a chest of drawers and a small wardrobe. What else did she need?

Though she tried not to think about home too much, the approach of Christmas inevitably brought back memories. She remembered lying awake on Christmas Eve, warm in a narrow bed with her sister Fanny beside her, trying to get to sleep; then Matty coming in from an evening with his mates, his boots noisy on the stairs. "Night, maws," he'd say as he went through their bedroom to the back room, where Sam and Joe, equally awake, had whispered their anxious hopes. 'No, he en't bin yet,' Matty would say in his loud, cheerful way. 'And he won't come, 'long as you're awake. If you don't go to sleep you'll get ashes in your stocking.' There'd never been ashes – an orange and a shiny new penny had been waiting by morning.

Suddenly overcome with longing for her family, Jess threw back her blanket and went to stand by the curtainless window. It had small panes of diamond-shaped glass and was hinged at one side, looking out along the walled vegetable patch and the path through the orchard, leading to the woods. A half moon shining on the snow made shadows black while everything else was almost plain as day.

Feeling the need of cold air to clear her head, Jess struggled with the rusty latch and opened the window, lifting her face to the welcome wash of chill night air. It smelled faintly of bonfires and stable dung, with no tang of the sea nor the underlying stench of excrement and fishy decay that had tainted Fisher's End. Distant on the cold night came a sharp, coughing bark. A fox, maybe. Wild things seemed close here.

She distinctly heard the scrape of wood on wood, like a gate closing. The sound drew her attention back to the garden three storeys below.

Moonlight illumined the path that emerged from the orchard and followed the line of the garden wall towards the house, and it was there that a figure appeared. He walked lightly, furtively, in such a way that Jess knew he shouldn't be there, not at that late hour when everyone was asleep. He was clad in a long, heavy cape that might have been leather, with a peaked cap on his head and a bag slung over his shoulder. At his heels, Jess made out the shape of a shaggy black dog.

Somewhere below, Gyp began to bark, alarmed at the approach of an intruder so late at night. The barking stopped suddenly, just as the man went out of sight below, hidden from Jess by the slope of roof under her window. But her ears were sharp and the night so still, the air so carrying-clear, that she heard the scratch of fingernails on glass, the opening of a door, the murmur of low conversation, and then the closing of the door. Someone had let the man into the house!

Realising that she was shivering, Jess closed the window and went back to her bed to lie curled under the blanket trying to get warm.

Next morning, she collared young Dolly and asked about arrangements in the house at night. She learned that Dolly slept in a corner of the kitchen and that Gyp usually spent the night in his basket by the kitchen range. 'Though if he're restless I bring him in along o' me,' said Dolly. 'Eliza get her rag up if he bark and disturb her beauty sleep.'

'Was he barking last night?' Jess asked. 'I thought I heard somethin', after the moon was up.'

'Yes.' But Dolly could no longer meet her eye. 'He musta had a bad dream or somethin'. Eliza come in a-swearin' and a-carryin' on, so I hushed him up and took him to bed along o' me, and there we both stayed till that was time for me to riddle the ashes.' She might as well have added, *and that's all I intend to say so don't ax me no more.* The scarlet in her cheeks, and the guilty sidling of her glance, betrayed her.

'Does Eliza sleep downstairs, too?' Jess asked.

Yes, said Dolly, Eliza had a room off the side passage – a room she kept firmly locked. Eliza was jealous of her privacy. When she'd caught Dolly trying to peep into her room she'd clipped her round the head and sent her off with a flea in her ear.

After what she'd seen last night, Jess didn't wonder that Eliza guarded her right to that room so conveniently near the side door, where she could let a lover in and out without anyone knowing – anyone except poor little Dolly, and light-sleeping Gyp.

–

On Christmas Day, Jess took part in family prayers for the first time. These were held in the staircase hall, where a plum-coloured curtain draped the front door, protecting the hall from the worst of the draughts. Morning prayers usually included all members of the staff and household, though, it being Christmas, on that day the boy Button and the outdoor man Fargus were both absent, having been allowed to take the whole day off. The maids would start their holiday later, after dinner.

There were chairs for Lily and Miss Peartree while Jess, Eliza and Dolly stood behind. They had little to do except repeat 'Amen' in the appropriate places while Reverend Clare rattled off words from behind a wooden lectern. Most of the time Jess kept her head down and her eyes shut, wishing she could pray.

In the kitchen later, in company with the two maids, Jess partook of the luxury of Christmas dinner – carvings from a fat capon, with all kinds of extra trimmings. Eliza managed to be polite, though hardly friendly, still wary of Jess but ready to put up with her for the present.

'Seems as how you'll be joining us for a time, then,' she remarked, helping herself to a sausage.

'Shall I?' Jess returned.

'So I hear. Well, far as I'm concerned you're welcome to the kitchen. Cooks and kitchenmaids get fat and ruin their complexions with the heat. That's not for me. Some day I expect to be a lady's maid, if not somethin' better. Howsomever, don't you never imitate to move into my room down here. That's mine, and mine that will stay, long's I've a place here. Keep you to your attic and we shan't fall out, together.'

She went back to her food, expecting no answer; she had laid down the rules and that was that.

Glancing at young Dolly, Jess encountered a pair of sympathetic eyes in a rosy round face topped by a mob cap. Dolly gave her a little conspiratorial grimace before ducking her head to stuff another roast parsnip into her mouth.

'I know Miss Lily have spoke up for me,' Jess informed Eliza. 'What don't yet fare to be settled is do I accept. I hen't made up my mind.'

'No?' Eliza's green eyes were narrow with suspicions.

'No.' Jess returned the stare levelly, thinking about illicit callers, and her lost ring. Perhaps her eyes reflected the bitterness of her thoughts, for something in her face made Eliza look away.

Eliza and Dolly were anxious to get away, to spend the rest of the holiday with their families, so Jess offered to help with the washing up that piled high in the scullery. Eliza seized the chance to slope off. Tearing off her apron, she threw it at Jess – 'You want the job, do you do it' – and she made for her room off the kitchen passage to change out of her working clothes.

Jess looked at young Dolly, who gave her a wry grin that said much about Eliza's well-known laziness.

'Run you off, too,' Jess said, 'soon's you've put them pans to soak.'

'Not until the work's done,' the child answered, her round, ruddy face set in determined lines. '"You can leave soon's you've washed up the dinner things and set everything out for tea and supper" – that's what Miss Peartree say to me and that's what I'll do, thank you, Miss Jess.'

Jess smiled. 'No, don't call me that. I'm Jess. Just Jess.'

The kitchen was in sad disorder, cupboards crammed in disarray, flour sieves with ladles, copper pans thick with verdigris, mouldy jars of jam shoved behind saucepans. In corners, the flag floor was thick with grime; cobwebs laced the backs of cupboards, and the larder shelves displayed a liberal sprinkling of mouse droppings. Jess was shocked. Neither her mother nor Mrs Bone, her previous employer, would have dreamed of allowing her kitchen to get into such a state.

'I never have no time to bottomfy it,' Dolly said. 'Eliza's alluss chasin' me to do somethin' to help her out and if ever Miss Peartree do mention the cleanin' Eliza alluss make out she're intendin' to do it. Trouble is, Miss Peartree's blind as a bat, even with them glasses, so she don't know how bad it is, and Miss Lily 'ouldn't notice 'less someone drew her 'tention to it.'

'If Mr Clare knowed, he'd do somethin', surely?' Jess said.

Dolly gave her a wondering look. 'Mr Clare don't never come near the kitchen. He're far too busy with more important things.'

'More important? Like what?'

'Well... holy things. Church things.'

'"Cleanliness is next to Godliness".' Jess had had that text drummed into her from babyhood. 'And elbow grease cost nothing. Shipshape, that's the way a kitchen ought to be, all tidied away and scrubbed down.' She rolled her sleeves up further in anticipation. 'Well, Dolly, that look as if you need me here, after all.'

She was tempted to start then and there, but since it was Christmas she contented herself with sitting by the kitchen range, sewing. Having the place to herself was nice. Restful. All she did for the rest of the day was set tea, clear up afterwards and tidy the kitchen, by which time she was ready for her bed.

Boxing Day was another quiet day. As it was a Saturday, the rector had granted his maids an extra day off, but Miss Peartree and Lily both helped Jess with the meals so work was light. On the Sunday Dolly dutifully appeared to light the fires at six a.m. as usual, but Eliza Potts did not turn up; one of her brothers came to inform Miss Peartree that Eliza was 'took sadly with the miseries in har stommick'. Recounting this tale, Lily shook her head, torn between amusement and vexation.

'Eliza's decided that she wants a few days off. Cousin Oriana is always complaining of her, but Papa says unless we actually discover her being dishonest…'

'Like taking my ring,' Jess said.

Lily flicked her a sidelong look and, sympathising, touched her arm. 'Yes. I did ask her about it, but of course she denied all knowledge. By now one of her brothers will have sold it, I expect. I'm sorry, Jess.'

'Well, that don't signify,' said Jess, resigned. But she promised herself that one day she'd get even with Eliza, or at least let her know that she knew who the thief was, even if she couldn't prove it.

Meantime, in Eliza's absence there was work to be done.

—

Later that day, with a rustle of taffeta petticoats, Lily erupted into the kitchen, astounded to find Jess on her knees, scrubbing the floor.

'Jess! Whatever are you doing?'

Jess sat back on her heels, cuffing sweat from her brow. She wasn't sorry for the interruption; she'd begun to regret her impulse to tackle the floor when she realised she was feeling faint, but stubbornness had carried her on.

'This here floor wholly need a good scrub, Miss Lily. That was a disgrace. This whole place—'

'I told you not to do anything strenuous! You're not strong yet. You were very sick, you know.' Holding her skirts clear of the wet floor, she came and hauled Jess to her feet, looking her up and down with a mixture of concern and annoyance.

'I'm all right, Miss Lily,' Jess muttered.

'You're not all right! Look at you – your skirt's all wet – and your sleeves! Go and get changed.'

'What about the floor?'

'It will dry itself.'

'Not in this weather it won't, Miss Lily.'

'Then… then mop it up, if you must. And then leave it. Oh… I shall never forgive Eliza for staying at home today! She doesn't deserve to have a place here.' As Miss Peartree appeared, Lily appealed to her, 'Cousin Oriana, it isn't fair that Jess should have to work so hard. She's still convalescent. If she doesn't rest, she'll be ill again.'

Miss Peartree came to peer into Jess's face, her myopic eyes huge behind the oval lenses of her *pince-nez*. 'H'm. You may be right. But young Dolly can't be expected to do it all, and *I* certainly can't do much more.' Turning away, she grumbled, 'That's the modern world for you – one can't get reliable servants. Nobody wants to work any more.' She blinked at Lily, adding fretfully, 'When I came here it was on the understanding that I was to be companion and nurse to your poor mama, not a general housekeeper, which is what I have become. At my time of life I had hoped to be taking things easy. Oh… yes, yes. Let the girl have an hour or two off. Didn't you say you wanted to go over to the Manor? Why not take her with you? But one day this week, Jessamy, we must have a baking session. We're going to need some pies for Thursday.'

'Thursday?' Lily queried.

'Your papa has been invited to join Sir Richard for a New Year's Eve shoot. We must contribute our share to the luncheon, naturally.'

Dolly was dispatched to alert the boy to harness up the trap, while Lily and Jess put on their outdoor clothes. Jess wrapped herself in several layers; this was the first time she had been out for almost a month and the first stab of the cold air near took her breath away.

The trap had a well-padded double seat and a plain wooden box, with a lid, at the back; this would take extra passengers, uncomfortably, or serve for luggage. The sturdy vehicle came under the charge of the boy, Button, a great lummox of a lad, with enormous ears and a skin erupting with pimples. He was employed to take care of tasks like cleaning knives and boots and he shared the outside work

– care of the rectory's large garden and outhouses – with the man Fargus, who also acted as the rector's coachman. Button and Fargus both slept in a garret over the stable which housed the two horses – the rector's black hackney and the gentle grey gelding, to which Button was evidently attached. Only with reluctance did he hand the reins to Lily, who insisted she would drive. Button had hoped to have that pleasure himself. He glowered at Jess under the peak of a floppy cap, his loose red lips twisting.

'That's supposed to be my job, the trap drivin',' he muttered. 'The mawther could go on the back.'

'She most certainly could not,' said Lily. 'Be off about your work and mind your business, John Button.'

As they drove away, the lad came slummocking as far as the gate, where he stood staring after them morosely.

'He's not the brightest of intellects, but he's harmless,' Lily said, and laughed, her face alight under the sway of a jaunty feather in a little red hat that matched her riding habit. 'Oh... isn't this wonderful, Jess? At last we're off on our own. Hup, Greyman. Hup!'

The horse picked up its pace, heading down a drive whose verges remained deep in spattered snow while the centre was flattened to ice. The temperature hovered just below freezing, the air making Jess's eyes run as she squinted ahead.

The east lodge entry of Hewinghall was flanked by tiny cottages that guarded the gateway. There were three ways into the park, Lily told Jess – this east gate, the main Lion Gates which led to Hewing village, and the smaller, north-facing Park Lodge gate, which gave access to the coast.

'The Fynchams were a very great family,' Lily said. 'They're supposed to go back to the Conqueror. But their fortunes have dwindled lately. Cousin Oliver probably has more money in the bank than Sir Richard, though of course he doesn't have half as much land. Or a title.'

Beyond the gates the lane ran into the village of Syderford, busy with people bundled up against the cold, carts and horses splattering wet mud where salt had been strewn, dogs wagging and sniffing. Shops and cottages stood around a broad triangle of trampled snow – the village green – which bore the remains of snowmen and evidence of snowball fights. At its centre was a well where women stood gossiping, wrapped in shawls, stamping their pattened feet and blowing on mittened hands as they waited their turn to draw water.

'You'll love the Manor, I know you will,' Lily said. 'And I'm sure you'll love Aunt Jane – she's blind and rather lonely, so I visit her to cheer her up. I can go any time – Cousin Letitia has said so. I don't need a formal invitation. Well, I *am* part of the family,' she added, almost defiantly.

In the centre of the village a small, round-towered church bristled with scaffolding. Some of the masonry from the tower had collapsed and gaping holes in the roof were covered with tarpaulins.

'They're having to put up temporary buttresses to keep the tower from falling down completely,' Lily said. 'The church is very ancient. That long row of yews behind it has a romantic history. It was planted by one of the Fynchams of Hewinghall.'

She chatted on as they passed between cottages with smoke trailing from chimneys. The inhabitants, busy about their chores, paused to stare at the occupants of the trap, curious to see the 'lost girl' whom the fey Miss Lily had found.

Jess huddled deeper into her grey-knit scarf – to keep warm, she told herself, though deep down she knew it was also an attempt to hide. Which was silly. No one here would recognise her as the girl who was wanted for questioning after a man was killed in Lynn…

Lily said that in the middle ages the young lord of Hewinghall, as it was then, had fallen in love with the daughter of his neighbour, the squire of Syderford. But the lady rejected him and married his rival, whereupon he decided to plant a yew hedge along the entire border between the two estates, to stand for ever as a symbolic barrier. He began by planting the section behind Syderford church, to shut from view the place where his love had made her vows to his enemy.

Seeing that the hedge extended only half way along the next field, behind the last of the cottages, Jess said, 'I 'spect he on'y got that far afore he come to his senses.'

Lily shook her head, her eyes full of tragedy as she empathised with the forsaken lover. 'The lady died. And soon afterwards the young lord of Hewinghall died, too – of a broken heart. Isn't that sad?'

'Seem to me as how he should have found hisself another lady if that one didn't want him,' said the practical Jess.

'Oh, Jess!' Lily was shocked. 'How can you say that? He died of grief. Of unrequited love. It was *romantic*.'

It wasn't romantic, Jess thought, it was plain foolish. A waste of a life. But it seemed Miss Lily had a fondness for tales with sorrowful endings.

The lane was buried between tall hedges, in frozen ruts of icy mud, hollows filled with stones picked from the fields. Beyond the hedges lay a landscape of rolling fields and hills, white with snow, marked with dark patches of bare trees in many woods and copses designed as coverts for game. They passed a cart fetching mangolds back to be chopped for the cattle, and further on there were two men with guns and dogs, but mostly the country lay quiet, resting between Christmas and New Year.

As they topped a particularly steep hill, Jess had a glimpse of the sea in the distance, a grey expanse whose edges were blurred by mist, blending into a grey sky. The sea…

Riding in the trap had begun to seem like a dream, as if she were floating – past strange fields, along foreign lanes, with never a fishing boat in sight. The few men about were all wearing fustian, or moleskin, most of them with linen smocks over winter warmers. No dark blue ganseys, knitted in the round – knitted tight so they'd be spray-proof. No great thigh-boots turned solid hard by salt. No thick white sea-boot stockings, nor sou'westers and capes, nor seal-skin caps. No smell of salt and sea. Oh, dear Lord. What was she doing here in this alien place? Was this her punishment – exile from everything dear and familiar? Exile for ever?

'The Clares are entertaining guests,' Lily's voice broke across Jess's anguished thoughts. 'A house party – Clemency said the house would be full to overflowing.'

So *that* was what this trip to Syderford was all about, Jess thought – Lily was hoping to find Ashton Haverleigh still at the Hall.

'They would have invited us too,' Lily chattered, both nervous and excited, 'but Papa isn't the social kind. He prefers his own company unless he feels it's his duty to be sociable. Like this shoot on Thursday – he's only going so as not to offend Sir Richard.'

Coming over another rise, she slowed the horse to give Jess a good view of Syderford Manor, waiting in its hollow half a mile away, a glow of unexpected sunlight gilding its red-gold carrstone walls.

'Isn't it magnificent? We shall go in by the front door this morning – usually I go by the side entrance, but as this is your first visit I want you to see it properly. They won't mind.'

Against a flow of snow-clad fields and dark winter copses, the house looked to Jess rather garishly rusty-orange, all turrets and towers and strange outcroppings of red-tiled roofs, standing in a flattened area of land where new gardens were being laid. The new shrubs and trees had had no time to grow and soften the harsh outlines of the buildings. Jess thought it wholly ugly.

'When Cousin Oliver saw what the Prince of Wales had done with Sandringham,' Lily said, 'he decided to make changes here, too. But he didn't just renovate, he built a whole new house. Wonderful, isn't it?'

A humped bridge, of that same orange sandstone, newly quarried with sharp edges, took the trap across a stream and into a semicircle cleared of snow. Brick steps led up to a terrace, flanked by statues – draped female figures which looked, to Jess, like churchyard effigies.

A man appeared to take the reins and help Lily down, doffing his cap to her. He gave Jess a sidelong glance from bold, appraising eyes, but she, feeling her scalp tighten, warded him off with a look as she followed Lily up the steps.

'Good morning, William,' Lily greeted the liveried footman. 'We're here to see Miss Gittens,' and she would have tripped past him had he not bridled, half barring her way.

'I'll announce you, miss.'

Lily paused in surprise. 'Announce me? But I'm family, William – you know that. There's no need for you to trouble. I know my way.'

'Nevertheless, miss. If you'll follow me...'

Nose in the air, he made his stately way across the marbled hall and up the grand, curving stairs. Lily pulled a face at Jess, deriding the man's formality but still upset by it.

'Are the rest of the family at home?' she asked. 'And their guests?'

The footman replied that, apart from Miss Gittens and her companion, no one was at home. Most of the party had gone to catch a glimpse of the Prince of Wales, who was riding out with the West Norfolk hunt; the others had gone walking, or looking at churches and historical sites. None was expected home until dusk.

Lily tried to conceal her disappointment, but Jess saw her droop, saw some of her animation and hope fading. Was that what this trip was about – had Lily hoped to see Ashton Haverleigh?

The inside of Syderford Manor was as sumptuous as the façade, all marble and polished wood.

At a door on the upper floor, the footman knocked and entered, saying, 'Excuse me, Miss Gittens, but Miss Lily Clare is here.'

'Lily?' a soft voice cried, full of pleasure. 'Well, ask her to come in, William. Don't keep her waiting outside like a stranger.'

Slanting him a gleaming look, tossing her dark curls and her long feather, Lily tripped lightly by and ran to greet the old lady who sat in an armchair by the fire.

Miss Jane Gittens, maternal aunt to Mrs Oliver Clare, had lived at the Manor since losing her sight to the cataracts which made her eyes milky-blue. Her skin had that same translucence, threaded with blue veins that were visible even on her scalp, under a fuzz of thin white hair. She looked as if the slightest breeze might blow her away, but her mind was clearly still active and full of fun.

'Come and sit by me, my dear,' she urged Lily, who brought a footstool and squatted by the old lady's feet, holding her hand as they talked. 'Goodness, you're cold! How did you come here? Did you walk?'

'I drove the trap.'

'Alone?'

'No.' Lily sent Jess a laughing look, her humour restored. 'Jess was with me. My foundling. My friend, now. You must have heard about her. I know those sharp ears catch every last word of gossip.'

Miss Gittens tutted, but she was amused. 'You're a wicked imp, Lily Clare. So… tell me all about your new friend.'

So Lily recounted the story, complete with the dramatic embellishments with which she loved to adorn her tales, making everything more exciting and romantic than it really was.

Told to sit down, Jess chose a hard chair by the wall, from where she could watch and listen. Another spectator was Miss Wilks, Miss Gittens's companion, an enormously fat person dressed in unrelieved brown. Most of the time she kept her eyes and her mind on the embroidery frame where she was working a cross-stitch calendar for the coming year, her fat hands deftly forming the daintiest of stitches.

Another occupant of the room was a sleek, cream-coloured cat, its paws and pointed ears tipped with darker brown. It lay curled on an embroidered cushion in a low chair and might have been sleeping except that its ears twitched now and then. Jess had never seen such a cat; it looked thin, but its coat was silky with health.

They rang for tea, which Jess poured. As she placed a cup by Miss Gittens's chair, the old lady put out a cool dry hand and caught her wrist, pressing it in an exploratory manner.

'You're small-boned,' she observed. 'But strong, I'd guess. Good blood in your veins.' Jess sensed another message in the thin fingers that pressed harder before the old lady released her, saying, 'Put some cream in a saucer for Ching,' and returned her attention to Lily.

As Jess floated cream into a bone-china saucer painted with roses, Miss Wilks gestured her to put it by the cat's chair. The animal stretched and yawned, showing perfect rows of sharp white teeth. Miss Wilks watched it, every muscle tensed as the cat got up, stretched, tested its claws on its beautiful cushion and indolently stepped down to lap at its cream. Having finished, it began to prowl around the room, causing Miss Wilks to follow its progress with her eyes, stiffening every time it turned in her direction. She was terrified, Jess saw, and the cat seemed to be tantalising her.

'Here, Ching,' Lily called, rubbing her fingers to attract the cat's attention. It came running lightly and allowed her to pick it up and place it on her lap, where it settled happily, purring under her stroking fingers, much to Miss Wilks's relief.

Lily was relaxed, as she seldom was in company. But of course the old lady, being blind, didn't react in any way to the queerness of Lily's eyes, only to her bright personality, Jess divined. Watching them, she felt protective – the same emotion she had sensed in Miss Gittens.

The feeling was confirmed when, eventually, they took their leave. 'And Jessamy...' the old lady said as Jess was about to close the door. 'Look after her.'

'I will,' said Jess, and for an instant it seemed that those milky eyes actually looked into hers, binding her to that vow.

She didn't see the cat slip out by her feet until Lily cried, 'Ching! Oh, you naughty...' and she hurried away in pursuit. 'He's not supposed to be out unless he's on his leash. Ching! Ching, come here, you wicked cat!'

As Jess was about to follow, a sound from somewhere behind made her pause and look round, puzzled. 'Psst!' the sound came again, and Jess saw a part-open door behind which a shadowy figure lurked. A maid, by the look of her, with her cap pulled down to cover all her hair. From beneath its floppy frill a pair of worried eyes stared at Jess as the figure beckoned frantically – *Come here, quick.*

Glancing around her, Jess saw that Lily was out of sight, gone into the staircase hall still chasing the cat.

'Quickly!' the maid hissed, beckoning again.

She was standing on a landing of the back stairs, bare treads lit by a skylight in an angle of the ceiling. Jess had just a glimpse of it before the maid was thrusting a piece of paper into her hands. 'Give it to Miss Lily,' she whispered. 'Oh— Help!'

A voice from above called sharply, 'Who's that? What are you doing there?'

The voice belonged to Clemency Clare.

The lawyer's daughter came running, in a flurry of petticoats, from the attics above. The housemaid fled down the bare stairs towards the servants' quarters, but it was too late for Jess to escape.

'Aha! What's this?' Clemency pounced on Jess, grabbing for the note. 'Passing secret messages, are you, Jessie Sharp? Well, we'll see...' She scanned the note with growing fury, her face contorting. 'No! Oh, this is too much!' Her hand came out and caught Jess's arm, her long nails biting painfully. 'Who gave you this? Who was it?'

Jess shook her head. 'I dunno, m—'

Next moment she was reeling back, a hand clapped to her stinging cheek. Clemency's hand had moved like lightning. 'Liar! It was one of the maids, I saw her skirts. Damn her! Damn all of you sneaky peasants, working against your betters.' In a passion of spite, she tore the paper across and across, tossing the pieces to scatter across the stairs and float down the stairwell. 'There! And you can tell dear little Lily that if she dares to meet him, I'll... I'll tear her in pieces, too. Mr Haverleigh hasn't the least interest in her. He's only using her. That's what it is. He's using her to make me jealous.' Ashton Haverleigh? Jess thought, outraged – he'd had the brass cheek to leave a note for Miss Lily?

From regions overhead, a younger voice called, 'Clemency? I can hear you talking. It's not fair if you don't hide properly. I'm going to count to a hundred again.'

'I was delayed by stupid servants,' Clemency called back. 'Start again, Evangeline.' In a lower tone, she added to Jess, 'And if you tell about this, you'll be sorry. There was no note, do you understand?' And she went on down the stairs.

As Jess started back along the main bedroom hallway, Lily appeared carrying the cat, laughing. 'You went in the wrong direction! Still, I managed to catch him by myself.'

Ching was delivered safely back to Miss Gittens, and Jess decided not to mention the incident of the note. Mr Ashton Haverleigh had no business sending secret messages. If Miss Lily knew, she'd only be upset. She might even try to contact him. Sometimes Miss Lily didn't think too clearly, especially where this Mr Haverleigh was concerned.

As they drove back across the bridge the light was fading, the clouds closing in, dropping thin fragments of snow. Lily's spirits drooped too, turning to sighs and frowns as she guided the trap along the valley. She showed Jess the site of the old Manor, half demolished now, its stone used for other purposes, its windows gaping, with ivy strangling its broken walls and shrubs growing unkempt around it.

'It was a nice old house,' Lily said. 'But the smoke used to blow backwards down the chimneys, and all the floors creaked. When I was a child I found it quite scary, and even now I hate to come past here after dark. I'm sure it's haunted.'

For her it certainly was haunted. By memories. 'It was here I first saw Ash – Mr Haverleigh. Five years ago, when I was twelve years old and he seventeen. I was sitting on the stairs when he and Dickon came in from riding. They sat in the hall drinking wine, laughing and swapping stories. Oh... he was simply the most amusing, daring, beautiful creature I had ever seen. From that moment on there has been no room in my heart for anyone but Ash.' Lily shuddered with the joy of her confession.

Why did Lily have this obsession with a young man she hardly knew? Jess wondered. She herself had had passing fancies now and then as she grew up, but she'd never believed such feelings were of much account. More important was a man's ability as a breadwinner – whether he could stay sober, be trusted, be faithful. If you wanted a good husband, you chose with your head, not your heart.

'Oh, I *wish* something good would happen!' Lily cried. 'I wish my real father would come.'

Five

Standing on an upturned milk-setting pan in order to see better, Jess watched intently as Miss Peartree measured out flour and kneaded lard in a mixing bowl on the scrubbed table.

'A light hand,' the plump lady declared. 'That's the secret of baking pastry and dainties, so my mother taught me.'

The day outside was dismal, bitter rain turning snow to slush. But it was pleasant in the kitchen, warm from the big fire in the range where Dolly was tending a leg of mutton on a spit. Eliza had returned that morning – been real poorly, she'd claimed.

Lily was in her room, writing her journal. Since the visit to the Manor she had been subdued and Jess wondered what words of misery were pouring into that private diary. Had she herself done wrong to keep her silence about the note Ash Haverleigh had sent? But though she was worried about Lily, she also had other preoccupations now she was a working woman again. She had to learn how to cook with the right ingredients, instead of making only soups and stews with whatever came to hand.

As they worked, Miss Peartree chatted about her life. She had grown up in Bristol, in what she called poverty – only one maid, and a woman to do the heavy work. She and her mother had existed on a pittance, her father having died young, so she had learned to cook at an early age. She had stayed at home, caring for her mother until she died, at which time Miss Peartree had been obliged to sell her family home. The money, invested, afforded her a minimal income; she had lived rather unhappily in various rented rooms until, seven years ago, she had been summoned to Hewing rectory to nurse her cousin, Mrs Hugh Clare, through an illness which had proved fatal.

'My cousin's death left a great gap here,' she said sadly, 'and I was the only one available to fill it. There was, anyway, little for me to return to. My mother gone, my sister married…'

One of the bells on the wall jangled briefly and hung quivering. In the same moment Dolly shrieked and leapt back, clutching her arm – the ladle had slipped, sending boiling fat down her apron and on to her wrist.

'Put that in cold water,' Jess ordered, jumping from her perch to drag the girl into the scullery and pump water over the burn.

'Jessamy! The door!' Miss Peartree cried.

Jess ran for the door, drying her hands on her apron, smoothing it and her hair, fastening the buttons on her sleeve...

In the twilight that pervaded the rectory in winter, the kitchen passageway was the most gloomy of all. Dim daylight filtered through a leaded window above the outer door. It had coloured glass, in a flower pattern, but since the door faced north it seldom saw sunlight and was, anyway, half obscured by the mat of ivy that covered the wall outside. When Jess opened the door all she saw at first was a figure with a hand raised, a dark shadow etched against grey daylight washed with rain.

He wore a thornproof cape that enveloped him from neck to knee, his lower legs being encased in buskins – leather gaiters with buckles all down the sides – his feet in sturdy brown boots. Everything about him looked strong and sturdy. Dependable, her instinct told her as she encountered a pair of lively hazel eyes fringed by thick brown lashes and set in a clean-shaven, heavily freckled face.

The force of her reaction to him shook her – an overwhelming feeling of pleasure, a feeling that cried in glad welcome, *Oh, that's you! There you are at last!* And yet, as far as she knew, she had never seen him before in her life.

He'd just taken off his cap to stand bare-headed under the drizzle of rain. Now he paused, in the act of sweeping back the thick brown hair that grew long on his neck. Dark lashes flickered as he swept a glance over her slight, slim body enveloped in an oversized apron.

Seeing herself through his eyes, she became aware of the mess she must look, splattered with water, dusted with flour. What must he think of her? But as she was stiffening herself defensively his eyes met hers again and, with a pang that was almost physical, she saw that he wasn't amused or derisive, as she had half expected; instead, those hazel eyes held a flattering interest, and a dangerous warmth.

'Morning,' he greeted with a smile that made her feel hot all over. 'Is Miss Potts about? Or Miss Peartree?'

As she recovered her common sense, her barriers went up, strong walls to guard her from the threat he offered to her peace of mind. Whoever he was, however attractive his smile, she couldn't afford to let him near.

'Who is it, Jess?' Miss Peartree called. Coming out of the kitchen, pastry-covered hands akimbo, she added with pleasure, 'Oh, it's you, Mr Rudd. What a day you've brought with you!'

'Aye, it's right lovely weather for ducks,' he replied with a rueful laugh. 'And if it freezes on top of this lot, we shall need to get our skates out.'

'Well, come along into the kitchen and get dry. Dolly, stop fussing over your arm and make a pot of tea.'

Jess stepped back, opening the door wider, wondering why she hadn't realised who he was. Mr Rudd, of course – the gamekeeper – the man who had carried her back from the wood. Remembering his strength and his warmth she avoided his eyes as he stepped inside the house and swirled off his cape. Under it he wore tweed breeches, with a belted tweed jacket with many pockets. Behind him, a shaggy black dog padded placidly at heel, though once inside it stopped to shake itself vigorously, throwing water from its coat. Startled, Jess jumped back, her long, starched apron spattered with muddy drops.

'Dash!' the man admonished, though there was amusement in his voice as he cast a gleaming look at Jess. 'Sorry, lass. Dogs do that.'

'You should have warned me!' She'd never had much to do with dogs and she was wary of this one – and its disturbing master.

'Aye, happen I should.' His eyes were bright with laughter, teasing her. 'Sorry, lass.'

Her awareness of him raised prickles along every tiny hair on her flesh. He wasn't a Norfolk man; his voice had more of the north in it – Yorkshire, perhaps. Jess had met fishermen from Scarborough who had that blunt burr in their voices. Or it might be Lincolnshire. Was he a Lincolnshire Yellow-belly, like her mother?

Evidently the gamekeeper and his dog were frequent and welcome visitors in the rectory kitchen. The retriever stretched out by the hearth, basking in the warmth from the fire; its master settled himself in a wheelback chair, chatting easily and pleasantly to Miss Peartree as Jess tended Dolly's arm, all the time aware of Rudd's bright hazel eyes on her. His interest made her fumble-fisted.

Dolly's burn, though not severe, was bad enough to warrant the use of cotton wool dredged with flour, applied to the spot and bound with bandage. The attention soothed Dolly and soon she was heading away with a tray of tea for the study.

'What a fuss over a spot of hot lard,' Miss Peartree commented.

'Poor little mawther'll feel better for a mite o' fussin',' Jess replied, stretching to replace the tea caddy in its spot on the high mantel. 'She don't get much o' that.'

Miss Peartree regarded her with surprise. 'Perhaps you're right.'

As Jess finally managed to get the caddy back into place, she caught herself sighing, as she often did, over the lack of an extra inch or two in height, which would have made her life so much easier. It hadn't been so bad in the tiny cottage at home, but the rectory kitchen seemed to have been designed for a much larger type of woman. She stepped back, cuffing her brow in relief, and caught a knowing gleam in the gamekeeper's eye. What did he mean, she thought hotly, watching her so close he seemed to be reading her mind? Her cheeks flushed to burning as she tipped her chin at him defiantly.

Miss Peartree was saying to Rudd, 'You remember Jessamy, I expect. Had you heard that she had joined our household?'

'Aye, ma'am, I did hear that,' Rudd replied. 'Took a while for me to realise she was the same lass, though. She looks a lot better now.'

The smiling hazel eyes were directed at Jess again, trying to make her look at him, but she avoided doing so. He made her feel confused and she didn't like being confused.

Handing him a cup of tea, she noticed his hands – strong brown hands, capable, with square-tipped fingers and neat nails, bearing the marks of scratches from thorns and, on the back of one thumb, a healing cut that must have been nasty not long ago. There was also a plain gold band, worn on his little finger. What was that meant to signify? Was he married?

As the last batch of pies went into the side oven, Miss Peartree was called away by a summons from the front of the house, where Lily demanded her attention. Jess found herself alone with the gamekeeper.

'Any more tea in that pot?' he asked.

Fetching his cup meant going near to him again but she made herself move slowly, so as not to trip or fumble, and retreated to the table to pour. She wondered what was keeping Dolly; she ought to have come back by now.

'Well, then,' he said. 'So it's Jessamy Sharp, is it?' She chanced a glance at him, wondering if the question held more than passing curiosity. '*Miss* Jessamy Sharp?' he added.

He was watching her as if deeply interested in her answer. Wanting to know if she was spoken for! What a nerve! Did her flush betray her agitation, or was she already red-faced from the heat of the kitchen? 'Just Jessie Sharp will do.'

As she took him the full cup, keeping her eyes on the level of the liquid, he said, 'I've got something of yours, Jessie Sharp.'

Surprise made her look fully at him, feeling again the jolt of her senses as her eyes encountered his bright hazel gaze. Instinct told her he was as alive to her as she to him.

'Leastways,' he added, 'I think it must be yours. Can't think where else it came from. Have you lost summat lately? Found owt missing, like?'

'Not as I've noticed,' she said, and turned away.

'You sure about that?'

Now that there was safe space between them, Jess tossed her head and spun to face him. 'Do you have somethin' to say, Mr Rudd, then say you your piece. I en't got time for foolery.'

The light in his eyes turned rueful as he shook his head, murmuring, 'Well named, Jessie Sharp,' and to her astonishment he reached for the ring on his littlest finger and took it off, holding it up to her between blunt-tipped fingers. 'What about this, then?'

Jess had thought it was his own ring. It was just a plain gold band, with nothing to distinguish it from others. But now she found her fingers at her throat, remembering a small weight hanging there from a thread.

Rudd said, 'It was on a piece of black thread. Got caught round one of my buttons, the day I brought you back here. I didn't notice it until after I got home, and then I wondered if it could be yours. I couldn't think where else it might have come from.'

Slowly, drawn by the sight of the ring, Jess stepped across the flagged floor to stand by his chair. Rudd too was staring at the ring, but as she paused beside him he looked up into her eyes, his own gaze almost sombre, the teasing light gone. Her senses jerked again as she fancied she was being allowed a glimpse of the real man behind the façade. 'I thought I'd best give it to you myself,' he said. 'You might not have wanted others to know… Is it yours?'

Jess was too full of emotion to speak. She could only nod, and reach out to take the ring, savouring the feel of it against her fingertips, smooth and still warm from contact with his skin. She had feared she might never see it again.

'That was caught round your button?' she managed.

'Aye, it was.' He looked down at his coat, touching one of the buttons fastening a breast pocket. 'This one. You can see how it happened. When I lifted you up...' He pantomimed the action and she, fearing for one panicky second that he was going to take hold of her, backed away and turned her shoulder to him, gazing again at the ring.

Oh Lord... All this time she'd believed Eliza to be a thief and thought hundreds of unkind thoughts about the girl. She'd have to find a way to make amends, somehow.

'I thought it was gone for ever,' she said, slipping the ring on to her own index finger – the only place it would fit and then not very securely; her mother had been a bigger woman than Jess would ever be.

'Where is he, then?' Rudd's north-country tones came close behind her.

The question brought her back. 'What?' She glanced round and saw his frown deepen as he glimpsed the moisture in her eyes.

'Your husband. Where is he?'

It took her a moment to understand what he meant; then she shook her head. 'That's not *my* ring. Not that way. I en't never been wed. Look – that don't fit 'cept on my first finger.'

'Then who—'

'That's my mother's wedding ring. That's all I've got left of her. She give it me when... just afore she died.'

'I see.' Though his expression asked questions it was also full of understanding; then he further disconcerted her by taking her hand, curling her fingers over to guard the ring and closing his own warm hand over hers. 'Then keep it safe, Jessie Sharp. I know how much a keepsake can mean.'

There was sadness in him, buried deep behind those steady hazel eyes, and she could feel the beat of a pulse where his flesh touched hers – her pulse or his, maybe both combined, awfully intimate. For one terrible compulsive moment she wanted to throw herself into his arms and cry her eyes out, and tell him everything that was troubling her.

Panicked by that impulse, she cried, 'Let go o' me!' and wrenched away with a force that made him stare at her in puzzlement.

Before either of them could say or do anything else, a commotion in the passage made Rudd retreat to his chair. Miss Peartree was back, with both Eliza and Dolly, bringing great trails of holly and ivy to throw out. Lily had decided that the festive season was over, here and now. She was getting rid of the Christmas decorations long before Twelfth Night.

Eliza was in a fine temper – any unexpected extra work put her in a passion – but when she saw Rudd her mood changed and she became arch and female, saying pertly, 'Well, Mr Rudd, I didn't know as you was here. You now goin' after them poachers?'

Shaking his head, lounging indolently in his chair, he smiled to himself and reached to scratch Dash's head, saying, 'A poacher'd have to be daft to risk trespassing just before a shoot, Miss Potts. I've got men out all round the woods.'

Eliza tossed her head, her cheeks touched with colour that made her eyes look extra green. 'You must be sure o' your hirelings, if you can afford to spend time here drinkin' tea.'

'I'm sure of 'em,' Rudd said.

Eliza's boldness was tinged with defiance, and Rudd's apparent ease was a camouflage for deeper, guarded thoughts. Sexual challenge thrummed in the air between them, loud as a drumbeat to Jess's perceptions, though obscured by murky undercurrents.

It was only then – and Jess never understood why it had taken her so long to see it, except maybe that she'd been stupefied by her own reactions to the man – only then did she realise the truth of what was going on: the man skulking along in the garden the other night – a man wearing a big heavy cape and tweed cap, with a shaggy black dog at his heels...

Rudd was Eliza's secret lover! The thought made Jess feel numb.

'Get on with your work,' Miss Peartree admonished and Jess hurried to get a pan of hot water from the boiler beside the fire, to scrub the floury table, while Dolly and Eliza made through the scullery to get rid of the foliage in the yard. Later, the boy Button would make a bonfire.

'Speaking of the shoot,' Rudd said, 'that's the reason I called, Miss Peartree, ma'am – to warn you that we'll be beating through the woods here,' a gesture indicated the rear of the rectory, 'probably late tomorrow afternoon. So don't be alarmed if you hear the noise.'

'That's most considerate of you, Mr Rudd,' Miss Peartree replied. 'Do you know yet where you'll be lunching?'

'We plan for the old barn at Soley's Low.'

'Good. I shall send over some of these pies and things. If you're at the big house, you might tell Mrs Roberts I haven't forgotten them.'

'I'll do that.' Easing himself to his feet, straightening his jacket, Rudd glanced at Jess. 'Why don't you send Miss Sharp over with the food? The fresh air might put some roses in her cheeks.'

'She doesn't know the countryside, as yet.'

'She has to learn some time. The way you get there, Miss Sharp, is—'

'Mr Rudd,' Miss Peartree interrupted, 'I'm quite capable of giving the girl directions, *if* I decide she's the one to come.'

He took the rebuke equably, murmuring with a smile, 'My apologies, ma'am,' and made her a little bow, rolling his cap up in his hand as he said to the dog, 'Come on, Dash, we've work to do.' At the door, he paused to add, 'Thank you kindly for the tea, Miss Peartree. Miss Sharp…' His glance was warm, sending messages of hope for future encounters, filling Jess with bitter thoughts of the faithfulness of men. She'd thought him so fine, but it seemed that the charming, smiling Gamekeeper Rudd had sordid black depths to him. Well, why should that surprise her? Hadn't she learned by now that men could wear two faces?

'Good day to you both,' he concluded. 'I'll see myself out.' And he was gone, leaving Jess wanting the answers to a million questions.

'Perhaps I should warn you,' Miss Peartree said as the back door was heard to close, 'Reverend Clare doesn't allow followers.'

'Then mebbe you should tell that to Eliza,' Jess retorted, stung. 'Seem as how there was sparks flyin' 'twixt him and her.'

'Sparks of animosity, Jess. Eliza's father is reputed to be the finest poacher in the district.'

Was that what the undercurrents had been about – poaching? Jess didn't believe it. A blind man would have sensed that other, more intimate tug between them. Eliza was a fine-looking woman and Rudd an undeniably attractive man. And he visited Eliza late at night.

'Is he married?' she heard herself ask.

'He's a widower, I understand. Lost both his wife and his boy to the low fever a few years ago. That was up north somewhere. It was what made him leave and take the job with Sir Richard.' She peered sharply at Jess through her oval spectacles. 'But, as I said, Jessamy, you'd be wiser not to think of him in a personal way. I hope you're not going to turn out to be the flighty sort.'

'Me, miss?' Jess almost laughed.

Something in her great tawny eyes made Oriana Peartree flush and look away. 'No, of course you're not. Forgive me.'

Flighty she was not, nor ever could be. But she was still a woman, despite emotional scars. She kept on thinking about Rudd, both scared and flattered by his interest in her. She knew she'd be wiser to steer clear of him, but she couldn't stop her thoughts from roaming in his direction at disconcertingly frequent intervals.

At least he'd done her a good turn – he'd brought her ring back. She found a piece of ribbon and hung it back round her neck, against her skin where she could feel its small weight brushing her when she moved.

–

When Lily heard that someone must take the pies to the shooting party, she found her own solution: 'Jess and I will both go. Well, gracious goodness, Cousin Oriana, if we send Eliza she'll be gone for hours – you know how she loves to abscond. Poor Dolly's hurt her arm. And if Jess goes alone she may get lost. I can show her the short cut. It will make splendid exercise for us both.'

Miss Peartree could think of no valid objection so they set out, warmly wrapped against the cold. The day had dawned fine and crisp, with pools of ice everywhere, making the going treacherous. Frozen ruts could easily break an unwary ankle, or there was the danger of slipping on the ice so Jess went gingerly, hampered by a heavy basket which banged against her thigh at every step and left her trailing behind an exuberant Lily.

'Of course I know why Papa decided to accept this invitation,' Lily confided at one point as she waited for Jess to catch up. 'One of Sir Richard's friends is a publisher. I expect Papa is hoping to persuade him to take one of his books of sermons. Or perhaps...' Her face was bright with excitement at the thought, 'it could even be that the Prince of Wales will be there. He does sometimes shoot at Hewinghall. Imagine meeting His Royal Highness!'

'I'd be frit to death,' said Jess, panting from exertion.

Lily laughed. She felt elated, though even to herself she hardly dared to admit why – it was because the Clares might be at the shoot, Cousin Oliver and Dickon, and if they were present then, perhaps, *oh please!* Ashton Haverleigh might also be among the Guns.

All morning, at intervals, they had heard the distant fusillade as the shoot progressed. But the lanes themselves were quiet. 'They stop all farm work on shooting days,' Lily explained to Jess. 'The men find work indoors – those that aren't used as beaters. No one's allowed to wander about.'

As if to prove the truth of this, up ahead they saw a man in a labourer's smock, a blue ribbon tied round his arm and another fluttering from his cap. Before he could see them, Lily grasped Jess's arm and pulled her into a field gateway, saying in an undertone, 'That's one of the marshals. They're supposed to stop people getting too close. If he sees us, he won't let us through until the beaters have gone by and then we shall be late. Come, Jess… we'll go across the fields.'

Pushing open the great five-bar gate, she let Jess and the basket through and eased the gate shut, so its noise didn't alert the marshal. Then, laughing and tossing her hair, she strode on across frozen furrows.

Once away from the tall hedges, the countryside opened around them, gentle hills and hollows, snow still lying in sheltered spots, the earth just on the thaw. A hint of mist hovered about the nearby woods, as if trapped by the net of black branches, but the sky was clear, a bright sun making patches of snow look blinding white while shadows lay inky.

In the distance something small and dark, just a shape on the frozen earth, crawled away to die. Seeing it, Lily noted the other wildlife that dotted the arable slopes, partridge, pheasant and hare – oblivious to the fate of their fellows not far away. The unwelcome thought made her hesitate. In her excitement she had forgotten that the whole purpose of the shoot was death for small, helpless creatures. But she mustn't be squeamish. Not today. She just wouldn't think about it.

Her face and hands were cold, but under layers of flannel and wool her body began to glow as she forged on, crossing the field to the far end where it bordered a stretch of open woodland and a track ran downhill. This was the quickest way to Soley's Low, whatever the rules of shooting etiquette might say.

Reaching the track, Lily followed it downhill, keeping the copse on her left, with the sun in her eyes making it hard to see. Ahead of her, in a fold of land, a tall hedge threw a shadow so deep and black that it was some time before she discerned the figures waiting there – the shooting party and their attendants – spread out in a line, waiting, with the dogs straining at leashes nearby.

Then all at once she heard the noise coming from behind the further rise – voices calling, sticks clattering… Lily stopped, dismayed, her mouth dry and her heart thudding. She'd never been this close to a shoot before. All at once she recalled hearing warnings of the dangers of being in the wrong place when a drive began. Why hadn't she thought of that before?

'What is it?' Jess asked, pausing a few yards away as she sensed the waiting tension in both Lily and the men below.

'It's the beaters,' Lily said. 'Perhaps… Perhaps we shouldn't have come this—'

With a mighty whirr and clatter of a thousand wings, with screechings, calls, cryings of pure terror, the birds burst into sight over the hedge. The guns leapt up, muzzles lifting skyward. And *bang – bang – bang-bang* came the staccato beat of sound. Lily cried out in horror and threw her hands to cover her ears as around her birds rained upon the earth, or were knocked off course to flutter wounded into the woods. Others flew on, impelled by fright. And still they came, wave on wave, grey partridge fast and low, pheasants sailing higher, slower, long tails streaming. *Bang – bang – bang.* Dead or dying they fell, crashing into trees and hedges, thudding on frozen ground, some bouncing to waist height with the force of their landing. On the ground, hares ran in panic, and halted, to roll dead. Puffs of blue smoke rose and hung on the still, cold air. Feathers drifted, swinging like fairground boats. *Bang – bang – bang – bang* the slaughter went on while Lily stood mesmerised by horror. Though her fingers stopped her ears she could still hear it, feel it in all her nerves – the noise of guns, the calls of terror.

Jess stared at the carnage in confusion, deafened by the noise. She could see that Lily was upset but she daren't move to help her. If she moved, she might get shot too.

A final pheasant soared, coming over the hedge. 'Fly. Fly!' Lily urged it. Then another gun spoke. Feathers floated free. The bird

71

halted, faltered, veering away from its course towards where Lily stood. With frantic efforts it tried to hold the air, but it was failing, falling. It hit the ground only feet away from Lily, rolled over, fluttering, one wing useless, plumage sticky with blood – trying to crawl to her, begging her to save it. Its harsh cries fell like despair on her ears.

Then she heard someone laugh, and through a daze of sick horror she saw Dickon Clare come running, his stocky figure garbed in tweed with thick woollen stockings. Saying, 'Mine, I think,' he set himself with feet apart, his gun bare inches from the struggling pheasant. The shot boomed, blasting the creature's head. Shreds of blood and flesh and bone spat sideways, splattering Lily's skirts. But when she lifted her shocked face Dickon was laughing, jeering at her timidity.

'You're so mew-hearted, Lily. So mew-hearted!'

Behind him, striding up the slope on his short legs, Lily saw her papa, his pink face flushed with temper. He grasped her arm in hurting fingers that made her squirm, saying in a low, furious voice, 'What are you doing here, Lily Victoria? Does it please you to make me look a fool by displaying your stupidity in front of all these gentlemen? You should know better. You don't get in the way of a shoot. You get to cover. *Behind* the guns. And if you don't know that yet—'

'Oh, come, Mr Clare,' another voice interposed, and through tear-dazzled eyes Lily made out the tall, concerned figure of Sir Richard Fyncham. His deep voice soothed her like balm and from under the brim of a flat cap his pale grey eyes spoke of his empathy. She was thankful he had appeared; she had always thought him a fine, kind man. 'Your daughter wasn't to know the birds would break this way,' he said, laying a hand on the rector's arm so that he released his fierce hold on Lily. 'Are you quite well, my dear?'

'Quite,' Lily lied. 'Yes, quite. Thank you, Sir Richard. Forgive me, please. I—' She felt nauseated, numbed. Around her the dogs were busy, searching the undergrowth for still-warm bodies. Somewhere not far away a wounded hare was crying, sounding like a human child.

Sir Richard sent a summoning look at Jess as he laid a kindly hand on Lily's shoulder. 'Go on with your maid to the barn, and rest there. Come, Mr Clare, let's go back to the others.'

'You're most gracious, Sir Richard,' the rector fawned, giving Lily a last searing glance. 'I can't think what possessed her. She knows better than to interfere with a shoot. What it is to have an ungrateful child…'

As they moved away, Lily was relieved to find Jess, all huge eyes and worried looks. 'You all right, Miss Lily?'

'Yes! Yes, of course. Silly of me. Stupid…' But it wasn't stupid. She just hadn't expected to witness such carnage, not so closely. She vowed she would never go near a shoot, nor eat pheasant, ever again…

An advance party from Hewinghall House had arrived and was setting out the luncheon in the disused barn in a corner of the next field. They had brought a portable stove and already had a huge kettle coming to the boil. A man was broaching a barrel of ale, another setting out bottles of porter and whisky. After the disturbing noise and confusion of the shooting, Jess was glad to get back to something she understood.

'Yes, I shall be all right,' Lily said. 'I just need to catch my breath.'

She paused to watch the Guns come ambling up the hill for their lunch. She had a headache behind her eyes and the thought of food made her queasy, as did the sight of the game cart that waited outside the barn, hung with dead birds and hares – like so many rags on a washing line: for Lily the shoot had lost its glamour. She would never forgive Dickon.

Even as she thought of him, she saw him approaching among a group of young men, waving his hands, miming the action of taking aim as he recounted some heroic moment from the day's sport. Sickened by him, Lily was slow in realising that one of his companions was Ashton Haverleigh.

Before she could move out of sight, their eyes met across fifty yards and she saw his interest quicken. As surely as if he had spoken, she knew he was eager to talk to her. And hadn't she come to the shoot in the hope of speaking with him?

But not now! Not when she felt so unsettled and ill. Not when he had the stench of blood still on him.

Six

The three maids who had walked from the big house with the food cart welcomed Jess among their number. She found herself carving cold roasts and cutting up game pies for the groups of men who came strolling up, and for the ladies whose carriage had toiled along the muddy track so that they might join their menfolk for the picnic.

At the centre of the ladies' group was Sir Richard's wife, Lady Maud Fyncham, a tall, plain woman, with hair like new chestnuts. She and her husband were matched in height, both thin and angular, more like siblings than spouses. 'First cousins,' one of the maids vouchsafed. The couple had one child, a five-year-old daughter named Bella, who was 'not strong. Else they might have brung her along today – she're the apple of Sir Richard's eye. He love to show her off. He ought to have more little 'uns, but since Lady Maud have shut him out of her bedroom...' Before she could impart any more gossip, she was called away.

The gentry, including Reverend Clare, kept to one side of the barn, while tenant farmers and tradesmen gathered at the other; outside, the beaters and keepers flirted with the Hewinghall maids amid much laughter and good-natured teasing. Among the company, Lily remained apart, as if trying to hide herself, Jess thought. Lily was habitually afraid of curiosity, or censure, or condescension – but on that day she was also trying to avoid the fair young man with the dark brown eyes.

For his part, though he kept glancing in her direction he made no attempt to join her. Jess had no doubt who he was: she'd heard one of his companions call him 'Ash'. Well, he was handsome, true enough. But Jess noted a weakness about his mouth, and shadows under his eyes. He looked a dissolute young man – 'nowt of a mucher' her mother would have said – and the group about him the same. Lily was better off without him.

The head gamekeeper, Rudd, came up to speak to the squire. Jess had been watching for him, but the sight of him still surprised and unsettled her – Rudd, with the cold sunlight striking red lights out of his brown hair, his freckled face alive with concentration. This was his day, the success of the shoot his responsibility. When he moved on, Jess noticed how everyone – from the gentry to the youngest beater – treated him with respect. Obviously Gamekeeper Rudd was a person of some consequence.

When he noticed her, his face lit in a way that both flattered and disturbed her. Breaking off from the group with whom he was chatting, he made a bee-line for the buffet table.

'Well, Miss Sharp,' he greeted her, his easy smile not entirely masking a touch of censure in those hazel eyes. 'So you managed to find your way here?'

'That weren't difficult,' Jess said.

'Pity you didn't come round by the lane, though. Weren't there any marshals about to stop you coming over the field?'

'Not as we saw,' Jess replied, stiff in defence of Lily.

'That's rum. I put some good men on duty in the lane.'

'Then they must have been takin' a nap,' Jess said.

Fixing her with gleaming eyes, Rudd decided to let it rest. 'Anyway, I'm right glad you made it. How're you enjoying yourself?'

'I come to work, not to gallivant,' she replied.

The gossipy Hewinghall maid stepped in, handing Rudd a large slice of game pie with a merry 'Got to keep up yore strength today, Mr Rudd!'

'Every day, Sal,' he responded with a grin. 'Every day!'

As he turned away, Sal gave Jess a sidelong look. 'Proper cross-patch, en't we? What's wrong wi' you? Most gals'd be glad to have Reuben Rudd pass the time o' day.'

'Mebbe I'm choosy,' Jess said loftily.

–

Lily had sought sanctuary in a shadowy corner of the barn. She envied Jess, whose diminutive figure she saw flitting here and there, busy as ever. Lucky Jess. She at least had a place in life. Which was more than Lily had. She didn't belong with any of the groups. She was an outcast with her mismatched eyes and her silly, sensitive nature.

Realising she was swimming into the deeps of self-pity, Lily shook herself and slipped out through a gap in the back wall of the barn, hoping to find some peace and quiet to ease her headache.

It was cold in the lee of the barn, deep shadow highlighted by frost, with the woods growing close. The broken walls of an old lean-to stood knee-deep in nettles and scattered bricks, providing a seat of sorts. Lily sat huddled in her coat and muff, eyes closed, thoughts in disarray as she breathed in the iced air and felt her head throb.

'Miss Clare?'

The voice startled her. As she looked up, pain lanced through her brain and she pressed her fingers to her temple, staring through misted eyes at the elegant young man who was the focus of her dearest dreams.

'Are you unwell?'

Slanting sunlight coming over the barn touched his hair to bright gold, and his dark eyes were full of concern as he gazed at her.

'I have a headache,' she croaked, her mouth dry with panic. She felt trapped, like a rabbit before a gun. Like that poor pheasant.

'Is there anything I can do for you?'

'No! No – thank you.' She could hardly breathe. She felt crowded by his physical presence. Much as she had dreamed of an encounter like this, the reality was alarming. 'Mr Haverleigh, please, I—'

'Did you get my note?' he asked.

Note? Lily's mind blanked with shock. She peered up at him under a shading hand, eyes aching, head pounding. 'Note?'

'I asked you to meet me. I wanted—'

Dismay brought her to her feet, where she stood trembling. 'And you expected me to come? Mr Haverleigh, whatever—'

She stopped, because Dickon Clare had stepped into sight, coming round the corner of the barn behind Ash. He raised his brows at her, a knowing smile making his eyes gleam. Alerted by the expression on her face, Ashton turned and, seeing Dickon, uttered a muffled oath.

'Forgive my intruding,' Dickon murmured, amused. 'We're moving off now, Haverleigh. Come on, leave the wench alone. We've other game to hunt. She'll keep.' He leered at Lily. 'Won't you, Lily Vee?'

'Don't call me that!'

'Now look here, Clare,' Ash began in a bored voice, 'this was hardly an assignation. I merely wanted to talk to—'

'Of course,' said Dickon, but his grin said otherwise. 'Oh, come, dear fellow, you don't have to explain to me.' With an insolence

76

calculated to insult, he looked Lily up and down. 'She *is* growing into a tasty little morsel. But now is not the time. Are you coming for the next drive, or shall I tell them you've found more interesting pursuits?'

Sighing his irritation, Ash flashed a look over his shoulder. He was going to say something, but changed his mind and, with a gesture of dismissal, strode away, brushing past Dickon, who grinned at Lily, tipped his hat in mock courtesy, and turned to follow his friend.

Somewhere a woodpecker was hammering, and a great tit flitted up to perch on a twig and sing his song. But otherwise the wood behind the barn was still and silent. Lily could feel the emptiness in it. The game was all fled, or dead. Like her hopes.

'Miss Lily?' Jess stepped out from the barn, from where she had witnessed the tail-end of the encounter.

'We're going home,' was all Lily said. She was pale as death, white to the lips. 'Get your basket, Jess. I want to go home. Now.'

–

Lily sat at the piano, singing songs with words of unremitting gloom in between staring out at the grey afternoon. She kept thinking about Ash, kept seeing the poor pheasant being blasted to bloody shreds by Dickon's gun. She hated Dickon. How could Ash be his friend? Sunk in depthless misery, she was surely dying of unrequited love and disappointed dreams.

But, even as she despaired, hope was still flickering. Suppose Ash did have some important message to give her? What might he have said, if that vile Dickon hadn't interrupted? If he didn't care, why had he sent her a note, wanting to meet her? What had happened to that note? To whom had he given it? Oh, if only they had been able to talk! She couldn't let go of her dream. Ash was not indifferent; he did know she existed. And one day, when circumstances fell right for them...

'Lily Victoria,' her papa said from the doorway. 'Can you not play something a little more cheerful? Tomorrow we begin a new year. A year when you will complete your schooling and begin a new phase of your life. You should be anticipating it with enthusiasm. A new beginning...'

'Yes, Papa.'

'Speaking of new beginnings,' he added, 'tell Miss Sharp I wish to speak with her. I shall be in the study.'

She looked up, torn between soaring hope and sudden icy fear. 'You want to see Jess? About what?'

His look was enigmatic but not, she fancied, unkindly. 'Ask her to come. Immediately.'

Lily ran at once to the kitchen where she found Jess engaged in polishing copper pans, her hands and apron blackened, even smears on her face where she'd rubbed her cheek.

'Oh, look at you!' Lily cried. 'But you'll have to do. Just wash your hands. There's no time for you to get changed.'

Jess stared, making Lily add impatiently, 'Papa has asked to see you. I believe he's going to offer you a permanent position. Oh, hurry, Jess!'

She led the way back to the hall where, in an agony of hope and anxiety, she studied Jess's appearance, tweaking at her apron and fiddling with her hair, looping it back behind her ear where the fine strands had come adrift from a loose chignon. 'Right. Now knock.'

Jess did so. They stared at each other, waiting, then from beyond the door came the rector's voice: 'You may enter.'

In the waning of a winter's afternoon a lamp on the desk shed golden light upwards across the rector's pink face, so that the shadows were all in the wrong places. He looked half demon, seated against a background of books and more books. 'Well, come in, girl, come in!' he snapped.

In an ashtray near his left hand a fat cigar reposed, drifting smoke. He picked it up, sucked hard on it and let smoke trickle from the side of his mouth. Bushy white eyebrows lifted slightly, but before he could speak Jess blurted, 'If you'll allow me, sir, I want to thank you most kindly for savin' my life. If Miss Lily han't brung me here – and if you han't let me stay, well... well, the Lord know what would've 'come of me. I want you to know as I'm wholly grateful, sir, and if there's any way I can show my gratitude... I en't never bin afraid o' hard work, sir.'

His eyebrows were eloquent, twisting like caterpillars though the rest of his face remained still as he looked her up and down, noting her birdlike slightness. 'Indeed. And I suppose we must take your word for that. My daughter seems to think we should not apply for references. You left your last place in haste, I believe. Under... shall we say "difficult circumstances"?'

'Yes, sir.' She set her chin stubbornly. She'd say no more, however hard he tried to make her.

'Do you cook?'

'Only plain food, sir, but I'm a quick learner. And, if I may be so bold, your kitchen was in a sadly state. That look like Miss Peartree need some extra help.'

'Indeed?' The cool eyes, glinting with golden lamplight, stared at her unblinking as he drew on his cigar and reached to drop the ash into a tray, tapping it with a pudgy forefinger.

Like fat pink worms, his fingers were. Jess shuddered as she imagined those soft, fat hands on her, shocking herself by the thought. Where had it come from? Lily's father had done nothing to suggest a sexual threat. Even so, something in the way he kept looking her over...

No! No, the fault was in her. Ever since Merrywest, every man she met had caused a shrinking inside her. *Any* man. Why, she'd even gone rigid when her beloved brother Matty had hugged her. He hadn't said anything – Matty wouldn't put a thing like that into words. But he'd noted it, just the same. It had made him wonder.

Matty, forgive me! she thought, suddenly longing for him. If only she could see him, talk to him, explain...

'What about children?' Reverend Clare asked. 'Do you know anything about caring for children?'

The question disconcerted her, since there were no children at the rectory. 'I've looked after little 'uns – brothers and sisters and such.'

'And you're a good Christian? You say your prayers, and go to church?'

She hesitated, wanting to be honest. Yes, she said her prayers – frantic, desperate prayers – but since she'd left Lynn there didn't seem anybody there to listen. 'I was raised in the chapel way, sir.'

'A pity. But we shan't argue about that, so long as you present yourself with the others at prayers every morning. Very well... You may stay as kitchenmaid and under-cook, helping Miss Peartree. Until something more suitable offers.' And he turned his attention to his manuscript, dipping his quill into the ink.

Jess hovered uncertainly, her mind working again. *Until something more suitable*... What did that mean?

'And the pay, sir?' Where she came from, that was the main question.

'We'll decide that in due course, when I see how much you're worth,' he said, and looked her in the eye. 'After all, I am taking you on trust, girl. For my daughter's sake. You would not be here if it were not for her faith in you. Be sure you don't abuse that trust.'

So that was it – he was letting her stay, under sufferance, because of Lily. But only for the time being. Perhaps, once Lily was gone back to school, Jess would be sent on her way.

Brushing the air with his hand as if chasing away a fly, he added, 'You're dismissed, Jessamy. Close the door behind you. I have work to do.'

Lily was waiting outside, hopping from foot to foot in the freezing hallway. She clasped her hands under her chin and gasped, 'Well? *Well*? What did he say? Are you to stay?'

'Yes, Miss Lily, I'm to stay.' For now, she added to herself.

'Oh, Jess!' The lovely, terrible eyes filled with tears as Lily threw her arms about the smaller girl's shoulders and hugged her, weeping and laughing. 'Oh, Jess! Happy New Year. Happy, Happy New Year!'

–

Lying flat on her back in her narrow attic bed, wide awake and strangely unsettled, Jess stared at the darkness and faced facts. There was no going back, that was for sure. Everything at Fisher's End was now lost to her – her brothers and sisters, her friends, familiar places… Tomorrow a new year began. Wasn't it sensible, then, to break with the past, to become Jessie Sharp and forget that Jess Henefer had ever existed?

Oh, she wouldn't really forget. Somewhere deep in her soul she'd always know who and what she really was: that was part of her punishment. But she wouldn't ever speak about it. Not to anyone. And she'd try not to think of it too much, either. Brooding never did no good. Work was the antidote. And there was plenty of that here. Starting tomorrow.

–

Returning to school was not a prospect Lily relished. She had come to hate Miss Waterburn's Academy for Young Ladies, though she had never told anyone how miserable her life was in Cambridge – until now. Now, she confided in Jess.

At school Lily felt even more of an outcast, an oddity. Not only because of her eyes but because of her background. Clemency hardly spoke to her when they were there; Clemency had her own close coterie of friends, daughters of the gentry and the *nouveau riche*. Lily anticipated her release from that life with pleasure.

'I can hardly wait for the summer. Then I shall be free. I can spend my time walking with Gyp, writing my journal, reading… Oh, and helping Cousin Oriana, of course. I think I shall write a book – about a little foundling child and how her real father searches for her and finds her at last, and takes her home… It will make a wonderful story.'

'Like a fairytale,' Jess said.

'Except,' said Lily, 'that *this* story may well come true. It *will*, Jess. Oh… you think I'm being fanciful, don't you? Dear Jess. You're so *good* for me.' Laughing, she went off about her amusements.

On the day Lily returned to school, Miss Peartree summoned the house staff to the front hall where they paid their respects as the young mistress left. She took a tearful parting of Gyp and of Jess, begging her take care of herself and the little dog. 'Oh, I shall miss you! I'll send you some picture postcards – I know you can't read, but you'll know I'm thinking of you. And when I come home I'll tell you everything that's happened, and you must do the same. I'll see you again at Easter, Jess. It's not too long. Oh – goodbye, Dolly dear,' and, tossed over her shoulder as she stepped outside, 'Goodbye, Eliza.'

As the Clares' carriage moved away, Jess caught a glimpse of Clemency Clare's beautiful, cold profile. Lily was waving a handkerchief, bound for the railway station at Hunstanton St Edmunds. Soon, she would be changing trains at King's Lynn.

Lynn – a wealth of memories and impressions flooded over Jess, childhood in the yards, safety with Mother and Dad around and Matty and Fanny as older siblings; the river, the Fisher Fleet, the boats going out, the anxious waits when storms arose… Hardening her mind against a wave of homesickness, Jess told herself her home was here now: Hewing rectory was all the home she had.

'Well!' Miss Peartree said gruffly. 'At least the house will be a little more peaceful now.' But as she turned away she blotted a tear. Maddening though Lily could be, she made the gloomy rectory feel alive.

The rector was standing in the shadows of the hall and as Jess made her way back to the baize-backed door she felt his eyes on her. When she glanced at him he seemed to smile a little, and nod at her in a self-satisfied way before he turned and went back to his work.

'*Now* we'll see how much longer you get to stay,' Eliza hissed behind her. 'Now Miss Lily en't here to plead your case.'

That night, Jess dreamed again of Salt's Yard and Fisher's End, seeing the tenements draped in shifting fog, where gas lamps hissed, monsters lurked, and roofs dripped. *Drip – drip – drip.* The fog was threaded with darker fronds of thickening, choking smoke through which her dream-self struggled until she came within sight of the glare of a great fire, a tower of flame against which figures moved and faces leered. One particular face ballooned in her mind, a face ugly with hate, covered in blood that drip-drip-dripped with a slow, terrible menace...

'You're dead!' she screamed at him. She woke with a shock, her heart thudding so hard it shook her whole body, her ears ringing to the echo of her own cry. He was after her. Haunting her. Wanting revenge...

She could still hear the dripping. It was hitting her pillow with soggy pit-pats. A thaw had started! Having lit her candle, she shifted the bed to a new position and put a jug under the leak, then threw her pillow aside and lay in the darkness listening to the musical *plink-plonk* in the jug. She was wide awake now. Awake, and facing memories she had hoped to keep at bay.

In fact, there had been no fog on the night it happened; the wind had been too strong. It had fanned the fire into an inferno. But there had been shadows, thick with whirling smoke, and a confusion of crowding people wanting to watch the spectacle as the new seven-storey grain warehouse, the largest structure in Lynn, had blazed itself to ruin.

Seeing her hated enemy standing near the edge of the dock, she hadn't stopped to think. It had been so easy. To edge closer. To wait for a surge in the crowd... He'd seen her at the last moment. But by then he was falling, arms flailing, between the dock wall and the side of the great ship riding there. The wind had shifted the ship, closing the gap. She'd heard the scream as he was crushed. Behind her shouts and alarm had spread, growing fainter as she pushed her way out from the crowd and fled.

For a long time she'd feared pursuit. But by now they probably thought it was an accident, a man slipping off the greasy dock in the excitement. Only she knew what had really happened. She, and a dead man named Nathanael Merrywest.

In Lily's absence, Jess set her mind to work, learning all the things that must be learned in order to run a kitchen and feed a household. Though her schooling had been poor and much-interrupted, under Miss Peartree's tuition she began to pick out some of the words printed in the recipe books. There were a few disasters, as when she confused 'teaspoon' with 'tablespoon' – the ingredient being mustard, it did make a difference!

Lily sent the first of the promised postcards, a sepia photograph of one of the Cambridge colleges. Miss Peartree read out the message and later Jess pinned the card up in her room, repeating the words to herself. She had particular trouble deciphering handwriting, but she was pleased with the card, and looked at it by candlelight last thing at night before she went to sleep. Try as she would, though, she couldn't imagine the sort of life Lily was leading.

Jess had her free afternoon on a Tuesday, a day when it suited Reverend Clare to leave the village school in the hands of his curate while he himself remained in his study. Since he liked to work without disturbance, it was also on that day that Miss Peartree did her local visiting of the poor, or took a trip to the Hall to see Miss Gittens, while Jess, Dolly, and the man Fargus had their half day off. Eliza remained at the rectory to see to callers – and to put her feet up, Jess and Dolly guessed – and John Button came into his own playing coachman for Miss Peartree. It made Jess smile to see the great lummox proudly driving the trap; you'd have thought he was a royal coachman from Sandringham.

At first Jess spent her free afternoon tidying her room and doing sewing and mending, and as the weather allowed she took Gyp out for a run in the snow. Without Lily, the poor little creature was lonely. Neither Reverend Clare nor Miss Peartree had time for him, though Dolly took care of him at night, keeping him quiet so as not to disturb Eliza.

One Tuesday, Dolly invited Jess to come and have tea with her crippled mother and fourteen-year-old sister Susan, who acted as their mother's nurse. Mrs Upton had fallen into a millrace when Susan was ten and Dolly only eight; her husband, trying to rescue her, had been killed by the wheel, which had broken both her legs and left them twisted. Another woman might have been bitter because of it, but Mrs

Upton believed God had a purpose in everything. After all, she said, she was fortunate to have two good daughters in Susan and Dolly, and good friends and neighbours, and a benefactor in Sir Richard Fyncham who, as owner of the mill and her husband's employer, had awarded her a pension that kept her out of the workhouse. Her ability to see good in everything made Jess feel humble.

'Why don't you come to chapel with us on Sunday?' Mrs Upton asked. 'You'd enjoy it, Jess, and you'd be made very welcome. It's a good way of making friends.'

Jess knew that was true. But she made excuses, fearing that the Lord might strike her down if she dared step inside a house of his.

She enjoyed her visit to the Uptons' cottage; it was as neat as any home on the Fisher Fleet and the warmth among the little family reminded her of how her own home had been, everyone drawn closer after Dad was drowned in the wreck of the *SARA GIRL*. More bitterly, she recalled that there'd been the light of faith there, too – that was another thing Merrywest had desecrated.

She felt she could become firm friends with Dolly and her family, but with Eliza Potts there remained a coolness. More and more this appeared to have something to do with the gamekeeper, Reuben Rudd.

As the cold weather continued, Rudd was a frequent presence at the rectory, bringing a brace of pheasant, or passing on a message from some villager, or simply looking in because he was passing. Whether he also called on Eliza at night Jess couldn't decide; she never heard or saw anything – which wasn't strange because generally she was so tired she slept like a wreck buried deep in mud.

One fresh morning when the earth lay frozen under a sky of hurting blue, Rudd turned up with a small step-up he'd made out of a crate. To Jess's amazement, the step-up was a present for her – to stand on at the sink or the table, whenever she needed the extra few inches nature had denied her. It was light enough to be easily pushed aside, out of the way, when not needed.

Disconcerted by the trouble he'd taken, all on her account, she muttered, 'I was alluss the runt o' the litter.'

'Best things come in small parcels,' Rudd told her with a smile, enjoying her surprise. 'Look, I've carved your initials in the side, so you'll know it's yours.'

Jess gazed unhappily at the neatly cut letters, seeing them like an accusing finger, pointing at her guilt – 'J.S.' of course, when by rights it should have been 'J.H.' It made her feel bad about lying, though he wasn't exactly honest himself, was he? Carrying on secretly with Eliza while making overtures to other women. The trouble was, Jess couldn't help but like him. If only he'd been the man he appeared to be on the surface things might have been different. But he was a deep one, this, a great dissembler. If she hadn't, with her own eyes, seen him coming to the house that night, with Dash at heel, she might have believed his blandishments were sincere.

When Eliza saw the step-up which Rudd had made for Jess, she flared her fine nostrils. 'We shall be fallin' over that now,' she complained. 'As if there wan't enough hazards in this kitchen.' She took to calling the platform 'Sharp's pulpit', and whenever she had the chance she tucked it away where Jess had trouble finding it.

Eliza was jealous, right enough. But if she exercised her temper on Rudd in private he gave no sign of it; he went right on paying attentions to Jess every time he visited the rectory. She began to wonder what sort of hold he had on Eliza, to keep her so tame.

There came a day when, having amused Jess and Dolly with a tale about Dash's antics, Rudd said softly, 'Why, Miss Jessie, I was beginning to think I'd never hear you laugh,' and she realised she'd forgotten everything else but her enjoyment of the moment. 'It sounds good,' he added. 'You should do it more often.'

From the doorway, Eliza said tartly, 'Nothin' better to do than listen to old tomfoolery, Jessie Sharp? And what're you a-doin' of in here, Dolly? I told you to polish them silver pieces in the drawin' room.'

'That's your job,' Jess put in. 'Dolly have her own work, she can't be alluss at your beck and call.'

'She're here to help out in any way needsome,' Eliza replied, slanting a look at Rudd. 'Anyhow, *I'll* say what she do. I'm senior here. Housemaid comes higher than kitchenmaid – and at least I don't need a *pulpit* to do my job. I'm not as fond o' preachifyin' as you be. Pour me a cup o' that tea, if there's any left. I'm spittin' feathers. And Dolly – go you now and do that polishin'.'

As Dolly departed, cloth in hand, Eliza settled herself in the chair across the hearth from Rudd, chatting with him in her usual half-flirting, half-challenging way. Rudd replied in kind, now and then tossing a remark to Jess to assure her she wasn't forgotten. They both played the game to the hilt. Jess had tried to tell herself she might be mistaken over the identity of the night visitor, but whenever Rudd and Eliza were together those sparks told their own tale. Something was going on between them. Something from the past, something presently in flood, or something building for the future: Jess couldn't tell, she only knew it was there.

She affected to be too busy to notice the interplay, though. She was glad when Rudd finished his tea and got up, wrapping his scarf around his neck and chest.

'Well, I'd best be off. Got to make sure the birds are fed and watered before nightfall. In this snow they find it hard to forage. Thanks for the tea, Miss Jessie.'

'You're welcome,' she said crisply, not looking at him but aware of a burning in her cheeks. As he left, she glanced at the window and saw snow pouring down in thick sheets driven by the wind. She hoped he could find his way safely home in all that weather.

'Gettin' notions about Reuben Rudd, then?' Eliza asked slyly. 'Tek you care not to set your cap too high, Jessie Sharp. He 'on't look twice at the likes o' you. He want a strong woman, who'll bear him strong sons.' She got up and stood with her feet apart, her hands on her hips – child-bearing hips, sure enough, wide and rounded. 'You're so little you'll have trouble bearin' a child for any man. I know about that sort o' thing. My mother, and her mother afore her, have delivered plenty around here – screamin', stillborn and strangled. And Rudd want sons. Well, any man do. He 'on't marry a woman as can't give him children.'

'And you think he'll wed *you*, then, I suppose.'

Eliza tossed her head. 'Huh! *I* wun't have him. Even if he did ax. When I come to wed, I'll have somethin' better than a gamekeeper in mind.'

Jess couldn't fathom it. What *was* going on between those two, then? 'I thought you wanted to be a lady's maid.'

Eliza's smile told nothing, except her contempt. 'You'll see,' was all she said before taking herself away.

Smarting, Jess stared at the window. It was blowing up a real raw blizzard out there.

Seven

The snowstorm swept on southwards, its outriders reaching Cambridge as Lily was leaving church after choir practice that evening. Crisp white flakes drifted down into cobbled streets where smoke from many chimneys hung on the cold air, haloing gas street-lamps.

Heading homeward through the dusk, Lily was just one among thirty girls, pupils of Miss Waterburn's Academy for Young Ladies, all dressed in capes and skirts of deep blue serge, with plain blue bonnets. They moved briskly in double file, bound back across the river Cam to the mansion which housed the school.

The acrid bite of the smoke and the quickening of an iced wind made Lily draw her muffler closer, to protect her throat. Her head was full of music, full of memories of the organ swelling and her own voice aiding the fullness of sound. Certain phrases in the harmony thrilled her, sending shivers down her spine as she recalled the way the notes soared towards the ornate roof bosses of the ancient church.

Beneath a group of bare trees which formed an island in the road, a band of young men sported, climbing on walls and swinging from branches, shouting and jeering at passers-by. They appeared to be undergraduates, in the loose, checked coats, cravats and slouch hats favoured by the fashionable young men of the university. More than one of them held a bottle which he drank from, or waved in the air as he hooted and called.

'Hurry, girls!' The order came from Miss Green, who was walking abreast of the column. 'Keep together. Eyes front. Swiftly, now!'

The young ladies quickened their pace and the wind did the same, gusting along the street, swirling among the thickly falling snow.

The young men mimicked the mistress's voice: 'Hurry, girls! Come along now. Quick march back to school, one-two, one-two.' One of them darted across the path and leapt to hang on a railing, swinging there as he doffed his hat and leered through the dusk, greeting teachers and pupils alike with scandalous familiarity: 'Hello, darling. Give me a smile, then. Like to come in a punt with me, eh?'

His companions laughed, adding comments that made the girls walk even more swiftly. Lily felt oddly light-headed, excited and repelled all at the same time. She drew her muffler even closer and kept her gaze on the ground for fear of fresh taunts if they saw her eyes.

And then, as she passed him, the young man hanging from the railings changed his note, saying in surprise, 'Well, hello!' and to her utter horror she heard him whistle and call loudly, 'Lily! Hey, Lily! Lily Vee!'

The other students took up the chorus, making the street echo amid the dusk and falling snow, while their ringleader came running after the column of girls. Though Miss Green tried to prevent him, he evaded her, peering at averted faces, calling, 'Lily! Don't you know me, my duck? Oh, Lily Vee, sweet Lily Vee! Meet me tonight. By the river, as usual, yes?'

Lily thought she might explode. No longer half-exhilarated, she felt her face burn, her spine alternately chilled and fevered. How could this be happening? She did not know the young man. She had not made the acquaintance of any undergraduates – who could, when the Academy kept its pupils so well guarded? Yet this man knew her, by a taunting nickname that Dickon Clare had coined. Distress strained the sinews along her throat as she fought with her disbelief and dismay.

Then one of the other students, apparently less far gone with wine than his fellows, grasped the loud one's arm and pulled him away. Two constables were approaching at a run, their boots heavy on the cobbles. The students scattered, leaving the swirling snow, the swift trudge of buttoned boots, the hiss of gas lamps, the clop of hooves – and a pulse in Lily's throat that beat like a trapped bird.

Around her, curiosity buzzed in whispers and stifled giggles.

'Well, I must say!' Ellen Pargeter breathed. 'Who on earth is that person? Where did you meet him?'

'I've never met him!' Lily denied frantically.

'Then how did he know your name?' Ellen demanded. Lily took a breath, trying to calm her unsteady heart. 'I don't know. Truly, I... I didn't know any of them.'

From behind her, Clemency Clare said, 'Oh, come, Lily, you certainly knew at least *one* of them.'

'And *he* knew *her*!' another voice added, causing more giggles.

Lily's face burned ever more painfully. Her stomach churned as she twisted round to look at Clemency but, before she could say more, her arm was grasped in pinching fingers and Miss Waterburn snapped, 'No talking! Be silent, all of you! Lily Clare, not one more word. Not one word!'

--

Being unable to provide an explanation for what had occurred, Lily was sent to spend the night in meditation in 'the turret', a curious excrescence built above the central part of the house, a place used as a punishment cell. Lily was conducted there by a maid bearing a lamp.

The turret comprised a single small room under a bell tower. It was meanly furnished with a plank bed, a deal table, and a cane-bottomed chair. On the table lay a Bible, no doubt intended to aid uplifting thoughts and penitence, and on the hard bed one single scratchy blanket was provided. An enamelled chamber pot reposed under the bed.

'Oh, please...' Lily began as the maid moved away, taking the lamp with her. 'Please leave the—'

The maid didn't even look at her but went away and closed the door.

Lily hated the dark. Monsters loomed up in her mind and she retreated to the bed, to crouch there listening to strange scrabblings in the ceiling. Rats! Oh, dear heaven... To bolster her courage, she began to sing John Bunyan's hymn 'To Be A Pilgrim'. It did help. It made her think that one day soon, when her real father came for her, all the people who had been unkind to her would be sorry.

After endless hours, dawn came grey against the high, narrow window that gave the only light to the room. Stirring herself, Lily set the chair beneath the window and climbed up to peer out across a roof where frost glittered on the surface of a soft counterpane of snow which had settled on all the world – on the trees in the school grounds and on nearby meadows, on church towers and rooftops with smoking chimneys, and on the pinnacles of college buildings which lifted above humbler structures. A scatter of snow drifted past the window as, with a flutter of wings, a couple of pigeons took flight from somewhere over her head.

Pigeons. Not rats. Lily sighed in relief, chiding herself for her vivid imagination.

A maid brought her a meagre breakfast, but all the town clocks had chimed nine before more footsteps presaged the arrival of Miss Rattray. Tall, thin, with eyes set close over a beaked nose, she was, inevitably, nicknamed Rat-face, though Clemency said she was all squeak and no nip.

'You're to come with me, Lily Clare.' As ever, she avoided meeting Lily's eyes as she spoke. Few people could face that pair of lovely, freakish eyes without some sign of disquiet. Many, like Miss Rattray, dealt with the problem by refusing to look directly at her at all.

She was made to wait outside in the hallway, staring at the print which portrayed an angelic young man on his knees by an altar twined with ivy. The picture was entitled, appropriately enough, 'Repentance' – Miss Waterburn's notion of softening the hearts of delinquents, no doubt. All it did for Lily was remind her of Ashton Haverleigh, because the man in the picture resembled the unattainable object of her dreams.

At last the study door opened and she was summoned, to find Miss Waterburn seated at her desk.

'Well, Lily? Have you anything to say to me?'

What was there to say? 'No, Miss Waterburn.'

'You still maintain that you did not know any of those young men?'

'Oh, Miss Waterburn, honestly and truly...'

The principal perused Lily's face, her own expression hidden by the light that hazed her; then she said, 'The other young ladies appear to be of the same opinion. You should be grateful to have such friends.'

Lily let out the breath she hadn't known she was holding. Friends? What friends? Had some of the girls spoken up for her? Which girls?

'I may have been hasty in my judgement,' Miss Waterburn conceded. 'I have never found you to be untruthful, Lily Clare. Over-imaginative, and over-impulsive, with many other faults that you must seek to amend, but... I cannot believe you to be mendacious. If I'm wrong – if you are lying to me – then it's clear that you are so far gone down the path of wickedness that nothing can redeem you. I trust you will reflect on that.'

'But I'm telling the truth!' Lily cried. 'Truly—'

'Then we must seek another explanation for what occurred. Your name was not plucked at random from the air. Tell me, do you know a young gentleman by the name of Haverleigh? The Honourable Ashton Haverleigh?'

Thoughts and emotions tumbled helter-skelter in confusion. 'He… he is a friend of my second cousin, Dickon Clare – Clemency's brother.'

'And did you not notice him among that ill-mannered band who accosted us last evening?'

Lily shook her head, numb with disbelief. 'I did not. Was he there?'

'It would seem so. Clemency Clare recognised him, so she informs me. I believe he is somewhat of an unruly young man. Given to practical jokes.'

'Is he?' Prickles of disquiet traversed Lily's spine. Surely it was Dickon Clare who liked to play unkind jokes? It was because of his behaviour that Dickon had been sent down last year. Ash had already graduated, but she had heard that he was considering undertaking post-graduate studies. Was he, then, in Cambridge? Had he been in the street last night? Out with companions, in drink and looking for amusement, had Ash seen his friend's freak of a cousin among the crocodile of girls? Had he told her name for his friends to hoot down the street?

According to Miss Waterburn, Clemency and her clique of close friends had pointed out that Lily was an industrious scholar, that during the day she was at her studies and at night she was safe in her bed. They had reminded Miss Waterburn that no girl of the Academy, even if she had a mind to mischief – which no girl of the Academy ever would! – no girl had any chance for illicit meetings with men: none could escape the vigilance of Miss Waterburn's benignly protective regime.

So they had argued, and so they were believed.

Lily felt light-headed with joy: Clemency and her closest friends had spoken up for her. It was wonderful! The senior girls – the cream of the school – the ones who had once avoided or scorned her, now clustered round, anxious for her favour, impatient to welcome her into their circle. It was as if, by achieving a measure of notoriety, she had suddenly become worthy of cultivation.

'It was unforgivable of Ash,' Clemency commiserated. 'But you won't say anything about it, will you? Not to Dickon, or to anyone? I mean… if Mama or Papa got to hear of it, there would be a dreadful fuss. You wouldn't want to make trouble for Ash. Would you?'

'Oh, no,' Lily assured her. 'No, of course not.'

'Bless you!' To her amazement, Clemency reached to kiss her cheek, her doll-pretty face flushed, her eyes sparkling. 'Dear Lily, I knew I could count on you. You see, Ash is a special friend. A very special friend of mi... Of my family.' Her lashes fluttered as she glanced away, confused by the slip she had almost made. 'I'm sure he wouldn't mean to embarrass you, Lily dear. He just wouldn't think of the consequences. Men don't, you know. It was just foolishness.'

–

In Norfolk, February drew on with more snowfalls, and then a day of gales that sent slates flying and rattled at the eaves even after Jess went to bed. She lay awake listening to it, praying that her brother Matty wasn't out in that awful storm. On just such a night, she and Mother and Fanny had watched until dawn, only to see the fleet limp in without *SARA GIRL*. All they'd found was a piece of board, with her name scrawled on it in white paint. They'd never found 'Hardlines' Henefer, or his best mate 'Ginger' Fysher. Dear God, let Matty be safe...

She must have slept at last for she came suddenly awake, wondering what had disturbed her. The night was silent. Still. That was it – the wind had died; it was the stillness that had disturbed her. Thank the Lord, the storm had ended.

But now she was wide awake. Times like this she hated – lying wakeful in the darkness, wondering how her family were, wishing she could see them and let them know she was well. Oh, such idle thoughts were stupid. Think of something else. Reuben Rudd, for instance... His face came clear in her mind, thick with freckles, brown lashes framing bright hazel eyes that asked questions about her coolness even while he was teasing her. He was puzzled about her, that she knew. And Reuben Rudd was no fool.

So why was he involved with Eliza? Jess would have sworn he wasn't the type of man to come sneaking to a woman's bed just for the physical pleasure it gave him. Or was it that she didn't *want* to believe he was that type?

Something broke into her thoughts like scissors cutting a taut thread. The night was dark, clouds hiding both moon and stars, and in the wake of the gale the earth was resting, waiting for the dawn in a silence so deep that any noise was magnified. Jess knew she had heard an alien noise, maybe the clicking of a gate latch.

Gyp must have heard it, too. Faintly, his barking came drifting up to Jess from the kitchen, sending her leaping out of bed to ease her window half-open. As she craned to listen harder, she distinctly heard the tap of fingernails on glass, followed by the drawing back of the bolt on a door below, and, the night being so dark, she saw a misty drift of lamplight as Eliza – it had to be Eliza – admitted the caller.

Hearing Gyp barking even louder, Jess didn't hesitate. She threw on her coat and crept out down the back stairs, moving softly on bare feet through the darkness.

The back stairs ended at a doorway which led into the side passage. It opened outwards, from the stairs into the passage. Carefully, hardly breathing, Jess turned the handle. It moved soundlessly. But the door stayed shut. Something was stopping it.

It was locked!

Momentarily baulked, Jess stood against the wall in pitch darkness. Evidently Eliza didn't want her interfering in whatever was going on. But for sure *something* was going on. Where she'd only suspected before, that locked door made her certain.

Going as swiftly and as silently as she could, she scrambled back up the bare, narrow stairs and let herself on to the upper landing. She could hear Miss Peartree snoring, but the rector's room lay silent behind closed doors. Jess glided by like a phantom, making for the main stairs where the carpet runner was thick under her feet, the banister smooth and polished. The parquet in the hall felt cool, then, as she let herself through the baize-backed door which led to the rear part of the house, she stepped on to flagstones whose cold caress made her gasp. Was that the sound of a closing door? Beyond the angle of the passage, a shadow moved in pale lamplight that was shut off as another door closed. Eliza's door. Had she let her visitor out again, while Jess was chasing through the house?

The side passage now lay dark and silent. The sliver of light under Eliza's door blinked out as Jess glanced at it. In the black stillness, she fancied that Eliza was laughing at her.

Turning to the kitchen door, Jess opened it quietly and found the room dimly lit by the embers in the range. There was no sign of Gyp – his basket was empty. She ran across to the side window, pressing her face to the glass with her hands shielding her eyes. Faint pre-dawn light showed up the pathway outside, with just the ghost of a figure disappearing into the shrubbery.

Annoyed with herself for indulging in such a wild-goose chase, Jess lit a spill from the embers of the fire and applied it to a lamp. The glow spread around the huge kitchen, sending her shadow looming up the walls as she made for the pantry and the marble shelf where a jug of milk stood under a beaded cloth. She poured herself a drink and let its creamy goodness slide down her throat to lie cool in her stomach. Oh, she loved milk. It was a luxury she'd always adored since she was a little 'un.

As she returned to the kitchen, she heard a faint noise in one of the big store cupboards. She flung open the door and stared at the huddled form of Dolly, miserably holding Gyp and trying to keep him quiet. The young maid was kneeling on a lumpy pallet, tangled in a ragged blanket, with an old and battered rag doll lying in a corner.

'He can't help it!' Dolly wept, curled over the dog as if to protect him with her own body. 'He's poorly.'

Sensing the child's abject terror, Jess knelt down beside her, touching her shoulder. 'Dolly. It's me – Jess. Oh, poor little mawther! Whatever's wrong?'

Dolly lifted a face drenched in tears and, seeing Jess, set the dog free and threw herself into Jess's arms with a cry of despair. Noisy sobs escaped her, but she fought to quiet them, muttering, 'Don't wake 'Liza. Mustn't wake 'Liza. If 'Liza comes—'

Neither of them had heard Eliza come in but all at once she was there, saying harshly, 'If 'Liza comes, what then, you blahrin' baby? You've now woke me up good and proper, you and that solin' dog. I keep a-tellin' you, I 'on't have my beauty sleep broke up on account o' that useless lapdog.'

She aimed a kick at Gyp, who cowered away and made for his basket. Dolly was still weeping, silently now, clinging to Jess for dear life. Jess stroked her back and her hair, trying to calm her.

'Hush now, little 'un. Hush now, that's all over.' She sat on her heels, holding the trembling Dolly and looking up at Eliza.

In the soft lamplight, the girl looked beautiful; she was wearing a softly draped wrap with her hair in a thick plait that trailed across one shoulder and on to the swell of her breast. But her expression was cold, her eyes hard.

'What's she bin sayin'?' she demanded. 'She're thick as a hedge. Tell lies, she do, soon's spit. Don't you, young 'un?' She swooped, reaching past Jess to snatch up the rag doll and carry it away towards the embers in the range.

Dolly screamed, surging to her feet to throw herself after Eliza and scrabble for the doll. Eliza held her off, keeping the doll out of reach.

'Leave her be!' Jess shot upright, prepared to do violence to defend Dolly. 'She say Gyp's took sick again, that's all. She were afraid he'd disturb you.' Something of her fury must have impressed Eliza for she thrust the doll at the sobbing child and moved away, muttering insults.

Jess went to rescue Dolly, drawing her back to her bed under the bottom shelf of the cupboard. 'Lie you down, Doll. Lie you down quiet now and go back to sleep. That's all over. She 'on't bother you no more. And if she do, we'll have a word with Miss Peartree. All right, now?'

Still snuffling with misery, Dolly allowed herself to be tucked up, clutching her doll. Jess left the cupboard door ajar, checked on Gyp, who was shivering in his basket, and carried the lamp into the passageway. Eliza was there, standing by the door to the back stairs, which was wide open now as if to prove it had never been locked.

'Do you harm that child once more,' Jess said, 'and I'll tell the master. "Beauty sleep", is it? You hen't been asleep, Eliza. Not lately.'

Eliza's mouth stretched in a cold smile. 'Who say I hen't?'

'Nobody say. I *know*. I seen him come. I heard him scratch at your window — and I heard you let him in.'

'Who? Who'd you see?'

The challenge baffled Jess: she hadn't actually seen anybody, and she certainly wasn't going to mention Rudd's name. 'A man.'

The smile widened, turning into a laugh. 'A man? What man? There wan't no man here.'

'Then who was it made them marks?' Jess pointed to the telltale signs on the flagged floor behind Eliza, where muddy bootprints and pools of dark wetness proved that someone had lately come in trailing water.

It took Eliza only a moment to lie, 'That was on'y Fargus.'

'I thought you said there han't been no man here.'

'Fargus don't count.'

'So why'd he come?'

'He was after a remedy for the boy. Button have a bad tizzick.'

'Oh, have he? Since when?'

'Since tonight. Likely it'll be gone by mornin'.'

'Must've been a powerful hummer of a remedy,' Jess commented darkly. 'I best tell the rector, come mornin'. He ought to know if Button's took sadly with a cough. Could be he's a-sickenin' for somethin'.'

Eliza's expression changed as she leaned forward. 'Don't you threaten me, Jessie Sharp! Do you imitate to get me into trouble with the master, I'll have a thing or two to say about you.'

'Such as what?'

'Settin' your cap after Reuben Rudd, for one thing. Rector 'on't think much to havin' a harlot for a kitchenmaid.'

'Rector won't believe your lies,' Jess said, comforted that, after all, Eliza knew nothing against her.

''on't he?' Eliza's smirk said she knew better. 'Well, we'll see. Good night, Jessie Sharp. Sweet dreams.'

When morning came, Jess didn't know what to do. She had no proof of anything. It was her word against Eliza's since Dolly was too afraid to speak up. She was too afraid even to talk about it to Jess.

'But if we both went to the rector...' Jess said.

Dolly shook her head violently, looking haunted as she glanced at the door, fearing Eliza might be lurking. 'He 'ouldn't believe us. 'Sides... she'd get even, Jess. It don't do to cross 'Liza. Please don't say nothin'.'

So Jess kept her counsel. She too was afraid. With so many guilty secrets in her past, she couldn't risk having an enemy start fresh enquiries.

—

Behind the gales, cold fronts closed in from the Arctic, gripping the land in talons of ice. Below stairs at the rectory a tacit truce was struck: young Dolly kept her head down while Jess and Eliza managed to maintain an outer politeness, circling round each other like barnyard hens.

Then, a week or so after the incident of the night visitor, Jess was summoned to the dining room where Miss Peartree was alone at breakfast, the rector having gone out early. The old lady was peering at the close print of the latest edition of *The Lynn Advertiser* and, with a pang, Jess wondered if the paper contained some threat to her safety.

But Miss Peartree folded the paper and laid it aside. 'Ah, Jessamy.'

'Was the haddock done wrong?' Jess asked anxiously. 'Or was it the eggs? I know I hen't yet got the knack of doin' scrambled eggs right.'

Miss Peartree shook her head. 'No, Jessamy. It's neither the haddock nor the eggs. However... I fear I must tell you that Reverend Clare... Reverend Clare feels that you are... not quite right – as a kitchenmaid.'

Jess's heart seemed to lurch in dismay. 'Not right, miss?'

'He feels that a kitchenmaid should be more... robust, let us say.'

'I'm strong!' Jess protested.

'Yes, I'm sure.' Miss Peartree blotted her upper lip with a lace handkerchief, her eyes behind her glasses looking pale and unhappy. 'But you aren't very tall... Now, don't misunderstand me, Jessamy. We've been pleased with your work. This is in no way a criticism. It's simply that we feel that you might be happier elsewhere.'

Taking a long breath to calm the churning of her stomach, Jess fixed her eyes on the cameo brooch which Miss Peartree habitually wore among a froth of lace at her throat. 'Do this have anythin' to do with Eliza, miss? If she've been sayin' words against me—'

'Eliza?' Miss Peartree looked genuinely puzzled. 'As far as I know, she hasn't said a word about you. Oh, come, Jess. I know the two of you are not exactly friends, but I'm surprised at you for harbouring such uncharitable thoughts.'

Jess wished she'd held her tongue – but she'd lay odds that Eliza's fair hand had taken a turn at stirring this brew. She might not have spoken to Miss Peartree, but had she talked to the rector?

'When do you want me to leave?' she asked.

'Come now,' Miss Peartree said, not unkindly. 'Don't look like that. We don't propose to throw you out into the street. Why, Lily Victoria would never forgive us. She's very fond of you, as you know. We hope to find you a new position, not too far away.'

And what did *that* mean? Jess squinted through her lashes, waiting.

'This afternoon, at three o'clock,' Miss Peartree said, 'you will present yourself at Hewinghall House for interview.'

Jess's head came up sharply. Hewinghall House?

'It so happens that Lady Fyncham needs a new nurserymaid,' Miss Peartree said. 'The present girl is about to be married, so they're anxious to find someone as soon as possible. When Reverend Clare heard about it, he put your name forward. You should be grateful, Jessamy – it was kind of him to think of you.'

97

'Yes, miss.' So *that* was what he had meant on New Year's Eve, when he asked her if she knew about children – this was the 'something more suitable' that he'd planned.

'He has even written a reference for you,' Miss Peartree added, picking up an envelope that lay near her plate. 'Now, Jessamy... Be sure to be very polite to Lady Fyncham – she has an abrupt manner, but don't let that worry you, you won't be seeing much of her. Your job will be to look after the nursery and help Nanny Fyncham with Miss Bella. I gather you've had some experience with children.'

'Yes, miss. With the little 'uns at home – my brothers and sisters.'

Miss Peartree's mouth suddenly pursed. 'I thought your family were all dead.'

'Well... No, miss, I never said that, exactly.'

'Quite.' The pale eyes shifted. 'It seems there are many things that you never said "exactly", Jessamy. That's another reason why I think you'll be better in a larger household. So long as you do your work and behave yourself Lady Fyncham won't trouble about your past, especially when she reads the kind words the rector has written. Be sure not to let him down. A position at the big house is something many a girl would think a great opportunity.'

'Yes, miss.' Jess twisted her hands together unhappily, wanting to apologise for her lack of honesty, but if she started down that road she'd have to go on and explain everything...

When Eliza heard the news she laughed, 'That'll put you in your place, Jess No-Name. From what I know of Nanny Fyncham she'll have you scrubbin' floors and cleanin' grates until you can't hardly straighten your back. Nurserymaid's one of the lowest forms o' life. See, I warned you not to cross me.' The green eyes were bright with malevolence.

That afternoon, dressed in her best grey print and faded black coat, with a pheasant feather set jauntily in her knitted hat and her letter of reference safely in her handbag, Jess set out to walk the long drive to the big house.

The north-east wind blew ever colder, and as she left the shelter of the trees she could hardly see for the watering of her eyes. The going was a bit easier, downhill now, with some kind of big wall off to the right. A gang of men were busy around an old tree which they had been felling. It had fallen awkwardly and smashed down part of the wall, causing a deal of shouting and cursing.

Half-blinded by tears of cold, she found herself suddenly near the service wing of the big house. The kitchen courtyard had been swept clean of snow and lines were strung across it, with sheets billowing like sails. One of the lines had just snapped; it was whipping about in the wind, wiping wet linen on the cobbles, much to the dismay of the maids who came running. Steam billowed from a laundry room; there was the sound of clatterings and bangings from other outhouses, the grinding of a knife-cleaning machine in operation, a cat spitting at a bored old dog. Over it all a courtyard clock struck the hour of three. Lord, Jess thought – she was late!

On the far side of the courtyard, tall windows looked into a huge kitchen where various aproned cooks and maids were bustling about. The back door lay in a corner by one of the kitchen windows, from where a scullery maid, up to her elbows in a sink full of pans, stared out. She must have said something about Jess for other servants came to glance out at the caller, curious to see what might be a new addition to the staff.

Wishing she were invisible, Jess approached the door. Outside it lay a dog – a black, curly-coated retriever. Gamekeeper Rudd's dog? With a little lurch of pleasure, she reached for the brass bell-pull, but before she could touch it the door opened and a man came out, stumbling backwards over the doorstep, tripping on the end of the heavy cape he carried.

He was pulling a grey cap on to his dark head as he protested, 'En't no need for violence, Mr Longman. I'm a-goin'. You know me, I'm not one to outstay my welcome.' As he turned, he saw Jess. He gave her a swift glance that swept her head to foot, and grinned at her, showing a missing front tooth. Maybe the dark moustache, waxed to sharp points, was designed to disguise the gap in his teeth, but to Jess it looked odd on a face that was otherwise blessed with regular features that some might have called handsome. 'I should run away, gal,' he advised her with a twinkle. 'They're a lot o' diddlers in this house.'

'Clear off!' the other man roared. From his dress, formal black and white with a tailcoat, Jess guessed him to be the butler.

The gap-tooth man swirled his heavy cape around his shoulders, snapped his fingers at the dog, said, 'C'mon, Bracken, we're not wanted here,' and winked at Jess as he went by.

Eight

'Well?' the butler snapped.

Jess jumped at the abruptness of his tone, so nervous she couldn't think. 'Please, sir… Milady's expectin' me. Jessamy Sharp.'

The man drew himself up, looking down his long, thin nose in a way that made her feel as small as the woodlouse that was crawling up the wall by the bell-pull. '"Lady Fyncham" is the correct mode of reference,' he informed her heavily. 'Or "her ladyship". Well, come in, girl. Don't stand there gaping. You're late, and her ladyship doesn't like to be kept waiting.' He caught his breath as she would have hurried across the doormat. 'Your feet, girl! Wipe them.'

She found herself in a long corridor with windows all down one side looking out across the park. The butler led the way into a windowless passageway where a lamp was burning in a corner alcove. A further door led into a lobby furnished with a marble table and a few chairs.

'Wait here,' the butler ordered, tapping at a huge oak door. A faint voice replied and the butler went inside, leaving Jess feeling tiny inside the vast house which seemed to have swallowed her up.

After a moment, the butler reappeared to inform Jess that her ladyship would see her now. He held the door open, with a lofty air of superiority, and closed it once Jess was inside.

She stared around her in awe. The morning room could have held three or four of the cottages in Salt's Yard, and still left space for smoke to curl out of the chimneys up to its high ceiling. A fire flamed bright in the enormous fireplace, and the oak-panelled walls were hung with pictures of stern-looking people.

Against the southern window, framed against the flare of daylight outside, a woman lounged on the window board, staring out as if waiting for something.

Jess made a curtsey. The movement seemed to distract Lady Fyncham, who glanced round, perused Jess in silence for a moment, then turned away, saying, 'My daughter is five years old. How old were your last charges?'

Charges? Did that mean her brothers and sisters? 'Well, milady... There was Sam – he's now twelve. Joe was... eight years old last April. And there was the baby.' She was going to add that baby Sarah-May had died before she was two, but Lady Fyncham wasn't listening. Lady Fyncham was impatiently watching for something beyond the window.

Remembering the letter Reverend Clare had written, Jess fumbled for it in her bag. 'There's this, milady. My reference.'

'H'm? Oh, yes. Well, bring it here, girl.' She clicked her fingers and Jess, shaking with nerves, forced her feet to cross the thick carpet.

Close to, Lady Maud Fyncham was an impressive woman with a taut, chiselled face. She hadn't an ounce of spare flesh on her. Her skin was fine and white to go with that rich chestnut hair, but her cheeks were blemished with broken veins and her lips were thin. Having received the letter, she waved Jess back with a peremptory hand, tore open the envelope and scanned the contents.

'Reverend Clare seems to think you'll do,' she said, and, 'Ah! Good!' as a movement outside drew her attention and a groom led a horse up to the iron railing and through the gate. The horse seemed unnerved by the wind, tossing its head and dancing sideways, but the sight of it made Lady Fyncham smile and get to her feet, swirling the skirt of her riding habit to one side. The skirt was split to the waist and beneath it she was wearing mannish breeches and high, polished boots.

Vaguely shocked at such unladylike attire, Jess stared up at her prospective employer. The squire's wife was very tall – Jess hardly came as high as her shoulder. Snatching up a riding crop from the writing desk, she strode across the room and tugged at an embroidered bell-pull with a silken tassel. 'I suggest you make arrangements with Nanny. If Reverend Clare thinks you'll do, that's good enough for me. You'll get the usual pay – whatever that is. You can start as soon as you like. Tell the girl to take you up to the nursery suite. I have business to attend to.' With which, she swept out.

Jess hovered, not quite sure what she ought to do. From the window, she saw Lady Fyncham run out to the waiting horse and, without assistance, leap up to the side-saddle. When the groom released the rein, the horse reared, but settled as its rider gave it a sharp crack with her crop and urged it at the railing, over which it soared as if sprouting wings. It landed with a thud that all but shook its rider free, and then she was off, with the wind behind her. The groom, who had sprung up to lean on the railing, waved his cap after her, admiring her daring.

'Maud?' The male voice sounded annoyed. As Jess swung round from the window, Sir Richard strode in, glanced round the room and said, 'Damn! Where is her ladyship?'

'She've...' Helplessly, Jess gestured at the window, which made the squire come striding past her on long, stalk-like legs to peer down the drive where his wife was rapidly disappearing.

'Damn!' he said again. 'That blasted horse...' and swung round as if recalling that he wasn't alone.

Realising that she hadn't curtseyed when he came in, Jess did so now, and waited. Unlike his wife, Sir Richard was looking her over with genuine interest and curiosity. 'You're the girl from the rectory, aren't you? The girl Miss Lily Clare discovered in the woods? Jessie...?'

'Sharp, sir – your lordship.' Miss Peartree hadn't told her what she should call him, only that if they met she'd better get out of his way and keep quiet.

'"Sir" will do,' he said with a wry smile. 'I'm not a lordship. Wouldn't even be a baronet if my two older brothers had lived, but there you are, that's the way life goes. Never know what it's going to throw at you next, do you?'

She was surprised that he should have such thoughts – and astonished that he should share them with her. Startled, she shook her head. 'No, sir.'

'What are you doing here at Hewinghall?'

'Well, sir...' She felt herself flush. He had every right to ask, if she was to be looking after his daughter, but she hadn't expected the question to be put quite so bluntly. 'I run away from Lynn, sir, because... because...' *Because I killed a man.* She was so unnerved she almost spoke the words aloud. Almost. It might have been a relief to do so and have it done with.

The smile in his eyes altered, first to speculation and then to a calm, waiting expectancy that said he was ready to listen and, perhaps, to understand. 'Yes, Jess? You ran away because...?'

He was interrupted by a voice from near the door, where a maid dipped a curtsey – the same maid Jess had met at the shoot. 'You rang, sir?'

He frowned his annoyance, snapping, 'No!' then, 'Yes. That is, I assume her ladyship rang for you to show Miss Sharp out.'

'Oh – no, sir,' Jess corrected anxiously. 'Beggin' your pardon, sir, but her ladyship said I was to go up to the nursery, sir. I'm to see Nanny Fyncham. About the nurserymaid job.'

His interest deepened as he stared at her again. 'Wait outside, Sal,' he said, and the other girl backed out, closing the door behind her. 'That was what I meant, when I asked what you were doing here – I meant today, not...' He stopped himself, shaking his head slightly, a gleam of wry amusement crinkling his eyes. 'It was my fault, for not making myself clear. So... the rector has decided to take up my offer, has he?'

'Offer, sir?' Not knowing what he meant, Jess shook her head. Could it be that he himself had suggested she have this job? Surely not. The squire of Hewinghall wouldn't concern himself over the fate of such as she.

He didn't explain, said only, 'Just tell me one thing – did you run away from your previous place because of something you'd done, or because of something that had been done to you?'

Jess stood there, searching his face. He was not a handsome man, but the grey eyes were bright and luminous, pale irises rimmed with a dark circle. Compelling eyes... 'Both, sir.'

'I see.' The flicker of amusement was gone. He regarded her gravely, reading her heart, almost. 'And tell me, Jess, if you had been treated fairly and kindly, would you have stayed? Would you still be there?'

'*Course* I would, sir. I'd never've run away from my home and everything if that han't a been for... for what he done. To my mother, sir – and to me.' She daren't say more. It was already more than she'd admitted to anyone else.

The grey eyes narrowed as he considered. He said, 'I pride myself on being a good judge of character, Jess, so I won't pry any further – everyone is entitled to a few secrets. If Miss Lily Clare trusts you, then so shall I. You see, it's my belief that people respond to trust by being trustworthy. Help me prove it, eh?'

Jess promised that she would, amazed at the way the interview had turned.

Dismissed from Sir Richard's presence, she found the maid waiting in the lobby. 'Hello!' the girl smiled. 'Remember me – Sal Gooden? We met at the shoot.'

'I remember.' Jess was glad of a familiar, friendly face. 'I'm Jess Sharp.'

'Yes, I know. We saw you arrive. Come on, the nursery's this way.'

She led the way back through the rear passages, explaining what various areas were and where doors led, though Jess didn't take in half of it. They came into a long, cold, flagstone-floored conservatory with tall windows looking out on to a grassed area between two wings of the house. Along the inner wall stood stuffed animals – strange animals with huge eyes and horns – and above them hung the staring heads of more beasts, among spears and shields decorated with beads, feathers and grasses.

'"Little Africa",' said Sal, pulling a face and shivering. 'Horrible, en't it? All those glass eyes starin'. I hate coming through here at night, and Miss Bella's terrified of the place – but then she're frit of a lot of things, poor little mawther.'

'What's it meant to be?' Jess asked.

'Well, it's a museum, en't it? Sir Richard's uncle was a great hunter. Liked bringin' his trophies home and havin' 'em stuffed for posterity. Poor gentleman died out there in the Dark Continent. Trampled by elephant, so they say.'

At the far end of the jungle-like corridor, another door led into another vestibule where the service stairs climbed steeply up, six flights of them, covered in a thin strip of worn brown carpet. The final flight led, via yet another door, into the attics, whose corridor was long and dark, with rooms off to one side. It was lit only by a single recessed window. Jess's head reeled at the height and the glimpse of a strange jumble of roofs and windows and courtyards far below. Beneath their feet the floor creaked under a thin carpet and overhead the ceiling sloped sharply, but the walls were decked in pretty papers and there was a fresh clean smell of soap and beeswax.

Tapping at a door that ended the corridor, Sal waited. The door opened a fraction, there was a whispered discussion, and with wishes for 'Good luck!' Sal went away, leaving Jess with the nurserymaid, who was wearing afternoon uniform of dark dress and apron. Glancing behind her, a finger to her lips enjoining silence, she beckoned Jess inside, hissing, 'I'm Kate. Come you in.'

The room was long, both sitting room and schoolroom, furnished with tables and chairs, a desk, books ranged on shelves, and a blackboard and easel. Beyond a magnificent rocking horse, two large dormer windows looked south across the park. But Jess's attention was drawn to the fireplace opposite the windows, where on the hearthrug young Bella Fyncham lay fitting the pieces of a jigsaw on a board. Beside her an elderly woman in black silk with a shawl about her shoulders and a blanket over her knees dozed in an armchair, her head at such an angle that her lace cap had slipped askew, falling over one eye. Her mouth was open, emitting loud snoring noises and heavy blowings. She made a comical sight. Jess had to bite her lip to keep from laughing.

The nurserymaid, bright eyes sharing the joke, breathed, 'Nanny likes to nap of an afternoon, poor old soul. She get wore out. Miss Bella's delicate and—' She stopped, realising the child had sat up and was listening.

Bella Fyncham's plain face was framed by long straight hair the colour of polished copper, which trailed on to the shoulders of a dark green velvet gown trimmed with lace. Her eyes were a calm, clear grey, like her father's, regarding Jess with wary solemnity.

Kate went to shake the nanny's shoulder and she woke with a jerk and a grunt, smacking her lips as she peered blearily about her.

'Nanny, the girl's here. The girl from the rectory – Jessie Sharp. Lady Fyncham sent her up.'

'Well, tell her to come over here where I can see her,' said Nanny, adjusting her cap.

Slowly, aware that every step was being examined by the narrowed eyes in that lined face, Jess crossed the room to stand on the hearthrug, glad of the warmth from the fire.

'You've seen Lady Maud?' Nanny asked.

'Yes, 'm. And Sir Richard.'

Wrinkled eyelids flickered. '*And* Sir Richard? Well, there's a thing,' she murmured to the child, who had come to stand by her knee. Nanny's hand came out to stroke the bright hair fondly. 'Shows how important you are to your father, my duck, so never you forget that. You're the apple of his eye.' She let her hand rest on the small shoulder, then straightened her back a little. 'Show her where everything is, Kate, and tell her her duties. She can come after supper on Sunday, while you're still here to settle her in. Come, Bella, get on with your jigsaw, there's a good child.'

Kate motioned Jess away, across the room to a further door and another angled passageway.

A room at the corner of the house was where Bella slept in a narrow cot under sloping eaves. Next door was a dressing room, containing chests of drawers, cupboards and presses for the child's clothes, with a hip bath and a marble wash stand. Near the head of yet another set of back stairs lay the room which was allotted to the nurserymaid. Jess was gratified to find it spacious, provided with old but decent furniture. The window looked into the kitchen courtyard where, Jess saw, the lines of linen had been removed. Snow was falling, driven on the wind.

'The stairs outside are the family stairs,' Kate said. 'They go down to the private apartments, but *you* mustn't ever use them 'cept in emergency. *You* have to go down the servants' stairs, the way Sal brung you. Seem like miles some days when you're cartin' coals and hot water. Nanny's room is over the other side, far end of the schoolroom. You see to that, too. You have to light the fire and keep everything clean, change the beds, help Miss Bella get dressed and undressed... Everything her and Nanny need. They're not much trouble. Nanny's getting too old to care and Miss Bella... well, she have her moments but mostly she're good as gold.'

'Then why're you leaving?' Jess asked.

Colour crept into Kate's sallow face and she unconsciously laid a hand to her stomach. 'I'm goin' to be wed,' she said with shy pride. 'Goin' to be Mrs George Hewitt. He's a blacksmith, in Hewing village. We're to be wed next Tuesday – first day of March.'

'I hope you'll be happy,' Jess said, guessing that Kate had captured her man in the oldest way known to womankind.

When they returned through the schoolroom, Nanny was napping again and Bella stood on the step below one of the windows, watching the snow. Troubled grey eyes followed Jess's progress towards the further door.

'Can you find your way down?' Kate asked. 'I'd best stay with her. See you Sunday, then.'

'I'll be here. Bye, Miss Bella.'

She thought Bella wasn't going to reply, but just as she was closing the door, a near inaudible 'Goodbye' reached her.

Jess felt sorry for the poor little mawther, left on her own with a tired old woman and a procession of nurserymaids to care for her.

She made it back to the rectory, arriving breathless and caked with snow, so cold her hands wouldn't work. Dolly helped her out of her outer clothes and she stood shaking in front of the kitchen range until her chilblains began to scream.

'Takin' you on, then, are they?' Eliza asked.

'They are,' Jess got out through chattering teeth. 'Lady Fyncham talked to me – and Sir Richard. Very nice them were, too. Real gentry.'

'Huh!' Eliza tipped her shapely chin in the air. 'That was all arranged, anyhow. Nothin' to do with you – 'cept Miss Lily'll be more likely to do as she're told if you're already there.'

Jess brushed aside a strand of soaking hair. 'What are you now on about, 'Liza?'

'If you don't know, that's not for me to say,' said Eliza, suddenly shifty, as if realising she shouldn't have said anything. 'You'll find out, soon enough.'

-

On the day before Jess was due to move to Hewinghall House, Miss Peartree came puffing into the kitchen in distress, eyes moist behind her spectacles. 'I can't believe it!' she gasped, a hand to her chest as she struggled for breath and blinked back tears. 'My brooch. My brooch is gone!'

Since Jess had her hands covered in flour, making scones for tea, it was left to Eliza to jump up from the chair where she had been enjoying a cup of tea. 'What brooch is that?' she asked in concern.

'You know the one – my mother's cameo brooch that I wear nearly every day. I *know* I put it safely away. I'm always exceedingly careful with it. It was in its velvet pouch, in my jewel box. And now it's gone. Gone!'

'Well, *I* hen't got it,' Eliza said, and sent a glinting look at Jess, who instinctively felt above her breastbone for the shape of her mother's ring nestling safely on its ribbon. Its small roundness comforted her.

Miss Peartree had lifted her tear-blotched face, horrified. 'Eliza! I said it was lost, not stolen. It never occurred to me to think—'

'Well, that seem to me as how that have to be the answer,' the maid replied. 'If you put that safely away, and now that's gone, well...'

Miss Peartree clasped her hands to her throat. 'You surely don't mean... Someone in this house?'

'Why not? Someone who mebbe thought that, you bein' so fond o' that brooch and all, that must be worth a lot o' money.' Again she looked straight at Jess, who this time felt her stomach go cold. She wanted to rush up to her room and search every crevice. This was how Eliza had planned her revenge – to brand Jess a thief.

Miss Peartree was trembling. 'Perhaps I just mislaid it. I *am* becoming a little absent-minded. I'll have another look for it later.'

'Let me do that,' Eliza offered. 'You have a cup of tea and sit still a while. You're all of a doo-dah. I'll go and look—'

'No!' Miss Peartree caught hold of the maid's sleeve. 'No! Oh… I don't know. I was sure I'd looked everywhere, but…'

'Who have been in your room lately?' Eliza asked.

'No one! That is… apart from you and Dolly – and Jess brings me my morning tea. You can't be suggesting that…'

'I en't suggestin' nothin', miss. I was on'y speckalatin' on the possibles. That leave just us three, then. Well, I'm sure you're welcome to look in *my* room.' And for a third time she turned her clear green stare on Jess.

You can search my room, too, Jess wanted to say, but the words wouldn't come. Her throat was thick with apprehension. Where had Eliza hidden the brooch? Perhaps if Jess could get to the attic…

'And what about Dolly?' Eliza's apron-draped skirts swished self-importantly as she strode across the kitchen and flung open the door of the cupboard where Dolly's pallet was kept rolled up.

'Eliza, please—' Miss Peartree protested, and Jess started across to intervene, but before she could get there Eliza had dragged the pallet out and unrolled it across the floor. Dolly's few pitiful belongings flopped and rolled on to the flagstones – her neatly darned nightshirt, a clean pair of drawers, a hairbrush, her rag doll… As the doll sprawled on the floor, something slipped from under its skirts and slid across to lie right by Jess's feet. It was a brooch, an oval of ebony framed in gold filigree, with a likeness of a woman carved in yellowing ivory.

'Oh, my Lord!' Eliza gasped. 'Honest, miss, I never dreamed…'

But she was lying, Jess knew. Of course she was lying! Eliza *had* taken the brooch and hidden it, but it was *Dolly* who was the innocent target for her malice.

Rushing to summon Dolly to the kitchen to answer for her crime, Eliza encountered the rector, who wanted to know what was going on. So the story was recounted for his edification. Jess never forgot the helplessness she felt as she stood by the green baize door listening to the rector as he stood in the hall lecturing young Dolly in his most kindly, deadly voice.

'My pity is for your poor mother, Dorothy. Your poor crippled mother. What will *she* have to say about this?'

'But, sir,' Dolly wept. 'I hen't—'

He went on as if she had not spoken, his voice crushing hers. 'To have one of her daughters turn out this way – not only a thief, but a liar. If only you would admit to your sin, it would go better with you, you foolish child.'

Dolly stood before him, apron bundled in her hands, tears streaming from her eyes, mouth working. She was too upset even to defend herself.

'You will leave the rectory, of course,' Reverend Clare decided. 'At once.'

'But Hugh!' Miss Peartree cried. 'You can't just dismiss her. How are we going to manage without her? With Jess leaving tomorrow—'

Swiftly, Eliza put in, 'My sister Mary Anne'd be glad to come, sir,' at which Miss Peartree flung her a wide-eyed, disbelieving glance.

Was that what this was all about? Jess wondered – a plot to get Eliza's sister a job at the rectory?

'Oh, I don't understand any of this.' Taking off her spectacles, Miss Peartree waved them helplessly. 'I can't believe Dolly would do such a thing. Not intentionally. It was a mistake, a moment's lapse.'

'To steal a valuable brooch and hide it away among her things?' The rector was incredulous. 'No, Oriana. Christian charity has its bounds. Dorothy has betrayed our trust. I will not have a *thief* in my house.' As Dolly began to turn away, he laid a big hand on her shoulder. Her eyes glittered like a frightened rabbit's as she twisted sideways to peer up at him. 'Before you go, Dorothy, I want you to clear your conscience. *Confess* that you took the brooch.'

For a moment Jess could hardly think. A red veil of blood blinded her as memory came – Merrywest, holding her as the rector was holding Dolly, speaking so low and meaning so vicious. Dear Lord!

Unable to bear the look on Dolly's face, she started forward, saying, 'Mr Clare, she—'

She was stopped by a look so sharp it felt like a lance at her breast. 'Don't interfere, Jessamy!' he ordered, and she saw his fingers tighten on Dolly's shoulder in a grip that made the child wince. 'Well, Dorothy?'

'I done it!' Dolly cried. 'I took the brooch. I do confess.'

His grip eased as a smirk of satisfaction played round his mouth and he glanced at the trembling Jess, and at the silent Eliza, as if to call them to bear witness to the truth of his justice. 'Very well. Since you admit your sin, and because of your poor mother, I shall not call the constables. Not this time. But if in future, Dorothy, I hear that you have repeated this crime, or anything like it, then I shall be forced to speak of what has happened today. Do you understand me?'

Dolly was sobbing into her apron. 'Yes, sir. Yes, sir.'

'Good! Then you may go. Gather your things and leave the rectory.'

Weeping wretchedly, Dolly wrenched away from him and came blindly down the hall, blundering into Jess, who threw her arms around the child and started to comfort her, but—

'Leave her!' Reverend Clare snapped. 'No one is to speak to her. She has betrayed my trust and now she must take her punishment. Stay where you are, Jessamy!'

Once, she might have obeyed, but this time she faced him squarely with her head high. She had nothing to lose; she too would be leaving tomorrow. And she hated bullies!

'You'll forgive me, rector, but the child needs someone to go with her. If you send her alone in all this snow, in the dark, Lord know what'll happen to her. No, I intend to go with her.'

His pink face seemed to swell and redden as he held his breath and suddenly made a chopping gesture. 'Very well! Then take your own things, too! Go now. Go – both of you! You make me regret my generosity in ever taking you in. If this is how you repay me, then… be gone, Jessamy Sharp.'

'Oh, Jess.' Dolly clutched at her. 'You shouldn't've…'

''Course I should,' Jess comforted, giving the rector a look of icy loathing as, with an arm round the child, she led her away.

Nine

As Jess told the gist of the tale, Susan Upton occupied herself brewing a pot of tea, while her mother rested on her couch and Dolly sat huddled on a little stool by the fire, her arms clutched tightly round her rag doll.

'We all know you didn't do it, Doll,' Jess said.

'Of course she didn't!' Mrs Upton was quietly furious. 'Miss Peartree have always been special kind to Dolly. Why on earth would the little mawther now steal her precious brooch? That's what hurt me most – that Miss Peartree do believe she'd do it.'

'She don't,' said Jess. 'Miss Peartree don't know what to think. She're an innocent old soul.'

Mrs Upton had been watching Jess closely. She said, 'It was that sly-boots, wa'n't it? Oh, you hen't said so, and that's to your credit, but I know. Eliza Potts took that brooch just to get my poor gal dismissed.'

'That seem so,' Jess agreed with a sigh. 'Trouble is, that was her word against Dolly's, and the rector believed Eliza.'

'He would!' Dolly muttered with venom, burying her face in the rag doll. The silence seemed to sing, waiting for her to say more, but she only rocked herself to and fro, curled in with her unhappiness.

Mrs Upton shook her head. 'She're wholly done up about this.'

But it was more than that. What, exactly, had Dolly meant? She knew far more than she was saying. Maybe that was why Eliza had got her dismissed – Dolly had been in the way; so she'd been dispensed with.

'It was good of you to stick up for her,' Mrs Upton said. 'You'll stop the night with us, of course. Yes, Jess, you will. And tomorrow we'll go to chapel and hold our heads up. We hen't got nothin' to be ashamed of.'

Mrs Upton slept on her couch in the living room while the sisters and Jess shared the bedroom above. It was warm from the chimney breast which came up from the fire in the main room, and it was companionable, talking quietly to Dolly and Susan, then listening to them breathe as they slept, reminding Jess of her own family home. But she herself remained wakeful. She was just beginning to realise that she'd left the rectory for ever. Tomorrow her new life at Hewinghall would begin…

–

Dolly was reluctant to face her neighbours and friends at chapel, afraid that they would believe her to be a thief.

'They'll think even more if you don't go,' her mother said. 'It'll do you good, Doll. Jess'll walk with you, too. Won't you, Jess?'

Though she was anxious to support Dolly, Jess hadn't been in a chapel since she fled from Lynn. 'Well…'

'Oh, good!' Mrs Upton beamed from the chair where she sat with her twisted legs covered by a blanket. 'Jess, that do my heart good to think of you bein' with us afore the Lord's table. You three girls can walk together. I have to go in the cart along o' Fred Trainer – on account of my legs. Howsomever, do you have good legs that's not so far.'

Jess was wearing the best of her clothes as she and Dolly and Susan set out to hike the four miles along snow-deep lanes, skirting Hewinghall estate, passing through Syderford village and on towards the coast. On the way they met up with other groups bound for the same destination, so a merry throng arrived in the village of Martham Staithe, which boasted the only Methodist chapel for miles around.

The little chapel, recently built of red brick, stood at the end of a row of cottages on the edge of the fishing village. Jess gazed with fond eyes on the boats lying in muddy creeks waiting for the tide, though here was no sheltered estuary haven like that offered by the Fisher Fleet. Here, the north wind blew direct from the Arctic. The inlets, and the sandy wastes between them, were dotted with wading birds, the skies awheel with gulls braving the cold wind. But inside the chapel a stove was going, offering a welcome. As yet, no word of Dolly's disgrace had reached beyond the rectory, so she was able to tell her own side of it, laying the blame squarely on Eliza.

'Well, what can you expect from a Potts?' was the general consensus. 'Never see *them* in chapel, do you?'

Jess was accepted with friendly curiosity and soon the harmonium was wheezing and she joined in gratefully as hearty voices raised praise in familiar words, to familiar tunes, stirring the blood. The preacher spoke of God's love and forgiveness and Jess prayed hard. But her prayers seemed to go up into nothingness. If God was there, he wasn't listening to her.

Maybe that was because she wasn't truly repentant. And if that was so, then she'd have to stay outside the fold. Because, deep in her heart, calmly and coldly, she knew that, if she had it to do again, she would still kill Nathanael Merrywest. She hoped he was even now burning in hellfire...

After the service, as gossiping groups gathered outside, still chewing over Dolly's misfortune, she saw a shaggy black retriever tethered to a fence. Just as she was wondering if it was Dash or the similar dog she had seen at Hewinghall, Reuben Rudd came up to untie the leash. She'd been so concerned about what folk might think or say or do that she hadn't noticed him in chapel. Dash was delighted to see his master. So, to her consternation, was Jess. But her instinctive rush of pleasure raised all her defences – she didn't want to feel that way, about him or any man.

Doffing his cap, he brushed back a lick of brown hair and stood smiling at her with those bright hazel eyes that had the power to make her feel as if she was the only woman he'd ever smiled at in quite that way – foolish, she knew. 'I thought it was you,' he said, 'though I was too far back to tell for sure, especially when you're wearing that smart hat. You look a bobby-dazzler. How are you, Miss Jessie?'

'Fair to middlin',' Jess replied with a shrug, watching Fred Trainer carry Mrs Upton to his cart while Dolly held the horse steady. 'And what're you doin' so far from home, Mr Rudd?'

'Far?' Laughing, he gestured expansively. 'Why, lass, this is all my beat – all Hewinghall land. Sir Richard's father built these cottages, and Sir Richard himself had the chapel put up only a few years ago. See, it's written up there in the brickwork – R.B.F., for Richard Baines Fyncham – and the date, 1886.'

She stared up at the letters and figures and when she glanced again at Rudd he was surveying her face and figure, admiring what he saw – and not the least abashed to have her catch him at it.

Hazel eyes alight, he said, 'Well, Miss Jessie, it's right good to see you. I hear you're joining the staff at the big house.'

'So?'

'So I think you'll enjoy it there. They're a good crowd of folk. You'll like Mrs Roberts, the housekeeper – and don't you already know Sal Gooden? She's a nice lass. Aye, you'll do right well at the big house.'

'I was doin' all right at the rectory,' Jess said.

Rudd's gaze held hers, seeming to read her mind. 'Were you?'

Tilting her chin, she said, 'Miss Lily liked havin' me there.'

'Miss Lily's a strange one, though, don't you think?'

'I'll not hear a word against her!' Jess retorted. 'She've been a good friend to me – whatever Eliza say.' Disturbed as ever by her reaction to the man, she glanced around for Dolly, hoping for moral support.

Gossip had stopped as all eyes turned to watch another man approach, a good-looking young man, sporting a fancy waxed moustache and one of the new 'bowler' hats. A proper toff, Jess thought – and one whom she had seen before.

His grin widened as his glance fell on her and, altering his course slightly, he made straight for where she was standing with Rudd beside her. As he came, he doffed his cap to the group of spectators. ''Morning, all.' Most of them turned away and resumed their conversations, though some continued to watch him from their eye corner. Only one man replied, with a courteous ''Morning, Jim.'

The newcomer must have noticed the extra frosting on the morning, but his smile didn't falter. He seemed to be enjoying the discomfiture he was causing. ''Mornin', Mr Rudd,' he greeted pleasantly.

'Potts.' The gamekeeper's reply was so clipped that Jess glanced at him and found him returning the other's smile with shuttered face and hostile eyes. This was another Reuben Rudd, a hard man – a man you wouldn't want to cross.

Potts turned his green eyes on her. Familiar green eyes, somehow. 'You must be Jessie Sharp, then,' he said. 'Our 'Liza's told me about you. Name's Potts, Jim Potts. Nice to meet you, Miss Sharp.'

Eliza's brother!

As Jim Potts held out his hand to her, Rudd said, 'Clear off, Potts.'

The sparkling green eyes held Jess's. 'Be he your keeper, then? I hen't heard as you was walkin' out, together.'

'I'm warning you, Potts!' Bristling, Rudd placed himself in front of Jess. 'Be on your way. This young lady wants nowt to do with you.'

To Jess's dismay, most of the people lingering by the chapel were now watching with increased interest, awaiting developments.

'Mr Rudd!' she objected. 'Next time I need a guardian, I'll know where to send. Until then, hold you hard. As for you, Mr Potts... where I come from, a gentleman do wait to be properly introduced afore he start makin' silly-bold remarks to a lady. Seem like folk hereabouts hen't got no manners at all. If you'll excuse me...' Nose in the air, she walked away.

Behind her, Jim Potts laughed out loud, though she fancied it was with approval.

Catching up with her, Dolly was agog over the incident. 'I thought Mr Rudd was a-goin' to sole him. I hen't never seen him so mad. My! That'll set Eliza's nose out o' joint. She think Mr Rudd have eyes for *her*.'

'Seem to me as how Reuben Rudd have eyes for anythin' wearin' a skirt,' Jess said loftily. It was flattering to have two men squaring up on her account – not that she was interested in either of them.

She glanced back to see Jim Potts stepping out of the way of the cart as it set off. Reuben Rudd was striding in the opposite direction, with Dash at his heels. He looked as if he was trying to put as much space between himself and Jess as was possible.

Jim Potts had other ideas. The girls and their companions hadn't gone far before he caught them up, saying, 'Mind if I walk along?'

'Yes, we do mind,' Jess retorted.

'Now, that en't friendly.' He caught her arm, managing to separate her from the others, who hurried on, in no mood to talk with Eliza's brother.

'That wan't friendly of your sister to get poor Dolly dismissed from her situation for nothin',' Jess said.

He frowned. 'What? I don't know nothin' about that.'

'No? Well, everyone else now do. Eliza 'on't get away with it.'

'Eliza can take care of herself,' he said with a shrug that dismissed the subject. Looking her over with fresh interest, he grinned. 'She told me you had a sharp tongue in your head. If I'd a known you was goin' to chapel I might a gone along myself. Not that I'm much of a prayin' sort of man, as 'Liza must've told you.'

'Eliza haven't even mentioned you,' Jess said with satisfaction, and walked on after her friends, hoping to end the conversation.

Jim Potts was not discarded so easily. 'What? Not mentioned her favourite brother? I shall have to have a word with the gal. She's told me about you. Plenty. On'y she didn't mention how pretty you was.'

Now Jess knew he was a liar.

'Howsomever,' he added, 'I couldn't a gone to chapel this mornin'. I bin workin'.'

Jess slanted him a look, curious in spite of herself. 'On a Sunday? Doin' what?'

'Bit o' this, bit o' that. Buy from one man, sell to another. I'm a trader, me. An enterprenner. My own master. Have my own business some day. Real business. A shop, prob'ly.'

Unimpressed, Jess increased her pace. She couldn't abide being near Jim Potts any longer.

'I better get back to my friends,' she said, and hurried on to rejoin the little gaggle of young folk walking home from chapel.

'What did he want?' Dolly asked.

'Nothin' that signify,' said Jess. 'Load of old squit. I give him short shrift, don't you worry.'

'You want to stay away from that one,' Susan Upton said. 'He's a wrong 'un. Everyone know that.'

'Just because he's a Potts?' one of the other girls demanded. 'Give a dog a bad name...'

'And what's it to you, Tansy Stafford?' someone else teased. 'Mashed on him, are you?'

Jess was unable to stop herself from looking round – to assure herself that Jim Potts wasn't following. He'd been watching for that. He saluted her merrily and turned aside on to another pathway, whistling, hands in his pockets, the subdued retriever following a few paces behind.

Great fool! Jess thought scornfully. But something about the man nagged at her. It had nagged at her when she first saw him, up at Hewinghall. But it wouldn't stay still long enough for her to see what it was.

–

After spending a companionable day with the Uptons, Jess walked across the snowy park to the big house, apprehension growing with every step. What did fate intend for her there?

The nurserymaid, Kate, was alone in the big schoolroom, with the fire burning low and just a candle on the table to see by. The candle flickered in several different draughts, making shadows lurch and loom.

'Miss Bella's in bed,' Kate told Jess. 'She's been a bit poorly and Nanny gave her some medicine that make her sleep. Nanny's takin' hot chocolate with Mrs Roberts, the housekeeper, and I was just finishin' some mending – Miss Bella's a terror for tearing her lace cuffs. You can now give me a hand, do you like, and I'll tell you what have to be done.'

She took Jess to leave her things in the back corner room which they would share that night. Tomorrow Kate was leaving and the day after she would be wed to her blacksmith, George Hewitt.

During the evening, Jess heard a lot about George Hewitt and, in odd words and phrases thrown in among the rest, she learned a little more about her new situation. Bella, she discovered, liked to be out and about but she had to be preserved from chills – she was a sickly child, prone to coughs and chesty infections; her inclinations for the out-of-doors had to be curtailed when the weather was cold or wet.

Lady Maud was an outdoor-lover, too, though she enjoyed a stronger constitution than her daughter. She bred horses and trained them to the saddle. 'George do all her shoein' – her ladyship say he's the best blacksmith in Norfolk. Pity of it is, she care more for her horses than she do for her little 'un. Or for her husband, come to that.' Sir Richard, in the nurserymaid's opinion, was at fault in the opposite way – he coddled and spoiled his daughter. 'Still, that's on'y natural, considerin' how they lost the boy.'

'The boy?' Jess queried.

'Oh, that was afore I come here. None of 'em talk about it. Nanny said I wasn't to gossip and put ideas in your head. Still…' She glanced round the cold expanses of the big, shadowed room and shivered. 'There's high sprites here. Can't you feel 'em?'

Jess shook her head. Ghosts were a load of old squit – especially when she was wide awake and with a light shining. If the dead returned it was mainly in folks' minds and troubled consciences, like hers about Preacher Merrywest. After a bad dream, she could believe that *he* might come back.

'Well, *I* can,' said Kate. 'I've heard 'em, too, up and down the passages at dead of night, and here, in this room. You can hear the floor creak. I don't stray out of my room in the dark, 'less I'm forced.'

Kate settled the fire safely and, having cleared up their sewing, leaving the schoolroom tidy, led the way back to the room they were to share that night. Since there was only the one bed they shared that, too, lying top to tail swaddled in the blankets, warming each other with their body heat.

'I used to lie like this with my sister, afore she got wed,' Jess murmured into the darkness.

'So did I,' Kate replied through a yawn. 'And two nights from now I shall be lyin' next to that lovely great warm Hewitt bor. Shan't be cold then. Nor never no more.'

Jess felt a coldness deep inside her. For her, the thought of lying with a man brought nothing but the memory of horrors.

Within minutes, Kate's even breathing said she was asleep. Not so Jess. Everything about her was alien – the draughts in the room, the smells, the feel of the bed, the faint moonlight falling at a different angle. Kate's gossip about ghosts had brought Merrywest closer. Her mind replayed frightening dreams she'd had, so that she was almost afraid to sleep.

She turned over, huddling closer under the covers for comfort, turning her thoughts to Lily. Lily was now safely at school but eventually she must come home to a house where Eliza Potts, her enemy, seemed to wield an increasing influence. Did she even know that Jess wouldn't be there? Had Miss Peartree written to tell her what was happening?

The wind blustered about the old house, making it creak and crack. Had Jess been more fanciful she might have been scared; sometimes it sounded as though there was someone walking right outside the door, making the floor creak. Sometimes it sounded as though someone was knocking, wanting to come in the window. But it was just the old house settling.

There! The floorboards moaned again, by the head of the 'family stairs' as Kate had called them. Was someone there, or was it only the wind? *Who* could be there? If it was anyone at all, he must be creeping about in the dark – no light showed under the door.

The board creaked again. This time Jess was sure she heard a sort of sigh, or was it a sob? Or was it the wind? Now thoroughly awake, she unwrapped the blankets from around her and, shivering in the cold air, sat up, swinging her legs out of the bed, moving slowly so as not to disturb Kate. There was a dull *pong* as her heel connected with the tin chamber pot under the bed. Jess held her breath, but Kate didn't stir.

Arms outstretched, Jess felt her way across the room. Her toes discovered the square of thin carpeting that covered the boards near the door and then her hand found the door itself. The latch lifted with the smallest snick, revealing deep darkness.

But something breathed in that blackness. Something snuffled and shivered. 'Who's there?' she demanded. 'Speak up, or else—'

A brain-piercing wail split the darkness, making her stop her ears. Behind her Kate woke with a start. 'Whassamatter? Who's that? Bella?'

The screaming paused for a short breath, then assaulted Jess again, louder and higher. A flare of misty light lit the room behind her as Kate struck a match. It let Jess see the terrified child who huddled in the passageway, her long hair in pigtails trailing over the shoulders of her nightgown, her face swimming against the darkness, pale as a dead dab floating belly-up in the Fleet, with staring eyes above a wide-open mouth. She was screaming like a steam engine's whistle.

Setting the match to a candle, Kate came hurrying, snapping, 'Bella! Stop that row!' She gave the candle to Jess and pushed her aside, advancing on the child.

'Don't—' Jess began, but Kate's hand was already connecting, hard, with Bella's cheek. The screams choked off. Bella stood shaking, staring at Kate, shuddering with both cold and terror, her arms wrapped tightly round her body as the nurserymaid grabbed her and shook her. 'What're you doing out o' bed, heh? Hen't I told you to stay in your room? You're a bad, wicked girl! D'you want old Harry to get you?' She glanced round at Jess. 'Her medicine should a made her sleep all night, but with you comin' when you did I forgot to bolt the door. Let's get her back to bed.'

With a hand guarding the candleflame from the currents of air that flowed about the attics, Jess followed the pair back to Bella's room. She blamed herself for the state the child was in, still shivering, teeth chattering, her arms locked round her own thin body. She was all wrapped in with herself, alone with a deep misery that called out all Jess's protective instincts.

'Here we are, then,' Kate said briskly. 'Here's your room. Get you into bed now, and do you stay there.'

'Shall I—' Jess began.

'Just wait.' She helped the child into bed and tucked the covers round the small, shivering form. Bella turned her face to the wall, curled up in a ball with her eyes tightly shut, excluding everything, pretending she was alone.

'She'll do,' said Kate. 'You'll have to remember – bolt the door every night, comewhatever. Can't have her roamin' about the house – Lord knows what Lady Maud'd say if little 'un turned up downstairs.'

'D'you think they heard her crying?' Jess asked.

'No, shouldn't think so. Anyway, her ladyship sleep like the dead when she've had a couple.' Shivering she rubbed her arms through her nightgown. 'I'm friz. Come on, Jess, let's go and get warm in bed.'

'I'll stay a while,' Jess said.

Kate stared at her in surprise. 'In here? On your own? It was this room where...' She stopped herself, with a guilty glance at the bed. 'Well, do you suit yourself, but I'm now goin'. Don't forget to bolt the door after you when you come.'

Jess was cold, too, but that was nothing new. A shawl lay across the end of the brass bedstead; she wrapped it round her shoulders and went to lift the curtain and look out at the night. Earlier clouds had parted, leaving bright moonlight sparkling in the frost on the parapet and lighting the snowy park.

'That look real cold out there,' she said quietly. 'Though that en't much warmer in here, is it?'

The only response was a change in the quality of Bella's breathing. It had been hoarse and fast; now it slowed – Bella was listening.

Jess went on talking, about nothing really, just letting the child know she was there. She sang bits and pieces of old songs and lullabies that came to her, songs she'd sung for Sam and Joe, and poor little Sarah-May, who'd died before she was two. After a while, when the cold got too much, she sat on the end of the bed and tucked her feet under the cosy eiderdown, curling up like a cat. Bella was resting now, her breathing even and relaxed. If she wasn't asleep she soon would be.

Jess was drifting, too comfortable to move and get chilled again, when a sudden thought shot her awake as if someone had prodded her. She was remembering Jim Potts, loping away from her that morning after chapel with a black dog trailing behind him – and on another day, wearing a tweed cap and a big weatherproof cape... She was also remembering another snowy, moonlit night, when she had seen a caped man come secretly to the rectory, loping down the path – with a black dog behind him.

She'd been so sure the night visitor was Reuben Rudd. But now she wondered if she could've been mistaken. Rudd strode out, while Jim Potts slouched along – just as the night visitor had slouched in the moonlight.

Had she been wrong all this time? Oh Lord! For weeks she'd thought the worst of Rudd – thought dreadful things, fended him off, been cool and clipped with him. Maybe he did have a kind of fancy for Eliza – many a man did, Jess was sure – but did that mean he would come creeping at night to have his sinful way? Oh, why hadn't she listened to her heart? Her heart had known all the time, from the first moment she saw Rudd, that he was a good, kind, honest man worthy of respect and trust and friendship...

No, it was more than that. The truth was, she'd taken one look at him and known he was a man she could love. And that had frightened her so much that she'd latched on to the notion of him and Eliza being lovers.

But what on earth would bring Jim Potts calling on his sister late at night? Something illegal? Smuggling, maybe. Plenty of that went on round these coasts – Jess's dad hadn't said no to a bit of extra cash in hand on account of the odd bottle of rum or brandy. Or maybe it was poaching – folk said Eliza's family were rogues, and hadn't Miss Peartree...

Jess sighed to herself. Whatever the way of it, sure as eggs was eggs she'd ruined any chance she might have had with Rudd. Not that she'd ever had much of a chance. Not she. Not with the weight of sin she bore on her conscience. If Reuben Rudd ever knew the truth about her – what she was and what she'd done – he probably wouldn't waste his energy even spitting on her.

–

Lily received a strange letter from Miss Peartree; it told a garbled tale of a disappearing brooch which had found its way into Dolly's pallet by some mysterious means which Miss Peartree didn't quite understand. She said that Dolly's place at the rectory had been taken by a sister of Eliza's, a girl of fourteen with a sullen expression and a constantly runny nose; her name was Mary Anne. Though she was slovenly, at least she was available to fill the empty place at once and Reverend Clare said she would learn, given time and patience.

Lily was perplexed. Why had Dolly been replaced by yet another member of the Potts family, whom most people regarded as little short of scoundrels? Was Papa demonstrating his Christian sense of charity towards the oppressed? A pity, then, that he couldn't show the same compassion for his adopted daughter.

Reading the letter again, Lily realised that it didn't mention Jess once. Usually Cousin Oriana had some story of Jess's prowess to recount, but this time – not a word. Perhaps she was growing forgetful in her old age. Oh, dear! If Oriana succumbed to senility it would mean yet more changes.

Near Easter, with the evenings lengthening and the weather turning mild, Lily looked forward to going home. It would be good to talk to Jess, to share the hope that, with her eighteenth birthday rapidly approaching, her real father might make himself known this very summer.

He had to come soon! He was her only hope of escaping from a life where she felt increasingly trapped. She didn't belong where she was. There had to be something else in store for her. There *had* to be. She had always known it.

One night she was dreaming about it, seeing a great carriage drive up to the rectory with a gold crest on its side, the footman climbing down, opening the door... Just as the passenger was about to reveal himself, she was startled awake by someone shaking her arm and hissing, 'Lily! Lily!'

She broke out of the dream with a shock, disorientated and blinking in the light of the forbidden candle Anne Ferrers was carrying, eyes flaring wide in a pale, worried face, fingers to her lips entreating silence.

'What?' Lily mumbled.

'The drawing room,' came the whispered reply. 'Someone's in there, climbing in through the window. I heard them.'

'Robbers, you mean?' Suddenly wide awake, Lily threw back the covers, reaching for her wrap.

'No!' Anne barred her way to the door. 'Oh, hush, Lily, don't wake anyone else. It's not thieves, it's... it's Jane and Clemency. I heard them. I couldn't sleep. I was going to find my book, and I heard their voices. They've been out. Now they're climbing back in. Oh... what shall we do?'

Ten

There came sounds – a sharp yelp, a faint clatter, a hiss of whispers – from the senior drawing room. As Lily hurried down the hall to investigate, two figures emerged in a rustle of petticoats, with long cloaks slung round them: Clemency Clare and Jane Lassiter, their hair curled and decked with pearls, jewels glittering at ears and throat, rouge on lips and cheek. They looked like the sort of common women one saw in cartoons, frequenting the balconies at Music Halls, except that their eyes were wide and frightened.

Clemency recovered first. 'Come, Jane, we must change.'

As she made to brush past, Lily caught her arm, saying, 'Clemency! What happened? Who cried out?'

'Don't touch me!' Clemency pulled away as if the soft hand on her arm were a spider, and darted into her room with Jane a pace behind. The door closed in Lily's face.

'Where do you suppose they've been?' Anne breathed. 'All those hints about secret beaux… Maybe it's true.'

'It's not!' Lily snapped. *It's not, it's not, it's not!*

But other matters needed her attention: someone was calling for help.

With Anne at her heels, Lily hastened into the drawing room. The shutters at the window were folded back and the window up, letting cold air lap into the room.

Three feet below the window lay the slope of the spined stone roof of the conservatory. Each spine ended in a spiked finial of wrought iron – except that one was newly missing. The voice came from somewhere below, an undertone edged with hysteria. 'Clemency! Jane! What shall I do?'

'It's Amelia,' Lily realised and, without hesitation, began to climb over the sill. Anne clutched at her in alarm. 'What are you doing? If you're caught…' But her warning was in vain; Lily was reaching her bare foot for the nearest stone rib.

The adventurers had used a knotted rope, looping it around one of the iron spikes, which had broken under Amelia's weight. Fortunately, the sharp finial had fallen to one side; it lay beside her on the paved terrace with the rope tangled about it.

'Pass me the rope,' Lily hissed.

Between them, she and Anne got the shivering Amelia back up into the senior drawing room, where Lily questioned her: 'What were you doing? You surely didn't go out with Clemency and Jane?'

'No, of course I didn't,' Amelia said miserably. 'It's my job to close the window and the shutter after them and wait for them to throw stones at my window when they get back.'

'You mean...' Lily could hardly get the words out, her throat felt so tight, 'this has happened before?'

'Oh, several times,' Amelia sighed. 'They find out when Miss Rattray's on landing duty – you know how heavily she sleeps – and then they make their arrangements. I think they meet...' she lowered her voice as her mouth shaped the forbidden word, 'men.'

Lily clenched her hands, wanting to beat something, riven with a wild mixture that included anger at their stupidity, envy of their daring, and bile-green jealousy. 'What men?'

'I don't know. I... I told them I wanted to go with them next time and they laughed at me. So I hooked the rope round the spike and let myself down, and... and the thing broke. They just abandoned me.'

'You were lucky to escape so lightly,' Lily said. 'You must promise me not to do anything so foolish again.' But a part of her envied Amelia and the others. If she herself had had the chance for such an adventure, wouldn't she too have been tempted? Especially if she were going to meet Ash Haverleigh.

–

As Lily and Clemency travelled home to Norfolk for Easter, there was not much chance for private talk, the train being crammed with people.

The Clares' coachman met them at Hunstanton station and as they rode along the edge of wild marshes haunted by seabirds the girls stared out of opposite windows, each busy with her own thoughts. Lily was torn between delight at coming home and despair because of the questions that gnawed at her heart, and Clemency must have been thinking of the same thing. Without preamble, she said, 'If you tell, I shall be disgraced, and it will be *your* fault. My family will never forgive you.'

'I would never tell on you!' Lily denied, turning her pale face and wide, liquid eyes. 'You know that, Clemency. But... you shouldn't take such risks. If you're discovered, your reputation—'

'Oh, a fiddle for my reputation!' Clemency scoffed. 'Who cares about that? I'm enjoying myself. I'm doing no one any harm.'

'Not even Amelia?'

Clemency shrugged and gazed out of the window, her fingers plucking at a fringed flounce that ornamented her skirt. 'Amelia's a fool. Anyway, she wasn't hurt, only frightened.' She flashed Lily a sidelong glance, her mouth tightening. 'And don't sermonise at me. Who do you think you are?'

Feeling that shrinking, curled-up misery inside her, Lily said, 'I'm – I'm trying to be your friend.'

'Well, you're not my friend! You're a gypsy brat. Your own mother didn't want you. And Uncle Hugh only took you in out of pity.'

'That's not so!' Lily denied.

'It is so. Aunt Helena was sorry for you – and she wanted a child. She couldn't have children of her own so she clung on to the only one that did come along. And she persuaded Uncle Hugh to keep you – against his better judgement. I've heard him say so more than once. If it hadn't been for him, you'd have grown up in the workhouse – or died in that basket where your own mother abandoned you. You owe *everything* to my family. Your home, your clothes, your food – even your education. You've been useful as a companion for me because I don't have any sisters. That's the only reason you were allowed to have lessons with my governess. And they'd never have dreamed of sending you to the Academy if I hadn't been going.'

Stung, Lily cried, 'They sent me because I showed promise! I'm as clever as you are. I have good brains – they came from my parents. My *real* parents. And when my real father comes for me—'

'Oh, really,' Clemency drawled, 'you don't believe that nonsense any more than I do. Your *real* father was some uncouth farmhand who bought the services of a gypsy woman for a penny and lay with her in a ditch somewhere. That's why you have those eyes – because you're a mongrel cross-breed bitch! And that's why your own mother abandoned you – even the gypsies were ashamed to own you.'

'That's not so!' Lily cried again.

'Isn't it? Then where *is* your "real father"? Why doesn't this fine gentleman come for you?' Seeing Lily flounder for an answer, Clemency supplied her own: 'Because he doesn't exist, that's why. Whatever man it was that fathered you, Lily Victoria Clare, he did it in a moment's fit of lust and then he forgot all about it. He'll never come for you. Never!'

Lily turned her head away, fighting the tears that boiled in her throat and blinded her eyes. The bitter truth in Clemency's words seemed to have curdled the air.

After a while, when anger overtook the pain, Lily's mind began to work again. Clearing her throat of a lace net of distress, she said, 'And where do you go, when you go out at night? Who do you meet?'

Clemency's long, slim fingers went on playing with the fringe of her skirt and she continued to stare out of the window, but the corner of her mouth curved in one of her irritating secret smiles.

'Men?' Lily asked. 'You meet with men? Students from the colleges?' One particular name was in her mind, but she daren't say it aloud.

Clemency looked at her sidelong through veiling lashes. 'A lady doesn't discuss her private life.'

'A lady doesn't sneak out at night to assignations with men,' Lily retorted. 'Not with her face painted like a... like a...'

A bubble of laughter escaped Clemency. 'The word is "whore", Lily dear.' Sparkling eyes scanned Lily's scarlet face. 'You're such a child. You don't know anything.' Her face contorted into ugliness and malice. 'You're to forget about it, do you hear? If you ever – ever! – repeat one word...'

She didn't complete the threat. She didn't need to.

'Anyway,' she added after a while, 'we shan't meet again until we return to school. Mama and I are going to London to be with Papa and do some shopping. So don't bother to come slinking along to the Manor trying to ingratiate yourself because we shan't be there. Except for Aunt Jane, of course. You can come and wheedle round her, if you must. Though I have to warn you you're wasting your time – she has no money to leave you.'

Lily said nothing. She sat staring out of the window, her face feeling stiff.

As always, when faced with rejection she sought refuge in her dreams, telling herself that when her real father came Clemency would regret her unkindness. And maybe it would be too late. Maybe, by then, Lily would no longer feel so forgiving.

Soon the carriage was turning in by the Lion Gate of Hewinghall, bowling along the tunnel of trees among thick growths of rhododendron, then climbing through the park to skirt round the church in sight of the big house before heading off down the east drive. Lily was desperate to be home, to tell Jess what had happened. Jess would listen, would understand...

They must have been watching for her. As the carriage drew up she saw the front door open. Gyp ran out, barking his enthusiasm, and Lily jumped down without waiting for the footman to help her, bending with a glad cry to gather the little dog into her arms, her face to his warm coat. He felt awfully thin, all bones beneath his silky coat. Had he been pining for her?

She looked up, smiling through her tears at the figure on the step. 'Oh, it's good to be home!' she said, opening her arms to embrace dear Cousin Oriana's plump shoulders and kiss her cheek.

'It's wonderful to see you,' Miss Peartree said, falsely bright. 'Come in, my dear. You must be tired.'

Lily looked up to where the maids were standing in the doorway, her smile dying as her eyes cleared. She recognised Eliza, of course, and the smaller, thinner girl, snuffling and blowing her nose, must be Mary Anne, who had replaced Dolly. But—

'Where's Jess?' Something was wrong: she could tell that from the way Cousin Oriana was cleaning her spectacles and blinking worriedly. 'Oh, gracious goodness – busy in the kitchen, I expect. She is *such* a worker,' she answered her own question, desperate now to avoid whatever the truth was.

'Lily...' Miss Peartree sounded anxious but Lily refused to hear it. She brushed past, hurrying into the house, through the passages to the kitchen. It was empty but for the boy Button bringing in the newly cleaned knives. He stared at Lily, slack-lipped.

'Where's Jess?' she demanded of him.

'Jess, miss?'

'Yes, Jess! Oh, don't stand there with your mouth open, boy. Are you stupid? You know who I mean. Jess. Jessamy Sharp.'

From behind her, Oriana Peartree said, 'It's all right, Button. Leave the knives on the table and go.' He did so, glad to escape. 'Now, Lily Victoria, my dear... Oh, perhaps I should have told you in one of my letters, but the fact is—'

Lily whirled to face her. 'She's gone, hasn't she? She's run away again. Oh, I was afraid of that! What happened, Cousin Oriana? Was it Eliza? Or was it Papa – he never did want her here. Did you try to find her? Where did she go? Oh, I *knew* I shouldn't leave her. I was the only friend she had. She must have felt so alone...'

'My dear. My dear...' Miss Peartree, not knowing what to do, stroked Lily's arm. 'Jess isn't far away. She... she has accepted a situation at the big house, as nurserymaid to young Bella Fyncham.'

Lily stared at her in disbelief, her mismatched eyes wide and accusing. 'What?'

'Well, my dear... she wasn't really suited to the kitchen. But your father wouldn't just turn her out – he knew how concerned you were for the girl. And so, when he heard there was a position at Hewinghall... She's quite happy there. Mrs Roberts sent word to say she's settling in well.'

'I see.' Lily felt numb.

Miss Peartree regarded the pale, beautiful face worriedly. 'There's no reason you shouldn't see her, my dear. I'm not entirely sure on what day she has her free afternoon, but we could get a message to—'

'It doesn't matter,' Lily said abruptly. 'I must go upstairs and change. Excuse me, Cousin Oriana. I'm very tired suddenly. The journey...'

Her journal that evening was scrawled with bitter jottings. She felt betrayed, bereft, bewildered and angry – the whole world had turned against her. Even Jess. She had so looked forward to talking to Jess!

But how could Jess possibly understand? She didn't believe in Lily's dream of having a real father – she hadn't the intelligence to comprehend how much that dream meant to Lily. And she had such working-class ideas of right and wrong; if Lily told her what had happened at school Jess would be shocked by the idea of such immodest behaviour among gently born young ladies. She'd be sure to say, yet again, that Lily ought to forget Ashton Haverleigh.

–

At the big house, Jess woke with the dawn, washed in cold water and dressed herself. In her morning uniform of a brown print dress and sacking apron, with a grey knitted cardigan for warmth, she went at once to unbolt Bella's door – from the outside – and check that the child was all right.

Bolting her in her room every night was wicked, but Nanny insisted it be done and since that first night, when Bella had walked in her sleep and frightened herself half to death, Jess hadn't dared disobey the rule. She compromised by staying with the little girl, telling stories and singing songs, until she was asleep. Once or twice, when Bella was extra restless, Jess had spent the night in her room. She hadn't won the child over, exactly, but at least Bella had accepted her in Kate's place.

Having seen that Bella was still sleeping, Jess set about lighting the fire in the schoolroom. She had learned to carry the coals up the previous night rather than leaving them to morning, when so much else had to be done. The grate had to be cleaned out and blackleaded, paper and sticks laid under the coals. While it was taking light, she finished sweeping the ashes and put them in newspaper in their bucket, to be taken down later, then washed down the hearth and began sweeping and dusting and polishing in the schoolroom.

Now, in April, the sun was rising as she took up the rugs and tossed them out of one of the dormer windows. The window had a step under it; you could climb out on to the roof – there was a little ladder on the other side that let you step down to the flat leads of a parapet edged with a stone balustrade. From there you had a wonderful view across the park. That morning a mist lay under the trees, with cattle moving knee-deep in it, and shadows stretched across the grass as the sun lifted. In the distance, a figure with a gun strode along the edge of the wood. Was it Reuben Rudd? He was too far away for her to be sure, but her blood beat faster anyway.

As winter's grip had eased on the land, the chill between her and Rudd had grown deeper. He came to the big house now and then, but she didn't often see him. At chapel he'd been as distant as the horizon, no longer teasing her, nor lingering to enjoy her company. He hadn't forgiven her for laying into him in front of Jim Potts.

As for Eliza's brother, well, he'd been there outside chapel every time she went to service, flirting and making eyes, but since he'd been at his worst when Rudd was about Jess had known he was playing games; she'd treated him to her loftiest disdain, turned a deaf ear to his foolishness, and decided that chapel-going was too much of a strain. Pleading pressure of work, she had taken to attending the church in the park. Miss Peartree had seemed glad to see her, though the rector regarded her much as he might have regarded a stray sparrow.

It wasn't important, though. None of it signified. She had the feeling that she was marking time. Waiting. As if there was a distant storm brewing...

Having finished the schoolroom she carefully closed the windows again – it was a rule that they be kept closed, for safety; then she took the ashes downstairs. She returned lugging two cumbersome enamelled ewers full of hot water.

Setting one jug down, she tapped on the door of Nanny's room, taking a deep breath. Holding that breath, she lifted the latch, said, 'Mornin', Nanny,' and went to open the curtains. She would have opened the window, too, but the first morning when she'd tried that Nanny had shrieked in horror: she considered fresh air and draughts to be unhealthy. With no fire in her room she held in every bit of warmth she could. Which meant also holding in her body odours and the aroma of her chamber pot and the underwear she seldom changed. Nanny's room stank.

''Morning, Nanny,' Jess called again as she poured hot water into the china ewer on the wash stand.

The mound under the covers stirred and, having done her duty, Jess slid out, glad to close the door and breathe easy again.

Carting the other jug across the schoolroom, she went into Bella's dressing room and filled the bowl before going to wake the child. Bella was sulky in the morning, but by the time Jess was fastening her into clean underwear, and wrapping her with the red flannel that protected her chest, the child was properly awake and wanting her breakfast.

'Can I have devilled kidneys?' she asked that morning. 'Papa has devilled kidneys. He told me so.'

'When you get to be a lady, then you can have devilled kidneys,' said Jess. 'While you're a little 'un, you must have your porridge.'

'Why?'

'Because you must, that's why. Your mama say so.'

Bella looked at her askance – mention of her mother always made her thoughtful. 'I don't like porridge.'

'Even with raisins?'

'I don't like raisins.'

'Then you can have your porridge plain,' said Jess, causing the little girl to give her another sidelong look. By now she knew that when

Jess said such things she meant them. Nanny was susceptible to tears and pleading. Jess was not.

Having made another trip downstairs, for a loaf of fresh bread and some butter, milk and eggs from the Home Farm, Jess laid a table in the schoolroom. As she was cooking porridge on the trivet by the fire, Nanny appeared wearing her usual black woollen gown. She and Bella sat at table. In between serving them, Jess broke her own fast, watching for the kettle to boil so she could make tea.

Later, she took the dishes all the way down to the scullery and washed them up. She was scrubbing egg from the plates when Sal Gooden came in and, in her usual cheerful way, informed Jess that Lily Clare was home.

Her immediate rush of pleasure surprised Jess – she hadn't realised how much she'd missed Lily. 'Where'd you hear that, Sal?'

'From the carter, Mr Witt, who heard it from the rector's boy, John Button. He was there when Miss Lily come a-flyin' in demandin' to know where you'd got to. Since then she've hardly spoke to nobody, so he say.'

'I feared she'd take it wrong,' Jess sighed. 'If she send a message, you'll let me know, won't you, Sal?'

Next in the routine came prayers. This daily devotion took place in the conservatory known as Little Africa. Mr Longman, the butler, officiated, though once a week Sir Richard would appear and read a piece from the Bible before addressing his staff with a few words of encouragement. Hard words, if needed, came later, from Mr Longman to the men and Mrs Roberts to the women.

Knowing that Lily was home gave Jess new energy. For the rest of that morning she worked with a will, cleaning the passages, the three bedrooms and the dressing room. She prepared a sago pudding for lunch, though the main courses had to be fetched up from the kitchen.

Nanny spent the mornings amusing Bella but after lunch the old woman needed a rest; then Jess was in charge. If it was fine they might go out into the garden or walk in the park, and then Bella was happy. Less easy were the cold, wet days when they were confined to the schoolroom.

Nanny often said that, one of these days, she ought to give Jess some instruction in reading. Jess would have liked that – she was beginning to see that reading might be a good thing – but somehow the day never came. Her chores kept her busy, and if ever she did have a spare moment Nanny was otherwise occupied, or tired, so Jess didn't like to remind her of her promise. She did, though, listen when Miss Bella was having her lessons and sometimes borrowed one of the story books with their big print, poring laboriously over the words late at night.

Most afternoons, when Nanny emerged from her nap, she took Bella down to spend half an hour with one or both of her parents – always allowing they hadn't more important business to attend to. Jess spent that time clearing up; then it was teatime, after which Jess hauled hot water to fill the hip bath and bathe the child before putting her to bed.

There had been no recurrence of the sleep-walking episode but each evening ended in the same way, with Jess feeling bad about slipping the bolt that locked Bella in her room.

Relieved at last from routine duties, Jess found something useful to do with the last few hours of the evening – mending torn linen, darning stockings, or sewing vests and drawers for whoever needed them, while the candle dwindled and Nanny's snores came loud through the wooden partition.

That April day was like all the rest, except that she spent most of it hoping for word from Lily.

But no word came.

–

That Sunday, Nanny Fyncham didn't feel well enough to attend service, so she sent Jess to sit with Miss Bella in the squire's box pew, along with both Lady Maud and Sir Richard. There was Lily, only a few yards away, but after a brief meeting of glances she kept her face averted, as if she had no other interest than listening to the long sermon. But the tightness of her pink lips, and the high colour in her cheeks, betrayed her. Jess guessed she was being ignored as a reproach for her desertion; she'd known Lily would take it wrong.

After the service, however, Sir Richard and his wife lingered to speak to one or two people. Since the squire had his daughter by the hand, Jess was obliged to hover nearby. She heard him welcome Lily back to Hewinghall and ask if she had met Bella, introducing them with charming informality before asking after Lily's prowess at school.

'I won the elocution prize,' Lily told him, though her veiled glance kept sliding towards Jess.

'Indeed?' His deep voice was both indulgent and amused. 'And what did you recite?'

'"The Lady of Shalott", and a piece by Miss Rossetti – "When I am Dead". Do you know it?'

Lady Fyncham put in, 'My husband has more weighty matters on his mind, Miss Clare, than poetry. For myself, I wonder what a young person like yourself is doing reciting dirges about death.'

'Oh, but it's not a dirge!' Lily protested. 'It's beautiful. So sad. So romantic. Perhaps you'd like to hear...'

But Lady Maud had already lost interest and was moving away, leaving her husband to make polite farewells.

'Say "Good morning" to Miss Clare, Bella.'

'Good morning, Miss Clare,' Bella repeated, then turned to her father to add in her clear voice, 'Why are her eyes different colours, Papa?'

A pool of embarrassed silence spread about the little group.

'Because that is the way God made her,' Sir Richard said, his patient tone belying the look of apology which he sent to Lily.

She was smiling one of her bright, false smiles. 'God's gift? Gracious goodness, yes.'

'She looks funny,' said Bella as she was drawn away towards the waiting carriage.

Lily's odd eyes encountered Jess's, her pain evident. 'I hope you're well,' she said with a little shrug. 'And happy at the big house.'

'Happy enough, thank you, Miss Lily,' Jess said, dipping a curtsey. 'But it en't the same. Please... Miss Bella don't mean nothin'. She're allowed to speak her mind too free, that's all.'

'Evidently.' The mismatched eyes flickered with momentary uncertainty, then Lily stiffened her resolve and lifted her chin. 'I can't stay to talk. My papa has invited Mr Dunnock and his mother to luncheon. I must not be late. Goodbye.'

Even as she walked away, Lily regretted her coolness to Jess. She'd hoped to inflict hurt, but the person she was hurting most was herself. She missed having a friend she could really confide in, and she knew Jess wasn't to blame for being sent away.

Oh, why did she do these things only to repent of them? Lily despaired of herself. She was sorry her recent moods had upset Cousin Oriana and annoyed Papa. After all, Papa might have sent Jess half across the county, had he the mind to upset his daughter. Determined to make amends, she returned to the rectory ready to put on a social face, even though the curate and his mother were tedious company.

Peter Dunnock was nervous, in awe of his superior and shy of Lily. An earnest, no-longer-young man in dark suit and dog-collar, he had a shiny, clean-scrubbed appearance and receding fair hair so thin that his scalp shone through like a yellow dome. His washed-green eyes peered from a frame of sandy lashes, begging for approval – much like Gyp, Lily thought, but far less appealing. Peter Dunnock was attracted to her, that was evident, but all she felt for him was a kind of irritated pity. She took refuge in reticence, replying in monosyllables when directly spoken to, and in consequence the curate's loquacious mother filled the gaps.

Mrs Dunnock was a small, well-corseted person, somewhat over-dressed for the occasion in a fur hat and stole, which she refused to remove – 'I have rheumatism in my shoulders. I feel the cold so easily in these great draughty rooms.' Her speech was punctuated by two recurring refrains: 'My brother, Canon Hargreaves, always says...' and 'When we were in Venice...'

'I think we've heard enough about Venice, Mother,' her son put in mildly at one point.

She shot him a look that had daggers in it, saying sweetly, 'Can one ever have enough of Venice, my dear? Or of travel in any form? So broadening, don't you think? So vital to a *complete* education. Have you ever been abroad, Miss Clare?'

Lily smiled, softly and regretfully. 'No.'

'Oh, but you should! It would be very good for you. Don't you agree, Rector? I would have thought that the summer after she finishes her schooling was just the time for a young lady to see a little more of the world. If she's to help with the village school next year—'

What? Lily's mind yelped, just as her father said, 'That hasn't been decided yet.'

'But I thought you intended to give more time to your writing, Rector? Peter certainly gave me the impression that Miss Clare would be joining him at the school after the summer holiday. Or did I misunderstand?'

The curate's neck and ears turned beetroot-red. 'I'm sure, Mama, I didn't intend to imply anything that might have led you to conclude—'

'The possibility has been mooted,' Reverend Clare said, delicately dabbing the corner of his mouth with a napkin. 'However, it's only one of several avenues Lily might follow. The principal of the Academy considers she would make an excellent governess if...'

Lily didn't hear any more. Her ears simply refused to listen to such nonsense. Her real father would be appalled if he came and found her employed as a schoolteacher. And as for being a *governess*... one of those sad, grey, sexless creatures, belonging nowhere, caught in the void between family and servants? Oh, no! She'd never be able to lift her head up again! How Dickon and Clemency would laugh. And Ash – what about Ash? He would never dream of marrying anyone as dreary, as hopelessly insignificant, as *a governess*!

In a passion of distress, she pushed her chair back and leapt up so violently that she sent the chair crashing over. They all stared at her in astonishment.

'Lily Victoria—' her papa began.

'How *can* you?' she threw at him. 'How can you arrange my life without even consulting me? I don't want to be a schoolteacher. And I certainly don't intend to be a governess! You can't make me. Oh... you're cruel, Papa. Cruel! My own father would never shame me in this way. Oh, I *wish* he would come. I hate living with you. I *hate it*!'

Eleven

As Easter Monday began, Bella was good as gold, not even making complaints when Jess towelled her dry after her morning wash. She was too excited.

'It's not raining, is it?'

'Set fair to sunset, if you ask me,' said Jess, throwing the curtains wide to let the child see the morning sun lighting the park. 'There was a red sky last night. "Red sky at night…"'

'"Sailors' delight",' Bella replied, jumping up and down for sheer joy. 'Then we shall go, shan't we? Nanny said so long as it wasn't cold or wet… I want to ride on the box with Abbot.'

'You'll ride inside with Nanny,' Jess replied firmly. 'Oh, do keep still, Miss Bella! I can't fasten your buttons.'

Bella ceased her jumping, but looked over her shoulder with shining eyes. 'I'm going to buy a leaping pole when we get to the beach. Papa said I could have a leaping pole.'

'Then I expect you shall. Long as you behave.'

A day in Hunstanton hadn't seemed the sort of thing Nanny would enjoy; Jess half expected the trip to be called off, but when she took Bella through for breakfast, there was the old woman, up and ready. She seemed determined to carry through her plan, though she grumbled all the while.

Jess couldn't decide whether she herself was looking forward to the day or not. Part of her relished the idea of going to the seaside for the first holiday of the year, but the rest of her was reluctant to face the crowds – some of them would, inevitably, come from Lynn; someone might recognise her, point her out, shout 'Murderess!'…

No! Don't even think it.

The coachman had prepared the yellow phaeton for the journey, with its hood up to shelter Nanny and Bella while Jess and the picnic hamper rode in the smaller railed back seat behind the bulge of the great yellow hood. Not that Jess minded: the seat was high enough for her to see over most of the hedges, with wide views over rolling farmland down to the lines of white foam-horses dashing on the edge of the sea a mile away.

By mid-morning they were in New Hunstanton, along with several hundred other people coming in by road and rail, some on the new-fangled bicycles, which made Bella stare and point. The town green, set on a slope above the sea, was merry with stalls and sideshows. Jess kept her new straw boater well down, but no one took notice of the phaeton as it went clopping down the hill.

Soon they were queuing to pay their toll to the uniformed pier-master and mingling with the crowds along boards that stretched hundreds of feet into the Wash, protected by wrought-iron railings. Jess had been to Hunstanton ten years before, on an outing with her family, but she hadn't been on the pier – Mother and Dad hadn't the money to pay for them all to go, so they'd settled for the beach, which was free.

Nanny Fyncham planted herself and the picnic hamper on the first vacant bench, while Bella dragged Jess off to explore the pier. It was lined with seats, and refreshment kiosks with bunting fluttering in the mild sea breeze. They went to the very end, where steamers from Lynn dropped their passengers. Green waves were breaking against the iron piles below. One or two hardy souls were emerging from the bathing machines, stripped down to blue serge bathing costumes as they ventured into the cold water. The sight made Jess shudder.

'*I* want to swim!' Bella cried.

'No, not today,' Jess said. 'That's much too cold for you, Miss Bella. But we'll go on the beach later.'

The sea was going out, leaving great stretches of sand and patches of rock where people wandered, some of them using long poles to help them jump across puddles or from rock to rock.

The sight made Bella cry: 'Let's go down to the beach, Jess. I want to go now! I want a leaping pole.'

'So you shall,' Jess said, keeping tight hold of the small hand. 'But behave you like a young lady and don't shout. Walk nice, like Nanny's always telling you.'

As they turned back along the pier the town on its cliff spread its wonders before them. At the highest point, half a mile off, Jess could see the white building that housed the light. An excursion train was pulling in to the station behind the Sandringham Hotel with much puffing and whistling and gouts of steam.

Having purchased a leaping pole from the nearest emporium, Bella's only desire was to return to the beach. The receding tide left shallow rock pools and runnels of water, over which Bella practised her leaping while an anxious Jess followed, trying to ensure the child didn't get too wet; Jess didn't want to get blamed for her falling sick.

Bella, however, fell in with a group of children all showing off their prowess and trying to outdo one another. Though she was one of the youngest, she could leap as well as most, much to her delight. Shouts of laughter, jeers and dares filled the air, joining the cries of gulls and the sound of a barrel organ from the fair.

'Jess…'

The soft voice made Jess spin round to see Lily standing a few yards away, dressed in a bright blue that exactly matched her blue eye. She looked strikingly lovely, but pale and uncertain – sad, perhaps.

'Oh, Jess!' Lily had planned to be a little cool – at first, anyway, just to show her displeasure at being deserted – but now she found herself flying to meet her friend, arms open to embrace her. 'Oh, Jess. Oh, Jess! I thought I'd lost you.'

Laughing, a mite embarrassed, Jess extricated herself from the hug. 'You don't get rid o' me that easy, Miss Lily. Hold you hard, though.' Straightening her hat, she glanced about her, checking that Bella was still safely playing. 'What'll folk think?'

'Why – they'll think we're glad to see each other.'

'Mebbe so. But you're the rector's daughter, and me… I'm on'y the nurserymaid from the big house.'

Lily blinked her strange, beautiful eyes. 'What difference does that make? You're my *friend*, Jess, the only real friend I have.'

'Oh, that's—'

'It *is* so! I'm discovering it more and more. Everyone else… even Clemency…' She stopped herself, eyes moist with distress. 'Oh, gracious goodness, there's so *much* I want to tell you! Let's try to get away on our own for a little. Nanny Fyncham says you're to bring Bella back to the pier – she says she'll get over-heated if she keeps jumping about like that. Bella must sit still and have a drink.'

Jess glanced up at the pier, unable to distinguish Nanny among the crowds lining the rails and benches. 'She sent you?'

'I offered to bring the message,' Lily amended. 'I left Cousin Oriana with her – they're old acquaintances. Both of them come from the West Country. In fact,' she added, 'if it wasn't such an absurd notion I might have thought they'd planned to meet today. Nanny Fyncham seemed almost to be expecting us—'

A scream from one of the children made Jess turn to see a youth swinging his leaping pole like a club, threatening the group of smaller children who were all backing away, forming a rough circle round him. Bella was standing wide-eyed, too astonished to move. Any minute now, that flailing pole was going to hit her.

Jess didn't stop to think, she went running into the circle and grabbed the pole, tearing it out of the boy's grasp. Before he could even protest, she had hurled the pole far out of reach, grasped Bella's hand and was hurrying her away. Behind her, the boy shouted something rude and went after his pole, while the others scattered back to their families.

'Gracious goodness!' Lily said. 'That was brave. You were like an avenging fury. Jess! Jess, wait!'

Jess strode on, pulling Bella along with her, the trailing leaping pole making a furrow in the sand behind them. She daren't look back. She'd suddenly realised that she knew the boy whose pole she had thrown away. He was nephew to Butcher Bone, at whose house Jess had once been maid-of-all-work. And if Freddie Bone was in Hunstanton then other folk from Fisher's End might be here, too. No, she daren't look back.

'Jess!' Lily complained, struggling after her across the yielding, slipping sand. 'Jess, stop!'

Bella too was complaining, hanging back, dragging on Jess's hand. As she reached the top of the steps that led up to the esplanade, Jess did stop. 'Now, come you on, Miss Bella,' she said crossly, stroking the child's tumbled hair back from her flushed face and resetting the straw hat that had fallen behind her shoulders on its elastic. 'Nanny says you're to have a rest. Look at you, all of a muck-sweat. That's no way for a nice young lady to be. We'll go back to the beach later, maybe.'

By that time Lily had caught up with them, out of breath. 'Goodness! What a race! We were supposed to help Bella cool down, not get her even more heated!'

'I'm sorry, Miss Lily,' Jess said, a swift glance telling her that the boy Bone had merged into the throng. No one was following her. No one had even noticed the small disturbance. 'I just thought it best to get Miss Bella right away. I shouldn't've let her play with them ruffians in the first place.'

'Why not? She appeared to be enjoying herself.'

Before Jess could reply, Bella pointed at Lily, piping, 'What is *she* doing here?'

'And who's "she"?' Jess demanded. 'The cat's auntie? Hen't you got no manners, Miss Bella? Why, your papa introduced you to Miss Clare only yesterday, at church. Have you forgot? I 'spect she've come to Huns'ton same as us – to enjoy the sea air.'

Bella squinted up at Lily. 'She's the lady with funny eyes.'

For the briefest moment, Jess and Lily exchanged a look of empathy, then Lily bent to be on a level with the child, who stared warily at her. 'You're right, Bella – I have odd eyes. One blue and one brown – see?' Only the faintest tremor in her voice gave her away. 'Do you know why that is, Bella?' With a conspiratorial air, she glanced about as if to discover if anyone was listening. No one was; the strollers on the sea walk were all intent about their own amusements. From the fair the robust, jangling rhythm of a barrel organ accompanied the movement of a roundabout, and the thin music of a street piper wove a silver thread through the gaiety.

'Shall I tell you a secret?' Lily asked in her special story-telling voice. 'Can you keep a secret?'

Bella, still frowning, unwillingly intrigued, nodded her coppery head.

'I have eyes like this,' Lily said, 'because I'm really a mermaid. A mermaid princess, from a kingdom under the sea.' Her gesture embraced the green expanse of the Wash, rippled by wind-whipped waves. 'And when we take human shape, we are doomed to show some sign of our true nature. Some of us have odd eyes. Some have scales on their hands and feet. Some… some of us have red hair,' and she lifted a lock of Bella's silky hair, 'red hair that looks green in moonlight – like seaweed.'

Dashing her hand away, Bella said, 'It doesn't! *I'm* not a mermaid!'

'Then you're very lucky,' said Lily gravely. 'Think how lonely it must be, to be different from everyone else. To be exiled from your own people and doomed to a world of mortals who don't like you because you're different. No one wants to be a mermaid's friend. A mermaid is always lonely, and often unhappy.'

Bella peered at her, thinking about it. Young as she was, she understood loneliness and unhappiness. 'Are you really a mermaid?'

Holding the child with her strange, mismatched eyes, Lily said quietly – as if she believed it – 'I really am.'

'Then why don't you go back into the sea?'

'I can't,' Lily sighed. 'I'm under a gypsy curse. I have to remain on dry land until I find someone who will love me and be my friend in spite of my funny eyes.'

Very slowly, Bella reached out a sandy hand and touched Lily's glowing cheek. 'I'll be your friend.'

'Will you?' Emotion made Lily's voice husky as she took the small hand between her own. 'Thank you, Bella.' She straightened to look at Jess with glittering eyes. 'Then that's two friends I have.'

'Can you go back to the sea now?' Bella wanted to know.

'Oh—' Laughing, Lily shook her head and dashed away her tears. 'No, not yet. You have to be my friend for... oh, at least a year. You have to *prove* you're my friend. And I must be your friend, too. Then – who knows? – I may not want to go back to the cold green sea.'

Taking Bella's leaping pole in one hand, she offered the child her other and the three of them moved off towards the pier. Jess glanced back again at the beach, but she couldn't see the butcher's nephew, or anyone else she recognised.

'Let's go and take a look at the fair!' Lily suggested after they had shared a picnic lunch, but the two older ladies demurred, pleading their age as excuse.

'But you go, my dear,' Miss Peartree suggested. 'You and Jess. You won't mind that, will you, Nanny?'

'*I* want to go,' Bella announced, rousing herself. She had been almost asleep, wrapped in a blanket and leaning on Nanny's ample lap.

'It's time for your rest, Miss Bella,' Nanny said.

'But I want to go to the fair, Nanny. You said I could.'

'Now, Miss Bella...'

The child was tired and her temper turned to tears.

'I'll stay with her,' Jess offered, not sorry for an excuse to stay hiding on the pier; folk from Fisher's End were unlikely to stray there, because of the extra pennies it cost.

'Oh, gracious goodness!' Lily exclaimed. 'Nanny Fyncham, it's you who need a rest, not Bella. *We* don't mind taking her with us, do we,

Jess? Let her come, if she wants to. But you must be very good, Bella. You must hold our hands tightly. Will you promise to do that?'

Bella's tears dried miraculously as she nodded.

Between Nanny and Miss Peartree there passed a covert look which puzzled Jess. Was it satisfaction that oozed between the two plump ladies?

In the afternoon sunlight the fair was in full cry. Vendors called their wares, waved frying pans and argued with each other to attract a crowd. Some wound garlands of unbaked toffee on hooks, above stalls piled with fair rock, candy, liquorice and butter fudge. It reminded Jess of the great February Mart in Lynn.

Lily bought some ribbons and lace, and some jaw-breaking toffee, and glasses of fizzy lemonade which gave Bella the hiccups; but that didn't prevent her from joining Lily on a roundabout with bicycles where you could sit and pedal, propelled round and round by a steam engine while a barrel organ played. Jess stood and watched, holding on to her straw hat and keeping covert watch on the people around her. She did see faces she knew, but they belonged to the present, not the past – people from Hewing and Syderford, others who went to chapel at Martham. She half expected to see Reuben Rudd, but if he was at the fair their ways didn't meet. Eliza Potts was there, though, with her brother Jim, among a laughing group of young men and women egging each other on to have a go on the roundabout.

Lily seemed determined to force as much enjoyment from the day as possible. She had something on her mind, Jess guessed. She had them marching along the clifftop in the wind, then down to the beach looking for shells and pretty stones among the rock pools. But the child was growing ever more tired and Jess was concerned: Miss Bella had a delicate constitution; she needed her rest.

'I think we ought—' she had started to say when a ball came whizzing between her and Lily, from a group playing cricket under the hang of the colourful cliff. A young man came after the ball, shouting with laughter, diving headlong to land at Lily's feet, while his companions cheered.

Jess had instinctively drawn Bella aside as the man sprawled in the sand beside them. His cap fell off, revealing an unruly, ill-kempt crop of brown hair – the sort of hair that took no notice of brush or comb. Like Matty's hair, Jess thought. His loud laugh reminded her of her brother, too. All in the same instant she took in his broad shoulders, his long legs, his strong body clad in an ill-fitting suit, and another burst of intemperate laughter as he righted himself and sat up, grinning at the startled Lily.

It *was* Matty.

Jess's ears seemed to go deaf, with a weird singing in them, as if a cloud had dropped round her, shutting her off from the rest of the world. Matty...

She found herself backing away, taking Bella with her, hunching her shoulders and trying her best to hide her face as Matty scrambled to his feet. Luckily he was so entranced by the sight of Lily that he turned his back on Jess. He stood like a fool, brushing sand off his suit and vainly trying to straighten that wild mop of hair. His ears and the back of his neck were slowly turning scarlet.

'And what,' Lily demanded, at her haughty, frosty best, 'are you staring at, you silly jackanapes?'

Behind him, his companions were starting to call to him, wanting to go on with their game. Among them were several of Jess's own friends.

Feeling ever more faint and sick, still trapped in her cocoon of shock, Jess moved further away, turning her shoulder, trying to watch what was happening and still keep her face averted. But the cricket players all had their eyes on Matty and Lily, ignoring the insignificant nurserymaid with her small charge.

'Well?' Lily demanded, a blaze of colour flaring on her cheeks.

Matty made some reply, but he spoke so low that Jess couldn't hear what he said. She only saw Lily's face contort with fury. She threw the shells she was carrying right into Matty's face, but though he flinched aside and flung a hand to his cheek he immediately straightened himself, saying, 'That's wholly the truth,' as Lily spun on her heel and ran away.

Unable to help herself, Jess stood and watched as her brother stared after the fleeing girl in blue; then he bent and swept up his cap, fitting it back on to his head as he turned back to where his companions were calling and laughing. Not once did he look in Jess's direction. It was what she wanted. Of course it was! But her heart wept lonely tears. Nobody must find her. Not even Matty.

She found Lily waiting near the entry to the pier, still fuming over the incident. 'That... that scoundrel! How dare he? He said I was the most beautiful girl he'd ever seen!'

Matty had said that? It didn't sound like him at all. 'Well, Miss Lily, that en't to be wondered at. You *are* a wholly beautiful—'

'I'm not! I know I'm not – I see that every time I look into a mirror. Besides… A man like *that*?' Lily shuddered. 'How dare he even speak to me?'

As she made for the pier entrance, Jess looked back, longingly and regretfully, to where her friends from Fisher's End were enjoying their game of cricket. By rights she should have been with them. By rights… but she no longer had any rights. On a cold December night, full of fire and hatred, she'd drowned her rights in the Alexandra Dock. Along with Nathanael Merrywest.

–

Abbot had promised to return at four o'clock to take them home and, sure enough, here came the big yellow hood. Jess was both glad and sorry to see it. She'd spent the last hour or so torn in two, wanting to see her brother but hiding instead on the pier.

'We must go, too,' Miss Peartree said. 'I told Fargus to be outside the Golden Lion by four thirty.'

But Lily cried, 'Oh, not yet, Cousin Oriana. Not yet!'

'But I'm tired,' the old woman complained. 'And my back is aching. Lily Victoria, I am not as young as I once was. We must go home. You cannot remain unchaperoned.'

'But Jess could stay with me. Couldn't she, Nanny Fyncham? It *is* a holiday. *Please* say she may stay. Oh, *dear* Cousin Oriana – couldn't you send Fargus back for us later?'

'I ought to go with Miss Bella,' Jess said, casting a look along the beach where the cricketers were beginning to disperse.

'Oh, but—'

'You're right, Miss Clare,' Nanny said. 'It's a holiday, after all. You're entitled to an evening off, Jessamy. Yes, you stay and take care of Miss Clare. I'll see to Miss Bella myself tonight.'

And so Lily had her way.

Linking arms with Jess, she bore her back up to the green to buy home-made rock, and plates of cockles and winkles with brown bread and butter, and cups of hot, sweet tea. The group from Hewing, including Eliza and her brother, were at the coconut shy. Seeing Jess, Jim Potts tipped his hat at her and called out, 'I'll win a coconut for you. Watch and see.'

The comment made another man nearby turn his head to look at her. Jess found herself staring into the disbelieving eyes of her brother's best mate – big, redheaded, slow-thinking Tom Fysher. Then the crowds between them closed, hiding her from his sight. She hurried Lily on, keeping her head down, praying that Tom Fysher would persuade himself he was mistaken. Knowing how slowly his brain worked, she hoped he wouldn't even think to mention it to Matty until later. Much later.

She increased her pace, taking Lily with her, putting more space and several stalls between her and the coconut shy. Oh, why had she stayed? They'd agreed to meet Fargus at the Golden Lion at seven, but he'd keep drinking in the public bar until Lily sent for him and Lily seemed to be in no hurry to leave.

'How do you know Jim Potts?' Lily wanted to know.

'I've seen him at chapel, 'times.'

Lily's brow knotted. 'He's not the sort of friend you ought to make, Jess. You can't trust a Potts. Cousin Oriana told me how Eliza contrived to get rid of poor Dolly. Oh... I *hate* Eliza Potts. And she hates me. Yesterday... yesterday she was unfastening my stays and she pinched me. I shall be bruised for weeks.'

'I don't suppose she meant to—' Jess began.

'Of course she did! Oh, don't you start defending her, Jess. You know what she's like. Not only did she pinch me, but she then managed to get the brush entangled in my hair and when I complained she...' she swung round, thrusting out her hand, 'she did *this* at me!'

Jess felt cold as she saw the shape Lily's hand was making: Devil's horns, the sign stupid, superstitious, ignorant folk used against the evil eye, to ward off spells.

'She's always doing it!' Lily cried. 'What does it mean?'

'That mean she're an ignorant fool. What did you do?'

'Oh, nothing. What was the point? Anyway, I was too upset about...' Glancing at the crowds around them, she went on, 'I can't tell you here. Let's find somewhere more private.'

They made their way back to the shore and along the sea walk. Jess felt safer there, with fewer people about. The tide was coming in, the breeze turning chill as the light waned. The sun dipped over the far side of the Wash in a welter of gold-edged clouds and patient horses plodded up the sand hauling the bathing machines in for the night.

After a while, Lily turned suddenly to Jess, saying, 'What am I to do, Jess? I've been trying not to believe it, but… Papa intends me for Mr Dunnock.'

'Oh, now—' Such a possibility was unthinkable.

'I know he does! But I shan't do it. I can't, Jess. I'd run mad, tied to that sad little man. And his *mother*…' The thought made her shiver and turn away, her arms wrapped about herself. 'My life is tainted, Jess. Blighted. I must resign myself to being a teacher. Or a governess – one of those grey, sad women who belong nowhere.'

Jess caught her breath, saying fiercely, 'That'll never be you, Miss Lily. Never!'

Her vehemence made Lily give her an odd look. 'You really believe that, don't you? You feel everything will come right for me?'

'I *know* it.'

For a moment Lily regarded her in utter silence, her strange eyes still. Then, springing to her feet, she hurried away, heading back towards the pier and the esplanade under the cliff, with Jess following.

Climbing the wooden stair that led up to the cliff top, they walked on, making for the lighthouse half a mile away. Jess cast a worried look behind her, at the fair where flares were being lit as twilight gathered. Was Tom Fysher still there? 'We ought to go, Miss Lily. You said we'd meet Fargus at seven.'

'Fargus won't care. All the more time for drinking ale in the Golden Lion.' She paused to take Jess's arm again and lead her on. 'Let's just walk for a little while. I don't want to go home yet.'

They walked on, slowly. As dusk gathered, the lighthouse blinked its bright light out across the Wash, answering the flash of the Lynn Well lightship. A little way from shore, the dangerous 'Roaring Middle' sandbank was illumined by a red glare thrown from the light through strips of ruby glass. Jess remembered the fishermen talking about it.

'We ought to go back,' she said, anxious to be away.

Lily sighed heavily. 'I suppose you're right.'

The market stalls were islands of light against a dark backdrop of houses and hotels. Naphtha flares leapt against darkness, sending shadows dancing on canvas, illuminating laughing faces. Smoke wove its acrid embroidery, while over the sea a great yellow moon rose and hung, whitening and brightening, in the cloud-scudded sky.

'It's almost barbaric, isn't it?' Lily said. 'Like something from the mystical east. Snake charmers and sword swallowers... Oh, if only we could be swept away on a magic carpet.' Moving away, she stood staring longingly out at the sea, where the moon laid a silver pathway across the swell. 'Or just simply float off with the tide...'

The night was so clear Jess could see lights on the farther shore of the Wash, and in the middle distance the red lantern of a fishing vessel rode homeward with the tide. Homeward – making for the Fisher Fleet. Well, at least she knew Matty wasn't out with the boats today.

Very softly, Lily recited:

Full fathom five thy father lies;
Of his bones are coral made:
Those are pearls that were his eyes:
Nothing of him that doth fade...

She let the words drift off as she watched the sea in silence for a moment, then whispered, 'It would be so easy, wouldn't it? Just to walk out into the water and keep going. Let it take you up in its arms and sweep you into its depths. Where it's all calm, and quiet. Where there's no more noise and strife. Where—'

'Where the crabs eat your eyes and you rot slowly, food for fishes,' Jess put in flatly.

'Jess!' Lily objected.

'Well, it's so. I'm sorry, Miss Lily, but you shouldn't talk that way. Drownin' en't a fairytale.' She stared at the sea, hearing the shush of waves against sandy shingle. 'My dad drowned. He's still out there somewhere.'

Lily was silent for a long time. She said at last, 'I didn't know. What happened? Couldn't he swim?'

'He wouldn't never learn. Most fishermen don't. If they're a-goin' to drown they want it over quick.'

'Your father was a fisherman? You've never told me that before.'

'There's lots I hen't told you, Miss Lily. But I know that don't do to mock the sea.'

'I wasn't mocking,' Lily denied. 'I was just thinking what a peaceful, romantic death it would make.'

'Death en't never romantic,' Jess said sharply. 'Death's cold and cruel. And final. Once you're dead, you're dead. You don't never come back.' A shiver ran through her, a chill more of the soul than the physical self. She didn't understand Lily's fascination for tragedy and sorrow, but it was always there, like a shadow in the background. 'Can we go now, please? If we don't go soon, Fargus'll get so bosky he'll have us in the nearest ditch.'

'Go and fetch him. Have him bring the carriage over here. I want to stay and watch the sea a few minutes longer.'

'I can't leave you alone.'

'Oh, of course you can!' Lily said impatiently. 'What could possibly happen to me?'

Jess started up the slope towards the Golden Lion, where figures moved against the light – men who'd been drinking; men still holding glasses of beer. Inside the hotel, other people were singing.

Worried about Lily, Jess looked back, seeing her friend as a shadow in the moonlight, standing near the edge of the cliff staring out to sea, her cape flapping in the wind. She was unhappy, that was evident; she was—

Jess stopped, her heart turning over, as two tall figures loomed out of the shadows either side of her. One of them said, 'I told you that was her.' The other reached out and grasped her by the arm, swinging her round so that her face was clear in the light falling from the hotel. 'Jess!' His hands came heavy on her as if to prevent her from escaping. 'Jess, what're you doing here? Where've you been?'

She felt as though a hammer had hit her chest, stunning her heart; then it was pounding. She heard herself say, 'Matty...'

'I told you that was her,' Tom Fysher said again. 'Your Jess. I told you I'd seen her.'

Jess was staring into her brother's open, honest, puzzled face. The sight melted behind tears that came hot and blinding. 'Oh, Matty!'

''S'all right, little 'un,' he soothed her in his old, old way, using words he'd used since she was two years old, reaching to pull her against him. He was a big man, like his father, but then all the Henefers were big – big, fair, amiable – except Jess, who was little and prickly, like Granny Henefer, so everyone said. The runt of the litter.

Oh, God! She tore free of Matty, fending him off with a shudder of revulsion. 'No! Don't touch me! Don't!'

'But, Jessie—'

'*Don't!*' She jerked away from his seeking hands. She saw his face – the hurt, the bewilderment... Suddenly she was weeping, words tumbling out of her, 'Oh, Matty, forgive me! It's not you. It's me. It's because of what he done to me. But I didn't mean to hurt him! I was scared. I never thought what it would mean. I was frit to death. Don't tell on me. Please! I don't want to be hanged for murder!'

Twelve

'What?' Matty made to take hold of her again, but when she backed away he let his hands fall and stood frowning down at her. 'Ha' you gone shanny, Jess Henefer? What're you now on about? Hanged? Why should you be hanged?'

'Because... because of Preacher Merrywest,' Jess managed. 'Matty, I didn't mean it. I must've lost my head. Seein' him there... It all seemed so easy. But I didn't mean to *kill* him.'

'Kill him? What – Preacher Merrywest?'

'That... that was me as done it.'

'Blast, girl!' He grabbed her, his hands on her shoulders gripping painfully tight, shaking her as if to waken her out of bad dreams. 'What d'you mean? Kill him? You din't kill him. He had a nasty fright, and a ducking, that's all. Caught a cold from it. But he en't dead. They pulled him out of that old dock right as rain.'

Jess felt cold, as if iced water was being trickled down her spine. Her brain seemed to have stopped working. 'Not dead? But...'

'Is that why you ran away? Why, poor little mawther. All this time a-thinkin'... That wan't your fault! You just happened to be a-standin' there. The crowd moved, and knocked you into him, and he fell...'

'Who say so?'

'*He* do! Merrywest hisself. He come and told us about it, afterwards.'

Jess couldn't seem to take it in. Merrywest was alive? Did he really believe his fall had been an accident?

'He *en't dead*, love,' Matty repeated. 'He en't even angry. He're real concerned. He keep a-comin' round every week or so, even now, to see if we have word—'

That was it! '*No!*' She threw up her hands and grasped his lapels in both her fists, her sight blurred by a red mist of terror. 'Don't tell him, Matty! Don't tell him where I am! Please don't. *Please don't!*'

After that, everything got confused amid flickering light and looming shadows. Some of the drinkers outside the inn had noted the disturbance and came running to intervene, the first of them wading into Matty and Tom. At the same time, a carriage rumbled up, its door open.

'Jess, run!' Lily shouted from inside the carriage. Jess did so, scrambling for safety. Lily's hands reached out to help her.

'Fargus!' Lily yelled.

The vehicle swayed as Fargus whipped the horses into motion. Jess was sent flying into a corner where she huddled in misery, hearing her brother calling, 'Jess! Jessie, no. Wait! Jess, where can I find you? Where'll you be? Blast, let me go! That's my sister! Jessie… Jess…'

The shouts died away as the carriage raced through lamplit streets and out into the darkness of the countryside.

'Those ruffians!' Lily gasped. 'Are you hurt? Who were they, Jess?'

'Nobody!'

'But they knew your name!'

Jess was shivering, huddled into herself, wishing she could wake and find it all a nightmare. She felt so cold, so sick. Her mouth was running with acid spit. Too much toffee and lemonade and ice cream and cockles…

She grabbed for the door handle and pulled it down, leaning out as her insides erupted in a bitter stream.

'Stop!' Lily screamed, banging on the roof. 'Fargus, stop!'

The conveyance drew to a halt, swaying. Jess hung from the handle by one hand, throwing up everything she'd eaten. Shivering and sweating, she thought dizzily that it was all up for her now. Matty would go home and tell, and then Merrywest would come after her. Merrywest…

She ought to feel relieved that she hadn't killed him. Well, she *was* relieved – glad not to have that guilt on her conscience. But if thinking him dead had been bad, knowing him alive was worse. She'd never forget the look on his face as he fell into the dock – it repeated itself in all her worst dreams. He'd recognised her. He'd *known*! He wouldn't forget that. Whatever he might have said to her family, Jess knew the blackness of his soul. Merrywest was a cruel enemy. He wouldn't rest until he'd found her.

'Jess! Why, you're cold!' Lily's hands came on her, helping her back to the seat, tucking her up with a travelling rug round her.

Jess closed her eyes, seeing red stars wheel in the darkness behind her eyelids. 'I'm all right, Miss Lily.'

'You're far from all right.' Lifting the trapdoor in the roof, Lily spoke to Fargus, telling him to drive on slowly and carefully. The vehicle moved away at a steady walk.

'Those men...' Lily said. 'I thought I heard one of them... He said you were his sister.'

'Yes, Miss Lily.'

'Then why—?'

'Don't ax,' Jess sighed. 'Please don't ax me nothin'. Not now. I'm sorry, Miss Lily, but I don't want to talk about it.'

To her relief, Lily let it go and silence closed in, the horse plodding along the lane, the wheels rumbling. Through half-open eyes Jess saw moonlight come and go, patched by trees' shadow. She was feeling sleepy, and growing warmer thanks to the rug, when she felt Lily move to sit beside her, taking her hand and squeezing it.

'Talk to me, Jessamy,' she said. 'Tell me everything.'

Though Jess didn't move, her brain woke up with a jerk. 'About what?'

'About you. You're so mysterious. I wish... I wish I could be inside your head and know what you know.'

'That'd be a disappointment, Miss Lily,' Jess prevaricated. 'You're the one as goes to school. It should be you teaching me.'

'But you know more about... about life. Jim Potts now... and there's Eliza... and your master who... who hurt you. People do... *do* things to each other. Men, and women. It's not supposed to happen until after you're married, but... I hear people whisper things I don't understand. There are girls in the village who've "fallen". What does it mean? If you're alone with a man, something happens. That's why respectable young ladies are guarded – to save them from that sort of danger. Isn't it?'

Jess remained very still, hardly daring to breathe. Her heart was pulsing in her throat and the carriage seemed airless. 'Yes.'

'But what happens? *What?*'

'Horrible things,' Jess said through a thickness in her chest. 'I can't tell you. You wouldn't want to know.'

Lily said no more until after they had turned in by the Lion Gate and were heading up the rise, when she asked if she should have Fargus take Jess up to the big house. Jess said no, the walk would clear her head.

'Very well. Oh, when shall we meet again, Jess? I have another week before I go back to school.'

'I get Thursday afternoon free.'

'Then... shall we meet on Thursday? By the church gate. We'll take a walk in the woods, if it's fine.'

Jess stood watching as the carriage moved away, heading off to the rectory with its lamps agleam in the night. Behind it, silence closed in. The night was quiet, with the moon climbing higher, lighting the way like a silver lantern. Jess stood and let the peace of the moment seep into her soul, calming her. The cool night air in her lungs helped too, though there was still a taste of bile at the back of her throat.

Was it time to move on again, before Merrywest came after her? Or should she stay and brave it out?

She looked to where the big house stood waiting for her, sprawling in its moonlit park. It was the only home she had. If she left, where would she go? From one or two of the windows, lights showed, and up in the attics her room was waiting – and Nanny and young Bella, and elsewhere Sal and the other maids, and friendly Mrs Roberts, and Lady Maud, and kind Sir Richard. Never forgetting blessed, vulnerable Lily. They all meant a lot to Jess; she felt a part of their lives. Besides, even if she had wanted to leave, her instinct said it was impossible: her fate lay here.

Reaching the attics, she heard murmuring voices from Mrs Roberts's room and went to knock there to let Nanny know she was back. Nanny spent many evenings playing cards with Mrs Roberts in her charming room, with its small, comforting fire.

Mrs Roberts smiled at Jess. 'Did you have a good day? I used to love the Easter Fair when I was younger. You really feel spring's well begun when Easter comes, especially when the weather's fine, like today.'

'That was a master fine day, thankee, Mrs Roberts.' It was a lie, but what else could she say? She wished with all her heart that she'd never gone to Huns'ton. She could hardly believe the hurt she must have inflicted on Matty.

'You'd best look in on Bella,' Nanny said. 'She didn't settle very well. I knew she'd had too much excitement. She'll be sleep-walking again, I shouldn't wonder, so be sure to bolt the door when you leave.'

The schoolroom was in darkness except for two patches of moonlight coming through the dormer windows, though the small lamp on the table was still warm – it had simply used up its oil. Jess went to replenish it from the storeroom near Bella's room, but before she got there something in the quality of the silence made her pause and listen at the child's door. Small sounds of snuffling came from close behind the wood.

Putting down the lamp, Jess unbolted the door and tried to open it. Something prevented her. She pushed harder and the door gave, but from the floor Bella gave a little moan. It was her body that was in the way!

As gently as she could, Jess pushed the door wide enough so she could slip inside. The child lay on the floor, where she had evidently fallen asleep after a long bout of crying. She was stirring now, but she was cold as cold. When eventually Jess got the candle lit, she saw Bella's tear-stained face and swollen eyes.

'I wanted Nanny,' she croaked. 'I shouted and shouted...'

And Nanny either wouldn't come or wasn't near enough to hear, Jess thought furiously, gathering the child into her arms. 'There, darlin'. That's all right now. Jess is here. Jess'll stay.'

Settling Bella into bed, Jess lay beside her, holding her to warm and comfort her.

'The moon was shining on me,' Bella said. 'Don't let it shine on me, Jess, please. It will turn my hair to seaweed.'

'Why, that it 'on't!' She hugged the child closer. 'Did you have a bad dream? That's all it was, just an old dream. 'Cos of what Miss Lily said. There en't really such things as mermaids. Miss Lily likes to make up stories, that's all. Do you go to sleep now, little 'un, and don't fret about it no more. I'll not let nobody hurt you.'

'Say that rhyme,' Bella requested.

Softly, Jess repeated the old nonsense rhyme that Granny Henefer had said to her so often:

Do you know what's in my pocket?
When, and where, and how I dot it?
Such a lot of treasures in it.
Listen now and I'll begin it:
Here's a handle off a cup that someone broke at tea,
And here's some pennies – one, two, three –

That... Nanny Fyncham gave to me.
Tomorrowday I'll buy a spade,
When I'm out walking with the maid.

'I bought a leaping stick,' Bella murmured sleepily.

'So you did. You had a masterpiece of a day, didn't you?'

Bella didn't answer. She was asleep.

Now that Jess felt calmer, she could think more rationally. Maybe she'd been wrong to fear Merrywest's vengeance. Maybe he wouldn't find out where she was. Matty didn't know her new situation, did he? It was even possible that Matty would hold his tongue and not tell that he'd seen her, though, knowing him, she doubted it: he'd be bound to tell Fanny, if no one else. They'd talk about it. The boys, Sam and Joe, would hear. 'Sprat' Fysher, Fanny's husband, would find out...

Sooner or later, Nathanael Merrywest would learn that she had been seen in Huns'ton. The question was – what would he then do?

–

That Thursday, Jess and Lily went walking, braving a stiff breeze and the threat of showers. After three days when nothing dire had happened, Jess was beginning to feel secure again. She was glad she'd seen Matty. At least she knew he was well, and that her family would know she was well, too; and her conscience was lighter for knowing that Merrywest wasn't dead. She did thank the Lord sincerely for that blessing – her soul was free of the taint of mortal sin, even if her life on earth was now shadowed by the fear of his coming in person to blight her new existence. Much as she argued with herself, deep inside she knew he would come. Merrywest had scores to settle. He wouldn't let it be.

But she wouldn't think about it. *Sufficient unto the day...* as Reverend Clare had it; or as Granny Henefer always used to say, *Never trouble trouble, 'til trouble troubles you. It only troubles trouble, and troubles others, too.*

The Hewinghall woods were beginning to spring with April life. Buds fattened on all the trees and bushes; snowdrops trembled in sheltered hollows and where the trees grew less dense a carpet of delicate yellow resolved itself into a thousand primrose faces lifting to the sun.

Lily knew the woods, every inch of them. She showed Jess where the first violets were peeping; she pointed out the places where seed and some sort of cooked mash had been scattered, 'for the partridges,' she explained. 'They're starting to breed, so the keepers like to keep them well fed. We must go quietly through here, not to disturb them. That's why I didn't bring Gyp. Mr Rudd doesn't like dogs running loose in his woods when the game birds are nesting.'

She moved on restlessly, all the time talking in a low voice so as not to disturb the birds that hid everywhere among the undergrowth.

The skies were changeable, one minute bright, the next shadowed by cloud. A larger cloud swept up and threw a brief shower of rain on to the earth, leaving everything dewed so that, brushing under a tree or past a rhododendron, Jess and Lily dislodged tiny waterfalls that damped their arms and skirts.

'"April showers bring forth May flowers",' Lily said, flashing a smile behind her. 'Keep up, Jess.'

Growing up on the edge of Lynn, Jess and her playmates had wandered along the river bank, into the marsh meadows and the tree-lined lanes. But she was not familiar with deep woods like this one. On her own, she might have been scared of the shadows and quiet places, and the sudden eruptions of hidden life, but seeing it through Lily's eyes made her aware of the pleasures of sharing this tangled world.

Even so, her own nature preferred the open fields, the sunlight. The wood was a dark excitement to be dipped into for a thrill, not a refuge in which to hide from the world, as it was for Lily.

She wondered what Lily was fleeing from now. Something was disturbing her, driving her on. Lily wanted to confide something, she guessed, but was afraid of doing so. So she kept walking, and talking. She showed Jess her favourite walks, especially one dark hollow she called the 'heart of the wood' where there was a pond so thick with frogspawn it was like gruel. In summer, she said, the leaves of the trees reached out to turn the place into a shady glade where she often came to read and think.

'Once I saw a deer come down to drink at the pond,' she added, brushing aside a trailing branch, 'and once— Oh, no!' Her voice was a moan of distress as she stopped, a hand to her mouth, and turned aside to hurry on, away from what hung from an ivy-clad oak ahead. It was, Jess saw, a rough framework from which were suspended the dead and decaying carcasses of birds and animals. She made out a hawk, and a jay with its flash of blue, a small fox, a cat...

'Come away, Jessamy!' Lily's face was pale, her eyes haunted.

'What was it?' Jess wanted to know. 'Whoever'd kill all them—'

'The gamekeepers would! Mr Rudd and his men. They kill everything that might harm their precious birds and hang them up in the hope of scaring away other predators. Oh... I know it has to be done, but that tabby cat... I'm sure it's little Cobweb, Mrs Tyler's sweet little cat. She used to come purring... She wouldn't harm their stupid pheasants! Oh, it's too horrible. Let's go. Let's go.'

They climbed a steep rise and reached a mighty blackthorn hedge whose blossom showed like drifting snow against dark branches. Here there was a stile leading to a field already green with young wheat.

Lily had evidently intended to cross the field, but the sight of people there – a work gang, bent to the task of weeding and picking stones – made her stop so abruptly that Jess, who was staring at the view of the sea, almost ran into her.

'We must go back now,' Lily said, and once again turned aside.

No, she didn't want to face people, to have them stare and point after her: *That's the Clare girl, the one with the funny eyes – the misbegotten gypsy brat.* Oh, why couldn't she forget what Clemency had said? Because she was half afraid it was true! Sometimes, at moments of cold despair, she herself had wondered if her dream of her 'real father' was a fantasy. But in the wood she was able to believe again. In the wood, anything was possible.

Today, though, Lily couldn't forget the imminence of her return to school. What would happen then? More escapades for Clemency? More sneaking out at night to meet Ash Haverleigh? Lily's conscience told her she ought to do something to stop it – for Clemency's own sake. She wanted to talk to Jess about it, but somehow the right moment never arrived and besides she *had* been sworn to secrecy.

Oh, she couldn't decide what was best! What was she to do? A distraction – she needed a distraction. A game, maybe. A little trick to play on Jess...

Behind her, Jess had paused, staring out across the field. The land sloped away before her, down to reedy marshes and a glittering inlet of the sea. A long arm of sandy, grassy hillocks spread out to protect the creek from the bright ocean beyond, where silver sunlight speared down between scudding clouds and gulls swept their white wings against the stormy sky. The view was familiar, though she'd never seen it from this height before; usually she saw it from near sea level, on the way to chapel. This would be a lovely spot for sitting and thinking, out in the air and sunlight but away from prying eyes.

She was sure she'd stopped only for a second or two, but by the time she turned to go on another cloud had shut off the sun. The wood looked darker than ever – and Lily was gone.

For the smallest space Jess was terrified. Calling, 'Miss Lily!' she plunged down a slope into deep thickets of rhododendron. The path twisted and turned. Within minutes she was lost. The further she went, the more the clouds closed in. Like twilight. Like the time she'd got lost back in December.

She blundered on, thrusting heavy branches aside, finding herself in a dim-lit space like a cave enclosed by greenery. Then something erupted right at her feet, springing into the air. Jess couldn't help herself. She screamed loud and long as the pheasant whirred away in fright, its call alarming all the other creatures in the wood.

Jess stepped in something that crunched and slid. Thrown off balance, she fell sidelong amid the undergrowth with a cracking of branches and another flurry of startled life. For a second it felt as if the wood was attacking her. She lay huddled, her arms over her head, waiting for everything to be still again.

Before she could recover herself, a black dog wriggled under a low branch and stood over her. It barked sharply once and was answered by a whistle. It looked like Dash. Or was it Jim Potts's dog? Jess tried to get up, but the dog bared its teeth at her, growling low in its throat, and barked again. Jess froze, too frightened to move.

'Good boy,' Reuben Rudd's voice approved, and the long double barrel of a shotgun parted the bushes, muzzle pointing straight at Jess, turning her rush of relief into fresh alarm. 'Now then,' the gamekeeper added in grim tones as he bent to fasten a hard hand round her arm, 'let's see what...'

He had come from the broader light outside so it took a moment for his eyes to adjust and only then did he recognise Jess. She saw the start that ran through him as he snapped upright, no longer threatening her – except by the look on his face. 'Bloody hell!' pronounced the good Methodist.

'I...' she began, wanting to explain. But as she got up, awkward and aching, she felt the wetness on her skirt and when she looked for the cause she saw egg-slime dripping, and pieces of broken shell, and on the ground she made out the shape of the nest she had destroyed.

In the half-light Rudd's eyes seemed to glow with furious fire. 'What are you doing here? Rampaging in my woods...' He seemed to be too angry for coherent speech. 'Do you know what you've done?'

Jess looked helplessly at the ruined nest. 'I've broke some o' your eggs. But I was frit! I fell over. I didn't mean... I'm sorry.'

'Sorry?! Blast it, woman—'

'Jessamy! *Jessamy!*' Lily's anxious voice called from beyond the thicket. 'Where are you?'

Affording Jess one last, tight-lipped look, Rudd ducked away and, as Jess followed, brushing uselessly at her egg-stained skirts, she heard Lily say, 'Oh, Mr Rudd. What has happened?'

'You may well ask.' His voice was thick with disgust and he cast a bleak look at Jess as she, stained and dishevelled, stepped out from the shelter of the rhododendron. 'Or ask Miss Sharp.'

One glance was all Lily needed to gather the gist. 'Oh, dear.'

'You know better,' he said flatly. 'You surely do know better than this, Miss Lily. When the squire offered you free run of his woods it was on the understanding you'd respect the game. You and anybody you might bring here. I must hold you responsible and I shall have to report it.'

'Must you?' Lily's strange eyes were wide with dismay. 'Oh – you're right, of course – it was entirely my fault. *My* fault. You mustn't blame Jess, Mr Rudd. She doesn't know much about country ways. Do you think... Will Sir Richard put a stop to my walking in his woods? If he says I mustn't come here I shall obey, of course. But... I do so love this wood. It's a special place. Like a magic kingdom where I feel free to be my true self. And you *know* how careful I usually am. This time... Oh, forgive me, but... I got it into my head to play a little game with Jess. I hid behind a tree and she... well, the joke went awry. She got frightened, I think – didn't you, Jess?' Allowing Jess no time to respond, she moved closer to Rudd, laying a pale hand on his sleeve, her face lifted in appeal. 'Oh, dear Mr Rudd, I most sincerely swear to you that it will never happen again. If you could find it in your heart to excuse me and perhaps not to mention it to Sir Richard...'

With anyone else, Jess would have called it flannel, but Lily just said what was in her heart, and acted accordingly.

Rudd was still frowning, though Jess saw he was not unmoved. 'Well, now...' he began dubiously.

'I know that won't mend the eggs,' Lily added, 'but it's early in the season. The hen may lay another clutch. And, you know, if we leave right now, the birds will all come back. Oh, Mr Rudd... won't you please overlook this unfortunate accident? Or shall I go up to the house and explain to Sir Richard myself? Perhaps if I offered to pay for any damages...'

Letting out a sharp breath through his nose, the gamekeeper shook his head. 'That'll not be necessary, Miss Lily. Just be sure and keep an eye on Miss Sharp in future. Now... happen you'll let me lead you back to the main path. Heel, Dash.'

He moved away with the dog close behind and Lily following. Jess trailed in their wake, feeling a fool and knowing that whatever he had said Reuben Rudd was still annoyed with her. Well, he'd hardly spoken to her since the day she first encountered Jim Potts, so today's disaster couldn't make much difference.

He led them back to one of the broad rides that ran through the wood and there took his leave, doffing his cap and making a bow to Lily but affording Jess only a nod and a brusque 'Good day' before he turned on his heel. Jess watched him go, wishing she knew what to say to mend matters, but soft, winning words did not come easy to her. Not the way they came to Lily.

'Thank you, miss,' she muttered.

'For what?' Lily seemed surprised. 'I only told the truth.'

'Not really. You've bin tellin' me all the time how quiet and careful we ought to be. I should've known better.'

'How could you? Gracious goodness, Jess, there are things about the countryside I barely understand myself and I've lived here all my life. To be honest... I never quite realised how horrid this whole game-rearing business can be. And to think it all happens solely to rear yet more beautiful birds whose only destiny is to be slaughtered.'

'Well, that's what he's paid for,' said Jess.

'Who?'

'Mr Rudd.'

Lily glanced round at her distractedly. 'You think I'm being foolish, don't you? But I can't help it. I hate the thought of all the blood and destruction. It's a desecration! Oh, I don't understand anything any more. The older I grow the more complicated life becomes. Why can't things be simple and straightforward?'

She pushed on, lifting her skirts to stride at a rapid pace down the path, leaving the shorter Jess struggling behind, more than ever concerned for what was really troubling Lily.

In the rectory garden, Gyp came bounding to greet them with little excited barks and cavortings. Lily bent and gathered him into her arms, kissing his head, smiling over it at Jess in that falsely bright way she had when she was covering desperate unease.

'I want to ask you to do something for me, Jess. I'm so anxious about Gyp. He seems awfully thin and nervous. I'm worried about leaving him. Cousin Oriana can't be expected to take him for walks, and I don't trust Eliza, or Mary Anne, so I wondered if you... Cousin Oriana says you may call for him any time you wish. It might amuse Bella, too.'

'Well... yes. I'm sure it would. Yes, 'course I'll do that for you. Glad to. But... look, Miss Lily, I better not stop for tea, if you don't mind. I ought to get back and change my clothes.'

'Oh... gracious goodness, then go, if you must.' Lily lost patience. She had hoped to share her worries about Clemency, but now she saw that Jess's instinct for social mores was right – it was hardly the done thing to invite an ex-servant back as a friend. Not that Lily had much patience with such nice distinctions. To her, people were people, divided into those she liked and those she did not. Jess was her friend and that was an end to it. But Cousin Oriana wouldn't see it that way, and neither would Papa. And since Papa had been ominously silent since she'd flung out of the luncheon party perhaps it was best not to risk annoying him again. This entire holiday had been a *disaster*. And what did the new term at school hold in store?

–

Jess left the rectory by the gate in the west wall of the kitchen garden. As she descended the far side of the hill she saw Reuben Rudd by the hedge, doing something to a trap, watched by the ever-alert Dash.

A soft bark from the dog made Rudd straighten and turn to watch her approach, though she had a feeling he'd already known she was there. The thought made a pulse throb in her veins, disconcerting her, for the look on his face was anything but welcoming.

After one meeting with a pair of challenging hazel eyes, she avoided looking at him directly. 'Mr Rudd,' she said and nodded, stepping off the grassy headland and into the young green wheat in order to get round him without going too close.

'Miss Sharp,' he answered, touching the peak of his cap.

She had a notion he'd leave it at that, but as she regained the headland and would have stepped out to get away, he said, 'You all right?'

Mystified, Jess paused and glanced back.

'You didn't hurt yourself, when you fell?'

'I've had worse.'

He gestured at her stained skirts. 'You've given yourself a job.'

'Well, that en't nothin' new,' she said, and heard him draw a swift, angry breath.

'I'm blowed if I've ever come across a woman as standoffish as you in all my born days! Blast it, Jessie Sharp, I'm trying to apologise.'

'For what?'

'For losing my temper earlier. It wasn't you I was mad at. Not really. I've been up every night this past week, keeping a watch for badgers. We've lost no end of eggs. Then, last night, a fox got into the rearing field and killed some of my poults, and a broody, and my chap's gun jammed and he shot himself in the foot and... well, you don't want to hear my tales of woe, but I've not been in the best of moods, as you'll understand. So when I found you taking a bath in egg yolk...'

'You'd a right to be angry,' Jess told him. 'I shouldn't've been runnin' about in your woods. Miss Lily told me to be careful.'

For the first time in weeks, she detected a hint of the old warmth in his eyes. 'Maybe you need a few lessons in woodcraft.'

'Mebbe I do,' she said, and watched a slow smile spread over his face, making her feel queer inside, like she was melting. The feeling took her unawares – she'd forgotten what effect he could have on her. It frightened her, too. Something inside her threw up barriers, barred doors, slammed shutters. 'I'd best get back,' she muttered, and turned to hurry on, knowing her behaviour puzzled him. No more than it puzzled her. She was in total confusion, drawn to him helplessly, wanting to explore the promise of what he seemed to offer – yet the thought of it terrified her.

Thirteen

With Clemency travelling to school from London, Lily made the journey alone, under the eye of various respectable lady passengers. She felt like a parcel being passed from hand to hand – a slightly suspect parcel: each chaperone was disconcerted to find her pretty, dark-haired charge was actually a changeling with defiant eyes that were not a matched pair.

Clemency was already in residence at the Academy, amusing the others with tales of the latest fashion and gossip from the capital while waiting for her best friend Jane Lassiter to arrive. Before long, however, they learned that Jane Lassiter would not be rejoining them – 'gone on a tour of the Continent with her parents' was the official explanation.

'Of course I knew about it,' Clemency claimed. 'Jane and I tell each other everything.' But she was lying. The news came as a shock to her.

After a period which Lily defined as a kind of mourning, Clemency emerged with renewed vivacity and set about rebuilding her court. Even Amelia was once again a willing acolyte.

'Amelia's a fool,' was Anne Ferrers's opinion.

Feeling more and more disregarded, Lily spent hours over her journal. She suspected that Clemency's nocturnal escapades had recommenced, but if she told she would be a sneak. Desperately she wished for the weeks to pass. Soon she would have finished with school. She would be free.

Or would she? The detestable Mrs Dunnock had assumed Lily would become a teacher in the village school. And Papa had mentioned her becoming a governess. Was he trying to frighten her into marrying the curate? Lily couldn't decide. She didn't want to think about it.

At night she prayed for miracles, and she dreamed – disturbing dreams of nakedness and desire. Those dreams had been coming to her for months but now they were growing stronger; she always woke with a terrible ache deep inside. To soothe the feeling, she had learned to stroke her body with her hands. At first the sensations had worried her because she knew it was wrong, knew she was wicked. But she couldn't prevent herself from repeating the experiment next time she woke in a hot sweat wanting... wanting...

Wanting she knew not what.

She justified her self-pleasuring as consolation for unhappiness – her secret alone. She felt guilty for it, but she couldn't stop it. It was her only source of comfort in a world that grew ever more alarming.

–

Spring drew on, April turning to May, heading for June.

At Hewinghall of an afternoon, while Nanny had her rest, Jess and Bella roamed the gardens and the park, playing ball, or hide-and-seek, or any other game Jess could think of. Often they called at the rectory to collect Gyp and give him a run. Eliza met them with sniffs and sour words – reasty because Jess was doing so well at the big house.

On free afternoons, the stile on the edge of the wood became Jess's favourite spot. There, out of sight of the world, she could perch and gaze across fields and marshes to the sea. There might be a coaster bringing coal into the harbour, or a fishing boat or two, with a white sail or a red. It made her feel a bit nearer to home, and that was a comfort.

She was able to think of home now without panicking; weeks had gone by since her meeting with Matty and nothing awful had happened. Maybe she was safe from pursuit, after all.

She didn't go through the woods, though – she'd found another way, round by farm tracks and the edges of fields. Occasionally she saw one of the keepers, though she never ran into Rudd. She fancied he was avoiding her.

Towards the end of May poor little Gyp was sadly again, lying in his basket by the hearth, thin as workhouse gruel. 'Can't seem to keep anything down,' Miss Peartree fretted.

'He shouldn't eat things in the garden,' Eliza said sharply. 'Lord knows what poisons Fargus do put down to kill all the rats and mice.'

But Jess had always thought Gyp was fussy about what he ate...

Worried about the dog, she made her way to the stile and sat looking over the fields to the distant sea. The brisk wind that tore the clouds and whipped up the sea's white horses came dancing on over the marshes, and teased Jess's hair out of its chignon. Tendrils fluttered on cheeks turned pink by the bracing air, and her brown eyes were bright as she heard a cuckoo fly, singing its forlorn song.

As she craned to see the bird, an iced finger touched her spine. Had there been a cry in the woods, faint and far away? Her ears sharpened to the memory. Yes, a cry. A shout. Two shouts. One sharp – of alarm – the other a wail of despair. But from where? Poised on tip-toe, Jess stared into the wood. Undergrowth grew thick and trees were putting out new leaves, an amazing variety of tender greens. The cuckoo still mocked from the distance, but the wood was silent.

Jess knew she hadn't imagined the cry. Her nerves were still alert to the peril she had sensed coming at her like a cold blast. Someone was in trouble. In danger. An accident? Rudd...

She found herself jumping from the stile, running down the main path into the wood, ignoring the rustle of disturbance as birds shifted in alarm. Once or twice she hesitated where the way divided, only to plunge on, guided by her sixth sense. It led her unerringly.

Through green branches she saw a boy standing by a big sweet chestnut tree, its trunk twisted with age, its bark deeply seamed and knotted, its branches hanging low. As she drew closer, she saw that the boy was rigid with fear, staring at something on the ground.

A body. A man's body. A shaggy black retriever was sniffing round him, whining. Dear God! She'd known. The moment she'd heard that cry...

The boy looked round as he heard her coming. Under the peak of an oversized cap his face was wet with tears, his whole body shaking.

'It's Mr Rudd,' he wept, wiping his nose on his coat sleeve. 'He fell outa the tree. What'll I do? I don't know what to do!'

Rudd lay sprawled on his side, one arm twisted under him, his skin pale as ashes under his freckles. Dash nudged at his arm as if trying to rouse him and Jess flung herself to her knees, pushing the dog aside, laying her hand to the gamekeeper's damp forehead. A pulse was still beating in his temple. He was breathing, thank the Lord!

'Is he dead?' the boy wept, hopping from foot to foot.

'No. Not yet. Run and get help. Run, bor! Quick!'

He hesitated a second, then set off at a charge. In his wake, the silence closed in around Jess. She was no nurse, had only her recollections of incidents she'd seen, and of things her mother had said. Keep

165

him still; keep him warm. She stripped off her coat and laid it over Rudd, tucking it round him. Then, feeling helpless, she sat and held his hand between her own, all the time watching his white face. It was terrible to see him like that, he who was usually so alive.

'Reuben, bor,' she whispered, clasping his hand to her breast. 'Come you on, now. Wake you up. Don't lie there like that.'

The quality of his breathing changed, deepening and quickening. A wince of pain contorted his face and his eyelids flickered, then snapped open. He stared at her uncomprehendingly and she, too full to speak, leaned to smooth the sweat-damp hair from his brow. None of their differences mattered at that moment. To see him conscious was enough.

'Jessie?' he croaked as if he didn't trust his eyes. 'Jessie, is that you?'

'I'm here, bor,' she managed. 'You'll be all right.'

She found herself caressing his face, stroking and soothing as if he were a child. He lay looking up at her wordlessly, his eyes saying he was glad she was there. In that moment heart spoke to heart, without evasions.

Then, as he tried to move, his face contorted and he bit back a cry.

'Lie you still!' Jess said anxiously. 'Where do you hurt?'

'All over,' came the wry reply.

'Can you move your legs?'

He stretched his legs cautiously, first one and then the other. The effort made him grimace but there seemed to be no bones broken. His left arm was stiff and bruised, too. But when he tried to move, to roll over on to his back more comfortably, the pain dug visibly into him, robbing his face of colour, breaking beads of sweat out from his forehead. He had injured his right shoulder, could scarcely move his arm. Jess helped him get as comfortable as was possible, and pulled her coat closely round him. Then she tore at the grass and weeds around her, rolling it to form a pillow for his head. Thorns ripped her skin and brought blood running, but she hardly noticed. Her only concern was for Rudd. By the time she had him settled he was lying with his eyes closed, his freckled face grey and dewed with sweat.

When he stretched out his hand as if reaching for comfort, Jess let her own hand meet his. He clasped her fingers briefly, letting himself relax, and she sat there, warming his hand between her own small ones, silently worrying while aloud she talked nonsense just to let him know he wasn't alone.

'That'll be Miss Lily's birthday soon,' she heard herself say. 'Eighteen, she'll be. I on'y hope Gyp get better afore she come home.'

'Gyp?' he mumbled.

'He took sick in the night, and again this mornin', so Miss Peartree say. I'd have brung him for a walk if he hadn't been feelin' so queer – we wouldn't have come through your woods, though. Not while the birds are breedin'.'

'You wouldn't do any harm. Not if you kept him on his lead.'

'That en't what you said when…'

His lashes lifted and through their dark veil the hazel eyes were heavy with pain. There was regret in him, too. 'I was right mad that day,' he confessed. 'I told you why, didn't I? Shouldn't have sworn at you, though. Forgive me for that, Jessie lass.'

Feeling the urgency in the way his hand tightened on hers, she bent closer to smooth his brow, concerned to find it hot and dry now. Where on earth was that boy? 'That don't signify,' she said softly.

Silent messages passed between them, through clasp of hands and beat of blood, through meeting of eyes and primeval instincts, man to woman, woman to man. She felt it strongly, a physical upheaval inside her, as if her stomach had turned over. It unsettled every sinew, changing everything for her. That was the moment she knew she loved Reuben Rudd, right or wrong, wise or unwise. She'd been fighting it since the day they met, but you couldn't escape fate, not when it was set on snaring you in its nets.

'Is it right you were with Jim Potts at the fair Easter Monday?' Rudd asked hoarsely. 'He said you were with him. He said he won a coconut for you.'

'What…?' She was outraged. 'Why, Mr Rudd, if you think I'd have anythin' to do with that fancy fool then… then you don't know Jess Henefer very well!'

The moment it was out she could have bitten off her tongue, but Rudd seemed too intent on his own train of thought to notice. A heavy sigh escaped him as he looked up at her with pain-clouded eyes and said, 'I'm the one that's the fool, Jessie lass. I let him wind me up like I was a clockwork clown. But… heck and go thump, I'm no good at playing those kind of games. Never was.'

'I'm glad o' that,' said Jess.

'I was plain jealous, that's what.'

Bewildered by the depths of emotion on whose shores she teetered, she backed away from danger, saying, 'And what were you a–doin' up that tree?'

Again Rudd tried to shift himself to get more comfortable, grimacing with the pain. When it subsided, he said with difficulty, 'Owl's nest... Nestlings in it. I've been watching the mother bird for days. Knew she had chicks somewhere. Today... today we saw her taking prey back to the nest. I'd nearly got there when she flew at me. Went for my eyes, blast her. I lost my grip. Fell... Young Bob was with me. Where's he got to?'

'I sent him for help. I told you. He'll be here soon, I reckon.'

He was slipping back into unconsciousness, she saw, the pain and shock overpowering him. 'I'm cold,' he muttered. 'I'm awful cold, Jessie.'

She clasped his hand, leaning closer, saying his name. 'Reuben. Reuben, can you hear me?' Getting no response, she stroked his hair, feeling it thick and soft under her fingers. 'Don't die. Please don't die!' Too many of those she loved had died. If Reuben joined them she didn't think she could go on. 'I won't let you die!' she whispered fiercely, and slid in beside him under her coat, trying to warm him with her own body, still holding his good hand between them, her other arm across him as she stared into his face. 'D'you hear me, Reuben Rudd? There's all your life ahead of you. You've got to go on. Got to keep fightin'. *I* did, and I had good reasons for wantin' to be dead. You've got a hundred reasons to live. You're young; you're strong; you're a fine, good-lookin' man. And what'll Dash do if you just give up?'

Suddenly his fingers were painfully tight round hers. 'Who says I'm giving up?' the hoarse whisper came.

Jess didn't know she was weeping until she had to brush her tears away to see his face and then she saw he too was moved to tears, looking at her with a tenderness that pierced all her defences.

'Giving up?' he said again. 'Nay, lass. Not when I've suddenly got everything to live for.'

It was happening again, the deep communion between them, the certainty and rightness that joined the two of them in ways far beyond words or sense or reason. This was her man and she knew it, just as her mother had predicted – *You'll know, when you find him, Jess. You'll just know.*

That she could never have him was somehow irrelevant at that moment.

She had an unbearable urge to bend and press her lips to his face, but before she could move a blackbird skimmed by, complaining, and she heard people coming. Carefully, she disentangled herself from Rudd and scrambled to her feet as a group of men appeared, led by Rudd's apprentice boy. With them came the doctor.

He diagnosed a broken collarbone and severe concussion. Within minutes he had immobilised Rudd's arm and shoulder. The activity made Rudd sweat again and Jess ached for the pain he was enduring.

'He'll be all right, 'on't he?' she asked anxiously as the injured man was carried away on a makeshift stretcher, swathed in a blanket.

'He has every chance,' the doctor replied. 'He's a strong man and you did the right thing, keeping him still and warm.' Only then did he pause to take full notice of her. 'You're the new girl at Hewinghall, aren't you? Jess Sharp, the new nurserymaid?'

'Yes, sir.' What was he thinking as he peered at her with intent brown eyes?

'I gather Miss Lily Clare has taken a liking to you,' he said.

'Why...' Surprised, she floundered for words. 'Yes, sir, that seem so. And me to her. She're a lovely young lady.'

'That's good. Miss Lily needs a friend. You'll be sure and look after her, won't you?'

Wondering at the reasons behind this instruction, Jess said, 'Yes, sir, I will.'

'Good,' he said, pulling on his gloves. 'Good,' and hurried away as if he was embarrassed for having mentioned Lily.

Jess watched him go, her mind on Reuben Rudd. If only she had the right to go with him! Instead, she was alone in the wood.

No, not alone – the dog was still there. Someone had ordered him to 'Stay!' and Dash had stayed. Now, lying dejected with nose on paws, he looked much the same as Jess felt. Maybe she ought to take Dash to the doctor's house. One of the men would know what to do with him and that way, too, she'd find out what was happening to Rudd.

Bending to pick up her rumpled coat, she said, 'Let's go find him, bor.'

The command 'find' animated the dog. He leapt up eagerly, tail going, and bounded away down a path which led in a direction Jess had not planned for. 'Dash!' she called, but the dog ignored her. 'Finding' was what he was trained for, and the person he wanted to find was his master, so he was going where he expected Rudd to be – he was going home.

Jess went after him. She called, but he took no notice. Now and then he'd pause as if to make sure she was coming, but he stayed well out of reach, imitating her pace and always keeping a little ahead.

Eventually, deep among shady trees, they came to a thatched cottage whose garden was neatly tended, daffodils fading in beds edged with tiny blue flowers, rose bushes waiting to bloom. One side of the garden was entirely given to wire-netted runs where hens were penned in crates, some of them with tiny pheasant chicks piping in the grass around them. She didn't see much more, at the time, because two great red dogs came snarling down the front pathway to launch themselves at the gate which, fortunately, was shut.

'Quiet down!' a male voice ordered from the cottage doorway and Jess saw a man emerge from the cottage. To her surprise, it was Sir Richard Fyncham, ducking his dark head under the lintel. 'Ah – good afternoon, Jess,' he greeted her. 'If you've come to see Rudd, you're out of luck. I called to see him myself, but he doesn't appear to be about.'

Jess dipped a hasty curtsey. 'Beggin' your pardon, Sir Richard, but Mr Rudd have been hurt bad. Broke his collarbone, so the doctor say. They've now took him to the surgery.'

'No!' His brow furrowed in concern as he came striding down the path. 'When did this happen?'

'Earlier this afternoon, sir. I was a-settin' with him while the boy went for help. Didn't know what to do about Dash – they left him behind.'

'Oh, I see.' He hunched himself down to greet Dash as an old friend, patting him and pulling his ears. 'Good old boy, worried about your master, eh? He'll be all right.' He roughly caressed the dog, murmuring comfort as if Dash could understand him. He had good hands, Jess thought, long and fine but with a strength to them that fitted with his tall, slender frame and broad shoulders.

He looked at Jess now, squinting slightly, his hands still ruffling the dog. 'Are you a friend of Rudd's, then?'

'I...'

A sudden boyish grin appreciated the reasons for her hesitation. 'Don't worry, girl, I'm not one of those employers who frown on followers. Always thought that was a bit unfair. Been young myself once, so I know how it is.'

He talked as if he was old, but he wasn't, Jess thought. Thirty-five or so, maybe.

'Rudd's a good man,' he added. 'I'd be happy to see him settled. A man needs a wife.'

Wife? The word startled Jess.

'Tell you what I'll do,' he said. 'These hounds could do with a run, so I'll take them with me, give them some exercise, and fetch one of the under-keepers to fill in here. That'll be best. Will you wait until he comes? Just keep an eye on the birds, that's all. Right – come along then, boys. Prince! Pacer!' He glanced again at Jess. 'I'll leave Dash with you. Anybody comes, let him deal with them. All right, boys, here we go.'

And he was gone, with the two red dogs after him.

Bemused, Jess made her way to the cottage.

It was clear at once that a lone man lived there – a loaf of bread lay on the side where it had last been cut, the knife by it, a cloth roughly thrown over to protect it from flies, and nearby there was an empty can that had once held beans; dirty crockery littered the draining board and the Lord only knew when the floor had last been swept, or anything dusted. Since she had nothing else to do, Jess set about what she knew best – cleaning up. Men alone were so helpless. She could just imagine what a pig-sty her brother Matty would inhabit, left to himself.

Oh, why couldn't she stop thinking about her big, soft brother and wondering what was happening to the family without her? Did they wonder why she had deserted them, and why she had run off when Matty found her?

No! She shook herself, closing out the thoughts. No, she wouldn't think about it. It hurt too much. Best get on. Do something. Work. That was right. Work was the best medicine for homesickness, and for worry.

The cottage was roomy for a man on his own – two up and two down, with a water-pump outside the back door and a privy at the bottom of the vegetable patch. Rudd lived mainly in his kitchen, from the looks of it; the parlour was unfurnished except for a couple of old armchairs, a dog basket, and traps of various kinds, in various states of repair. Did he spend his lonely evenings mending them? There were a few books on a shelf – books that looked as though they'd been well read. Jess took one down, opening it to stare at the pages of print. Frowning, she made out the title: 'The Moons—' but the word defeated her. She replaced the book with a little sigh. Here was another barrier between her and Rudd – he was an educated man and she knew nothing.

Cleaning the place properly would take more time than she had, so she contented herself with giving it a lick and a promise. She washed the pots, put the food away, swept the floor and scrubbed the table; then went upstairs where, sure enough, the bed was unmade and clothes tossed anyhow. Jess tidied up until she saw a photograph on the chest of drawers. That stopped her, made her sit down on the bed, the cheap frame in her hands as she stared at the two people pictured in stiff studio pose – a young woman, plain and unsmiling under a severe hat, and on her lap a child of about two, all bonny blond curls and big eyes. Rudd's wife and son?

Hearing the gate clash, and Dash bark in response, Jess sprang to her feet, feeling as guilty as if she'd been caught stealing. Replacing the photograph, she hurried for the stairs and reached the kitchen just as the newcomer let himself in.

He was one of Rudd's assistants, a dour, slow-witted man named Obi. He spoke in a slow, slurred voice, with a blankness behind his eyes as if his mind was trying to follow what his mouth was saying. He said he'd transfer the coops, with the broodies and the pheasant poults, to the main rearing field, which was near his own cottage. He'd look after Dash, too. Jess needn't worry. She could go now; he'd take over.

Jess was glad to escape. Obi seemed harmless enough but his blank eyes unnerved her.

On her way back, she called at the rectory to relay the news of Rudd's accident. But the rectory was already agog with the news. Mary Anne, off on errands, had heard Mrs Michaels, the doctor's wife, gossiping with Mrs Crane, the laundress. It seemed Dr Michaels had gone with Rudd on the train from Hunstanton, bound for the hospital in Lynn.

A fresh buttered scone turned to bran in Jess's mouth. 'The hospital?' That terrible place. Where Granny Henefer had died screaming in pain, and little Sarah-May had been snuffed out by diphtheria. 'Why?'

'Because he've cracked his skull,' Mary Anne snuffled. 'They might have to operate. On his brains.'

Dear Lord, Jess thought. Oh, dearest Lord... Across the table she caught Eliza's jaundiced eye on her. Eliza said, 'Well, so that's how you spend your afternoons off, Jess Sharp – in the woods with Reuben Rudd. I 'on't ask what the pair of you were a-doin' of.'

'Blast, and I wish he *had* been with me!' Jess said fiercely. 'If he had, he wouldn't a fallen out o' that tree!'

Her vehemence silenced even Eliza.

–

Since Jess's thoughts were all of Reuben Rudd that evening, it was hardly surprising that he got into her dreams, too. She was lying entwined with him in the wood, under her coat, and they were both naked, happy to be so. But as he lifted himself to possess her his face changed – no longer Rudd but Merrywest. She felt the tearing pain as he forced his way into her. She screamed – and came awake with the echo of her cry fading across the attic room. Her body was running sweat, her hair damp, her flesh throbbing and her heart unsteady. She sat up, throwing aside the sheet, gulping cool air to calm herself. Was she never going to be free of her fear?

She became aware that Bella was calling. Throwing a woollen wrap around her, Jess hurried through the darkness to the child's door and unbolted it. Bella was sitting up in bed, weeping with fright.

'I heard something,' she muttered, reaching to wind her arms around Jess as Jess sat beside her and held her, stroking her hair. 'It was the ghost, Jess. The dead boy.'

'Oh, now, Miss Bella—'

'It was! It was my brother Harry. Kate told me about him. He threw himself off the roof in a fit of temper and now he prowls about the schoolroom at night. It's true! Kate said it was true. That's why they bolt my door, and lock the windows – because if I'm naughty he'll come and get me and throw me off the roof, too. Oh, Jess... I heard him. I heard him call out!'

Wondering what other awful tales Kate had told the child to frighten her so, Jess hugged her and whispered calming words. 'That was me you heard. I was havin' a bad dream – yes, I have 'em, too, 'times. There en't no such things as ghosts, Bella. I've been in the schoolroom in the dark, late at night, lots of times, and I hen't seen nothin'. 'Sides, do he come, he'd have to get past me to get at you.

That's what I'm here for – to look after you. Never you fret, my darlin'. You're safe as safe.'

Rocking and singing, repeating favourite rhymes, she soothed the child back to sleep.

Eventually, when Bella was soundly resting, Jess laid her down and, wide awake herself, went to the window, drawing back the curtain. The window was screwed shut – she'd found that out weeks ago and wondered about it. But maybe now she'd discovered the answer. If Bella had had a brother who had fallen to his death from the parapet outside, then maybe it was understandable that she was over-protected.

The night was dark, lit only by fitful stars behind skeins of drifting cloud. She laid her head against the window, feeling the coolness of the glass on her brow as she remembered the wood, and Rudd. *Oh, Reuben, Reuben… where are you? How are you? Are you awake, too? Are you thinking of me?* Before the image of Merrywest intruded, her dreams had been sweet.

A sound outside the door made her whirl and stare through utter blackness. A board had creaked. Boards often creaked, or mice scampered, or plaster shifted in the old house. Generally Jess paid no heed to such noises, but tonight she was on edge, and tonight she saw a flicker of lamplight form a pale mist between floor and door as someone went by. A moment later, straining her ears, she heard the faint *snick* of the schoolroom latch.

The ghost? Jess thought, but dismissed the nonsense at once. Ghosts didn't carry lamps, or need to open doors. But no wonder poor little Bella was scared half to death, what with nurserymaids filling her head full of old squit, and folk wandering about at dead of night…

Moving as soundlessly as she could, she crept out of Bella's room and through the darkened lobby. The door of the schoolroom was ajar, a cold draught of fresh night air blowing through it. Jess peered round the door, stifling an exclamation as she saw a tall female figure, lamp in hand, in the act of clambering through the window.

It was the squire's wife, Lady Fyncham, known more familiarly below stairs as Lady Maud, or even 'Mad Maud' on occasion. Long hair flowed down her back, on to a dark wrap that hung loosely from her shoulders. Beneath it, she wore a long, voluminous, near-transparent nightgown that showed the outline of naked legs as she ducked out through the window and gained the leads where, every morning, Jess shook out the mats.

What was Lady Maud doing up here alone in the middle of the night?

As the mist of light faded from the room, Jess tip-toed as close to the open window as she dared. She could feel the night breeze on her face. To judge by the lamplight that faintly glowed in the darkness, the squire's lady had gone to the far end of the parapet. Doing what? Jess couldn't imagine.

She jumped back as a movement startled her. Then she stared in disbelief. Lady Maud had climbed up to the stone balustrade that guarded the roof. She was walking along it, very slowly, talking to herself, and weeping.

Fourteen

After she had scuttled back to her own bed in dismay, Jess remembered she hadn't bolted Bella's door. She daren't go back for fear of meeting Lady Maud; so she lay awake, worrying. At last that board creaked again – there was just one, that you couldn't seem to avoid however you walked – and the glow of light passed by her door as Lady Maud made for the family stairs. Having given her plenty of time to depart, Jess returned to Bella's door only to find that the bolt was fastened, after all.

Next morning, one of the under-housemaids arrived to summon Jess to attend the mistress in her bedroom. 'She's in a mood! Mind yourself.'

Wondering what she had done wrong – had she been seen last night? – Jess went down.

Lady Maud sat at her dressing table having her chestnut hair brushed by her personal maid, Gresham. She was wearing a dressing gown of quilted satin whose pale pink colour made her white skin look grey and lifeless as, through the mirror, she regarded Jess with cold eyes.

All Jess could think of was seeing the squire's wife parading on the parapet, talking to herself. Maybe she'd been sleep-walking, like Bella. Maybe it was a family trait. Maybe the dead boy had had the habit too.

Lady Maud's harsh voice clipped out: 'You left my daughter's door unsecured last night!'

'Milady, I—'

'I know you did! I went up to check, as I frequently do – ah, does that surprise you? I won't have my child harmed by your stupidity. Her door is to be bolted *always* when you leave her. *Always!* Do you understand?'

'Yes, milady.' Jess bit her tongue to stop herself from saying that it had only been for a few minutes. The least said about what had gone on last night, the better.

'Then remember it. While Sir Richard and I are away in London, we expect our daughter to be safe here. That's all. Now go away.'

Later, Sal Gooden told Jess that, before Bella was born, there had been a son and heir to Hewinghall – Harry Fyncham, a lively, bold little boy. One day he'd evaded his nursemaid and, laughing, scrambled out to the roof and up to the parapet where he'd danced in defiance of both his nursemaid and gravity. Gravity won.

'He was killed,' Sal added. 'Well, that's sixty feet or more. They say the nursemaid never got over it. No more hen't Lady Maud. She don't never talk about it, though, and there's orders none of us should mention it, either, so don't let on I told you.'

Jess was pleased to know, at last, what lay behind the tales of ghosts in the attics, and the reasons for bolted doors and nailed-shut windows. Not that she agreed with it. Locking Bella in and turning her into a nervous mouse, afraid of shadows, would not bring her brother back.

–

When Sir Richard and his lady departed to enjoy the London social season, their personal servants, including Longman the butler, accompanied them, but Mrs Roberts remained in charge of the house. Nursery life continued as usual, except that Nanny and Bella were spared their duty visits to the family drawing room and the whole atmosphere was more relaxed.

Gyp recovered from whatever had been ailing him, though he was never again quite so bouncy and inquisitive. He reminded Jess of Lily, whose bright gaiety had also wilted since Christmastime; she'd been so troubled at Easter that Jess still worried about her.

News of Rudd's progress filtered through to her. He was doing well; then he developed an infection and was real poorly, needing to be kept longer in hospital than expected. Jess fretted and wished she could see him, or write to him. Just to be in contact in some way, though she knew nothing could ever come of what she felt for him.

On one of her free afternoons she got a few necessaries together in a basket and set out for Rudd's cottage. Cleaning was, after all, what she knew best, and someone had to do it – when he came home he'd have more to think about than scrubbing floors and cleaning cupboards, or so she would say if anyone discovered her. Her real reasons were something personal, between her and Rudd. Her heart believed that, even if her head reminded her that she couldn't be sure. Maybe he *was* just a tease, using his smile and his easy ways to get round foolish women, but Jess didn't believe it. Her instincts told her Rudd was good and true.

Leaving her basket on the edge of the woods, she called in at the rectory to collect Gyp and take him with her.

'You're welcome to him,' Eliza said. 'He en't nothin' but a pest.'

'It's no wonder he don't thrive, with your bile alluss pourin' over him,' Jess returned.

Eliza merely stuck out her tongue; then as Jess was leaving she came after her to the door to say, 'By the way, somebody been axin' after you.'

By the time Jess looked round she had her face under control. 'Who'd that be?'

'Some chap. Reckoned he'd met you in Hunst'on a few month back. You in the habit of givin' strangers your address? Do Rudd know about it?'

'I hen't given nobody my address,' Jess denied hotly. 'What'd this chap look like?'

Eliza shrugged. 'Can't say I noticed. He wan't nothin' special. Hen't you seen him, then? Well, that must be two, three week ago now. I 'spect he've found other company.'

'Just as well,' said Jess. 'He sound like a chancer to me.'

But as she moved on, with Gyp trotting beside her on his lead, her heartbeat was unsteady. Someone looking for her? Who could that be? Matty, maybe? Or someone much less welcome?

She continued to fret about it until she arrived at Rudd's cottage, when all other thought was banished by the strange, eerie quality of the silence. The breeze had dropped, so that even the trees seemed to be holding their breath. No dogs came barking down the path; the pheasant pens were empty. And the cottage's curtains were all pulled across, as in a house where death had entered.

Rudd was dead? – the thought made her stop, her stomach like cold lead. If he had died in that hospital... She shook herself, taking long draughts of air to calm her stupid heart. Of course he wasn't dead. *That* kind of news would have spread into every corner. Still, she didn't like the way the cottage felt. What was more, as she discovered when she tried the door, it was securely locked. Where Jess came from, nobody locked a door. Do that and someone would soon want to know what you were hiding. Who had locked Rudd's cottage? And why?

As she stood on the doorstep wondering what to do, a voice behind her said, 'He en't at home.' The underkeeper Obi approached the gate, peering at her. 'Oh, that's you, miss. I din't reckonise you.' He dragged off his cap, hair flattened all anyhow across his brow.

'D'you have any news of Mr Rudd?' she asked.

He stared at her with flat, colourless eyes, as if trying to work out what she had said. 'Mr Rudd fell out a tree. He're in th'infirmary.'

He knew even less than she did.

When Jess asked if he had a key to the cottage, he produced one from under a flower-pot by the pump.

'Thought you might be one o' them thievin' warmints come to do more mischief,' he said as he set the key in the lock. 'Let me catch 'em and there'll be a fine to-do. From now on, I s'll come by here reg'lar. If they do do any more o' their nonsense, I'll do 'em!'

He unlocked the door and showed her what he was talking about – furniture upturned, rugs thrown about, flour and sugar scattered from the cupboard, butter smeared on linen. There were flies and ants everywhere. In the front room the armchairs had been slashed, the bookshelf toppled and the books torn. It made her so angry she could have wept.

'If I'd a known… I come to clean up, but this…'

Upstairs, drawers had been emptied, the bed stripped of the clean sheets Mrs Obi had put there, the mattress tossed to the floor.

'Have the constable been here?' Jess asked.

'Sir Richard sent for 'em, fust thing this morning, when I went and told him about it. They reckon some poacher done it – prob'ly Jim Potts, I told 'em.'

'Jim Potts? Oh, surely—'

'Or one of his kind. Keepers en't wery popular hereabouts, as I do have cause to know, bor.'

Jess was hardly listening; she gazed with despair at the ruination of Rudd's home, planning how to clean up the mess and get things shipshape again. 'Would your wife do the washing?' she asked.

'I 'spect she will, do I ax her.'

So Jess collected all the soiled linen and bundled it inside a sheet. As she was tying the knot, she saw a button on the bedside mat. Now, how had that got there? Last time she'd been here she'd shaken all the mats and swept every inch of this floor.

The button was made of silver metal, stamped with a trellis pattern, with a wavy edge that might have been cut by a tiny biscuit-cutter. There must be hundreds like it, but the sight of it gave her a turn because her father had had a Sunday-best waistcoat with buttons just like this. If he and Rudd had similar taste, maybe that was a good omen.

She put the button deep in her pocket, for safety. But she kept thinking about what Obi had said. Was Jim Potts a poacher? Had he done the damage here out of spite?

–

A few days later, Jess sat knitting under a tree in an arbour of the gardens behind Hewinghall. On a small patch of lawn Bella played in the sunlight with a kitten that had appeared from the stable.

Lately the laundrymaids had been all of a twizzle over a new recruit to the gardens, a newcomer to the area, young, presentable, and – what was most important – still single. Jess fancied that the figure she could see hoeing the flower beds beyond a blaze of azaleas must be the man in question. She couldn't see much of him, but he looked big and strong. Not that Jess was interested. The only man she thought of in that way was Reuben Rudd.

She went on knitting, keeping an eye on Bella, dreaming about Rudd. In the back of her mind she was aware of the gardener coming closer, but she took little notice of him. 'Look, Jess!' Bella squealed.

She had taken off her straw hat, dangling its blue ribbons for the kitten to play with. It had leapt up and caught its claws in the satin, hanging there, but as Jess looked up she saw it drop, safely on all fours, and get distracted by a passing butterfly. Kitten and Bella went chasing after the flutter of bright wings.

'Miss Bella!' Jess called. 'Do you now put on your hat, else—'

From behind a rose bush only a few feet away, the gardener straightened himself, looming against the brightness of the sky. She threw a hand to guard her eyes, peering at a face framed by the brim of a big, battered hat.

'Well, Jess,' he said flatly. 'Are you goin' to say "Hello" this time, or do you have more bullies to set on me?'

She jumped to her feet, spilling her knitting. 'Matty! What...
What're you doin' here? If someone see you—'

'They won't pay no regard. I now work here. Didn't 'Liza tell you?'
His usually placid face wore a truculent expression.

Jess flung a hand to her buzzing head. ''Liza? Eliza Potts?'

'That was her and Mary Anne as told me where you were.'

'What? Was that *you* at the rectory axin' after me?' Relief made her
angry. This last few days she'd been worrying herself silly about that.
'Blast, Matty—'

A voice from the distance roared, 'Henefer! Get on with your work,
bor!' and at the same time Jess realised that Bella's laughter was fading
into the distance.

'Meet me tonight,' Matty said urgently as she turned to look for
the child. 'On the path to the beach. Past Park Lodge. I'll wait there.
We've got to talk, Jess.'

For the rest of the day Jess was in a puckaterry. She questioned Sal
Gooden and learned that the new gardener was lodging in the village
– with Jim Potts's aunt. Since Jim Potts also had lodgings in the same
cottage, the head gardener, Mr Sparrow, was trying to find a more
suitable place for his new recruit.

'Anyhow, why're you so interested?' Sal wanted to know.

'Just nosey,' said Jess.

'Oh, yes? Then why didn't you ax him yourself this afternoon – I
was doin' out the Chinese bedroom, and I seen you from the winder,
flirtin' with him.'

'All that way? And through them trees?' Jess retorted. 'You know
no more about it than a crow do about Sunday, Sal Gooden.'

She returned to the nursery in an even worse mood. What was
Matty up to? How had he come to Hewing in the first place? And
how on earth had he managed to get mixed up with the Pottses?

Nanny gave permission for Jess to go out that evening, on condition
that she didn't leave until Bella was safely asleep. But Bella, sensing
her mood, started putting on her parts, refusing to eat and being as
disagreeable as she knew how.

When eventually Jess escaped, however, the midsummer sun was
still hanging above the horizon. With its light blazing into her eyes, she
walked down the west drive, towards the handsome cottage called Park
Lodge, where the old butler lived in retirement. He was pottering in

his flower-filled garden and peered shortsightedly at Jess, bidding her, "Evening, young woman."

'Good evenin', Mr Tomalty,' Jess replied, comforted by the thought that his eyes were so bad he wouldn't be able to identify her. Not that she was doing anything wrong. It was just that she *felt* guilty, even though she was only going to meet her own brother!

Outside the gate lay the coast road, a broad lane kept in good order by Sir Richard's workers, and beyond it a plantation of young pines grew well over head height. Where the pines ended, Matty was waiting, his big straw hat discarded for a more familiar cap. His hands were big and horny from salt and ropes and hauling shellfish, his shoulders broad, his face square, with a wide mouth given to laughter.

He wasn't laughing that night, though. He'd been lounging against a tree, chewing on a long grass. As he leapt up, Jess instinctively took a backward step, making it clear that she didn't want him hugging her. Matty read the gesture rightly – it puzzled and hurt him.

Taking refuge in irritability, she said, 'So how did you find me? If you've been and told 'em all where I am, I—'

'I didn't tell nobody,' Matty said. 'Only our Fanny, and the boys. Well, I had to tell them, they've all been worried half to death. But I made 'em swear to keep it secret. Not to tell nobody. Nobody at all. Not 'til I give 'em leave.'

'Well, that's one sensible thing you've done,' Jess said crossly. 'Lord, Matty, d'you know what trouble you could've caused me? I hope you hen't told nobody here at Hewinghall as I'm your sister.'

'No, 'course I hen't. What d'you take me for, our Jess – a fool?'

'You act like it, 'times.'

As they walked, he told her how easily he had traced her – through Lily. He hadn't had to ask further than the men outside the Golden Lion before he'd learned who the girl with one blue eye and one brown might be, and where she could be found – many folk in Huns'ton knew of the beautiful but blemished daughter of the Hewing rector.

Matty had gone home that Easter Monday evening and given the family the glad news that Jess was alive. He'd planned to come and find her when he had the time and the chance had come a few weeks ago when the fishing was poor and the Fyshers, for whom he worked, had had to lay him off. Failing to find a place on another boat, Matty had decided to tramp over to Hewing and call at the rectory, with the excuse of looking for work.

Eliza had invited him in to the rectory kitchen for a cup of tea. But when he'd mentioned a girl named Jess, she'd turned cagey, curious about his interest in 'Jess Sharp'. That name had warned him to be careful, so he'd told Eliza a few tarradiddles during which Mary Anne had blurted out that Jess was now at the big house. After that, Eliza had started to butter him up, trying to find out more about him, but he'd been too canny for her. She'd then sent him to see Mrs Kipps, where he'd taken lodgings and met Jim Potts.

'Jim's a good old bor,' said Matty. 'He'll learn me a thing or two.'

'He'll get you into trouble more like!' Jess fretted.

'Jess, I en't a complete fool, you know. Any road, now it's your turn. Why'd you come here? Why'd you change your name? Why din't you let us know where you were?'

'You know why, Matty. I thought I'd killed Merrywest and they'd be after me.'

'Well, you didn't, and they're not, so all that time you were afeared for nothin'. You could a been at home with us and we could a kept our own cottage – you and me and the young 'uns – 'stead of crampin' in with Fanny and "Sprat".'

Not when Merrywest was our landlord, Jess thought. But she couldn't tell that to Matty.

'I'm doin' all right,' she said. 'Got a good job – better'n slavin' for the Boneses. As for Sam and Joe, why… you and me can both send money home to help Fanny raise them.' As they crested the dunes the beach stretched out before them, sheets of wet sand reflecting the sunset sky in a welter of gold and flame and inky blue. A fisherman was checking his drift nets, and further out small boats had grounded on the banks, their crews out on the rocky scalps after cockles and mussels.

'Don't you wish you were with them?' Jess asked, gesturing at the fishing boats.

Matty shrugged. ''Times, maybe. Though gardenin' pays better. And you can't get drowned diggin'.'

'No,' Jess answered, and knew he was thinking about their father, lost for ever to the deeps of the North Sea. Was he also remembering Mother? She was glad he'd been away fishing when it happened. Only

Jess had been there when her mother's life ebbed on a shameful tide of blood.

All because of Merrywest, God blast his black soul! Lord, how she hated him. The strength of her feeling frightened her and she had to force herself to listen to what Matty was saying.

He planned to stay at Hewinghall, and she was glad of that. Yes, she was. Glad to have her brother back.

Why, then, did a small voice deep inside her cry warning and wish that Matty had never come? Jess couldn't have said. She only knew that his presence set a cold breeze blowing slantwise across her instincts, raising prickles of foreboding.

'Tell me about Miss Lily,' Matty said.

Jess shook herself, forcing her mind back to the golden evening. 'Oh, she's a dear soul. She found me wanderin' half dead and she took me in, bless her sweet heart. If that han't been for Miss Lily, I wouldn't be here now. She're a friend, for all our difference in station.'

'She wan't very friendly to me that day at Huns'ton.'

Jess laughed. 'You startled her, throwin' yourself down at her feet. But don't take no account of the way she was then. She get the miseries, 'times. Then other times she'll be light and happy, full o' fun. I can't never fathom the way she think. I reckon it has to do with her eyes – she feel as if she're different from everybody else. Cast out. Like a sideshow freak.'

'Well, she en't!' Matty said stoutly. 'Whoever made her feel that way should be... should be slung overboard and drug along the scalps 'til he's skinned alive!'

Jess squinted at him sideways. 'Oh, hum?'

He hunched his shoulders and looked at the sand, his neck turning red. 'I know she wun't look cross-eyed at me, but ever since I looked up and seen her there, I keep a-thinkin' about her. All the time, Jess. I hen't never felt that way about no other girl. I reckon I'm in love with her.'

'Don't talk squit!' Jess was alarmed. 'That don't do to raise your eyes above your station. She en't for you, Matty.'

'Why en't she?' he demanded. 'I can't help a-feelin' what I'm feelin', Jess.'

As she drew breath to argue with him she saw the futility of it. Wasn't she herself guilty of the same stupidity? One smile from

Reuben Rudd and she'd been lost. And there was Lily, yearning after Ashton Haverleigh.

'Feelin's can't alluss be trusted,' she said, and linked her arm through his in a gesture of mutual comfort. 'You'd better not think about Miss Lily. She have dreams way out of your reach.'

'Maybe she do. But a governess en't so far I couldn't reach if I wanted.'

'A governess? Who told you—'

''Liza Potts did. She say Miss Lily might be glad of somebody to sling a lifebelt, some day.'

What was he talking about? 'Miss Lily 'on't never agree to bein' a governess. She hate the very idea.'

'That don't signify. That's all arranged. The rector and the squire do have it all planned, so 'Liza say. I thought you'd a known about it, Jess, seein' as how you was sent ahead to prepare the way.'

Stunned, Jess could only gape at him.

'That's been understood for ages, so 'Liza say,' Matty told her. 'Miss Lily's comin' to Hewinghall, to be governess to Miss Bella. Well, didn't you know that, Jess?'

No, Jess hadn't known it, but now she realised what many hints and signs had been pointing to. *Understood for ages?* Then Lily wasn't going to be given a choice. When she found out, whatever would she do?

—

Though Lily, at school, continued to brood over what the future might hold, her spirits were lightened by one of the summer spectacles in Cambridge – the Procession of Boats on the river. This finale to the 'bumping' races rowed by the various colleges was a gala occasion of flags and picnics, with people lining the river banks and all manner of craft crowding the river to see the fun. Miss Waterburn allowed her pupils to attend, wearing blue summer capes and straw boaters with blue ribbons, accompanied by most of the teaching staff as chaperones.

Lily was cheering with the rest when she noticed a familiar figure in one of the crews, a fine athletic form in his clinging rowing costume, golden-fair, youthfully handsome, a smile of triumph on his face. Ash Haverleigh! The huzzahs died in her throat as she experienced a wave of physical longing that frightened her and left her with the familiar ache which, until now, she had experienced only while alone with her dreams in her bed.

Tearing her eyes away, she glanced about her, looking for Clemency, to see if she had seen him, too. But Clemency wasn't there. She didn't appear to be anywhere among the group of blue capes, nor among the crowd nearby.

Lily didn't think much of it; she was too preoccupied in watching Ashton Haverleigh and thinking all manner of delicious, sinful, throat-catching thoughts. She watched him until he and the rest of his crew rowed their boat away down the river, out of sight.

Only then did she think to look again for Clemency, in vain. By the time the young ladies gathered for the return march to the Academy, it had become obvious that Clemency Clare was missing.

'Perhaps she's eloped to Gretna Green,' Anne Ferrers said as the seniors gathered in their drawing room. 'Well, it wouldn't surprise me. She's been risking her reputation for months, sneaking out at night to meet men.' To Lily's horror, she went on to tell the others of Clemency's night forays.

Lily wondered if this was all her fault. Perhaps she should report what she knew. Perhaps she should have done so before: if Clemency's earlier adventures had been known, this latest disaster might have been prevented.

Not knowing what to do for the best, she found herself on the stairs, listening to a mutter of voices from below, where the teaching staff were gathered in the hall.

'They're here!' someone gasped as the main door opened and a glowering Miss Waterburn strode in. Behind her came Clemency and Miss Rattray.

'See her to her room,' Miss Waterburn snapped. Miss Rattray took Clemency's arm, propelling her towards the stairs.

Lily hung there, wanting to offer a word of comfort, but the words died in her mouth as Clemency directed a look at her. Beneath her plain straw boater her eyes were bright with scorn and a little smirk tugged at the corner of her mouth. She almost pushed Lily aside as she passed.

'Lily Clare!' Miss Waterburn was removing her gloves, breathing hard through her nose as was her habit when angry. 'What are you doing there? Return to your room at once. There will be no discussion. No discussion, no speculation, no indiscretion. It never happened. Go!'

Her veto on discussion was in vain: for days, in private, the senior girls talked of little else but the mystery of Clemency Clare.

Clemency herself was locked in the turret, overnight and into the next day. Then, shortly before luncheon, Lily saw the door of Clemency's room open and looked in to find the maid Perkins strapping up a trunk.

'What are you doing with my cousin's things?' Lily asked.

'Miss Clare's leaving,' came the reply. 'Being sent home in disgrace.'

'But... *why*? What has she done?'

Perkins shrugged. 'Search me. Miss Lily. I'm just doing what I'm told. Now, what do you suppose she'd want to travel in?'

Knowing that, if she were in Clemency's place, she would want to look her best, Lily picked out the travelling dress which was Clemency's favourite, a blue worsted poplin trimmed with darker flounces.

'I must see her,' she said. 'Perkins... Let me take the clothes.'

'Not on your life, Miss Lily. I'd be dismissed if—'

'Then let me come with you. I'll make it all right for you, I swear. But I *have* to see Clemency.'

Perkins was a simple soul, easily swayed by a pair of earnest eyes, one blue and one brown, set in a lovely face shining with sincerity.

Seeing the maid. Clemency snapped, 'About time, too! Oh, that bonnet's wrong, you stupid fool. Still, it will have to do. Has my father arri...?' She had noticed Lily, but her surprise turned to disdain as she demanded, 'And what, pray, are you doing here?'

'I was concerned about you,' Lily said. 'I know what it's like being locked up in here. I know how you must feel, Clemency.'

'You haven't the least beginning of a notion about how I feel,' Clemency retorted. 'Save your concern, I don't need it. I'm only too pleased to be getting out of this cheerless prison. *I* know why you're here. You're here to pry, to find out why I'm being dismissed. Well, I'll tell you – I'm being thrown out, Lily dear, because I'm pregnant.'

The word drenched Lily in horror. She stood staring, wide-eyed.

Clemency's laugh rang like a cracked bell. 'And *you* know whose baby it will be, don't you?'

Her mind didn't seem to be working. 'No.'

'Oh, of course you do, Lily. Think about it. A gentleman with whom we are *both* acquainted. But it's me he prefers, you see. Perhaps you'll believe that now. Very soon, I shall have the pleasure of becoming the Honourable Mrs Ashton Haverleigh.'

Fifteen

Desperate to know what was happening at Syderford, Lily wrote to her papa, expressing her concern. She didn't specify what disaster had befallen but alluded to it only as a tragedy that must cause the Clares great sorrow. The Reverend Hugh's reply was cool: 'It was *thoughtless* of her to be found in a punt with a young man, but I do feel that Miss Waterburn's reaction may have been a *little* extreme.

'However,' the letter went on, 'my nephew and his wife have decided that it will be good for Clemency to go away for a while, so they are taking a house on the Yorkshire coast for the summer.' Judging by his letter, even he had not been told the full, shameful truth.

The tale of the student and the punt had been spread at the Academy, too, to explain Clemency's expulsion.

One thing was horribly evident – Ashton Haverleigh had no intention of doing the honourable thing. If a marriage had been arranged, Papa's letter would have said so. Ash was nothing but a vile seducer and here was the proof of it.

Lily promised herself she would despise him for the rest of her life.

—

At Hewinghall, too, below-stairs gossip spread rumour about Clemency Clare. She'd come home from school and been whisked off to Yorkshire, for her health, so it was said. But Jess was more interested in the news that Reuben Rudd was to be released from hospital.

The last Thursday in June dawned bright, with a brisk drying wind. Having prepared lunch for Nanny and Bella, Jess begged an early start to her free afternoon and set off through the woods eager to resume her cleaning at Rudd's cottage.

Soon the fire in the small range was blazing. While it heated the water in the side boiler, Jess made the bed and put away Rudd's freshly

188

washed and ironed clothes. Then she donned a thick hessian apron, rolled up her sleeves, and took down the lace nets and the worn velveteen curtains.

By mid-afternoon she had the nets draped over bushes and was hanging the darker curtains on the line in the back garden. Being a long line, it sagged in the middle with the weight, so she was obliged to use only the higher ends, getting her sleeves and front soaked in the process.

She was stretching to get the last curtain over the line when, with a bark that broke her concentration, Dash came charging down the path. Jess's aching arms dropped. The wet velveteen swung in a bundle on the line and fell into her waiting embrace, further soaking her bodice and skirts as she stood hugging it.

'Rudd knew what he was a-doin' when he named you Dash,' she chafed at the dog, adding to the man who had appeared by the corner of the house, 'Can't you keep him under control, Obi? Now look...' Only it wasn't Obi.

Her heart seemed to want to jump out of her breast as Reuben Rudd came slowly down the path. He was carrying his cap, so that the wind flicked a lock of tousled hair across his brow. Under it his freckles stood out against the pallor of his skin and his face was still, his eyes asking questions.

'Miss Sharp,' he greeted her gravely.

Jess's heart dropped. What had happened to *Jessie, lass*?

'Looks like you're getting wet,' he added, and stepped in to help her.

'There's no need,' she protested, but he ignored her.

She being short, and he having the use of only his left arm, it took both of them to toss the curtain over the line and get it straight. By the time Rudd had fixed the curtain with pegs, Jess's face was burning from the effect of his nearness.

Had she really held his hand and lain next to him under cover of her coat, warming him with her body? She'd never been that close to any man except her dad and Matty – and Merrywest, her haunted mind added. But Rudd was different. She'd never felt like this, her senses filled by the sight, the scent, the feel of this man. But... *Miss Sharp* put her in her place. How had she ever imagined it any other way?

Torn between shouting at him and bursting into tears, she emptied the rest of the water, saying crossly, 'What are you a-doin' of, anyhow? Should you be out?' She was furious with herself for getting into such a stew. She almost wished he hadn't turned up. Almost.

'No law against a man taking a stroll, is there?'

'That depend. What do the doctor have to say about it? Do he know you've left the hospital?'

'They let me out of that place this morning. Not a minute too soon. I was going crackers, cooped up like a broody hen. Sir Richard sent his carriage to fetch me home. He wanted me to go to the big house for a few days, but I've had enough of that. I wanted to be home. Went by Obi's place on my way, to fetch Dash, and got invited to dinner. I gather there's been a bit of trouble – intruders, or summat.'

Jess slid a sidelong glance at him. 'That's so.'

'When I got here, it looked more as though a good fairy had been about. Then I saw you – at the window.' His gesture indicated the upper window, the bedroom window.

So he knew she'd been in there. Oh, Lord! But she'd meant it for the best. She hadn't meant to poke and pry into his private business.

'And then,' Rudd said in a different, softer tone that sent ripples of awareness along every nerve in her being, 'then I thought maybe it was true, after all.'

She waited, but he said no more so she was forced to look directly at him for the first time in minutes and say, 'What was?'

He didn't move, but the intimacy of his look made him seem very close. 'You being there with me in the woods, after I fell. Taking care of me. Keeping me warm.'

For a moment she couldn't speak. It felt as though her heart had swollen to fill her throat and stop her breath; what she read in his eyes was everything she'd ever dreamed of.

Jess Henefer had been through too much to let tears come easy ever again. But they came now, misting huge brown eyes in her plain, pointy-chin face. Feeling her lips tremble, she sank her teeth into the bottom one.

'Jessie, lass...' It was no more than a whisper as he reached out with his free hand and stroked her cheek with the back of a curled forefinger, the lightest of touches, like the sweep of a butterfly's wing, but it set her whole body on fire.

Unable to bear the sweetness of it, she ducked away, making for the door. 'I'll put the kettle on. I'll make us some tea.'

Rudd didn't protest, only followed her and sat himself down at the table, legs stretched out across the worn linoleum as he watched her going about her domestic chores.

Wiping her hands on her skirt, she felt the small shape of the silver button in her pocket. She'd brought it with her half intending to discover which piece of his clothing it had come off, so she could sew it back. Now she brought it out, holding it on her open palm.

'Is this yours?'

The brush of his fingers as he picked up the button set her heart off again. She considered his bent head, admiring the way his hair grew in strong waves, and remembering its thick, soft texture. Then he looked up, shaking his head. 'No. Where did it come from?'

'That was on the floor.' Nervous of being so near him, she snatched the button back and moved away again. 'I thought I'd sew it back on if... well, it don't signify.' Embarrassed, she thrust the button back into her pocket. She felt downright shy of him.

She got the teapot, warmed it with a dash of hot water and reached down the tea caddy from the cupboard which she had scrubbed and tidied.

'You look like you're at home,' Rudd commented.

Sensitive to criticism, Jess flung him a wary look.

'I like it,' he assured her.

Her blood beat an unsteady rhythm in every vein and her hands were all thumbs. She could hardly think what to do next – and all she was doing was making a pot of tea! But her mind was full of him sitting there, watching her with bright eyes, much as Dad had sat and watched Mother move about the tiny kitchen at Salt's Yard. Was that how it would be, she and Rudd together, maybe with their children about them and—

The sugar bowl slipped out of her hand as she put it down. It fell on its side, sending a little landslide of sugar across the table. Jess cried out at her own clumsiness and turned to the sink thinking dizzily about brushes and pans. But—

'Jessie.' Rudd was there behind her, his hand on her arm turning her to face him. He tipped up her chin, making her look at him and see the tenderness and understanding in his eyes. That – and the sudden longing he couldn't control as his glance slid to her lips and rooted there. 'Jessie...' he muttered again, and bent to kiss her.

Fleeting though the contact was, it scorched her. All at once, all she could think of was Merrywest. Merrywest's grinding mouth. Merrywest's hairy body...

'No!' She tore free, thrusting at him with all her strength. 'No!' And she whirled and fled from him.

She was out the gate before he got breath enough to roar after her, 'Jessie! Jessie, come back. I didn't mean... Jessi-i-i-ie.'

When eventually she stopped running she found her face flooded with tears. She was on the path that led down to the beach. Desolate, she walked on until she sank exhausted into a sheltered hollow. And there she stayed, soaked to the skin, hugging her knees and wishing herself dead.

She must have fallen asleep, for she came awake to find herself shivering. The weather had changed. A mist from the sea now surrounded her sandy nest like a damp grey blanket. Voices had disturbed her – male voices, calling and laughing as the men made their way up from the beach. Before Jess could move, a figure rose above the edge of her skyline, a dark figure blurred by the mist. He stopped, seeing her, saying softly, 'Blast...' then to his hidden companion, 'Go you on, Jim. I'll see you at the "Nelson" later.'

Jess peered up at her brother, suddenly aware of the state she was in, her clothes soaked and caked in sand, her face swollen and reddened by weeping. What story could she tell?

Matty slid down into the hollow, carrying a heavy basket which he plonked down beside her as she sat up and rearranged her skirts. The basket was full of live crabs. 'Look at you,' he said, seating himself on the sand. 'Where've you now been to get in that state?'

'Oh, I... I was doin' my washin' and had a fallin'-out with one o' them laundrymaids. Botty little mawther. Shouldn't've let her upset me.'

'That en't like you, our Jess,' Matty said. 'You can usually give as good as you get.'

Jess cast a look at his bucket. 'You been crabbin'?'

'No, we've been pannin' for gold,' her brother returned dryly. 'And that's not so far off the truth, neither.' He touched the cloth bag that hung at his waist. It jinked and clinked as he patted it. 'Jim knows a man as pays good money for whole sea-shells – to sell to ladies that like decoratin' boxes and such.'

Jess wasn't listening. She'd noticed the waistcoat he was wearing, hanging open over the darned linen shirt their mother had made. The waistcoat was grey, made of woollen stuff. Jess had often seen her father wearing it, and when he died it had been handed on to Matty, who'd slowly grown broad enough to do it proper justice – a waistcoat with six silver buttons with wavy edges, stamped with a pattern like a lattice.

Jess slipped her hand into her pocket, feeling the hard round shape of the button she had found on Rudd's bedroom floor – a button that would match the remaining five on the waistcoat Matty was wearing.

All at once she was afraid for him, and bitterly angry. 'You shun't listen to Jim Potts! I've told you afore, Matty, he en't a fit friend for you. D'you know how he earn his money for them fancy clothes and doin'ses? And don't tell me it's from findin' shells on the beach.'

'He's a businessman! A dealer,' Matty argued.

'So he say! Nobody hereabouts do trust him, nor any of them Pottses. One of the keepers told me Jim Potts is a poacher – and worse. They even reckon...' Again her eyes were drawn to the place where the button was missing from his waistcoat. 'Some say as how he's a... a housebreaker.'

'Huh!' said Matty. 'Give a dog a bad name. He've told me how folks about here hen't got a good word for him, or any of his family – just because his uncle got sent to prison once for stealin' a few old pheasant when his little 'uns was starvin'.'

'Do you believe that, then you *are* a fool.'

'Well, he en't a burglar!'

'I didn't say he was. I said "housebreaker". On'y last week...' She glanced again at his waistcoat, at the shank of black cotton sticking out from the grey wool. 'Somebody wrecked Mr Rudd's cottage.' She lifted her eyes to his face. 'You'll've heard of Reuben Rudd, Matty – he're the head gamekeeper at Hewinghall. Jim Potts's mortal foe.'

Matty could never lie convincingly, especially not to her. His face was a study of guilt and defiance. 'What're you now yarnin' about, our Jess? Yes, that so happen I have heard o' Mr Rudd – Dan Sparrow told me he're in hospital in Lynn, after havin' an accident. Fell out of a tree, din't he?'

Jess could hardly speak for the fury that boiled up in her, at Matty's stupidity and Jim Potts's evil ways. 'You've no more sense than a May gosling, our Matty! Jim Potts'll let you swing for him, see if he don't.'

'I don't know what you're prattlin' about,' he said stubbornly, though the red tide in his neck rose all the way to his hairline.

'This!' She showed him the button from her pocket. 'This was on the floor in Rudd's bedroom! Just thank the Lord it was me as found it and not the police. Dad's waistcoat. You went and wrecked Reuben's cottage wearing my dad's waistcoat!'

'Jess—'

As he reached for her she jerked away. 'Don't touch me! I don't want to talk to you. Now I'm goin' to have to lie to Reuben some more – as if there weren't enough I can't tell him.'

'You make it sound as if you and him—'

'And what if we are? He's a fine, good man. You don't know the half of it, Matty. You've let that Jim Potts spin you a yarn and you've believed it, and gone shywannickin' off without thinkin' of consequences. Oh… how could you do it, Matty? And you reckon you're a fit mate for my Miss Lily? You'd do better with a female dickey. You're such a blasted great fool!'

—

Jess hardly slept for worrying about Matty and wishing things had gone different with Rudd. She felt worn out the next morning, hardly in a mood for being 'lent' to the rectory, to help prepare a party for Lily's homecoming. Miss Peartree had asked Nanny if Jess might be spared for a day or two – which only made Jess wonder afresh at the close links between nursery and rectory.

Miss Peartree was excited over Lily's homecoming. After all, today Lily was ending her schooldays. And since she hadn't had a proper party for her birthday, being away at the time, a feast was planned, with custard tartlets and strawberry jelly, all her favourites.

Eliza was mostly upstairs, making final preparations to Lily's room, and Mary Anne too found jobs which kept her out of the kitchen.

'They're both bone idle!' Miss Peartree confided. 'That's why I asked Nanny if she could spare you. Besides… I know Lily will be happy to find you here. Lately her letters have been… Oh, I can't explain. I just feel she's unhappy. I'm worried about her. And when she discovers—'

She was interrupted. The door burst open and Mary Anne rushed in to announce with snuffling venom, 'It's that grinnin' bor, Gooden. He say he have to see Jess and he won't go away until he have.'

'The boy Gooden?' Jess queried.

'Mr Rudd's apprentice,' Miss Peartree supplied. 'I can't imagine what he can want. Can you? Mary Anne, ask him—'

'I have. He 'on't say. He say, "I have to see Miss Sharp and on'y Miss Sharp," he say. Stupid fool of a bor, he be. Alluss got a silly grin on his face.'

'Perhaps you'd better see to him, Jess,' Miss Peartree suggested.

On the doorstep, Rudd's apprentice stood clutching his cap, fidgeting from foot to foot – and grinning, as Mary Anne had said, though Jess guessed an excess of self-consciousness caused that nervous grimace. The boy was out of breath and red in the face, as if he'd been running. He tugged a forelock in greeting and produced a letter from inside his cap.

'That's for you, miss. He said I was to wait for an answer.'

Jess didn't need to ask who 'he' was. 'How did he know I was here?'

'He din't, miss. He sent me up to the big house and they told me.'

Feeling as though everything had stopped – even her heartbeat – she stared at the envelope. On it was written, in an unsteady hand, 'Miss Jessamy Sharp'. She could read her own name easy enough, but she doubted if she'd be able to read the letter and she didn't intend to try with the boy watching. Simpler to say brusquely, 'There en't any answer,' even though the words near choked her.

'Right, miss.' Clapping his cap back on his head, the boy turned to hurry off as if the rectory held terrors for him, while Jess put the letter carefully away in her apron pocket, where it stayed like a live thing, tormenting her.

During the afternoon, she was preparing the jelly moulds at the big table. Miss Peartree had been called away and Eliza and her sister were drinking tea in chairs placed either side of the open sash window, through which a cooling breeze came idling. Eliza was looking at a newspaper while Mary Anne sat with one leg curled under her, twiddling an end of her hair into lank ringlets, and sniffing.

'Mary Anne, hen't you got a hanky?' Jess said eventually, sick of hearing the girl snuffle.

'I've now lorst it,' the girl replied.

'Well, find you another one quick sharp!'

The newspaper rattled as Eliza folded it, saying, 'Sit you still, Mary Anne. You don't take orders from her. She're on'y the nurserymaid from the big house, and no better'n she oughter be.'

'You tryin' to say somethin', Eliza?' Jess asked.

'If the cap fit...' Eliza shrugged, fanning herself with the folded paper as she leaned in the wheelback chair. 'I hear you been visitin' Rudd's cottage, cleanin' up for him. And then there's that new gardener at the hall what come after you all the way from Huns'ton. Heard talk about him, too. Hen't we, Mary Anne?'

The only answer was another sniffle before Mary Anne wiped her nose on her sleeve.

'Go git you a handkerchief!' Jess snapped.

'Poor little mawther can't help it,' Eliza said. 'She was born with the snuffles. Anyhow, there's worse habits than that.'

'Such as?'

'Some folk might say that leadin' on two men at the same time was a nasty habit. *Some* folk might think a woman was axin' for folk to talk.'

'Some might,' said Jess hotly. 'Unless they knowed the folk in question better than you seem to do, Eliza Potts. *Some* folk have their minds higher than their belts.'

Eliza greeted this in silence, her green eyes narrowed with a speculation that turned slowly into sneers as she interpreted Jess's indignation correctly. Then she began to laugh, softly at first, breaking into loud peals of mirth that made Jess's face burn. She was about to reply when the door opened.

Eliza's face changed; her laughter stopped and she got to her feet as Lily whirled in, wearing a light travelling cape designed to keep out the summer dust. She paused near the threshold, her mismatched eyes darting round the three faces before her. 'What's going on? What's the joke?'

'Just kitchen gossip, Miss Lily,' Eliza murmured, dipping a brief curtsey. 'Come on, Mary Anne, we've work to do. 'Scuse us, Miss Lily. Nice to have you home.'

This piece of insincerity was answered by a look from Lily that would have kippered herring. Then Eliza was shepherding her sister out, bound for some quiet corner where they could sit and do nothing unobserved.

Giving Jess a tight smile, Lily came nearer. 'Cousin Oriana told me you were here. Are you well?' She glanced at the door as if to make sure it was closed, then added in a lower voice, 'I wanted to see you as soon as possible. I need to know...' She couldn't wait to ask; all the way home it had been burning in her mind. 'What are they saying about Clemency? I want to know every detail. Cousin Oriana has written to me, of course, but it's not the same – her ideas of what's interesting don't always coincide with mine. Besides, I want to know everything, Jess. Tell me *everything*.'

Jess did her best. Officially, word was that Clemency had been ill and had been taken to convalesce on the Yorkshire coast. However, gossip at Hewinghall whispered that she had come home in disgrace and that she'd been whisked away in hopes of saving her reputation. What she had done was not known, though some fancied it had to do with a young man.

'Oh, gracious goodness, of *course* there was a man!' Lily cried. 'But are they mentioning any names? Have there been rumours of a marriage?'

'Not as I've heard, Miss Lily.' Jess was bewildered. Why did it matter so much?

'Then maybe you haven't been *listening*! Sometimes you're so *dull*, Jess.' Stormy-faced, she swirled away in her loose cape, only to stop, her back to Jess. When she swung round her lovely, faulty eyes were abrim with tears and her soft mouth trembled. 'Oh, Jess... I didn't mean that. I'm just so... Oh, forgive me!' She rushed to throw her arms around Jess, who instinctively embraced her friend, stroking the heaving shoulders, while Lily sobbed against her. 'Oh, Jess, I'm desolated. *Desolated*.'

–

Lily was in no mood for a party, especially one with custard tartlets and strawberry jelly – Cousin Oriana treated her as if she were eight instead of eighteen. She was even more wearied by the prospect when she discovered who the guests were to be – Cousin Oriana's friend the widowed Mrs Anderson, from the Mill House, with her two horse-faced daughters; the curate, Peter Dunnock; and, possibly, Dickon Clare.

'Oh, not Dickon!' Lily cried.

'Why not?' Miss Peartree replied. 'We must have more than one young man or Mr Dunnock will feel overwhelmed. Dickon has promised to bring a friend with him, so—'

'A friend?' Lily's heart quite skipped with dismay. She pressed a hand to its palpitations. 'Who?'

'He didn't say who, my dear. Does it matter? I thought you might go walking in the afternoon, then after tea we could have a musical soirée. You love to sing, and Tilly Anderson plays piano tolerably well.'

Lily wasn't listening. She was thinking that if Ashton Haverleigh were to come to her party with Dickon that would mean he was not responsible for Clemency's disgrace, in which case Lily would be free to adore him with renewed fervour. Perhaps that was why no rumour had so much as breathed his name – because he was innocent. Oh, please God, let it be so!

–

As Jess undressed that night, she heard the rustle of paper and remembered the letter in her apron pocket. Rudd's letter. With unsteady hands she lit a candle and sat down on her bed to open the envelope.

Sadly, the writing inside wasn't half as clear as her name on the front – of course, he'd had to write it with his left hand – and the few words she could pick out didn't convey any clear meaning. She always had special trouble with handwriting. She would have to get Nanny to keep her promise about those reading lessons, if ever there was time. Oh, why couldn't she read! Here was an important message from the man she loved and she couldn't understand more than a few words of it!

–

The day of Lily's party opened with a thunderstorm which settled into a steady downpour. As she left for the rectory, Jess encountered Sal Gooden in the passageway. Sal spread her arms, barring the way, saying with a grin, 'Well, and now who's a sly-boots, then? Quiet little Jess Keep-myself-to-myself, gettin' secret messages from Mr Rudd, heh?'

'How'd you know—'

'Ah, I do have my spies,' Sal laughed. 'Why, din't you know Bob Gooden was my brother? I heard as he'd been here askin' after you, so soon's I got home last night I got hold of his ear and made him tell. Fancy! You slopin' off cleanin' up Mr Rudd's cottage and never sayin' nothin'. What's he now say in that letter, then? Thankee kindly for all the hard work?'

'Somethin' of the kind,' Jess said, glad of the shadows that hid her heated face. She had the letter with her, tucked inside her bodice where its corners scratched her tender flesh, making her feel closer to Rudd. She didn't know what he'd written, but she was sure it was something more personal than a simple thank you. 'Howsomever, that's atween him and me, Sal Gooden. So don't try startin' a flood when your pump en't primed.'

'What, me?' Sal beamed. 'Why, I en't never been known to gossip. Well, not for more'n ten minutes a time!'

—

Lily spent the morning in alternating hope and despair, staying mainly in her room staring out at the grey day. It was almost July, but it seemed more like November.

In the afternoon, the Andersons – Mama, Tilly and Jane – arrived too early as a result of a misunderstanding. Miss Peartree assured them this was of no matter; she welcomed them in and sent to the kitchen for sweet biscuits and elderflower wine, which Jess served.

'Send Mary Anne to tell Miss Lily that her guests are here,' Miss Peartree instructed her.

Since Mary Anne was on her knees cleaning up the crock of pork lard she'd dropped, Jess herself went up to deliver the message.

Lily was seated at her dressing table, her black hair flowing round her shoulders in a curling cloud, soft from washing, but she was leaning on her elbows, staring glumly at her reflection.

'En't you ready yet?' Jess asked.

'I'm not sure I can face anyone.'

'That you can. Let me help. There's friends waitin' for you.'

Lily sat up hopefully. 'What friends? Has Mr Dickon arrived?'

'No, not yet.'

The light in the strange eyes died as quickly as it had come. 'You mean the Andersons. Cousin Oriana fondly hopes their sober influence will rub off on me. Oh… Yes, Jess, stay and help me. Stay and make me calm down. I'm all aflutter.' She pressed her hands to her breast, closing her eyes as she took several deep breaths while Jess began to dress her hair. 'I can't think what…' Her gaze met Jess's through the mirror, blue and brown both equally agonised as she said hoarsely, 'Ash might be coming with Dickon. If he does… If he does, then everything will be all right. Won't it, Jess?'

Sixteen

A calmer Lily was dressed and down in time to greet the arrival of the curate, Peter Dunnock. The company gathered in the drawing room, making awkward conversation. Lily was on edge, anticipating further arrivals.

Dickon arrived at last, just as tea was being served. And he did bring a friend. But the friend was not Ashton Haverleigh. The two young men had been out with the mole catcher, laying traps and poison, and, to judge by the stink of their breath and their disgraceful behaviour, they had been freely imbibing from their hip flasks.

'Papa ordered them to leave,' a distressed Lily told Jess later. 'The Andersons also departed, in great dudgeon. Papa begged Mr Dunnock to stay, but I couldn't have borne his sympathy so I said I felt unwell. Oh, Jess… I was a fool to imagine that Ash would come, wasn't I? But then I am a fool — I always let myself believe what I want to believe.'

After Jess had finished clearing up and gone back to the big house, Lily was climbing the stairs when her father emerged from his study. 'Lily Victoria,' he said. 'I regret if your day has been spoiled. Dickon had no right to come here in that state.'

'Dickon's a buffoon,' Lily said dully. 'I've tried to tell you that before, Papa.'

'You may be right,' he conceded. 'Be that as it may, that is not what I wished to say. I wished to speak about… about your future. It's time we began seriously to consider what you are going to do with yourself now that you have completed your education.'

'Oh.' Her stomach turned to lead. She felt herself sag and her fingers tightened on the shiny banister. 'Yes?'

'The thing is…' His glance shifted away from hers as he hesitated, in a way that puzzled Lily; uncertainty was not usually a trait of his. 'On reflection, I realise how much you enjoy being about in the summer, so I suggest we delay any decision. Enjoy the fine weather while it lasts. Later… later we shall speak again.'

He turned away, going into his study, closing the door. Lily was bewildered. Uncertainty – and consideration of her feelings! Gracious goodness, what was wrong with Papa?

–

A few days later, when the rain had gone and the summer resumed its smiling course, Lily and Gyp walked up to the big house. They were both invited in and shown up to the nursery suite.

'Gyp!' Bella came rushing to hug the little dog, who leapt up and licked her face.

'Cousin Oriana suggested I should come,' Lily said as she peered curiously about her, wrinkling her nose at a vague, unpleasant odour.

'I'm delighted that you did,' Nanny said. 'Now, Miss Bella, why don't you show Miss Clare your drawings – and your writing.'

Lily was interested, curious both about the child and the nursery suite. She went to the window and peered out at the leaded balcony and the stone parapet, with the park spreading far below. 'Gracious goodness – isn't it high? Can we go out there?'

'No!' Alarmed, Bella backed away, her hand seeking Jess's for comfort. 'I'm not allowed out. I – might fall.'

'Not if—' Lily stopped, the warning looks on both Jess's and Nanny's face reminding her of poor Harry's fate. 'Ah, well,' she added with a smile, 'it's nicer in the garden, anyway. Shall we go for a walk? Would you like to go to the beach? If that's in order, Nanny Fyncham?'

'I'm sure Miss Bella would love it,' Nanny said, settling into her chair beside the fire, which Jess lit every day, come heat or freeze. 'Jess will come with you. Get the things together, Jess.'

As they were making down the attic corridor, Lily looked back, wrinkling her nose. 'Whatever is that smell?'

Before Jess could reply, Bella said, 'That's Nanny. Her room smells of pinkle-pot. So Kate used to say.'

'Ah…' said Lily, her pretty face eloquent.

She led the way, via a path new to Jess, through the woods behind the house and past a strange hummock with steps leading down to an iron gate.

'That's the ice-house,' Lily said. 'They fill it with snow and ice in the winter and freeze meat there. They also use the ice for ice cream. Brrrr! It's a cold, cold place. Do you like ice cream, Bella?'

'Oh yes!'

'So do I,' said Lily, licking her lips. 'With honey on it!'

The path ended at a little gate in the perimeter wall, from where Lily crossed the coast lane and skipped lightly down into another stretch of woodland. The sun glimmered among tossing leaves, on to fronds of bracken and bramble, and grass thick with flowers. Lily pointed them out to Bella, telling her about the birds and animals they glimpsed. She would, Jess thought, make a fine governess, if only her hopes and dreams hadn't set her heart on a totally different direction.

'Oh!' Lily stopped so suddenly that Jess walked into her. 'Gracious goodness!'

Following her gaze, Jess too saw the little group of brightly painted caravans. They stood in a clearing, around a fire whose smoke drifted up through the leafy canopy towards the clear summer sky. A couple of horses were tethered under the trees, and on the steps of one caravan an old woman dressed in black was intent on some handiwork.

Lily had an almost hungry look on her face. 'They're back! Did you know, Jess? Why didn't you say?'

'I didn't know,' Jess denied. 'Come, we'd best go on, Miss Lily. Don't want Bella gettin' near no diddicoys. There's no tellin' what could happen.'

'But I want to know...' Frowning distractedly, Lily glanced at the child who had come back to see what was keeping them. 'Now is not the time, I suppose. But I must talk to them before they leave. One of them might know...'

Bella piped up, 'Is it gypsies? They told Kate she was going to get married – she told me so. Do you want to get married, Lily?'

'I'd like to find out whether I'm a gypsy princess or only a fairy changeling,' Lily said.

'I thought you were a mermaid,' the little girl responded.

'That, too,' Lily smiled, and moved on slowly, with many lingering, backward glances.

By the time they reached the beach, the tide was coming in, almost reaching the line of seaweed and flotsam it had left behind early that morning. Throwing off her shoes and stockings, Bella went to dig in the sand and play with Gyp, while Jess spread the blanket and got out her mending. Lily remained on her feet, glancing back the way they had come.

After a while, she said, 'I think I'll go for a walk.'

'Not to see them diddicoys, miss,' Jess warned.

Lily flashed her a look. 'And if I am?'

'Nothin', Miss Lily.' Shaking her head, Jess went on with her sewing, aware that Lily was standing uncertainly.

At last Lily stamped her foot. 'Oh, sometimes you make me so *angry*, Jess!' And she whirled away, to go running down the sandy slope to the beach.

Gyp went yapping after her, and Bella joined the game. The three ran off along the sand, just above the tide line. Concerned, Jess stood up so that she could see better. Bella was calling to Lily, who eventually stopped and allowed the child to catch up with her, taking her hand. She would calm down soon, Jess knew, and probably come back and say she was sorry. Well, that was Lily – changeable as the weather.

As she was about to sit down and carry on with her mending, Jess glanced back landward. A movement among the dunes drew her attention to where an old woman was making her slow way through the sand. She had a big basket over one arm, and as she came she kept pausing to bend and pick some of the ling that grew here and there, white-flowered and purple.

With a sick feeling of alarm, Jess realised that the woman must have come from the encampment in the woods. She had probably seen the little party go by, and followed them. Jess knew instinctively that her presence was no accident.

Making a show of being surprised to find anyone there, the woman tipped up her face and looked at Jess, saying, 'Afternoon, miss.' She was bent of back and had a thick streak of coarse grey in her hair. Some accident had twisted her spine and her left arm, and robbed her of her left eye, leaving a livid scar slashing across her face. To disguise the injury she wore an eye patch embroidered with sequins, a gaudy oddity against a drab black gown, with a blue and black paisley wrap draped round her hair and shoulders.

'You've a kind face,' she told Jess. 'You won't turn me away, I can see that.'

'Then you're wrong. Clear you off!' All Jess's nerves were on the alert, scenting trouble. It wouldn't do for Lily to come back and find a gypsy here.

'You must need some pegs,' the wheedling voice argued. 'Or perhaps a yard of lace – a pattern of my own making, with luck woven into every knot. Lovers' knots. You are in love, girl, aren't you?'

'No, I en't,' Jess denied, though her mind flew at once to Reuben Rudd.

The gypsy seemed to read her thoughts. 'Sew my lace on your drawers, girl. It will bring your lover to see you. Or...' the single dark eye, practised in reading faces, scanned Jess's blushes with interest, 'perhaps it will *make* him your lover.'

As she spoke, she fingered the contents of the wicker basket slung over her arm and balanced on her hip. She had shapely hands, dirty and stained with nicotine though they were, with a ring on each of the long fingers that sifted through a bag of coloured stones, letting them tinkle together suggestively. 'How about a lucky amulet? Dipped in the healing waters of Our Lady's Well at Walsingham. Some have the power of healing. Some will bring you sweet dreams of absent lovers. Take your pick. Only a ha'penny. Or, for your kind face, you can have one for nothing if you run and bring the young lady.' The dark brown eye told nothing in response to Jess's sharp look. 'I hear she's kind to poor gypsies,' the woman added.

'She don't want to see the likes of you,' Jess said. 'And I en't got no money, so—'

That was the moment Gyp chose to come charging up the sand, barking like fury until the gypsy bent and offered him her outstretched hand. Gyp paused, sniffed, and backed away, sneezing.

'Gyp!' Lily's clear call came. She appeared round the side of a dune only a few yards away, holding Bella by the hand. She was remonstrating with Gyp for his naughtiness, but the words died as she saw the gypsy and stopped, staring.

There was nothing Jess could do to stop the encounter. The woman began to move towards Lily, saying, 'I've got lucky charms, young mistress. And lucky white heather brought from the moors of Scotland. Or I could tell your fortune. The blood of Egyptian Kings runs in my veins. I'm gifted with the Sight. I can see right away that you haven't been happy lately.'

Any fool could see that, Jess thought – especially a canny old gypsy whose one good eye was trained to read small signs. Besides, she had probably asked around the village for tit-bits of gossip and thanks to Eliza and Mary Anne there'd be plenty of those to be had.

'You'd best leave now,' she told the gypsy sharply. 'Do you annoy Miss Clare I'll report you to the constable and he'll soon see you off.'

But the gypsy wasn't listening. The gypsy was watching Lily, her eye bright and beckoning. Releasing Bella's hand, Lily gestured her to go and join Jess. Bella did so, sidling round the gypsy with a frown of deep distrust as she made for the shelter of Jess's skirts.

'Miss Lily—' Jess began.

'It's all right, Jess. I want to speak to her.'

'But, miss—'

'It's *all right*, I said.' Lily's eyes flashed with temper. 'You're supposed to be looking after Bella. She's *your* charge, not mine.'

Stung, Jess desisted.

The gypsy was holding out a sprig of white-belled ling. Slowly, she walked towards Lily. Her dirty, bejewelled fingers picked under her shawl and came out holding a long pin with which she reached to fasten the heather to the collar of Lily's blouse. 'That'll guard you, lady,' she muttered, cocking her head to slant a look across her sequinned eye patch. 'That'll keep you safe from harm. Old Bathsheba's luckiest charms have been spoke over. They'll last you all your life, so long as you keep the heather— Ah!'

She had pricked her finger. A smear of bright blood showed among the grime; it had left a mark on Lily's blouse. The gypsy apologised fulsomely, taking out a dirty handkerchief and spitting on it, dabbing with it at the bloodstain on Lily's blouse – much to Jess's disgust.

'Leave it. Leave it!' Lily was impatient. She fingered the prickly heather sprig and the soft flowers on it while she stared into the woman's face. 'I need to talk to you, Bathsheba. I need to know so much. Walk with me.'

Jess would dearly have loved to follow, but she couldn't, not with Bella dragging at her hand and wanting to go for a paddle in the sea. Well, as Lily had so curtly reminded her, it was Bella who must be her first concern.

-

Seeing the gypsy, Lily had felt her heart jump with hope, then plummet with despair. The woman was so old, so dirty. Even so, she might know something about a child who had been left here eighteen years ago. *You haven't been happy lately*, her words repeated in Lily's mind. But how did this gypsy know it, unless she truly had the gift of second sight?

'What is it you want, lady?' the woman asked. 'The future? The past?'

'Oh… both! Everything!' Lily was near bursting, questions tumbling together incoherently in her brain. 'Do you know anything about a stolen child that was left here eighteen years ago? She was left in a basket, on a doorstep. I've asked so many times before, whenever I've met any of your people. But none of them will tell me anything. Oh, please… I must know. I must know where the child came from – who her real parents were. Can you tell me? *Please*… Tell me everything you know.'

'Everything?' In the ruined face the single eye both mocked and pitied. 'That would take long, cost much. More than you could afford, lady.'

Money, Lily thought. Of course! She searched in her pockets for her little pouch purse, and found there a silver florin which she offered impulsively. 'That's all I have with me. But there's more at the rectory. If you call this evening, I'll give you… I'll give you a guinea!'

'Well…' Holding out her dirty hand, the gypsy accepted the florin, spat on it and closed her long fingers round it. Then she cocked her head like a bird, staring at Lily with her one bright eye. 'A stolen child, you say? Eighteen years ago? A long time, lady. Give me your hand. Let's see if it will tell us…'

—

Jess would have given much to know what was being said behind the sand dunes, but from her station where rippling shallows caressed her bare feet she could hear and see nothing of either Lily or the gypsy. Bella was squealing with delight, kicking up little showers of the cool water to annoy Gyp, who barked and dodged away. But Jess's mind was on her friend.

Suddenly afraid, she started back up the beach, going as fast as she could in the soft sand.

The pair were not far away, standing in a dip among the dunes deep in conversation. Seeing Jess coming, Lily turned to her, eyes shining, cheeks pink. 'She knows, Jess. She knows!'

Jess didn't need to ask: she knew what the gypsy had claimed to know – anything that Lily wished to hear. But the woman returned her look with blank defiance.

'I shall have my heart's desire!' Lily sighed happily. 'She says that my real father is close by, that he's been watching over me all this time. Isn't that right, Bathsheba? He's an important man – a wealthy man. But he's weighed down with responsibilities. That's why he hasn't revealed himself yet. But he'll come for me when the time is right. And it will be soon. She foresees him coming soon! Oh, Jess...' She was ecstatic. 'Don't you see...? It's all coming right for me. Just when I'd begun to despair. But when I saw her standing there... Oh, I just knew she'd been sent to help me. Where's Gyp? Where's Bella? I want to hug both of them!'

As she flew away on lightened feet, Jess turned on the gypsy: 'What've you now been sayin' to my young missus?'

'She's happy, isn't she?' Bathsheba returned.

'On'y because you took advantage! I know your sort. Get you out o' here afore I chase you out, you lyin' diddicoy!'

The gypsy drew herself up as straight as she could with her twisted back, her one good eye glittering. 'I am going, *Gorgio*. I've had my say. I told her the truth, the way it came to me.' She took a step forward and lowered her voice. 'And I'll tell *you* the truth, Jess No-name. You can run away from the past, but it always catches up with you. *Your* past is in hot pursuit.' As she spoke she came closer, until her single, baleful eye was glaring into Jess's. 'Can't you feel its hot breath on your neck? It's coming. Your fate. Your Nemesis. Very soon now. Very soon.'

How did she know about Jess's past? Why did she say *Jess No-name*? Before Jess's guilt-addled mind could reason that the gypsy had been garnering gossip and making clever deductions, the woman had gone.

–

The gypsy did not appear at the rectory that evening to collect the promised guinea, so next day Lily went down to the encampment in the woods, only to discover that the caravans had gone. All that remained was trampled grass, the ashes of a fire, and some horse dung.

To Lily's mind, the gypsy's leaving without more money only proved that her intentions had been honourable, though she did wish she had been able to show the woman the engraved gold bangle and the necklace of amber beads.

Feeling light as ashes on the wind, she returned home and sent for the trap to be harnessed while she changed into a prettier dress and cape. She intended to visit dear Aunt Jane Gittens and cheer her up in her solitude. Being alone at the Hall with only the enormous Miss Wilks for company must be such a bore.

As it turned out, Aunt Jane was in need of a sympathetic ear. Her prized Siamese cat, Ching, had been missing now for two days and the old lady was distraught at his loss.

'He can't be lost, Lily,' the old lady said, plucking fretfully at her skirts. 'He's a very resourceful cat. I'm very much afraid something dreadful has happened to him.'

'Oh, I'm sure he'll come back,' Lily comforted, settling on her usual stool beside the old lady's chair. 'Don't worry, dear Aunt Jane. I shall look for him myself. I shall find him for you.'

The servants had been searching, too — a small staff had been left to care for Miss Gittens, the rest being divided between the London town house, where Oliver Clare was staying, and the rented house in Yorkshire to which Mrs Clare and Clemency had departed.

'You will have heard the gossip, no doubt,' Aunt Jane said. 'They gave out that she was ill and had to convalesce, but you know the truth — she was discovered boating on the river — with a young man.'

'Yes.' Lily was glad Aunt Jane couldn't see her face, which would surely have betrayed her.

'Foolish child to be so indiscreet,' Aunt Jane said. 'But then — unlike you, dear Lily — Clemency was never the most biddable of girls. Any more than Dickon is the most biddable of young men. He's supposed to be here overseeing the estate, but we hardly ever see him. He often stays out all night, though...' Sighing, she shook her head. 'What can I do? Letitia's children are both so wilful. And now to lose my darling Ching...'

Miss Wilks looked up from her embroidery. 'They've no right to expect her to worry about Mr Dickon. It's making her ill. If you're writing to them, Miss Clare, I hope you'll say so.'

'Yes,' Lily said at once, laying a hand on Aunt Jane's. 'Yes, I shall tell them. Perhaps they'll send for Dickon to come and join them, or tell him to go to his papa in London.' Somehow she didn't think Dickon would be wanted in Yorkshire. Not until Clemency's problem had been dispensed with. Oh, she couldn't bear to think about it, it made her want to *scream*. She jumped up. 'I'll go and look for Ching, shall I? Oh, yes, I shall. He'll be frantic by now. If he's shut in somewhere, I shall hear him crying.'

Searching the house gave her something to occupy her mind. She didn't want to think about Clemency and Ashton now, not when she'd been feeling so happy. Ash was lost to her, but there would be other young men – more handsome, more noble – once she came into her true heritage. The gypsy had promised, *Your heart's desire...*

There was no sign of the cat, though she looked in every room that lay open to her, in closets and cupboards and behind curtains, working through the house until she came to one of the rear passageways. The door of the gun-room stood ajar. Lily pushed it further and went in, calling, 'Puss, puss, puss, puss,' before she smelled cigar smoke and realised someone was there before her.

Dickon Clare was dressed for riding, his gingerish-fair hair tousled. In his fingers was poised a cheroot whose aromatic smoke twined enquiringly towards Lily as if it were alive.

'Why, Lily Vee,' he greeted. 'What a delightful surprise. Do come in.'

'I was... looking for Aunt Jane's cat.' She glanced around the room, seeing on the table a new shotgun and oily rags, a box of cartridges open beside it. Reminded of the way Dickon had blasted the pheasant at her feet, Lily said uncertainly, 'Well...'

As she backed for the door, Dickon moved quicker, barring her way, still smiling. 'Don't go, Lily dear. Stay and talk to me.' She instinctively stepped away from him, further into the room, and almost fell over a pair of muddy boots lying on the floor. Dickon stood there, letting smoke trickle from his nostrils as he smiled at her. She had never liked him. Now she feared him.

'You had better let me go, Dickon,' she said, her attempted firmness marred by the tremor in her voice.

'Let you go? But, my dear Lily, what can you mean? I only wish to apologise for the nuisance Torrance and I made of ourselves at your party. Truth to tell, we were a little the worse for drink. But I'm sorry for it. Wouldn't have embarrassed you for worlds.'

'Then you should never have come.'

'Indeed. It was a little inconsiderate of us.' His smile deepened as he began to stroll towards her. 'At your birthday party, too. How old have you become, suddenly? Eighteen? My, how time does pass.' He looked her over in a predatory fashion that sent goosepimples along her skin.

Lily stood uncertainly, her pulse quickening until she could feel it throbbing in her throat. Under his sensual blue gaze her whole body seemed to have come alive with awareness. 'If you'll excuse me, I—'

'*I* let the cat out,' Dickon said with an indolent gesture. 'Blasted thing was at the french window, yowling to get out. So I let it go. Pity not to let it use its killer instinct for a while, eh?' Now his grin looked wolfish. 'Cats can fend for themselves. And they have nine lives. While you and I, Lily my dear, have only one. Surely you can spare me five minutes of yours?'

'For what?'

'Why...' He ground his cheroot into an ash tray on the table. 'To get better acquainted, of course.'

When he stepped closer, Lily backed off, awaiting her chance to slip past him. Most of her was terrified. But some deep, errant part of her was curious, a little excited. And that alarmed her even more. How could she even *think* of Dickon in that way? She feared and detested him. Yet he was a man. He might supply the answers to...

She gasped as her back encountered the edge of one of the gun cases. She edged sideways, slipping into a gap between two cases, up against the wall. With nowhere to go.

'What is it you're afraid of?' he asked, faintly teasing, faintly triumphant. 'Come, Lily Vee, let's be friends.'

'Don't call me that!'

'Why not? It's fondly meant. We all refer to you as Lily Vee, didn't you know?' He lifted a hand, touching her face with fingers that smelled of tobacco smoke. She felt as if she were choking.

'I should like to leave,' she managed. 'Please, Dickon—'

'Hush!' The fingers moved across her cheek, his eyes following the movement, touching her lower lip.

So she bit him. She grabbed his hand and sank her teeth into his thumb until she fancied she felt bone crunch. He cried aloud, swore obscenely, and jerked away – far enough for Lily to dart past him and run for the door just as it opened and the butler said: 'Excuse me, Mr Dickon, sir, but—' He goggled at Lily as she pushed him aside and fled.

A stable lad was in the courtyard, watering Lily's pony, Greyman. She didn't even give him time to put down the bowl but leapt up to the seat, gathered the reins and was away, hating Dickon Clare with all her heart. Hating herself, too, because there was a familiar throbbing in her body and she knew that as soon as she got home she'd have to shut herself in her room and try to soothe that ache. But it would not be Dickon she was thinking of. It would be Ash. Faithless, dissolute, deceiving Ash...

She drove at haste over the bridge, her bonnet flying off and bobbing on its ribbons behind her nape. But the fresh air helped to calm her. She was more under control as she made down the drive, allowing the pony to slow to an easy trot while she began to plot vengeance on Dickon. He would be sorry for what he'd done. When her real father came, soon now...

She had utterly forgotten about the lost cat until she saw something dart across the drive into the undergrowth and spreading trees that veiled the ruin that had once been Syderford Manor. Ching! She slowed Greyman to a walk. Was that where the cat was hiding, somewhere in the ruin of the old house?

Leaving the pony tethered to a branch, Lily picked up her skirts and ventured in among the undergrowth, where the remains of a path led to the ivy-grown frontage of the old house, its windows broken or missing, the left wing torn ragged where the stone had been removed for use in the new house. She'd always had the feeling that Syderford Manor might be haunted, but on this bright day the shades were sleeping. Consciously daring, a pulse beating heavily in her throat, Lily approached the main door.

She was vaguely surprised to find the door locked, obliging her to enter through a window whose lower panes were all smashed, with leaves lying dry on the bare board floor of what had once been an elegant room. Leaves, and bird droppings. There was even a dead bird. Newly dead – Ching's work, by the looks of it. Grimacing her distaste, Lily ventured further.

'Here, Ching. Here, Ching! Puss, puss, puss...'

The further door opened into a hallway, where stairs curved upwards into dusty gloom. Was it only five years since she had sat on these stairs and watched Ash and Dickon in the hall below?

Slowly, Lily began to climb, remembering occasions when she had been in this house believing she was accepted as a member of the family. These last few months had proved to her how wrong she had been. Well, it didn't matter. Soon her real father would set everything right for her. The gypsy had promised.

Hearing a sound below, she froze, then snapped her head round to look down into the hall. A shaft of misty sunlight penetrated from somewhere overhead, dancing with dust motes, making the rest of the hallway momentarily hazy before her eyes adjusted and she saw the figure standing there dressed in riding breeches and fitted coat. For a second she fancied it was Dickon come after her, then, disbelievingly, she recognised Ashton Haverleigh.

'Forgive me,' he said with a laugh. 'I didn't mean to startle you. I saw the trap and wondered who could be here.'

Ashton! As she felt the blood drain from her head, her hand stretched out to grasp the banister for support.

Ash took a step nearer to the foot of the stairs, his fair head tipped back as he looked up at her. 'Miss Clare? Are you unwell? You look so pale. Why...' He began to mount the stairs. 'You're trembling. Are you ill? What's wrong, Miss Clare?'

'Don't come any closer!'

He stopped, frowning at her. 'You're not afraid of me, are you?'

In front of Lily's eyes rose a vision of Clemency's face, contorted with hatred as she spat, *I'm pregnant. And you know whose baby it will be.*

'No, I'm not afraid of you,' she denied, though her feelings did include an element of fear. Mostly she felt sick – sick with bitter disappointment at the way he had betrayed all her dreams. 'The truth is, Mr Haverleigh, I hate you! *I hate you!*'

The force of her words made him back off a step, staring at her with narrowed eyes. 'Why?'

'Why?' Lily repeated in a voice that shook. 'Because I know the truth about you, Mr Haverleigh. I know how you treated Clemency. You led her on. You used her, and then you abandoned her – to bear your child, alone and in disgrace.'

He regarded her strangely, his eyes wide and dark. 'Who says so?'

'*She* said so!'

'Then she's mistaken.'

'*Mistaken?*' She almost choked on her disgust. 'Mr Haverleigh, that... that's a disgraceful thing to say. It's unworthy of you. No lady would lie about such a thing.'

'But a gentleman would? Is that what you're implying, Miss Clare?'

'Yes!'

'Thank you!' His lip curled as he drew a deep breath and quietly, furiously, he said, 'I appreciate this demonstration of your true opinion of me. However, since my good name appears to be at stake, let me assure you, Miss Clare, that I do not recall a single occasion when

I have been alone with Miss Clemency Clare for even a moment. Perhaps you should report the matter to the bishop. Evidently a miracle has taken place – a second immaculate conception!'

Seventeen ·

He descended the stairs with swift dignity, two at a time, then strode across the hall, boots loud on bare boards, and pushed open the door to the morning room so violently that it slammed back into the wall. Hearing the bang echo through the house, Lily winced and, driven by distress, fled on up the stairs and through the first open doorway she came to.

It had been a bedroom. Now it was dark, the shutter closed across the tall window with faint gleams of light showing only emptiness – though somehow a rug had been left by the hearth, and near it a worn armchair. On the chair, something moved, and mewed.

'Ching! Oh... Ching...' Lily threw herself down, her head in her arms as she leaned on the chair, and wept.

She never knew how much time passed; it might have been a minute or an hour before she heard the step in the doorway. She stifled her sobs, but kept her face hidden, not caring who had come to find her, whether it was Dickon, or some village urchin – she was too unhappy to care.

A hand touched her shoulder, caressing and comforting her. 'Lily... dear girl, we can't go on with so many misunderstandings between us.'

Ashton's voice, sounding tender and regretful. What had he said? Misunderstandings? Lily forced her aching head to lift, blinking at him through her tears, unable to see him clearly in the twilight of a room lit only by fitful gleams through cracks in the shutters.

'Clemency lied,' he said firmly. 'Believe me... Clemency Clare would lie about anything that suited her whim. Though why she should have told you such a terrible thing I do not know. *Is* she having a child?'

Lily bit her lip, not knowing what to make of this. She felt so confused...

Sighing, Ash sat himself down beside her on the dusty floor. 'Why was she expelled from school?'

214

'It...' She licked her dry lips and swallowed to clear her throat, though her voice was still croaky. 'It was a silly indiscretion. She slipped away from us during an outing, on the day of the Procession of Boats. She was found, later, with—'

'Found in a punt, with a man,' he finished for her. 'Yes, I heard that story, too – from Dickon.' As a stray thought intruded, he paused to study her tear-blotched face. 'Were you there, at the Procession? I was one of the oarsmen, in the third crew.'

'Yes, I saw you.' She flushed as she remembered the sight he had made in his close-fitting rowing costume, his body tall and lithe. So male... It had made her think shocking, intimate thoughts. The same thoughts came again now, beckoned by his nearness.

He turned towards her, kneeling, eager. 'Was it the truth? About the student and the punt? Let us be honest with each other.' His dark glance caressed her face, settling on her lips with almost the intimacy of a kiss. 'What did Clemency tell you?'

Unable to repeat the calumny, she stroked the cat which still sat on the chair in front of her, stirring sensuously under her hands.

'Miss Clare...' Ashton said. 'Lily...'

He reached for her chin, to make her look at him, but before he could touch her she jerked her head away, staring at him wide-eyed, questioning both him and herself. She wanted him to touch her. But she was afraid of it, too.

His fingers curled into a fist and he withdrew the hand, saying, 'Suppose I tell you I hardly know the girl, hardly noticed her, hardly ever spoke to her, let alone... Lily, if she implied there was anything else between herself and me, it was a falsehood. I swear – it was a lie.'

Reading the candour in his dark brown eyes, she believed him. Oh, she believed him. Hearing it from his own lips, how could she doubt? Her heart had always known it. 'Then who did she meet? If it wasn't you, then—'

He leaned closer. 'You know she went out at night?'

'Yes. But how did you?'

'Men talk about such things! And because... I was there, the night they called after you in the street.'

The memory of that humiliation made her scramble to her feet, crying, 'Oh, I know you were there! Clemency saw you. It was you who told them my name.'

'It was not I!' He too scrambled up to deny the charge with a passionate gesture. 'I didn't know you were among those girls. I swear I did not. The truth is… The truth is, I was too drunk to know much at all that night. But it wasn't you they were cat-calling. The girl my friend recognised was Clemency Clare.'

Lily was shaking. 'I – I don't understand.'

'She used *your* name during her nocturnal escapades. That's what I discovered when I questioned my friends when we all had clearer heads: when she and her friend went out at night she called herself "Lily Vee". So you see, it was Clemency they were calling after in the street that night, not you.'

Swaying where she stood, Lily threw a hand to her buzzing head, hardly able to take it in.

'I tried to warn you,' Ashton said. 'I took the risk of writing you a note, to ask you to meet me. But you didn't come. And then when you refused to speak to me at the shoot… I gave up trying. You evidently had no wish to listen to me.'

'Oh, Ashton…' Fresh tears stung her eyes as she lifted a trembling hand, instinctively reaching for him. 'Ashton…'

'Lily.'

After all her torment and heart-searching, it was as easy as that. She opened her heart to him and found him waiting to welcome her. As if it were the most natural thing in the world, he drew her into his arms, bending his fair head, letting his lips meet her soft, willing mouth.

Under the onslaught of that first kiss, her lips parted and she found herself clinging to him, her arms twined around his neck and shoulders as he held her ever tighter, pressing his body to hers. She didn't try to stop him when he lowered her to the rug. She even helped him, excited by the air that lapped round her lower body. Such was the burning need that filled her she could think of nothing else. Feeling the shape of his manhood against her thigh she almost fainted. So this was how it happened. This was what a man was.

'Please…' she heard herself whisper.

It happened all at once. A spear of pain, then the pleasure began to spread, claiming her, overflowing to roll over her in waves of such incredible delight that she wept at the sheer release of it. Thank you, Ash. Thank you, my darling. Oh, my darling…

She expected him to leave her and allow her to savour the ecstasy of it, but Ash was oblivious to her. His body still thrust inside her, deeper and deeper, scraping her backside on the rug as he rode roughly to his own paroxysm, shuddering over her before clamping his hot mouth on hers in a final, punishing kiss.

As he rolled away to lie on his back beside her, breathing heavily, Lily stared at the distant ceiling, seeing it veiled in dusty gloom. Every vein in her body seemed to be throbbing with hot blood. At last she knew the secret of the great mystery of life. No, she wasn't sorry. She was glad it had happened. Ash loved her. She knew that now. *Your heart's desire*, the gypsy had said. Only twenty-four hours ago.

A sob erupted from somewhere deep inside her.

'Don't cry!' Ash was all concern, moving to bend over her and stroke her face, wiping her tears on his fingers. 'Oh, my dear... You were a virgin. I didn't realise. You seemed so eager. You were so ready—'

'I was!' she wept. 'Oh, Ash, I have wanted you for ever!' Blindly she reached for him, burying her face against his throat. 'Oh, Ash, I love you. I love you so! Do you hate me now? Do you think me wicked?'

'Lily...' His voice was unsteady, though whether with laughter or concern she couldn't tell. 'Lily, my sweet girl... No, of course I don't think you wicked. I *love* you. You're a warm and generous girl, not afraid to show your feelings. So many girls are cold, but you... You have made me very happy today.'

'Have I?' She blinked up at him, glowing with a joy that seemed to bathe her from toes to scalp.

Ash smiled down at her, stroking her cheek, playing with the little curls of hair that framed her ears. 'Indeed you have, my love. Did I make you happy too?'

'Oh, yes!'

'Then will you meet me here again tomorrow?'

'Tomorrow?'

'Or any day you say. I'm staying for a few weeks with my uncle at Martham Staithe. He has a cottage there. He paints, so he's often out, and I'm left to my own devices. I was about to call on Dickon to see if he could ease my boredom, but I should far prefer to spend time with you.'

'Oh, Ash... Ash... You do love me, don't you?' Gazing into her eyes, he slid a hand up under her skirts to caress her thigh and let his thumb graze her most intimate parts. Lily caught her breath, and saw him smile. 'I love you with all my heart,' he said. 'Would you let me do this if it were not so?'

'No.' She shook her head convulsively. 'No. No one else has ever...'

'I know,' he murmured, bending to kiss her again. 'And no one else ever shall, my love. You are mine now. All mine.'

—

Through the most awesome moments of Lily's young life, the cat Ching had remained curled in his chair, apparently oblivious to what was happening only a few feet away.

Ash offered to take the cat back to the Hall and Lily watched from a broken window as he made his way back through the overgrown gardens to vanish under the trees. She hoped he had hidden his horse well. If anyone had seen her trap and Ash's horse, waiting together so near to the ruin... But no one had. No one knew. Only she, and Ash.

Only then did she realise how hot and dishevelled she felt. And dusty. Her clothes were covered in it; there was even dust in her hair. Not that it mattered. Nothing could spoil the glorious consummation of her love for Ashton. The memory made her long for him to touch her again. She would never get tired of it. Oh, how long it seemed until tomorrow, endless hours of nothingness before she could see him again. And he loved her – that was the wonder of it. After all her doubts and despairings, Ashton loved her.

—

'It's true, Jess!' In the gardens at Hewinghall, a radiant Lily shared her joy. Most of it, that is. She didn't say that she and Ash were lovers, but she did tell Jess about the misunderstandings over Clemency and the ways Ash had tried to warn her, because he cared about her. 'All this time!' she cried. 'If only I had known! How much heartache I could have avoided.'

Jess wondered if she'd done wrong by not telling Lily about the note that Clemency Clare had torn up in a jealous rage, but it was too late now for regrets.

'You ought to be careful, though, miss.'

'Careful?' Lily laughed. 'Why? Oh, Jess, you don't understand. Ash loves me. He wouldn't harm me. He *loves* me. Oh... I really believe

I am the happiest, most ecstatic, completely *alive* woman in all the world! I simply had to tell you. But you'll be discreet, won't you? No one else must know. If Papa, or Cousin Oriana, discovered that I'm seeing him, they would not understand. They'd only try to stop it. And nothing can stop it, Jess. This is what I've been waiting for. The gypsy said it would happen, didn't she? My heart's desire.'

As she talked, her face alight, her glance had been flicking beyond Jess, to where in dappled shadow, one of the under-gardeners had stopped in his work and was staring at her.

'What *is* that man looking at?' Lily demanded.

Glancing round, Jess saw that the distant onlooker was Matty. 'Well, miss, you know what some on 'em are like. Nosey.' She waved at him, gesturing him to go away, and with evident reluctance Matty turned to trundle on along the wooded path, pushing a laden wheelbarrow.

'What's his name?' Lily asked. 'I often seem to see him about. If I didn't know better I might think he was spying on me. And I'm sure I've seen him somewhere before. How long has he worked here?'

'Started a few week ago. Name's Henefer. Matty Henefer.'

If Lily had shown any real interest Jess might have told her the truth, but in her present state a mere gardener, however importunate, was no more than a momentary distraction. What really occupied Lily was her romance with Ashton Haverleigh; everything had to be ordered so that she could see Ash as often as was possible.

'Aunt Jane Gittens is lonely,' she told Jess, 'so I shall be spending a lot of time with her during the summer. Which means I shall have to leave Gyp behind – he's not welcome at the Manor.' The dog and Ching shared a mutual loathing and Lily was afraid her pet might get badly scratched. So she wondered if Jess would continue to take him for walks. He was not well, was occasionally sick for no reason. Even Miss Peartree had begun to wonder if it wouldn't be better to have the poor animal put out of his misery.

'But I shall *not* have him put to sleep!' Lily said with a mutinous thrust of her lip. 'He has a delicate stomach, that's all. But he loves you, Jess. If you'll take him out for me, I know it will do him good.'

'While you… visit Miss Gittens,' Jess said.

Lily looked at her, parti-coloured eyes bright with mischief. 'But of course!' she declared with a conspiratorial grin. 'Where else would I be?'

On a bright hot Saturday morning, little Miss Bella was sadly out of sorts. A bad head cold had turned into a chesty cough that confined the child to the stuffy nursery suite where Nanny was fussing over her – and making things a good deal worse, in Jess's opinion; Bella would have benefited from some good fresh air.

'Perhaps I ought to send word to Sir Richard,' the old woman fretted. 'If anything should happen to Miss Bella he would never forgive me.'

'She en't that bad,' Jess said. 'Look… would you like me to stay in with her today?'

'No. No – you've made your arrangements, you go off as we planned. The carter will be expecting you. I need those messages run in Hunstanton and, while you're there, you can bring another bottle of Lanham's Elixir – it's the only thing that seems to clear her congestion.'

The messages weren't all that urgent, though, not that Jess could see, and there was already a full bottle of the elixir in the cupboard. 'Well, if you're sure…'

'Sally Gooden can manage well enough. You have a quiet day to yourself for once. You deserve it. And here's a shilling for you to spend.' Nanny couldn't wait to get rid of her, it seemed.

Thinking that a trip to the sea would be good for Gyp, Jess called at the rectory to collect him. She saw, briefly, an elated Lily, who was in such high spirits that Jess guessed she had an assignation with Ash Haverleigh that day. Sighing to herself, convinced it would all end in tears, Jess departed and, with the little dog trotting beside her on his lead, went on her way.

In the fields the corn was high, the root crops green, and gangs of workers bent to hoe and pick the never-ending weeds. One of the girls Jess saw hoeing along with the rest was Dolly Upton. She wore the standard linen bonnet, a broad brim shading her face, a frill guarding her neck, but her arms below rolled-up sleeves were red with sunburn and even as Jess watched the girl paused to look ruefully at her hands and spit on a broken blister before once more bending over her hoe. Jess might have called out to her, but didn't want to rouse the curiosity of the others. One or two of them had already stopped to stare at her, wondering what she was doing out walking so free when they were all slaving away.

One of the women called, 'If yew hen't got nawthin' better to do than stand there a-starin', Lady Muck, come yew hare an' tek a turn wi' my hoe while I tek a piddle.'

Jess moved on, followed by raucous laughter, glad when the tall thorn hedge hid her from sight. 'Lady Muck' indeed, and her in her second-hand grey print and a straw bonnet Mrs Roberts had given her. True she had trimmed the hat with velvet violets and a piece of green ribbon, but she knew she looked the same plain old Jess, nurserymaid to Miss Bella Fyncham. Still, that position was better than some. Jess didn't envy Dolly her toil in the fields.

–

In the fine new seaside town of Hunstanton St Edmunds, Jess's errands were soon done. Her shopping basket remained light, especially after she'd eaten her bread and cheese picnic and washed it down with homebrewed ginger beer. And she still had the whole afternoon ahead of her before she must start the long walk back. That itself would be a pleasure on a day like this. Oh, God bless dear Nanny Fyncham for allowing her this freedom!

She and Gyp headed for the beach, which was stony in places, formed of big, rounded flint pebbles that were hard to walk on and took all Jess's concentration in placing her high-buttoned boots. Lucky she had small feet, she thought as she stepped from one rock to another and wished she had a leaping pole. Further on there were stretches of wet sand, and pools left among flattish red rocks as the tide receded.

Under the shelter of the cliffs, Jess paused to let Gyp free and watch him patter among the rock pools, curious over crabs, startled by seagulls. She herself perched on a low outcrop of orange rock which, though above the tide line, was surrounded by damp sand. Not far away a governess was watching three small children play in the shallows while an older boy, in knickerbocker suit and straw boater, sat frowning at an easel trying to capture the colours of the cliff. Seagulls swooped and called and a squadron of waders hunched motionless on the sands, facing into the breeze as they waited for the tide to expose their favourite feeding ground.

It was all too tempting. Jess unbuttoned her boots and set them neatly beside her basket, then reached up under her skirts to the garters above her knees. Glancing round to make sure she was unobserved, she pulled off her black woollen stockings and tucked them inside her boots. How cool the sand felt under her stifled feet, oozing between her toes as she curled and flexed them.

Hearing Gyp bark, she looked up and saw him chasing a seagull that lifted lazily and flapped away. The dog's charge took him into a shallow pool where he stopped, surprised to find his feet wet, looking so comical that Jess laughed out loud. Feeling suddenly carefree, she unpinned her hat and pushed it into her shopping basket so the wind wouldn't catch it, then jumped up and went to try her toes in the nearest pool. It was only inches deep, but so cool and refreshing, alive with tiny shrimp. Holding her skirts bunched in one hand, she wandered on, lost in the magic of the seashore.

After a while, Gyp came splashing by, playing a game of chase with another, bigger dog. A black dog. A curly-haired retriever. Dash? Or Bracken? Jim Potts, or...

Squinting against the brightness, she saw Reuben Rudd standing by the rock where she had left her basket and boots. The sight of him made her heart hurt. His right arm was free now, no longer in its sling, and he was wearing his usual boots and breeches, leather gaiters replaced by long socks. As concession to the heat he'd removed his jacket and slung it over his shoulder, leaving himself in waistcoat and shirt, with loosened collar and tie.

Jess wanted to run to him; she wanted to wave like an idiot and call his name. Instead, she stood as if rooted, like a sea anemone in the pool, the strong beat of her pulse sending out little ripples in the water. Rudd had a knack of catching her unprepared. She was aware of her bare legs and feet, skirts all crumpled and splashed, hair flying loose from its knot.

Although she knew he had seen her, he made no sign, only bent and tossed his jacket near her basket, then calmly squatted on the low rock and took off his cap, ruffling his hair to let the breeze cool his scalp. He wasn't looking at Jess, he was watching the sea. Just sitting there, leaning on his knees. Waiting. Every line of him said he was prepared to stay there for as long as it took.

Jess delayed a little, pretending not to have seen him, pretending to be searching for more shells and stones, but a meeting with Rudd could not be avoided and, since she couldn't think about anything else with him sitting there only yards away, eventually she made her way towards him.

'Mr Rudd.'

He tossed her the briefest of glances, said, "Afternoon,' and went back to staring at the sea, his gaze following Gyp and Dash as they romped in the receding shallows.

Jess watched his tousled hair and sunbrowned profile, wondering if she should grab her things and go. Make it clear to him, once and for all...

Rudd squinted up at her. 'If I'm not welcome, I'll go. Right away.'

Then go. She opened her mouth to say it, but the words wouldn't come.

Silence stretched, and it was again Rudd who broke it: 'Why don't you sit down, lass?' When she didn't move, he added gruffly, 'I'll not bother you, if that's what you're afraid of. I want to talk, that's all. I should have done that before, I know, instead of... I just thought... well, any road up, I was wrong and I'm sorry. I'll not be making any more foolish moves, that I promise you.'

'That wan't your fault,' Jess managed, suddenly remembering, in vivid detail, how his lips had felt, soft on hers.

'Wasn't it?'

'I was... took by surprise.'

Again he cast a narrow glance at her. 'Aye,' he said softly. 'Me too, lass.'

The meeting of their eyes said more than words. He knew he'd made his move too soon, knew he'd startled her; he wanted leave to go back and start again, assuring her that this time he'd be less hasty. Perhaps he, too, needed time to adjust.

The answers he read in her face made his expression soften. 'Here,' he invited, patting the place beside him. 'Sit you down, lass. You're giving me a crick in the neck.'

Jess lowered herself carefully, her back to him as she began to dry her feet on the underside of her skirts. She wasn't touching Rudd but she could feel the living reality of him only inches away from her spine. Her flesh remembered the way he felt, lying next to her, and her lips still echoed the imprint of his gentle kiss. It had made her run away from him. No, not from him – from her own fears, her own dark memories...

'I tried to tell you in that letter,' he said. 'I wanted to explain. When you told the lad there was no answer I thought to myself, "Blast it, Rudd, you fool, now you've gone and torn it, rushing in like a bull in a china shop and frightening the girl." I was right wretched. Been that way ever since, thinking I'd offended you so much you wouldn't even look at a letter that came from me.'

Again he let the silence lengthen, the tension between them growing with every second, until Jess blurted, 'I did look at it. On'y...'

'I know,' Rudd said.

She twisted round to look at him and found him watching her with a tender regretfulness that made all her good resolutions scatter. Her insides turned weak with love for him.

He said, 'Why didn't you just tell the lad you couldn't read?'

'I dunno.'

'What – too proud?'

She shook her head. 'That just seemed easiest. I was wholly upset.'

'Because I'd taken liberties?'

'You didn't,' she heard herself say, without intending any such thing: it was her heart that had answered for her.

'You sure about that?'

He was much too close for her to think straight, bright hazel eyes caressing her face, his mouth barely a whisper away. Cheeks burning, she presented her back to him again and rubbed vigorously at her sand-caked feet. 'I en't sure of anythin', if you want the truth, Mr Rudd,' her voice echoed her prudent head. 'I'd just as soon not talk about it.'

'If you say so,' he agreed at once. 'So what shall we talk about?'

Jess bent over her legs, rubbing them more for comfort than anything, since they were mostly dry now. But at least it took her a few inches further away from the burning presence behind her. She couldn't think of a subject. All she could think was that if he were to touch her right now she'd probably turn and reach for him and to hang with the consequences. She badly wanted to be held, warm and safe.

'I didn't come chasing all this way after you to sit silent,' he said.

'Chasing all this way?' Jess repeated.

It was Rudd's turn to flush and glance down at his boots as he dug hobnailed heels into the sand. 'I was waiting for you – going to ask to walk along and ride on the cart with you. But I saw you stop and talk to that... that tatty-headed Matty Henefer. So I didn't show myself.'

'Oh,' said Jess flatly. 'I see.'

'I hear you've been seeing quite a bit of him lately.'

'He work at Hewinghall. I've on'y to step into the garden and—'

'You know what I mean, Jess Sharp.'

'I know you've been listenin' to gossip! Who've now been flappin' her mouth? Sal Gooden? Or was it Eliza Potts? Or Mrs Roberts? Well, whichever it was, she're wrong. And so are you, Reuben Rudd. You were wrong about Jim Potts and you're wholly wrong about Matty.'

'Do you deny you knew him before?'

'No.' She tipped her chin proudly, defiantly, knowing exactly who had told him *that* piece of news – Eliza Potts. 'No, I en't denyin' it. I do know him. I've known him a long time.' Was this the moment to tell him Matty was her brother? She wanted Rudd to understand, wanted to be honest with him. But, if she confessed her true relationship to Matty, Rudd would ask questions – why had she used a false name? Why hadn't she ever mentioned her family? What had made her run away?

Maybe she'd best just tell him and get it over with.

But before she could speak, Rudd said, 'They say Henefer is from Lynn. Used to be a fisherman.'

'That's so.'

'Is that where you knew him?'

'Yes.'

'It wasn't him that… that caused you to run away?'

'Him? Lord, no! No, he don't know *nothin'* about that.' She didn't want Rudd questioning Matty, for fear of what Matty might let slip. 'You en't to ax him about it, neither.'

He let the silence lengthen, perhaps expecting her to explain some more, perhaps giving himself time to consider the puzzle she presented. At last, in a gentle voice that made her throat choke with emotion, he said, 'Were things really so bad for you back there?'

Jess rubbed at her arm as if it itched. 'Yes. Bad.'

'So bad you ran away and didn't care if you died?' Wondering where these questions were heading, she slid him a sidelong look. How did he know that?

'That day in the wood,' he said. 'After I fell out of that tree. You said summat then. I can't remember what, exactly, but it made me wonder.'

'Yes, it was bad. Terrible bad.' Her voice was hoarse, making her clear her throat. 'And I en't ready to talk about it, Reuben. Not yet.'

'I understand,' he said gravely. 'But – blast, I'd like to get my hands on 'em. Folk shouldn't be allowed to have servants if they can't treat 'em right.'

Jess nodded, biting her lip as she stared into the distance. Thank goodness he believed the tale of her being ill-treated by previous employers. That was good. He didn't need to know any more, not yet. Maybe not ever. If their relationship ever got really close then, for fairness, she'd have to confess. But for now she was happy to let it rest.

After a while, as she sat watching the sea and the birds, her curiosity began to quiver. What had Rudd said about seeing her talking to Matty that morning? Keeping her face still, her tawny eyes wide and clear, she looked at him, saying, 'So how'd you know I was goin' to meet the carter?'

The blood that darkened under his tan told her a good deal, as did the flicker of his eyes. 'I heard somebody mention it.'

'Who?' she challenged.

'Come to think of it, I believe it was Nanny.'

'Oh, hum? Seem to me Nanny have lately been takin' uncommon interest in things as don't concern her.'

'She's fond of you. She means it kindly. And any road, lass,' he added with a deep, intimate look, leaning so that his shoulder just brushed hers, 'how do you think I got to know you couldn't read?'

'She *told* you? You've been axin' her about me?' She didn't know whether to be flattered or offended.

'Had to, didn't I? Well, I couldn't seem to get *you* to talk to me.' His eyes were gleaming, warm with a humour that she found irresistible. 'Had to employ a go-between, didn't I?'

Bending over to hide her smile, Jess rubbed at legs that were well dry by that time. So he hadn't been put off by her sharpness, or her evasions. He'd seen through all her ruses. She felt just a bit giddy with delight. Maybe she'd better stop fighting him – Reuben Rudd was evidently a very determined man.

Eighteen

For the first time, Jess and Rudd were able to share thoughts touching many things of shared interest. Inevitably, they talked about Lily.

'She's always been different,' Rudd said. 'A changeling, happen.'

Lily had used that word, too. 'What's a changeling?'

'A fairy child, left in place of a human child they've stolen away.'

'No – don't say that!' She didn't like the idea, especially when Lily really had been abandoned on a doorstep.

Drawn by the shadows in her eyes, he laid his hand over hers. 'You care too much, Jessie lass. Miss Lily's not your concern. Not since you left the rectory.'

'Yes, she is,' she said, and gently eased free of his touch.

Rudd noticed, took his hand away, but said only, 'Why?'

'That just is so. She're... oh, breakable! A little hurt thing that won't let you get too close in case you hurt it some more. She often remind me of Dolly Upton.'

Rudd had heard the tales about Dolly and had been as shocked and dismayed as anyone. But, 'It's not fair of folk to blame everything on Eliza,' he said. 'That poor lass can't do owt right. Miss Peartree's always on at her, chafing at her for nowt. You must have seen it yourself.'

'Well...' Jess didn't know what to say, not if he was going to defend Eliza so stoutly.

'Of course you have. You're too loyal to say so, happen. Trouble is, Miss Peartree's tarred Eliza with the same brush folk use to blacken the other Pottses. Lord knows old Effram's a scoundrel, and I'd not trust Jim Potts further than I could throw him with one hand behind my back. But Eliza's not to blame for the trouble her menfolk have got themselves in. Oh, she has a forward way with her, but that's no reason to stamp her as a scapegrace, too.'

'No,' said Jess, toying with the folds of her skirt, feeling scratchy. She'd all but forgotten about the feeling she'd sensed between him and the green-eyed maid from the rectory. 'All the same, Reuben, she en't no saint.'

'I never said she was.'

'You're... fond of her, are you?'

'Fond?' He frowned over that, considering his answer. 'No, it's not fondness. I feel sorry for the lass, that's what.'

'Oh, yes? It en't that she're a handsome woman?'

About to deny it – heatedly – Rudd stopped himself, a twinkle growing in his eyes. 'What if it was? You're not jealous, are you, lass?'

'No, I en't.' It was her turn to get heated. She jumped to her feet, her cheeks burning. 'What a silly-bold suggestion! Go you off for a walk now. I need to put on my stockings. Can't do that with you gawkin' on.'

'I'll give you five minutes,' he said with a grin, and took himself off to collect the dogs.

The tide was well back from the rocks and still ebbing, leaving expanses of gleaming wet sand. Jess pulled her stockings over her gritty feet, trying to retain decorum against the whims of a breeze that swirled under her skirts. Having no button hook, she couldn't fasten her boots properly, but they fit snugly enough and with her skirts so long only she would know the hightops were flapping against her ankles. Once decently attired again, she tidied her hair as best she could and anchored her bonnet with a long hat-pin.

'Fancy a cup of tea?' Rudd asked as he returned.

Later, with the sun hovering over a wedge of golden cloud, they started the long walk home, via cross-country paths and tracks that Rudd knew well. They talked about nothing much at all that Jess could remember later; she only remembered being shanny with happiness. Rudd was in high humour, too, teasing her and watching with bright eyes as she laughed. She wondered if he would like to hold her hand, but she kept both of her own hands folded round the handle of her basket. She didn't want to give him the impression she was leading him on in any way.

Rudd said he was from Lancashire. He'd done his apprentice work on grouse moors, then moved to Cumberland where he'd learned about raising other game and earned a reputation. Four years ago, Sir Richard Fyncham had visited the estate where he was working and had been so impressed that he had offered Rudd the job as his head keeper. Rudd put it more modestly, but Jess read between his words.

He did not, however, say much about his private life, nor mention his wife and boy. He, too, had aspects of himself that were as yet too deep to share.

'And what about you?' he asked eventually. 'Tell me summat about yourself, Jess. I want to know. Not to pry. Just to know a bit more.'

'En't much to tell.'

Troubled, needing a diversion, she turned to see what the dogs were doing. Dash was still at Rudd's heel, but to her dismay Gyp had fallen some distance behind and was limping visibly.

'Reuben!' Without thinking, she laid her hand on his sleeve, stopping him. Rudd took one look and started back to help.

Gyp had a sore cut on his pad. It looked as though he had stepped on some glass. Rudd cleaned it as best he could, bound it with his handkerchief, then tucked the little King Charles inside his jacket.

'He's nowt but skin and bone, poor old chap.'

'I know. He's not hisself at all. He've been like it for ages. Sick and sadly, 'times, and not eatin' like he should. 'Course, Eliza don't like him much.' She hoped he might ask what she meant, so she could tell him of her suspicions, but Rudd dismissed the subject with:

'She prefers a working dog to a lapdog. Anyway, he's not her concern.' He stroked the dog's soft ear, frowning down at it. 'Happen I should take him home with me, see what I can do. He shouldn't be like this.'

'We'll have to ask Miss Lily,' Jess said, 'but I don't think she'll mind. She've been worryin' about him, too.'

The sun had gone but the sky remained light, streaked with pastel clouds. Bats came swooping from trees in whose shadow twilight was gathering.

'*You're* limping now,' Rudd observed dryly.

'That's my boots rubbin'. I couldn't fasten 'em properly.'

'Want me to carry you, too?'

The thought made her brain spin and as she floundered for a reply, he slanted her a grin. 'Maybe not.'

All at once Jess was so happy she wanted to sing – and her with a voice like a crow. She was growing blisters, she knew. Still, it had been worth it: paddling in the sea had been wonderful. The whole day had been wonderful, even this – with her feet aching and her whole body longing for home, walking beside Rudd in the twilight was more than she'd ever dared hope for. As if they were a pair. Walking out together.

Even if it ended right now at least she had something to remember. She could dream on this day for months to come. Years, even.

With the last of the sun's light gilding a cloud behind the Hewing-hall woods, they reached the rectory gate. Jess took the sleepy Gyp into her own arms, petting his silky head. 'I'll speak to Miss Lily about you takin' him for a little while.'

'When shall I find out? Tomorrow?'

'Tomorrow's Sunday.'

'I know that. I wondered… would you be going to chapel? We could go together. If you're willing.'

She ought to say no. She knew she should. 'It's not that I'm not willin', Mr Rudd, but if folk see us together—'

'We needn't arrive together,' he said. 'We could split up before anybody sees us. I know some paths where no one else goes, not on a Sunday. Please, Jess. I'd like a chance to get to know you better, and… though I'm not a gambling man, I'd lay odds you feel the same.'

Looking into his earnest eyes, she couldn't deny it. Perhaps the dream might go on, just a little longer. Just one more day… She arranged to meet him in the morning.

—

Lily agreed that Gyp might benefit from a sojourn under Rudd's care and after a week or two the little dog regained his health and returned to the rectory with some of his spirit restored. At Rudd's suggestion, rather than sleeping in the kitchen those warm summer nights, Gyp was given a place in an outhouse off the yard, where he slept easier.

It became their habit for Jess and the gamekeeper to walk to chapel and back together, though they tried not to be seen keeping company. And there were evenings, and her free afternoons, when Jess went walking and encountered him 'accidentally on purpose' as Rudd called it with one of his grins.

In time, she overcame her shyness enough to start visiting his cottage on occasion. Reuben knew so much, about the birds he kept and the woods and fields that were his kingdom. He often laughed at her constant 'why's and 'how's, though in an affectionate, teasing way. He was never condescending. More than that, he never once overstepped the boundaries they'd silently agreed upon. There were times he wanted to – times when she was tempted to let him – but she always drew back before any further commitment could be made. She was still afraid of plunging in and finding the water too deep. Rudd seemed to understand that and his patience made her love him all the more.

For Jess it was a magical time of peace and happiness. She lived it as it came, accepting each day as a gift, aware that it couldn't last for ever but no longer worrying about that. The storm she had sensed brewing since she came to Hewinghall seemed to have retreated into the distance, and for most of the time she could forget it.

The same, she believed, was true for Lily. For both of them, love was a sweet new adventure.

–

Lily went about singing, merry as a mudlark; not that she spent much time at home those summer days. Mostly she was off 'visiting Miss Gittens', or 'walking' in the woods, collecting flowers and stones and all kinds of natural curiosities. She came home with her clothes streaked with dust or spattered with mud, or torn as if she'd gone through a brier-patch. Miss Peartree tutted over it, and shook her head indulgently. Dear Lily. Such a thoughtless flibberty-gibbet, but such a dear child. And naturally she always had a good explanation ready.

'Gracious goodness!' she would laugh in that breathy way she had, all pink cheeks and bright eyes. 'It was so dusty I slipped on the path,' or, 'I simply had to pick some beautiful flowers and I didn't notice I'd caught my sleeve. It only needs a stitch or two – Eliza can do that. I don't care how much she grumbles,' or, 'Yes, I am a little crumpled. I just lay down for five minutes in the grass and fell fast asleep.'

Hearing about it all, Jess suspected that Lily was lying. Nor did it need a great brain to deduce why – to Jess, Lily's moods were transparent, and when they were alone Lily was unable to keep from chattering about what was most on her mind: whatever they talked about, Ashton Haverleigh's name always managed to be mentioned.

Oh, it was all wrong. It would end badly. Jess felt it in her bones. But what could she do to prevent it?

'Miss Lily seems in fine fettle lately,' Rudd commented one golden evening as they strolled homeward through the wood.

'She is.'

'The dog, too. Though I'm foxed to know what was up with him, exactly. It wouldn't surprise me if he hadn't got hold of some poisoned bait in the woods. I'd rather trap, but we sometimes have to resort to poison. I'll have to ask Obi if he's been careless. Or the lad. Maybe it was the lad, while I was off in that blooming hospital.'

Maybe that was so, Jess thought. Maybe, as she had begun to suspect, it had nothing to do with Eliza and her night visitor, after all.

'Anyhow,' she said, 'Gyp's near his old self again. Happy 'cos Miss Lily's happy.'

He shook his head at her, laying a hand on her shoulder to stop her and make her look at him. 'It's always Miss Lily. You think the world of her, don't you?'

'She've been good to me.'

His fingers rubbed her shoulder, kneading and caressing, sending little darts of delight all through her as his smiling gaze slid to her mouth and hovered there. 'Jessie, lass...' he said under his breath. 'Do you know what a powerful notion I have to take you in my arms and carry you away and take care of you for ever?'

Though her heart was jumping, she said lightly, 'Not afore Miss Bella's party, you 'on't.'

Sparkling eyes teased her. 'But afterwards. Will you consider it?'

'You'll have to join the queue.' Laughing, she shrugged away. 'Don't come no further or someone'll see.'

'I don't care who sees,' said Rudd, but he let her move away from him all the same. 'I'll see thee Sunday?'

'If I can.' She always had to make that proviso; her duties might not let her free. But if it was possible she'd be meeting Rudd and if the day was fine they might give chapel a miss in favour of walking and talking.

One of these days, she knew, she'd have to tell him about herself. But she kept delaying, and delaying. Leave it 'til another time. One day soon. But not quite yet. Once he knew the truth about her, it would alter everything. And not for the better.

A man like Rudd might not want another man's leavings.

–

On the first Sunday in September, Lily made excuses not to attend morning service. Her father was away for a few days and, with the two maids off on their own Sunday diversions and dear Cousin Oriana so easy to befool, it would have been wicked not to take advantage of the opportunity to have yet one more sinful, thrilling meeting with Ash. He was going to the Manor to meet Dickon before heading off for a luncheon engagement, but on the way he had a short time to spare and so they had arranged an assignation, right there in the rectory garden. Lily felt sorry to have to lock Gyp up in the house, but he might have been a nuisance – Ash didn't really like having the dog around when they were together, and if she did take Gyp with her and had to tie him up he fretted and sometimes yowled, which annoyed Ash even more.

However, she didn't worry about Gyp for long. She was too excited by the prospect of making love with Ash in her very own secret place where she often came to sit and think. No one else knew the haven was there.

This secret place lay in a dark corner of the shrubbery, far away from the house, where rhododendron and laurels grew over head height. Daylight filtered greenly through spiky leaves and old gnarled branches and the ground was hard and dry, littered with old leaves. It was hushed and silent here, caught in a spell that separated it from the rest of the world. Lily loved it.

From this day on, now and for ever afterward, it would hold wondrous memories of Ash. She would be able to come here and relive that memory whenever she wished.

She had taken off her stays before leaving the house and while she waited she loosened the rest of her clothes, feeling the need build in her. Just thinking about Ash roused her to readiness.

He was on time, bursting into the tent-like space with burning eyes as he reached for her, sweeping her into his arms to kiss her. He had brought a blanket. He laid it down on the ground and undressed himself hurriedly, though he kept on his undershirt and drawers as always. Lily longed to see him naked, longed to touch and caress him as she did so often in imagination. But there was never time. Ash always seemed in a hurry, called away by unspecified 'business'. She understood that he had other concerns, but…

'Do you love me?' she would ask.

'More and more,' he would reply, reaching for her to bare her breasts and her aching thighs and touch her in the way that set her aflame. 'Lily… Oh, my sweet darling…'

He the smouldering coal and she the gunpowder, their meeting igniting an explosion of emotion and physical delight of which Lily

233

knew she would never tire. But it was over all too quickly. She groaned aloud as her body shuddered under him, then lay waiting for him to complete his own release. Replete with love, yet vaguely unsatisfied, she lay and watched through discontented eyes as he dressed.

'Will there ever be a time when we don't have to hurry?'

'Of course there will, Lily. One day.'

'When?'

'Soon.'

'How soon?'

She fancied his mouth tightened, but a moment later she knew she must have imagined it for Ash came and knelt by her, kissing her eyes and her mouth. Ash would never be impatient with her. 'Darling, you know we have to be discreet. Your papa wouldn't approve – I'm a penniless youth as yet. And if *my* family found out they'd send me away in the hope that I might forget you.'

'Ash!'

He gathered her more closely, gazing at her with ardent eyes. 'I never would, my love. Oh, how could I forget my sweetest Lily? But we'd be separated. Perhaps for years. I shall have no inheritance until my uncle dies – I could be thirty or more before I'm free to marry. Of course, if you prefer not to wait so long—'

'For you, I shall wait for ever!'

'Then be patient, love.' He eased free of her and went on with his dressing. 'Be thankful we have this time together. Enjoy it. It's only a sample of the time we'll have later.'

'When we're married?'

He paused to smile at her. 'We're already married, in body, heart and spirit. No ties of church and law can bind us closer than we are. Let that be enough for now, Lily my sweet.'

'It is enough.' Sighing, she lay back and stared at the branches laced above her. 'My heart's desire – that's what the gypsy said. And it won't be long, Ash. When my real father comes for me, he'll provide me with an allowance. We can live on that until you have your inheritance.'

'Of course, my love.' Coming near to her once more, he kissed her tenderly. 'And until then we have many meetings to look forward to.'

'And the ball – the "Belladay" Ball, at Hewinghall?'

'The what?' he laughed.

'That's what they call it, because it's for Bella's birthday. Until now I've only been invited to the tea party, but this year we have all been asked to attend the ball. You have received an invitation, have you not?'

'One came for my uncle, though he won't go. He doesn't care for such occasions. He did say I should go in his stead, but...'

'Oh, you must! Ash—' Her dismay gave way to smiles as she saw that he was teasing her.

'Of course I shall be there, my love.'

'And you will put your name on my dance card, will you not?'

'A dozen times.'

Lily let out an ecstatic sigh. 'Oh... I can hardly wait! We shall be together, in front of them all, and only we shall know that we are promised. Bound to each other. For ever. Ash, I love you so.' She twined her arms around his neck and leaned on him in utter contentment.

'And I you,' he said, holding her for a moment before he eased her arms loose and stepped away. 'But I must go, my love. Until Tuesday?'

'Tuesday. Yes.'

The glow of his lovemaking was still on her, like a magical shield. It made her invulnerable. She felt safe from all assault, a castle fortressed by thick walls, defended by a hundred bowmen. And if some enemy dared attack, then she was ready for them. Nothing could hurt her now. Nothing.

—

Jess, too, spent time that day with the man she loved, though for her there were the softer pleasures of strolling along unfrequented lanes, sharing conversation and quietness in the late afternoon sunlight.

'Shall we give chapel a miss tonight?' Rudd asked. 'There's a visiting preacher – a good speaker, so they say. But I'm not rightly in the mood for thundering speeches about hellfire, not on an evening like this.'

'Nor me,' Jess agreed. She'd already had taste enough of hell here on earth, without any more reminders of what waited beyond.

The summer was ending, and with it the time of peace they had enjoyed. Tomorrow the squire and Lady Maud were due back from London and in a few days' time the house would be full of guests. Jess would be less able to get away, and for Rudd one of the busiest times of his year lay ahead. The birds were at their most plentiful; poachers would be busy. This month saw the start of partridge shooting, and in

October there'd be the pheasants. Sir Richard liked his guests to have good sport, which meant long hours for his gamekeepers.

'Would you say you're happy, lass?' Rudd asked.

'Right now? Oh, yes.'

'I meant… Are you happy with your life the way it is?'

'Happy as I've any right to be.'

They'd paused where the lane allowed a sight of the sea, always a magnet for Jess. The tide was far out, leaving acres of sand runnelled with receding streams, and in the huge arc of sky layers of cloud moved at different speeds, high banners stretched by wind, puffs of cotton wool floating over veils of light floss scudding so low you could almost touch them. Harvest was well under way, the fields dotted with stooks of corn sheaves.

'What does that mean?' Rudd asked, moving closer.

Jess watched the sea, part of her wanting to run, part of her longing to lean on him. The need for physical contact had been growing stronger between them lately. Once, he'd taken her hand as they walked, but she'd found excuse to break free, on the pretext of wanting to pick some wild flowers. Rudd had noticed. He hadn't tried again to touch her but she knew he was only waiting his moment.

'Why do you shut me out, lass?' he asked now, his voice soft and sad. 'We've been walking out for weeks, but I know no more about you than when we began. I know you've got your reasons. I know you've been hurt. Can't you trust me, just a little bit?'

Pain made her turn to look at him, feeling the sting of anguish behind her eyes. 'I do, Reuben. 'Course I do. It's just… There's things about me I'm afeared of you knowin'. Once I start to tell you…'

'We've all got secrets.'

'Not like mine.' Unable to bear the sight of his beloved face, and the tender concern in his eyes, she turned again to the sea as if it might comfort her. It didn't; it only reminded her of what was lost.

Now she must lose Reuben, too. If she failed to be honest with him he would know, and that would spoil everything between them. But if she did tell him the truth that too would mean the end for them.

'Jessie…' He moved closer, and though he wasn't touching her she felt the warmth of his love surround her like the light of a rainbow, piercing dark clouds, holding a promise. 'I'm not daft, lass. Nor am I a simple, untried lad that expects his girl to be perfect. I know what goes on.'

She doubted that, somehow. Reuben was a good Christian man. He hadn't ever plumbed the black depths where she had been.

He said, 'I'm not stainless myself, tha knows.'

A laugh breathed out of her. 'Why, what have *you* ever done that—'

'I married a lass because I was sorry for her. And I regretted it. I had to lie to her, every day, not only in words but in actions, too. I had to pretend. And I hated myself for it.'

'You made her happy.'

'It was built on sand.'

Now she looked at him, saying fiercely, 'No, Reuben. That was safely founded on rock, 'cos you're a rock – a fine, steady, sturdy man. Did she ever know you didn't love her?'

'No.' But his eyes were shadowed. 'No, she died believing I cared about her. Even so, I feel badly about it.'

'You were the one as got hurt.' She could feel that hurt, buried deep inside him. She'd had glimpses of it before, but now it was showing clearly. 'Was it because of the little 'un – your boy?'

In his hesitation, she sensed his inner struggle. He was not a man to speak easily of his deepest emotions. As if the words were being dredged out of him, he said gruffly, 'That boy was the joy of my life. Weren't for him... well, if he hadn't been born happen I wouldn't have stopped with Gwennie. He gave me good cause to stay. Then the sickness came, and that was my punishment. The Lord took them both away from me.'

Hurting for him, she laid her small hand on his sleeve. 'I on'y wish I had words to comfort you, Reuben.'

'You comfort me just by *being*!' He grabbed her hand, pressing it between his own as he held it near his heart. 'Jessie, you don't know how much you comfort me. Just to see you – to watch you – to hear you laugh... Having you near me...' He gave a shaky laugh. 'Always asking questions, wanting to know everything. Jessie, lass, I was lonely before you came. I never knew how lonely. Now...'

He was interrupted by the sound of approaching voices. Muttering, 'Blummin' hummer!' Rudd released Jess and stepped away.

People were coming along a path that met with the track Rudd and Jess were on. Through a veil of leaves and branches, Jess recognised the Syderford blacksmith, big Henry Pratt, and his well-fed family – his fat wife Becky, and their five ruddy children, ranging in age from fifteen to seven, all dressed in their Sunday best, bound for chapel. There was another man with them, dressed in black with a broad-brimmed hat.

The blacksmith was one of the exhorters for the chapel and, having a large cottage, he often gave hospitality to itinerant preachers; so, even before Jess saw him clearly, she guessed the stranger must be the visiting preacher for that day. Walking next to the burly blacksmith he made a neat figure in his dark Sunday suit and white shirt with its high collar, with his big black hat, and his thick black beard...

She must have made some small sound in her throat. Perhaps she swayed. Certainly she stepped backwards, feeling Rudd's hands come at her waist to support her as the world grew vague and grey around the face of the visiting preacher.

He wasn't a stranger.

She closed her eyes, trying to rid her brain of the apparition, but when she looked again he was still there. The beard was new, but the face was frighteningly familiar.

The man was her enemy: Nathanael Merrywest.

Nathanael Merrywest, more surely than ever. Merrywest in the living flesh. Oh, dear Lord!

He had recognised her. After a moment of shock that mirrored her own feelings, his close-set black eyes had narrowed with speculation, and then with satisfaction and cunning as his quick mind reviewed the situation, seeking to exploit it to his own advantage.

Panic jolted through her, weakening her knees. 'Reuben,' she turned to him, clutching at him for support, wanting to tell him...

His 'What's wrong?' came thick in her ears as if through feathers. She was incapable of replying. His face came and went behind veils of mist. Blood roared in her ears. She thought she might faint.

She didn't faint – nothing was to be spared her. That first surge of blood merely opened the floodgates. Behind it, nausea boiled in her stomach, bubbling up to scorch the back of her throat. And then the memories came pouring full and fierce – grief, and pain, and puzzlement; a bed soaked in scarlet lifeblood, a beloved body lying in a cheap deal coffin; disgrace and betrayal, and yet more pain, and shame – all building together into a black, black hatred. That hatred battered round her like vast wings beating at her brain, blotting out thought.

The blacksmith was greeting them heartily, introducing 'tonight's preacher, Mr Merrywest, from the Lynn circuit. He've been passing the day with us, thanks to the Lord's grace. This is Mr Rudd, Mr Merrywest – he work for Sir Richard Fyncham at Hewinghall. And this young person—'

'I know who this here young person is.' Merrywest's voice, even when he spoke softly, was deep and resonant, all the more powerful for emanating from a slight, short figure. The sound of it seemed to curl into Jess, take hold of her insides and squeeze until she couldn't breathe. She read her fate in his face: Merrywest had not forgotten. Nor was he the man to forgive. The small black eyes bore into her, burning cold. He had her in his power now. With a word, he could ruin her life yet again. He would do so with exquisite, vengeful pleasure.

'Well, Jessamy. So this is where you've run to, then?'

'You know each other?' Rudd said, looking from one to the other in puzzlement.

'That we do, sir. That we do. Jessamy was part of my flock in North Lynn. Her, and all the other Henefers.'

'Henefers?' Rudd said, and Jess felt his faith in her falter. Oh, why hadn't she told him Matty was her brother?

Mrs Pratt, being helpful, put in, 'She've been callin' herself "Miss Sharp" ever since she come to Hewing.'

Sorrowfully, Merrywest shook his head at Jess. 'Ah, Jess. Has it now come to this? You even deny your own name? Fled from your family and friends – left them weeping for your fate. For shame, girl. For very shame!'

Nineteen

Jess felt as though she were caught in quicksand, being dragged under slowly but inevitably. Unable to save herself. Unable to speak in her own defence. He'd twist whatever she said. He always did. That was how he controlled people – with words. That was how he was now influencing the Pratts and, far worse, Reuben Rudd. As if through his eyes, she saw herself standing shaking, pale to the lips – pale with guilt was how it must look. Her own silence was damning her.

The preacher's soft, thunderous voice went on, slicing deep. 'It's not too late to repent, Jess. Repent the lies told, and the pain inflicted.' He turned to his fascinated audience, emphasising his words with gestures. 'The sorry fact is, friends, that after her poor mother died Jess Henefer lost all sense of decency. Maybe an evil spirit got into her. In all charity, I'd like to believe that. Fact is, when I tried to bring her back to the straight and narrow, she turned her wiles on me. Laid temptation in my way. Like Eve. Like the serpent in the Garden.'

'No,' Rudd said softly.

'Oh yes, Mr Rudd.' The preacher's face was all sincerity and sorrow. 'I'm obliged to say it plain – she tried to tempt me into fornication.'

'Oh, my Lord!' Mrs Pratt flung a hand to her mouth and at the same time tried to cover the ears of her youngest.

'And when I refused,' Merrywest went on, 'she threatened to tell a whole swill of lies about me. En't that, Jess?'

She couldn't speak. She felt as if she were strangling. She *refused* to deny his damnable lies and give him more ammunition against her. She only stared at him with hate in her heart. Where was his conscience?

Rudd had let her go, looking at her as if she were a stranger. She could see he was remembering the sins she had half confessed to him. *It wasn't this*, she wanted to cry. *Not this!* But it was too late. The preacher's poison had already started its work.

'I couldn't hardly believe it myself,' Merrywest said with a sorrowful shake of his head. 'She look so young and innocent, don't she? Like butter wouldn't melt in her mouth. But they're the worst, Mr Rudd. Girls who look like angels but have deceiving devils in their soul. Nor en't that the worst of it. When I warned her she was riskin' her immortal soul with her sinfulness, the devil in her then tried to kill me.'

Mrs Pratt shrieked and put her fist to her mouth.

'But yes!' Merrywest turned his fire-dark gaze on the woman. 'She struck out at me. Tried to have me crushed and drowned, time the fire burned down the great warehouse on the docks. Last December.'

December... Jess saw the significance of that hit Rudd as he recalled finding her in the wood, in December. Oh yes, she was drowning. The quicksand was up to her neck and gaining.

'You surely heard about that fire, Mr Rudd,' Merrywest said.

Rudd's horrified eyes said, yes, he had heard about it. So had the Pratts. They were nodding, murmuring. All of them were looking at Jess as if she were unclean.

'She came at me in the crowd. Pushed me in the dock.' Merrywest shook his head, his black eyes piercing, remorseless. 'Thought she'd killed me. Didn't you, Jess? Then she ran for her life. But you see...' His voice rose as he lifted a hand, accusing and condemning her, 'That's written in the Word of the Lord: Be sure your sins shall find ye out. For the Lord knoweth the secrets of all hearts. *I'll* not bring charges, but the Lord surely will. You'll answer to Him at the Day of Judgement. Why wait? Do it now, girl, and free your soul of the burden. Repent!' He lunged at her, catching her arm. His fingers dug into her flesh, his gaze ripping at her soul. Mesmerising her, as he had before, with that voice, with threats of hellfire and damnation unless she obeyed him. 'Come with us to the chapel. Confess your sin. Come and tell your crimes aloud. It's the only way.'

'Jess...' Rudd was staring at her, wanting some sign of denial from her, puzzled by her silence. 'Jess...'

But it was too late. She'd always known this would happen some day. Hadn't the gypsy warned her? How could she fight fate with such an enemy against her? Merrywest had the gift of words. He was the preacher, the swayer of crowds. In his mouth the vilest lies sounded like truth.

'No, never!' With a mighty effort she wrenched free. 'I *don't* repent. I en't sorry I did it. I *still* wish you dead, Nathanael Merrywest. And when I get to hell I'll wait for you – if you en't there before me!'

241

As she turned and fled, Merrywest's voice boomed after her, 'We shall pray for you, Jess. We shall pray that you see the light.'

This time, Rudd didn't even call after her. This time, it was final.

–

Back in the nursery, Jess set to with grim energy, determined to polish every piece of furniture. What kind of sermons were being preached at the chapel tonight? She'd heard Merrywest at work before, damning some poor sinner from the pulpit while pretending to exhort him to repent for the sake of his immortal soul. But what hurt her most was that Reuben had believed the lies.

'Whatever are you up to, Jess?' Nanny asked, coming in from enjoying a nightcap with Mrs Roberts. 'Is something wrong?'

'Not as you'd notice,' said Jess, her softest cloth circling a round table; she could almost see her face in its glossy surface.

'Had words with Rudd, have you?' Nanny said with a knowing grin. 'Ah well, it'll pass over. I'm going to bed. Don't work too long.'

It was nearly midnight before Jess calmed down enough to go to bed.

She hadn't expected to sleep, but she found herself trapped in a nightmare maze. Memories that she'd hoped one day to share with Reuben Rudd came screaming. She woke from them, and heard Bella call, and went rushing out to find the child teetering on the parapet, the wind tearing at her nightdress and hair. Jess lunged for her, and herself toppled over, and fell – only to wake, shivering thankfully, in a bright morning that drew her out into the familiar yard – Salt's Yard – where sheets billowed in the sunlight and she heard her father calling her. She ran to him, and saw him – flesh dripping off him, clothes in sea-bleached tatters, fronds of seaweed dangling from his mouth, crabs crawling in his eye sockets; then shock jerked her awake again, to find herself lying in a pool of sticky blood and Mother cold and still beside her…

Finally, she did wake up, in her room in the attics at Hewinghall. Sweat drenched her and the night wrapped its coolness about her as she sat up, listening, sure she'd heard something. The wind had risen; it was banging a shutter somewhere. Shuddering, both with cold and with the horror of her memories, she lay wakeful until the blessed dawn came.

Having lit the fire and washed the hearth, she swept and dusted the schoolroom, shaking the rugs out on the leads as usual. There was already a touch of autumn in the trees, a golden tinge to the light, with rain-clouds gathering from the west. It only increased her melancholy.

She took the ashes downstairs and returned with two ewers of hot water, taking one in to Nanny as usual, holding her breath against the stink of the room. ''Mornin', Nanny.' Even in warm weather Nanny wouldn't keep her windows open at night – she said bats might get in – though she did allow them open during the day. With relief Jess drew the curtain and unfastened the latch, throwing the window wide and taking a good breath of the fresh, rain-damp air. The early sun had gone as clouds closed in. The room was grey with shadows.

As was her habit, Jess went to pour hot water into the bowl on the night-stand, saying again, 'Good mornin', Nanny.'

Nanny hadn't stirred.

It was only as Jess went to shake her that she realised how quiet the old woman was, no sound of snoring or open-mouth breathing. The mound under the covers lay unmoving. Gingerly, Jess drew back the sheet. The nightcap was askew, down over one eye. The other eye was closed.

'Nanny?' But Jess knew as she spoke that she wouldn't be heard.

–

'Better keep Miss Bella out of the way this morning,' Mrs Roberts advised Jess. 'Go in the morning room.'

Since a steady, seeping rain had set in, Jess was happy not to venture out of doors, but she felt overawed by the hugeness of the morning room, with all those solemnfaced people staring down from their fancy frames. She hadn't been in there since the day of her interview. She kept Bella amused by helping her with a jigsaw and by drawing. Bella scribbled a big black blob of a figure with stick arms and fingers. 'Look – that's Nanny. Who've you done?'

Jess had been drawing a slender figure in a frilled dress.

'It's Lily Clare!' Bella cried. 'Is she going to a party? Yes! *My* party. Next Saturday. Belladay. I'm to have a real ballgown. Papa said so. When are they coming, Jess? Is it afternoon yet?'

The Fynchams were due home on the afternoon train.

Jess and Bella both lunched in the servants' hall, a treat which delighted the child. She was the focus of attention and had them

243

all amused with her remarks and sayings, ending up standing on her chair reciting for them in pure Norfolk: 'Do you know what's in my pocket....?'

Well, it took their minds off the shock of Nanny's passing, as Mrs Roberts remarked. The village carpenter had brought a coffin and the midnight woman had seen to the laying out. Nanny was resting now, in her deal box, on trestles set amid the greenery and stuffed animals in Little Africa. Since she had no relatives that anyone knew of, the rest must be for Sir Richard to decide.

'I've sent her bedding to be burned,' Mrs Roberts said. 'I know she didn't like having her things disturbed but I didn't realise it had got quite so bad. You should have told me, Jess. That room will need a good scrubbing before the next occupant comes.'

Did she mean Lily? 'D'you know who that'll be, Mrs Roberts?'

'There's been talk of a governess being appointed, but that's up to Lady Fyncham. Whoever it is, I imagine it may be some time before she comes, so in the meantime you'll have to cope.'

'Lord – look at the time!' The coachman, Abbot, leapt out of his chair, draining a last drop of beer from a pewter mug. 'I'll be late. Train gets in at half past.'

His departure broke the party up, reminding everyone that they had duties to attend to now the squire was coming home.

It seemed deathly quiet in the attics as Jess put Bella into a clean dress. Bella wanted to know where Nanny was, so Jess told her the old woman was sick and had had to go away for a while.

'When is she coming back?' Bella asked.

'Well... that depend how soon she get better.' Jess had decided to prepare the child bit by bit for the fact that Nanny was never coming back.

She hurried Bella downstairs to wait in the porch, while the household lined up in order of precedence to greet the squire and his lady. Fortunately, the rain had all but stopped. The carriage bowled up the drive, in through the gate that guarded the front court, and halted in a flurry of damp gravel. The footman leapt down to open the door and pull down the step for her ladyship to alight in a fluster of silver-green flounces with feathers swaying in her hat.

'Mama,' Bella breathed to herself, clutching tightly to Jess's hand, then: 'Oh, Papa! Papa!' and she launched herself at the tall figure who ducked out of the carriage and, laughing, swept her up in his arms.

Lady Maud looked on with a tight smile, saying, 'Well, Bella,' before scanning the welcoming party. 'Where's Nanny Fyncham? Not sick again?'

A silence fell, spreading to include the entire party. Mrs Roberts, speaking for Lady Maud's ears alone, told the sad news.

'Dead?' The lady of the manor had a shrill voice that carried for yards. 'When? Good heavens… Richard, did you hear that? Nanny—'

'I heard,' he said, and bent to set Bella on her feet, telling her to run and stay with Jess.

Bella's copper hair flopped against her back as she came running to grasp Jess's hand and lean against her skirts, looking up at her with wide, worried eyes. Smiling, speaking reassuring words, Jess stroked the child's head, but that didn't prevent her from hearing Lady Maud say:

'She'll just have to come at once, that's all. I won't have our daughter left solely in the care of a common nurserymaid, especially when I shall have a houseful of guests to worry about. You must send to the rectory and have Miss Clare come. At once!'

—

With Gyp lying on the rug beside her, Lily sat at the pianoforte in the drawing room of the rectory, playing and singing love songs. 'The Heart's Secret Song' was her favourite, pitched just right for her mellifluous contralto. The bad times were over. From now on everything was going to be sunlight and sweetness for Lily Victoria Clare.

She was aware that someone had called at the front door and that Eliza had gone to the study to speak to Papa, but since it didn't concern her she ignored it. Tomorrow, she thought, she would see Ashton again. Tomorrow – a Tuesday, when Papa liked to have the house to himself and Cousin Oriana went about her neighbourly calls. For once, Lily and Ash could spend the whole afternoon together.

''Scuse me, miss,' Eliza said from the doorway, interrupting a particularly pretty phrase of the song. 'Your father now want to see you.'

Sighing heavily, Lily turned to look at her. 'You have no appreciation of music, do you, Eliza?'

'Got better things to do with my time,' Eliza said, her face like stone as she turned her back and left the room, without the least attempt to pay respects.

Really, that girl was getting above herself! Lily thought as she swirled her skirts straight and made for the study.

'Papa...' He wasn't at his desk. He was standing in front of the firescreen, holding a letter in his hand. 'Papa, I really must ask you to speak to Eliza. Every time she addresses me—'

'Sit down, Lily Victoria.'

'But you must listen, Papa!'

'I said – sit down!'

Lily drew a deep breath, letting it out slowly through her nostrils as she lowered herself on to the edge of one of the leather chairs beside the fireplace. It was always the same – he would never hear a word against Eliza. Oh, but what did it matter? Nothing mattered now she had Ashton's love. Conjuring up a picture of her lover, Lily relaxed and put on an obedient, attentive face as she looked up. 'What is it, Papa?'

'I'm afraid there's some bad news from Hewinghall. Nanny Fyncham was found dead in bed this morning. Her heart...'

'No! Oh... how very sad. Poor Nanny. She was a sweet old thing, too. Bella will miss her. But... she was quite old, was she not?'

'Her age is irrelevant. But her death does affect us. Lily Victoria... I had intended to speak to you about this very soon, but circumstances now compel me... The fact is, my dear, that the Fynchams have been looking for a suitable governess for their daughter. When I mentioned your name to Sir Richard, he agreed that you would be eminently suitable – much better than a stranger. I hope you're suitably flattered by the immense trust he places in your ability.'

Lily stared up at him, colour draining from her face. This could not be happening! Not now, when she'd been so happy, so sure that everything was coming right.

'We had intended for you to go in a few weeks' time,' he said, 'but Nanny's death has forced Sir Richard to request that you should go at once. Now. Today. I've sent Eliza to pack a few of your things, so you'd better go and give her proper instructions. Just take what you need for a day or two and we'll send the rest later.'

'Papa...' she managed faintly.

'I don't intend to argue about it, Lily Victoria. The arrangement is made. You will go. I myself will, in any case, be leaving soon. I've accepted a post at York Minster.'

What? He was leaving Hewing? Why had no one told her? Hardly able to think, she said, 'What will Cousin Oriana do?'

'She's hoping to secure a place as companion to an old friend. In Weston-super-Mare, I believe.'

'But… she's said nothing to me!'

'Because nothing is settled as yet. Besides, I asked her not to mention any of this. After your outburst earlier this year, I thought it kinder to allow you to enjoy the summer without further unpleasantness. I was considering *your* interests, my dear.'

Oh, what a hypocrite he was! Lily thought. He simply hadn't wanted to tell her until it was most convenient to *him*.

'After all,' he went on, 'you made it very clear that you had no wish to be with me. I was therefore obliged to conclude that you prefer to remain here, among your friends and familiar places. Or would you rather try to find a place elsewhere? We could advertise your services in—'

Appalled, Lily shot to her feet and stood trembling, her hands clenched by her sides, her thoughts like darting fish. Advertise? Never! Oh… this was all a bad joke. It could not be true.

Anyway – the thought steadied her – she couldn't leave Hewinghall. She needed to be here to see Ashton. And if she went away her real father might not find her. Of course she must stay.

'I see,' she managed. 'I see. Then… very well, Papa.'

She saw his surprise as she turned away, but she felt too numb to do other than obey him.

In the shadows of the hallway she stood for a moment, taking a long breath, her eyes so tightly closed that coloured stars and flickers of lightning showed in the blackness behind her lids. Yes, of course it was a joke. A temporary hiatus, that was all. It might even be fun, being with Bella and Jess – just for a while. Just until her real father came to take her with him, to where she belonged. Oh, it wouldn't last. It couldn't last. A governess? Oh, no. Not Lily Victoria Clare.

When she reached her room she found Eliza there, carefully placing clothes in a valise. That, too, was unreal. Ignoring the maid, Lily went to the window and stood staring out. The clouds were breaking, pools of sunlight moving across the shadowed stubble field, briefly gilding the church tower. A covey of partridge pecked among the stubble. Waiting for the guns to strike them dead, Lily thought.

No, it wasn't happening.

'Shall I put in your best, or just the darker things?' Eliza asked. 'Pity you hen't got something grey.'

'I shall never wear grey!' Lily snapped. Grey was the colour of nothingness, of lost hopes and endless servitude.

'That'll be up to Lady Fyncham, I should think,' said Eliza, holding up Lily's new ballgown, a rustle of kingfisher silk. 'Shame you'll not be wearin' this, miss. Such a waste. Well… I hen't never heard of no governess attendin' no ball, have you? 'Cept in the servants' hall, of course. Maybe you can wear this there, and dazzle all them footmen, and boot-boys, and gardeners.'

Lily didn't stop to think. She picked up the nearest weapon – a hand mirror – and flung it. Eliza ducked, throwing up her arms. The mirror cracked on her elbow. She howled, rubbing the place, backing away for the door. 'You'll be sorry for that! You see – you'll be sorry. That's the last time you throw things at me, you boss-eyed witch!'

Later, when Lily picked up her hand mirror, she found it cracked right across. Seven years' bad luck, she thought. The gypsy hadn't mentioned *that*. Her distorted reflection stared back at her, her eyes swollen and sore, her face puffed. The crack ran right across her face, dividing it into two unequal pieces. Blue eye in one part, brown eye in another. Changeling, she thought bitterly.

Then, straightening herself, she put the mirror aside. She would *not* succumb to hopelessness. Her papa had abandoned her, that was clear. But the gypsy had foreseen coming happiness and *that* was the truth. Lily already had Ash, and she had her hopes of her real father. This change meant a little alteration in plans, a brief delay, nothing more. It would not affect the ending. Not at all.

She sat down and penned a letter to Ash.

–

Fargus brought the carriage round as Lily came down the stairs wearing her best costume, of turquoise and white. On her hair she wore a perky little plumed bonnet, and she carried a turquoise parasol. She was Lily Victoria Clare, the rector's adopted daughter, *not* a grey governess.

She saw Cousin Oriana blinking tearfully in the doorway of the drawing room, a handkerchief to her mouth. Her washed blue eyes widened as they took in Lily's attire, and the reasons for it, but she didn't remonstrate. She was feeling much too guilty.

'Lily… my dear, you must know this is not the way we had hoped—'

'I know. Nor I. But *c'est la vie*, Cousin Oriana. I do not intend to be a governess for long. My fortune lies elsewhere. I am perfectly sure of that. So please don't worry about me.' Smiling her brightest smile, she stepped lightly across the polished floor and placed a kiss on Oriana's cheek, tasting the wet salt of her tears. 'Dear Oriana, I shall miss you. I hope you'll be happy in Weston-super-Mare.'

Miss Peartree shook her head, more tears spilling down her soft, lined cheeks. 'I fear my friend is unable to offer… I must look elsewhere. But with only the income from my small inheritance…'

'I see.' Lily's smile had died. All at once she was bitterly angry with her papa. 'He's abandoning you, too.' She glanced along the hall and saw Eliza standing by the baize-backed door with a cold smirk on her face. Raising her voice a little, Lily said, 'He's abandoning us all, it seems. And what shall *you* do when my father goes to York, Eliza? Hope that the new rector needs a lazy… I mean, a *lady's* maid?'

The baize door slammed, with Eliza behind it. But the look on her face remained with Lily. How very odd. Eliza knew many things that she wasn't supposed to know, but she hadn't known that the rector was leaving. The news had dismayed her. Serve her right, Lily thought.

'She'll do well enough,' Oriana Peartree said, and reached to hug Lily. 'Oh, my dear, you deserve better than this. If your poor dear mama were here to see… I do hope you will find happiness.'

'I shall,' Lily said. 'This is not goodbye, Cousin Oriana. I shall call and see you often. Take care of Gyp for me, will you?'

'You're not taking him?'

'Not until I'm sure he's welcome. I shall ask Sir Richard if I may have him with me, and I may well enlist Bella's help to persuade him.' Her mouth quirked at the thought. 'He won't be able to resist her plea, even if he can resist mine. Sir Richard is a dear, *susceptible* man.'

Miss Peartree looked worried. 'Oh, Lily…'

But Lily only laughed and went out to the waiting carriage, hoping that her papa might be watching. She would not glance at his study window, nor send him word of farewell. She would never forgive him.

Arriving at Hewinghall, she instructed Fargus to drive up to the front door – she had no intention of going to the back like a servant when she had more than once accompanied her papa here as a guest.

The butler let her in but, rather than leading her into the great hall as she had expected, he took her through to a small lobby and thence to a lamplit corridor which she had always assumed was servants' territory. A door let on to a flight of shallow stairs which soon took a turn, climbing up to a suite of rooms which were much smaller than the state rooms Lily had previously seen. She realised she was seeing the less sumptuous private apartments. Less sumptuous? Shabby might be more the word: the carpet runner was worn, the furniture bore evidence of much use...

In an angle of a passageway lay a door at which the butler knocked and was bidden, 'Come in, Longman.'

Inside lay a long, low-ceilinged room furnished more for comfort than splendour, with potted palms and stuffed birds under glass, a harmonium in one corner, and two red setters sprawled on the floor. Lily had seen farm parlours that had more pretensions to grandeur. Sir Richard Fyncham rose lazily from a horsehair couch, stretching to his full lanky height, and the dogs too got up and came eagerly to sniff round Lily, who stroked their heads, thinking them beautiful animals.

'Miss Clare,' the squire greeted with a smile, strolling across with his hand outstretched. 'Welcome. I hope you'll forgive us for summoning you in this rude manner, but, as you'll appreciate, Nanny's death...'

'If you had listened to *me*,' his wife said from the far side of the room, where she sat at a desk writing letters, 'Miss Clare would have been well settled in by now.'

For the merest second his smile withered, then he was surveying Lily with renewed kindness. 'We had not anticipated losing Nanny in this way. I had hoped she would enjoy a long retirement in Park Lodge.'

'Is Mr Tomalty leaving?' Lily asked, making conversation.

'He has decided to go and live with his daughter. Will you sit down, Miss Clare? Longman, have someone bring some tea.'

Lily took the chair the squire had indicated and the two dogs followed, wanting to be petted. She obliged them.

'This is Prince, and that's Pacer,' Sir Richard said. 'Gun dogs. Rudd's been training them for me and we're about to find out what they can do when the shooting starts. Oh, but... you're not enamoured of shooting, are you? That unfortunate incident at New Year... I shall not be inviting your cousin Dickon to shoot on Hewinghall land again. Not until his sportsmanship is improved.'

At this, Lady Fyncham got up from her chair and, settling her bustle under rustling skirts, said, 'Miss Clare is here to be informed of her duties. Perhaps you would let *me* see to that. Dogs! Down! As for you, Richard, I thought you had a meeting with Frazer.'

Her tone, addressing her husband, was much the same as that she employed for the dogs. But he answered mildly, excused himself, and took the dogs with him.

'Well, Miss Clare.' Lady Maud's voice was as hard as her expression. She was so pale, her face so gaunt, she looked ill. 'Perhaps now we can have it understood – you are here to teach my daughter, as a governess, not a family friend. I want us to be clear about that from the beginning, however familiar my husband has chosen to be until now. He was brought up in a somewhat relaxed manner, being the youngest of three brothers and never expected to amount to much. But I warn you, you must not try to take advantage of your previous privileged position. The transition may not be easy. Indeed – let me be frank – despite excellent recommendations from your school principal, I am not entirely convinced you are a good choice. I give you three months in which to prove your worth.'

Three months was about right, Lily thought. By the end of that time, everything would have changed, in ways that would astonish the haughty Lady Maud. The squire's wife would regret her condescension when she discovered who Lily really was, and that she was to be married to the Honourable Ashton Haverleigh.

A maid appeared with a tray of tea for three. Lady Maud bade her put it down on a side table and, 'Take Miss Clare up to the nursery suite. But first...' Taking a paper from her desk, Lady Maud held it out. 'Here is a list of your duties and the lessons I wish you to introduce. We shall pay you twenty pounds *per annum*, to begin with. You will bring my daughter to see me every afternoon, unless I decide otherwise, and I shall keep a close check on her progress. Very well, you may go.'

At the door, a thought made Lily turn and look her new employer directly in the eye. 'May I... may I ask one question, please? About the ball on Saturday. My father and I were invited...'

Lady Maud's look was cold, her voice toneless. 'Naturally you will be there.'

'Oh!' Lily almost sagged at the knees, so intense was her relief. 'Thank you!'

'You will be there to look after my daughter,' her ladyship amplified with a wave of her pale, bony hand. 'Not as a guest, Miss Clare, but as a governess. On duty.'

Through a mist that veiled everything but her new mistress's face, Lily stared her disbelief. Not to wear her kingfisher gown? Not to have the chance to dance with Ash, in front of all the neighbourhood?

'And, by the way, Miss Clare, you will address me as "milady"; you will pay me the respect that is due to my rank; and, the next time you wish to enter my house, you will use the side entrance, or the kitchen courtyard door. The front door is for friends and persons of rank.' She allowed herself a slight, patronising smile. 'I fear you have a good deal to learn. The rector's charmingly quaint little daughter has been allowed many liberties which a governess must learn to forgo.'

—

Whatever other privations Lily was to endure, no one expected her to use Nanny Fyncham's room until it was properly scrubbed out. Indeed, Mrs Roberts had asked the squire if the room might be painted and he had agreed to have it done when the weekend's jollifications were over. In the meantime, the men had brought an extra single bed into Jess's room.

Lily didn't mind that; she was glad to be with Jess, and with Bella. She was all false smiles and brittle gaiety.

'I don't expect to be here for very long,' she kept saying. 'But while I *am* here it will be fun.'

When Bella asked questions, Lily told her bluntly that Nanny had been taken by the angels to live with them in heaven; she would not be back. Lily had come to take her place, 'for the time being.'

'Why didn't you bring Gyp?' Bella wanted to know.

'I wasn't sure he'd be welcome, but Mrs Roberts says that your papa has kindly agreed that Gyp may come to join us. We'll go tomorrow and fetch him, shall we?'

For Bella, it seemed, Lily and Gyp were ample substitutes for Nanny. She didn't mention the old woman again. But perhaps she thought about her; she was restless, unable to settle, demanding stories and rhymes. It was late before Jess was able to leave her and return to the schoolroom.

Lily was standing by an open window with one hand on the coarse mane of the rocking horse, making it sway gently. The sun was low, glinting on a distant edge of the sea, stretching shadows from the trees in the park.

'You weren't surprised when I arrived,' she said quietly.

'I… I'd heard them sayin' as how—'

Lily swung round. 'You *knew*, Jess!'

'I heard rumours,' Jess admitted. 'I din't wholly believe them, though, miss. It wun't have done to worry you if—'

'"*Ettu Brute*",' Lily muttered. 'It seems that everyone knew except me. Very well… So be it.' Reaching into her pocket, she brought out an envelope. 'I want you to take this for me. Tonight. You should be able to get to Martham and back before it gets completely dark.'

'Martham, miss?' Jess took the envelope, puzzling over the scrawled writing.

'It's for Mr Haverleigh,' Lily said. 'And don't look like that, Jess! How else am I to tell him what's happened?'

'But, miss—'

'Please, Jess! Just do this for me. Please!' Her voice turned husky, her eyes bloomed with bright anguish. 'I'm trying very hard to hold myself together. I simply *refuse* to give up all hope. You *must* help me, Jess. You know Martham Staithe, don't you? The cottage is on the edge of the creek. To get there, you go…'

Jess was on her way before she had time to think about it.

Twenty

By the time Jess reached Martham, dusk was gathering. Inside the pretty cottage by the creek, with hollyhocks growing up to thatched eaves and the door trailed over with roses, lamps sent out a soft glow of welcome. The door was ajar and she heard voices inside, conversing easily, laughing, but Lily had said not to wait for an answer, so she laid the envelope on the mat inside the door and hurried away.

The light was fading rapidly, the stars blinking on one by one as the sunset glow died behind dark bands of cloud. A great flock of starlings passed overhead, heading for their night's roost.

She daren't use the shortcut by which she'd come – by night the wood was a terrifying maze of pitfalls and clawing branches; she stayed on the road where the worst risk was a twisted ankle. Sometimes trees closed on either side, making everything dark; then the way would open and let her see better. Not far away was the small gate Lily had shown her, and the path through the woods where the gypsies had camped. Soon be home safe. The trees closed in again, reaching to touch tips overhead, forming a lightless tunnel. But at the end of the tunnel she could see the outline of trees in the pine plantation, black spikes lifting against the starry sky. Not far beyond them a light gleamed from one of the windows of Park Lodge. From there it was only a mile to the house.

As she stepped out with renewed confidence there was a sound among the trees ahead, the crack of a stick, a mutter of reprimand, a hiss of irritable excuses. At least two men were hiding there. Jess stopped, fearing they might hear her footsteps. If she went on she'd be seen. It wasn't full dark with that moon climbing, brighter every minute.

Was it poachers lurking in the wood? Rudd had told her how bad the thieving could be at this time of year, when the season was starting and folk in London would pay good money for fresh game birds. Jess recalled the cornfield beyond this copse. It was stubble now, just the spot for a covey of partridge to spend the night, easy prey for a couple of men with a swift net – unless the keepers had got there first and strewn thorn branches to guard the birds and snag the nets.

One of the hidden men muttered something. The other hushed him. Without wanting to, Jess put faces to those voices – Matty, and Jim Potts. It could easily be them. Waiting for the sky to get really dark before they crept off after the birds. Oh, that Jim Potts was a wrong 'un. And Matty was a foolish great lummox, easily led. If they got caught—

Something swooped at her out of the night, a pale shadow against the trees. It almost brushed her hair. She cried out in fright and threw up her arms, wrapping them round her head.

'What the—' the exclamation came from among the trees. With a flurry of undergrowth, the two waiting men erupted into the lane only to stop in confusion.

'What the bloody hell do you think you're a-doin' of, mawther?' one of them demanded.

'I...' Jess managed, swallowing her panic. 'There was an owl. That came at me and—'

'Jess!' The quiet, half-accusing, half-relieved voice belonged to Reuben Rudd. She could see moonlight slant on the barrel of the shotgun he was holding crooked across his arm. 'What are you doing out at this hour?' He glanced behind her, at the shadowed woods, and though she couldn't see him clearly she knew he was frowning. 'Are you alone?'

'Who'd you think I might be with?' she retorted fiercely, relief turning to temper, fuelled with hurt because of the way they had parted. 'I been runnin' a message.'

'At this time of night?'

'I couldn't get away afore. Things en't normal at the big house today.'

'No,' Rudd answered gravely. 'I'd heard. I'm sorry. Nanny Fyncham was a good old lady. I liked her.'

'So did I,' Jess said. 'And I can't stand here—'

She was interrupted by a shot. It came from beyond the wood, in the direction of the cornfield. A faint cry of 'Mr Rudd!' was followed by the bang of the second barrel.

'Blast!' Rudd bit out. 'That's Obi. Blast, man, we've missed them! Come—' In the act of turning away, he stopped dead, staring at Jess. She saw the flash of his eyes, a glint of bared teeth as he muttered bitterly, 'You!... Damn it, Jess... You wait here!' and he was gone, his companion after him. Jess caught a glimpse of Dash bounding alongside as they vanished down the path that led to the cornfield. She heard the pursuit for some distance, heard voices calling, a dog barking.

'*You!*' she thought dazedly. What had he meant? What had she done now to make him swear at her? Oh, she had no business being out here all alone in the dark. No, she wasn't going to wait.

She started away, heading for the light that beckoned from the lodge.

—

Lily was reading by lamplight, curled in Nanny's chair beside the embers of the fire as Jess took off her coat and went to warm herself.

'Did you see him?'

'No. But someone was home. I left the letter on the mat.'

'Good. Is it cold out?'

'No. I just... Just felt in need of comfort, that was all.'

'I know.' Lily glanced around, at the deeply shadowed corners of the big room, where the lamp didn't reach. She pulled the shawl she was wearing closer round her throat. 'It's this place. It feels as if there are eyes watching us.'

'I don't believe in ghosts, Miss Lily.'

'Don't you? I do.' She shivered. 'I can feel them here, all around us, hiding in the shadows. There was a boy who was killed, you know – Sir Richard's son and heir. Harry, he was called. I remember it happening. I was about ten years old at the time. There was a dreadful to-do, and a huge funeral. The procession went on for miles. And now there's Nanny...'

'Nanny wun't hurt no one,' Jess said firmly. 'Dead or alive.'

'Ghosts don't have to *hurt* people, Jess. They *haunt*. They hover around in the ether. I was beginning to be sorry I'd sent you off tonight, but then Mrs Roberts came and asked me to have a cup of chocolate with her. She expected to find you cleaning Nanny's room, but I said I'd sent you to the rectory for something, so remember to say the same if she asks.'

She seemed calm. Too calm, maybe.

'Jess!!' The sound of Bella's voice, calling her in terror, took Jess scurrying out to the landing to unbolt the door. Bella was out of bed, shivering. She'd been having a nightmare about Nanny and had woken herself up by walking into the wall – she had quite a bump on her forehead. Jess stayed with her until she went back to sleep.

It was only after Jess and Lily both went to bed, in the room they were sharing, that Lily gave in to her distress. She wept for a long time. Jess lay silent, sympathising but not knowing what to say. She herself felt too empty for tears.

Everything had gone wrong. For both of them.

–

The following morning, as she made along the attic corridor to fetch hot water, Jess was surprised to hear Mrs Roberts call her name rather sharply. The housekeeper stood in the doorway of her room, fully dressed but with her long plaits still hanging down in front, waiting to go into their usual coil about her head.

'Jessamy,' she repeated, her pleasant face set in unusually severe lines. 'Come here, please.'

With a sinking heart, Jess did as she was bid, being beckoned right inside the room before Mrs Roberts closed the door firmly. Something serious was afoot.

Nanny's death had given the Hewinghall staff plenty to gossip about, but now, it seemed, a new subject was fuelling whispers – rumours that emanated from chapel, from the Pratt family in particular.

'I am astonished by what I'm hearing,' Mrs Roberts said, perplexed. 'I don't understand… What is the truth of it, Jess? Why should this preacher say such things if—'

'He says 'em so's to hide the real truth,' Jess said flatly. God rot Nathanael Merrywest, she would *not* submit to his ruses. How could she explain, though, without going into damning detail? 'Mrs Roberts… When I first come here to Hewinghall, I told the squire… He axed me about my past and I told him… I told him there'd been trouble, on account of what someone did to me – not for something I'd done. The squire believed me. He said a person was allowed a few secrets. So if you now reckon I've got somethin' to answer for, then… then I'll answer to the squire and nobody else.'

Mrs Roberts peered at her with narrowed eyes. Evidently she didn't want to bother the squire over a few unsubstantiated rumours, which was all the gossip amounted to, as yet. And she seemed impressed by the frank way Jess returned her gaze, with her head up high and her eyes steady. After a few moments' thought, the housekeeper said, 'Very well, Jess. I'm willing to give you the benefit of the doubt, for now. In the short time I've known you, I've come to think of you as a girl I can rely on. But I may need to speak to you again. Some very serious charges appear to have been raised. If these rumours don't stop...'

'I understand,' said Jess. But she knew she was going to be on trial from now on. The ordeal by gossip was only just beginning.

–

For Jess, however, hard work had always been an antidote to worrying; she was not sorry to have an extra job, cleaning Nanny's room, to occupy her mind. It wasn't a pleasant task, but since it had to be done she'd sooner do it herself. She and Nanny had been friends, in their way.

By mid-morning she'd emptied all the cupboards and drawers and put the contents in boxes to be sorted later; then she'd moved all the furniture to the middle of the room, covered it with dust sheets and set about clearing cobwebs from the ceiling; she'd swept the walls down, washed the paintwork and scrubbed the linoleum area by area, leaving it to dry while she went down to bang the mats in the kitchen courtyard. She might have done it on the roof except that Lily was in the schoolroom finding out how well Bella could read and Jess didn't want to open the windows with the child in there. Besides, guests were beginning to arrive in the gravel court below and she couldn't risk showering dust on any of them!

Mrs Roberts and her kitchen staff were up to their eyes preparing food, sweating cobs in the heat from the ranges. As she belaboured her rugs on the cobbles outside, Jess could see them busily rolling pastry, turning spits, chopping vegetables. She didn't envy them, but she did wonder what was being said about her. Suspicious glances came her way through the big windows.

No sooner had she replaced the rugs than it was time to wash her hands, change her apron and think about dinner – or luncheon, as it was called in the big house. As usual, she prepared a milk pudding for dessert and fetched the rest from the kitchen.

'I want you to look after Bella this afternoon,' Lily said, pushing away her dish of creamed tapioca. Delicately dabbing her mouth, she laid her napkin aside and looked at Jess with clear, guileless eyes. 'I need to go home, to fetch a few more of my things – and to collect Gyp.'

'Oh, yes!' Bella cried, all excitement. 'Let's fetch Gyp. May I go, too? I want to go!'

'Well, you can't!' Lily said sharply.

'Why not?' The child's flailing fist – mostly by accident – landed on the edge of her dish. It flipped up and turned over, depositing her pudding on the cloth.

'Naughty girl!' Lily cried, and leapt to her feet in a rage that made Bella blanch and cower down in her chair, arms up as if to ward off blows.

'She din't mean to!' Jess swooped to whisk the child out of her chair before she could get tapioca over everything. She set her down on the floor and swiftly cleared the table, cloth and all, on to a tray.

'She *did* mean to,' Lily said angrily. 'Nasty little beast. Now she's given me a headache. Oh… I must have some fresh air. It's so stuffy in here. *Why* can't we open the windows?' She knew why, though she didn't see the sense in it. 'It's unhealthy. I shall have to go out. I'll go and change my shoes and—'

'Miss…' Jess ventured as Lily made for the far door. 'Do you go out on your own, Lady Maud'll find out. 'Sides, I'm supposed to be clearin' out Nanny's room today, not lookin' after Miss Bella.'

'Can't you do both?'

'I could try, but if someone come up here…'

'I have to go, Jess!' The strange eyes were suddenly desperate, on the edge of tears.

It wasn't only Gyp she was anxious to see, Jess realised. Was that what that letter last night had been about? Had Jess been used, not to cancel an assignation but only to change the arrangements?

Lily didn't even try to lie. 'I told him I'd be there, if it was humanly possible. I need to explain to him…'

'That en't possible,' Jess said quietly. 'Not today. Please, Miss Lily, don't…'

Lily hesitated, chewing her thumb nail as she agonised over it, changing her mind ten times in the space of as many seconds. At last, she let out a sigh. 'Oh… very well. You're right – and I *hate* you for it, Jess. But I can still go to the rectory and fetch Gyp.' She looked at the child on the floor, forcing a smile. 'Well, Bella, it seems you have got your way after all. Shall we go for a walk?'

–

To Lily's utter astonishment, there was no one at home at the rectory and all the doors were locked. On a *Tuesday*, of all days. That was the one day of the week her papa always stayed at home, working quietly in his study with as few distractions as he could manage, with only Eliza at home to make tea and answer the door. Eliza, of course, loved those days, when she could laze about as she pleased.

But she wasn't there today. No one answered at any door.

'Where have they all gone?' Bella asked worriedly. 'Where's Gyp?'

'I don't know.' If Gyp had been in the kitchen he would have come barking when she looked in the window. He wasn't in the walled garden, or the kitchen yard.

Not believing that there could be no one in, Lily hammered again at the side door. This time there was movement inside and the bolt was drawn, the door opened a fraction. Eliza peered out, holding a wrap close to her throat, her hair dishevelled, her face puffed and bleary – but her green eyes remained sharp.

'I en't well,' she said flatly. 'You've now got me out o' my sick bed. There en't no one else here, they're all gone out.'

'Even my papa?'

'Someone came after him. There's somebody poorly in the village.'

'I only came to get Gyp,' Lily said. 'Where is he? I'll take him and then you can get back to your bed, if you really are ill. You don't *look* ill. You look as if you were sleeping.'

Eliza regarded her with undisguised hatred, mouth compressed and eyes burning. 'The dog en't here, neither. We let him out to have a run afore we shut him up last night, and he never come back. He're run away.'

'Run away?' Lily repeated, so incredulous she almost laughed. 'Gyp *never* goes out of the garden!'

'Well, he have this time. Must a got out through a hole in the fence somewhere. Now I have to shut this door. I'm gettin' cold stood here in my bare feet.'

The door actually closed in her face. Lily stared at it, then pounded on it. 'Eliza! *Eliza!*' But Eliza didn't respond.

'What's happened to Gyp?' Bella wanted to know.

'What?' Lily had all but forgotten the child was there. A hand to her whirling head, she looked down at the small pale face. 'I don't know.' What was going on? Had the world gone mad? Gyp vanished, the house empty, Eliza behaving as if she were the mistress and Lily a beggar at the door.

All Lily knew was that she had to talk to someone about it. She had to talk to Ash. In her letter she'd told him she'd be there, if she could get away, at their frequent rendezvous in the old ruined manor at Syderford.

Well, it wasn't far to walk, even with Bella tagging along. She could find some tale to still the child's curiosity. She simply *had* to see Ash.

–

Nanny's possessions were pitifully few, as Jess discovered when she came to sort them out. There were her clothes – mostly black – and other personal bits and pieces; cheap jewellery, a photo or two, some folded papers with childish scribblings on – Nanny had kept mementoes of several old charges, it seemed, though Jess could only guess who they might be. One piece of paper proved to be an envelope. It said 'Harry' on the front, and it contained a bright ginger curl of soft hair...

When she thought about it, Jess realised she knew little about Nanny, not even her real name. She must have been young once, with a family, and friends. Yet she had died alone, anonymous, with only these few pitiful things to testify to her long life. Was that how it was with women who gave their lives to the children of the rich?

Was that what Lily feared?

Footsteps along the outer landing preceded a knock at the door, which opened to reveal Sal Gooden. 'Her ladyship want Miss Bella taken down to the red drawing room this afternoon. She're goin' to show her off to the company. You're to tell Miss Clare...'

Oh, Lord! Jess had known there'd be trouble if Lily went out. If she'd gone to meet that Ashton Haverleigh...

But just at that moment Lily appeared, dragging an equally breath-less Bella with her. She looked about fit to burst with either fury or misery, but on learning that she had been summoned she said, 'You see to Bella. I must get changed,' and disappeared.

261

Hurriedly, telling Bella that she was in for a real treat, taking tea with the grown-ups, Jess managed to wash the child and put her into clean clothes. She was brushing the coppery hair when Lily reappeared, garbed in black unrelieved but for a frothy white jabot at her throat. Above it her face was pale, her eyes bright with defiance.

'I've been told to dress like a governess, so will this do? Shall I merge sufficiently into the background – assuming I keep my eyes demurely lowered? Well, I shan't! I shall hold my head up and let them all take a good look. I don't care what they think. I *know* who I am. Come, Bella, let us go down. Your mama will be waiting.'

She endured the next hour with impatience, ignored by the company. They were all anxious to please their hostess by admiring her daughter, though after a while Lady Maud tired of the game and Bella was made to sit still and be quiet while the adults resumed their own conversations and took tea. Bella's huge, nervous eyes remained fixed on her mother most of the time, as if she expected reprimands.

Lily sat in a chair by the door, unregarded. Despite her earlier bravado, she took care not to meet anyone's eye. She couldn't bear to, in case someone remarked on her affliction. She wanted to be left alone, to think about Ash.

He hadn't been at the old manor, but she had found the message he had left tucked behind the loose piece of panelling which had become their letterbox. It had told her that he, too, had altered his plans, that he couldn't get away to meet her; he had been called away for a few days. But he hoped to see her at the Belladay celebrations. *Hoped to?*

'Miss Clare!' Lady Maud's call jerked her attention back to the room. 'You can take Bella back to the nursery now. Come here and kiss your mama, Bella dear.' Bella did so, with obvious reluctance, made an awkward curtsey to the company, and came to take Lily's hand.

'Pretty little thing,' one of the gentlemen remarked with more sentiment than truth.

All eyes were on the thin, plain child as she left; no one looked at her governess, much to Lily's chagrin. Being ignored was almost worse than being stared at. Didn't any of them realise she was a human being with feelings?

They buried Nanny Fyncham that evening. Most of the Hewinghall servants were busy because of the guests, but Mrs Roberts managed to get away for half an hour and Jess also made it her business to be there at the church in the park; she left Bella sleeping, in Lily's charge. The gardeners, including Matty, acted as bearers. Reverend Clare conducted the brief ceremony and Miss Peartree attended, weeping copiously for her friend. Sir Richard also put in an appearance, though he arrived late.

As Jess turned to follow the coffin out of the church, she saw another late attender in one of the rear pews – Reuben Rudd, with lamplight warm on his bare head and a black band around his sleeve. Her heart seemed to jump as their eyes met, though his expression told her only that the coolness remained between them. He fell in beside Mrs Roberts as she passed him, and she said something about having to get back to the house to be sure the food was all ready.

At the graveside, Jess found herself standing beside Rudd in the cool damp of the night. A rising wind swung the lantern that one of the men carried on a pole, sending light waxing and waning across the rector's pink face and white hair as he intoned the words. Matty and the others lowered the box into the freshly dug grave, then Sir Richard and Miss Peartree each tossed a handful of earth to thud on the wooden lid. Jess and Rudd did likewise and the four gardeners copied them. The sexton moved in to fill the grave almost before the sorry little party turned away.

'Didn't she have any relatives?' Rudd murmured to Jess.

'Not as anyone know. Not much to say for a whole life, is it?'

'No. Not much.'

Sir Richard strode by, bidding them good evening. The gardeners were making for the gate, too. As Jess turned to follow them, Rudd said in an undertone, 'I need to talk to thee. About last night.'

'What about it?'

He took a breath, as if to steady himself, then: 'I could shut my eyes, just once. Happen I could put it down to chance, on account of what's been between us. But I have to warn thee, Jess, I won't let the memory of fondness sway me if it happens again.'

Mystified, she glanced back at him, feeling the first soft flurry of rain on her face. It made her shiver. 'If what happen?'

'Jess?' Matty loomed up out of the shadows. 'D'you want me to see you back to the house? We're then a-goin' to have a jar or two, to see the old girl on her way.'

'And get your courage up for another night's poaching?' Rudd asked in a hard voice.

Matty peered at him, as if he'd only just realised who Jess was with. 'Poachin', Mr Rudd? What – me?'

'Yes, you.' Low as it was, Rudd's voice expressed his bitter fury and even in the darkness Jess saw his eyes flash as he turned on her, saying, 'Was it you dug the shot out of him? Or was it Jim Potts that Obi hit? He got one of them, he swears. Well, next time, Henefer, you might not be so lucky. Next time, it might be *me* behind the sights. And I shoot straight. Good night to you both.'

As he strode away, Matty let out a soft laugh. 'He'll have to catch me first. Blasted gamekeeper!'

Only then did Jess realise what Rudd had meant by his veiled accusations – he took her for a poacher's decoy! He thought she'd been helping them last night! Blast… didn't he know her better than that? She turned on Matty furiously. 'Was it you? Was it you after them birds last night? Oh, Matty… I warned you about Jim Potts.'

'Jim Potts weren't nowhere near that field last night,' Matty said. 'No more was I. We heard there was some trouble, but that wan't us as caused it. Fact is, we was in the back room of the "Admiral Nelson". You ax anybody who was there – half a dozen on 'em will swear to it.'

Jess only wished she could believe him.

'Will they swear he din't do any harm to Miss Lily's dog, neither?' she demanded. 'Or was it Eliza that let him out to get hisself lost, off her own bat?'

'What, have Gyp gone missin'?'

'Got loose and run away. So Eliza say.'

'I'll keep a look out for him, then. Miss Lily'll miss him. Is that why she're unhappy? I saw her today, walkin' through the woods as if she was shanny, and tears all down her face. Wish she'd of talked to me, but when I showed myself she ran away. You tell her I'll find Gyp if I can.'

Did he really believe that would make Lily think more fondly of him? 'I don't reckon nobody'll find him,' Jess said. 'That wun't astonish me if Eliza han't give him a grain too much poison this time, and killed him.'

'Jess!'

'Well, it's so! If he're dead, that'll certainly keep him quiet and let her get her beauty sleep – or whatever else it is she do of a night.

Maybe you know what that might be, Matty. Do you and Jim *both* call at the rectory after you've been out poachin'?'

'Jess!' Matty said again, and glanced around as if fearing listeners, but the graveyard was empty except for the sexton filling the grave by lanternlight, too far away to hear above the scrape and shush of his spade in the earth. 'D'you want to get me in trouble?'

'That en't *me* as'll accomplish that,' Jess said bitterly. 'You keep in with them Pottses, you'll soon find out where real trouble come from. And speakin' of trouble...' She too looked at the sexton, then drew Matty away towards the gate, heading back to the big house through the windy, rain-spitting night. 'I better tell you, else you'll hear it from somebody else. That's a wonder nobody han't told you afore this. Matty... Merrywest was here Sunday. Preachin' in the chapel. We ran into him as he was headin' back.' She pulled her coat collar up around her neck, huddling into it more for comfort than warmth. 'Now the rumours are startin'...'

'What rumours? What'd he say? I told you he din't hold a grudge.'

'Oh, but he do, Matty. Whatever he've said to you and Fanny, he've said it on'y to keep you sweet. Hopin' you'd let on where I was. See, I know things about him he wun't want spread around.'

'What things?'

'Don't ax, Matty. That's not something I can ever tell. Funny thing is, he ought to have known that. I didn't tell then and I en't a-goin' to tell now – not for my own sake but for someone else.'

'Who?'

'If I told you that, you'd know as much as me. I won't tell, not even to you. But Merrywest reckons I might. So he're goin' about tellin' lies about me. He say I played Jezebel and tempted him, and when he spurned me I tried to kill him.'

'Jess!'

'He said it to my face, Matty! And some of it's true – I did push him into that dock.'

'Jessie...'

'I did, Matty,' she confirmed in despair. 'I did want him dead. If it han't a been for him...' No, she couldn't say that. She turned away, squinting against the rainy darkness with eyes that were suddenly painful. 'Oh, I don't know, Matty! The night of the fire... I ran mad. I hated him so much... I saw the chance, so I pushed him. And I ran. I darsen't come back. I thought they'd be after me for murder. All those months, I was frightened sick. I still dream about it. And, if you want the truth... I still wish him dead.'

'Don't say that, Jess.'

'Why not? It's the mortal truth.'

'I can't believe it. That en't like you. *I'm* the one's too handy with the rough stuff. *You*... you was alluss a sharp 'un, but not in that way.'

'No?' Jess looked into her heart, finding black depths she didn't care to plumb. She couldn't tell Matty the whole truth: if he discovered what Merrywest had done, he'd probably do for the man himself and the last thing she wanted was her brother dragged to the gallows in her place. 'Well, that's what he done to me – he learned me how to hate. Now he're shoutin' his poison from the rooftops. He've already turned Reuben against me, and most of Hewing village, and... Oh... let's not talk about him. That make me sick thinkin' of it.'

–

The whispers continued. Conversations stopped when Jess hove into sight; eyes followed her, assessing her in new lights; and there was a new coolness in the air that had nothing to do with the weather.

'Whatever is this gossip I'm hearing?' Lily demanded. 'Something about a preacher?'

'An old enemy. He'd say black was white if he thought it'd hurt me.'

'I thought so. I said as much to Mrs Roberts. My friend Jessamy a scheming, murdering Jezebel? Really, what nonsense! One has only to look at you to know that you'd never do anything wrong – you're as sweet and innocent as... as Dolly Upton.'

Jess kept her face straight, though she wanted to laugh, or was it to cry? If only she could be 'sweet and innocent' again. 'Thank you, miss.'

'The man must be mad,' Lily said. 'But then, all of those ranters are slightly unhinged. Oh – I know you go to their services sometimes, but you're not really one of them, are you? Especially not now. I mean, they're the ones who're repeating these rumours. *Very* Christian of them.'

Blessed Miss Lily. At least Jess had one friend left.

On the night before her birthday, Bella woke screaming and when Jess and Lily went rushing they found the door of her room open. Lamplight glowed, illumining the form of Lady Maud, clad in nightwear whose flowing folds seemed to emphasise her thinness. It was hard to tell who was most startled – she, or the child she had terrified by her presence.

Jess reached Bella first, clasping the shivering body to her. Bella had stopped screaming but she was shaking, stuffing a favourite teddy bear against her mouth.

'I only came to see if she was well!' Lady Maud said, glaring about her as if she'd been accused of some crime. Her hair was wild, her eyes too. Her breath smelled strongly of gin and cashews. 'Can't I even visit my own daughter now?' Gathering her nightrobe round her, assuming an air of dignity, she stalked out, dodging the doorjamb by a hair's breadth.

After they'd settled Bella down and returned to their own room, Jess and Lily lay awake in the darkness. Lily was curious; she kept asking questions until Jess reluctantly told some of what she knew.

'But it's mostly kitchen gossip. Tittle-tattle.'

'Quite, and I know how unreliable that can be. But don't be annoying, Jess. Tell me! If I'm going to be living here, I have a right to know.'

It was no secret that the Fynchams used separate bedrooms, but gossip added that Lady Maud invited her husband to her bed only rarely. Their personal relationship was a mystery to Jess. All she knew for certain was that, as a mother, Lady Maud didn't have much natural ability, and Bella was cowed and subservient with her, which further irritated Lady Maud.

'I reckon she've tried to be more of a mother to Bella because she feel bad over what happened to Harry,' Jess said. 'That prey on her mind, how that boy died. She blame herself. That's why she keep comin' up here to check on Bella in the night. She're a sad lady.' She didn't add that she'd seen her ladyship go out on the roof one night and walk the parapet; she was beginning to wonder if she'd dreamed that particular piece of madness. 'I don't reckon she have it in her to love anything human. She save it all for her horses.'

'Poor little Bella,' Lily said sadly. 'Thank goodness she has a father who loves her. He does, doesn't he? And doesn't care who knows it.'

Sighing long and deeply, she turned over to lie on her back, saying quietly, 'That's what I always dreamed *my* real father would be like – kind, and loving. Oh, Jess... he *is* going to come. One day soon. I still believe that. Bathsheba promised me I should meet him soon.'

'I wouldn't dream too hard on gypsy promises if I was you, Miss Lily,' Jess said.

'Why not? She was right about Ash, wasn't she? She told me I should have my heart's desire, and so I have. He loves me. Oh... knowing that, I can endure anything!'

—

They were at breakfast the next morning when Sir Richard arrived with two of the footmen laden with bright packages. Lady Maud was 'indisposed', so he'd come alone to cheer Bella's birthday morning with gifts – toys and books, and a party dress which was a froth of pale pink silk trimmed with rosebuds. The dressmaker had taken measurements weeks ago, but Jess was to do last-minute alterations to make it a perfect fit.

From the park came sounds of hammering as men strung bunting around the marquee that had been erected, and flurries of shot could be heard now and then from misty fields where the gentlemen were shooting partridge. The shots made Jess think of Rudd as she plied her needle, making small adjustments to Bella's party gown. As head gamekeeper, Rudd would be in his element that day, enjoying the outcome of months of effort. Would he even give her a thought?

Lily was restless, silent for half an hour at a time, then full of false brightness. She kept being drawn to the window to stare out at the mist. The weather had suddenly turned mild, forming condensation from the cold sea and the damp earth, making a fog that swirled and eddied, reducing visibility now to twenty yards, now to a hundred. Might Ash be with the Guns?

And what of poor little Gyp? Was he out in this mist, lost and pining for her? She'd been back twice to the rectory to ask after him, but Cousin Oriana had only blinked worriedly and said there was no sign of him.

From the rectory she had also brought some more clothes, including a blouse or two – the garment seemed a good compromise for morning lessons in the schoolroom, worn with a shawl for extra warmth and one of the plain skirts which she usually kept for walking in the woods. After lunch she usually changed into her black silk.

That day she agonised over what to wear, deciding eventually on the black silk. No one then could complain that she was being defiant or unreasonable, not Lady Maud nor even Papa. But she mourned her kingfisher silk. She had brought it with her, just to look at it and wish...

After luncheon, Jess was commandeered to help the kitchen staff. She found herself with all the heaviest or dirtiest jobs, hauling crockery out to the marquee and helping the scullery maid scour greasy pans. Nothing was said aloud but she was aware of undercurrents which seemed to be encouraged by a clipped Mrs Roberts. Nathanael Merrywest's serpent tongue was working its evil well.

Villagers began to gather in the park, the men, women and children of the estate all being invited to share in the 'Belladay' celebrations. From them, too, Jess received more than her share of hard looks. She heard one portly woman say, 'What, that scrawny mawther? Well, now, she had *no* chance. Not wi' *that* there preacher man. He look to me like the sort as prefer more meat on the bone. Now, if that had been *me* after him...' Jess slipped away, but the sound of raucous laughter followed her.

'Jess Sharp!' Sal Gooden beckoned, her usually merry face shadowed by the doubts that troubled many of Jess's erstwhile friends. They wanted to believe her innocent; after all, in spite of the rumours she was still walking free, not languishing in a police cell awaiting trial, but even so when a preacher claimed things against her a certain mistrust couldn't help but linger. Jess tried to pretend she didn't notice but it wasn't easy.

'What is it, Sal?'

'I been lookin' for you. Someone want to see you. He say he'll be waitin' in the walled garden.'

'Who?'

Sal looked blank. 'The boy din't say.'

'What boy?'

'Well, how'd I know? I don't know all the village little 'uns. Go you and find out. If Mrs Roberts ask for you I'll tell her some tale.'

What was up now? Jess wondered. Was it Matty wanting to see her? Or – the thought made her heart skip – was it Reuben Rudd?

Throwing her hands up to tidy her hair, she stole away, glad of the mist that soon separated her from the activity in the park.

Beyond the stable block, a great oak tree spread its branches over the entrance to the so-called 'shrubbery walk'. A maze of pathways twined among bushes and trees which on a hot day provided a cool place to stroll. On that day the walk was wet, branches dripping with droplets of the mist that seemed to hang heavy on thick air. Jess was not sorry to be through the shrubbery and on the path that led to the walled garden. Beneath an archway in the wall a door stood ajar.

Feeling like an intruder, Jess pushed the door wider and stepped inside. The garden was divided by tall walls and connecting gateways. Here grew vegetables, and figs and cherries trained against southern walls. Apples and pears hung ripening; box hedges defined flower borders bright with dahlias and chrysanthemums; greenhouses sheltered grapes and oranges, all serviced by wide gravel pathways kept neatly raked. It was quiet there, an enclosed and secret world made even more secluded by grey mist.

Then the door shut behind her with a hefty *thunk*, and as she whirled a hand grasped her wrist in punishing fingers. It wasn't Rudd, or Matty. She stared in disbelief and growing dread into the narrowed black eyes of Preacher Merrywest.

'Well now, Jess,' he said softly. 'After all these months. Alone at last. Just you and me.'

Twenty-One

'There's no one else here,' Merrywest informed her as she glanced behind, hoping for help. 'I made sure of that. Didn't want to be interrupted. But don't worry, I won't keep you long.'

Jess strained away from him, her eyes fixed on his bearded face – that hated face! Her wrist burned from the hold he had on it. He was not a big man but he was strong. A gasp escaped her as he squeezed tighter, rubbing her bones together.

'Please!'

The pressure eased but the light in his eyes said it would resume if she resisted. 'That's just a reminder,' he said in a calm, reasonable voice that held infinite menace. 'I hope you're going to keep on being a sensible girl, Jess. Just keep our secret to yourself, eh? If you tell...' His hand tightened again, threatening to break her small bones, sending spears of pain up her arm and into her head. 'If you tell, then it will be the worse for your family. Think what I could do to your Fanny and that new husband of hers, and the young 'uns – Sam, and little Joe. As for Matty...'

'Blast your eyes!' she got out, hardly able to think past the pain in her wrist. 'You don't have to threaten me. I hen't said nothin' yet. I won't *ever* say nothin'. Not 'cos I'm afeared o' you, though. I'll keep quiet to stop my brother from comin' after you. If *he* knew what you'd done—'

He swung her round, slamming her against the garden door. Her head cracked on the wood with a blow that dizzied her.

'You open your mouth, girl, and I'll kill you. Hear me! I'll kill you and I'll ruin your family, every one of them. Remember that.'

He let go her wrist and she hugged it to her, cradling it with her other hand, leaning against the door with her eyes closed and tears seeping from under her lids. She heard him leave, his feet scraping on the gravel, walking at first, then breaking into a run.

Letting her shaking legs give way, she sank down into a huddle beneath the archway, her whole body hurting with this and the memory of previous assaults. No, she'd never tell on him. She'd never dare. But she'd pray every day that he would die, horribly and slowly.

For as long as she lived, she would wish him dead.

–

As part of the 'Belladay' Celebrations, the steward had organised games and races. The gentlemen came back from shooting and the ladies emerged from their luncheon party to applaud as Sir Richard and Lady Maud helped their daughter to award the prizes.

Lily stayed nearby, applauding with the rest while her gaze roamed, seeking one particular face among the crowd. But presumably he was not coming until the evening. Well, she could wait. She would see him soon. She was living for the moment when she would be with Ash, dancing with him in front of the assembly, declaring their attachment…

Later there was tea in the marquee, with the ladies and gentlemen of the company helping to serve the villagers. Bella sat at the head of the table, flanked by long lines of children who all drank her health in homebrewed lemonade and ginger beer. But the excitement tired her. Dark circles showed under her eyes and she began to grow fretful.

'We'll take her up to bed, I think, Miss Clare,' Sir Richard said, lifting his daughter into his arms. 'She must have some rest if she's to enjoy the ball this evening.'

One of the footmen stepped in and would have taken the child but the squire brushed him aside and strode on, long legs carrying his daughter rapidly towards the house with Lily hurrying in his wake. Thank goodness the afternoon was over. Now she could really look forward to the night.

Worn out by the excitements of the day, Bella went to sleep almost as soon as her father laid her down on her bed. He extricated himself from her with care and straightened to smile at Lily.

'I believe she enjoyed her day.'

'I believe she did,' Lily agreed.

He regarded her with perceptive eyes. 'But you did not.'

'It's not my place to enjoy myself.'

'Is it not?' About to argue, he stopped himself and made a gesture that drew attention to her gown, 'Is that for Nanny?'

Lily looked down at the black silk. 'It's the only suitable garment I possess. With so little warning of my change in station…'

'Of course. Yes. We must have the dressmaker call. Mrs Roberts will see to it.'

Mrs Roberts will have me garbed in plainest grey, Lily thought dully, though aloud she said, 'You're very kind, Sir Richard.'

His hand came out, as if to lift her chin and, startled, she looked up at him, backing away. The hand fell and his smile turned to concern as he saw her face. 'You're not happy, Miss Clare. Is something wrong?'

'No, sir.'

'Do you regret your… what did you call it? – your "change of station"? I understood from the rector that you were willing to come to Hewinghall. If I thought otherwise…'

'Oh… yes. I was… quite willing,' Lily lied. 'Just a little… unprepared. Forgive me. I'm sure, when I am more accustomed to my new position…'

'I want you to be happy,' he said. 'You must be sure and tell me if you are not.'

Lily could not imagine any circumstance in which she would be likely to tell him any such thing, but she answered again, 'You're very kind, Sir Richard. I'm only sorry…' She knew she ought not to mention it, but the words burst out of her anyway: 'The thing is… I had a new gown made for the ball this evening. A *beautiful* gown! I was so looking forward to…'

The gentle smile in his eyes said he understood. 'Then you must wear it. Of course you must.'

Lily stared at him, feeling herself sway a little, as if she were dizzy. 'May I? But Lady Fyncham said… I'm not to be a guest. I must play the governess. Looking after Bella.'

'My dear Miss Clare… You were invited to attend the ball as yourself. You must come as yourself. In the circumstances, I think we can flout convention, just a little, just for once.' His smile widened, asking her to collude with him. 'I'm already considered eccentric because I adore and spoil my daughter. If I allow some extra privileges to her new governess, it will be in character, don't you think? And we'll have your friend Jess on hand, too – she can take Bella to bed when the excitement grows too much for her.'

Lily's face brightened with incredulous joy. She could have kissed him. What a lovely, understanding man he was! Oh, she'd been an

273

idiot to worry so, she should have known all would be well – the gypsy had told her so. Now she could wear her gown, and dance with Ash. 'Oh... *thank you!*'

'We like to keep a happy household,' he said with a smile, and, enjoying the sound of alliteration, emphasised the aspirants: 'A *h*appy *h*ousehold, *h*ere at *H*ewinghall.'

A soft laugh broke from Lily as she added, 'A *wholly* happy household.'

'Splendid!' he laughed. 'We shall teach Bella to enjoy words, too.' Nodding at her, he moved away. 'I shall see you later, Miss Clare.'

While Bella slept, Lily found herself pacing the schoolroom in a fever of hope and anxiety. It was all working out – she was going to the ball, as a guest, in her new gown. Now, all that was needed was for Ash to come, as promised. Oh, of course he would come!

She would be Cinderella at the ball, appearing in her glory despite the efforts of an evil mistress to clothe her in subservience. Whatever the consequences, nothing else would matter once her prince appeared and swept her into his arms, claiming her before all the world.

–

For Jess, the remainder of the afternoon passed in a haze of sick fear. Merrywest hated her because of the wrongs he had done her. Would he harm her family, even if she kept her silence? She'd never be sure. She'd go through life wondering, fearing...

She managed her chores somehow, though her wrist was sore and her head aching. When Sal asked what had happened, Jess shook her head and moved on, knowing the other girl was curious about the marks of strain on her face.

As she was carting a last basket of crockery through the kitchen courtyard, the boy Gooden came running across the cobbles, doffing his cap with one of his nervous grins, saying, 'Miss Sharp... can you come? Mr Rudd want a word. If you please.' His glance indicated the game larder at the far side of the courtyard, where Jess saw Dash sitting outside, and Rudd's sturdy figure just visible in the shadowy interior.

'I'm busy,' she said dully, though she longed to share her worries with Rudd. How lovely it would be to tell him the truth and have him comfort her and... oh, she was as bad as Miss Lily, dreaming hopeless dreams. 'What do he want?'

'Just a word, he say. That 'on't take long.' He'd stopped grinning. He looked as if he might burst into tears. 'That's important, miss.'

Suddenly apprehensive, she glanced again to where Rudd was waiting inside the outhouse: What was this? Dear Lord, she couldn't take much more, not today. 'Carry you this basket in for me,' she instructed the boy, glad to relieve her aching wrist. 'Mind, now, that's heavy. Don't drop it, or Mrs Roberts'll have your hide.'

She crossed the yard with her eyes on the ground, watching her feet because the cobbles were uneven. Peering against the half-light, she stepped over the threshold into the game larder, where Rudd was writing in his tally book while Obi reached to hang yet more of the kill. Dozens of small feathered bodies hung in rows, dangling from hooks in the beams of the ceiling, and there was an odd, sickly odour that made Jess's nose wrinkle.

Rudd gave her a sidelong glance. 'Never been in a game larder before, Miss Sharp?'

'Never had no call – Mr Rudd,' said Jess. 'That wholly reeks.'

'It's the death sweat you can smell. You get used to it. Don't you, Obi?' But Obi only nodded and went on tying the birds in pairs and hanging them up. Rudd cast a bleak look at the carcasses. 'Wish I could get used to seeing 'em slaughtered, though. It's what I raise 'em for, but it right grieves me to see my beauties like this.'

'Didn't know you was mew-hearted,' Jess responded. 'Thought you was the hard man. Scourge of poachers – and their helpers.'

Another hooded look answered this sally. The uncertainty in it only annoyed her more, as did the tears that came hot behind her eyes. She denied them, tossing her head, saying defiantly, 'Well, hear you this, Reuben Rudd – I was out on a message on Monday night, and that's all I was about. If there was poachers after your birds, that wan't nothin' to do with me. Do you doubt that, then... then you can go hang! I hen't got time to spare jawin' about it. What'd you now want with me?'

He had opened his mouth to reply to her attack, but her final question made him pause. He glanced at Obi, who went on with his work. 'I thought you might want to know – we found Miss Lily's Gyp.'

His voice and grave expression told her that the news was bad. 'Where? He's not...?'

'Looks like he got into a poacher's snare.' The hazel eyes held hers, full of speculation. 'Tell Miss Lily I'm sorry. I'd have brought him to her, but it might have upset her to see him like that.'

'His neck was broke,' Obi said. 'Strung him up on our gibbet, they had, along of all the stoats and jays and weasels. Blasted warmints, poachers.'

'Obi!' Rudd snapped.

The man desisted, but Jess had the full sickening picture; it would stay with her for a long time, poor little Gyp strung up among the rotting carcasses of predators, with his head lolling and blood on his silky coat. 'Lord rot that Eliza Potts!' she muttered to herself.

Rudd's eyes narrowed, hardening. 'That's a right lousy thing to say. Eliza wouldn't—'

'Oh, yes, you'll defend her,' Jess flared, flinging up her head, not caring if he saw her tears. 'Most men do. But *I* know her. She've alluss hated Gyp. And she hate Miss Lily. She threatened to do somethin' against Miss Lily and now—' Oh, what was she saying? Unable to bear the growing anger in his eyes, she turned away. She had no proof of any of it. Just because she disliked and was jealous of Eliza she had no right to make accusations. Besides, it was only confirming Rudd's low opinion of her.

'I thought you cared about Miss Lily,' he said roughly.

'I do!'

'Then don't repeat this wicked slander to her. In fact, don't tell her any details. No need to upset her. Just say we found him. Tell her it was peaceful – natural causes.'

'I'll try.' She shivered a little, knowing how upset Lily was going to be. 'What did you do with him?'

'Buried him in the wood. I thought she'd like that. I can show her where, if she wants to come and say her goodbyes.'

'I'll tell her.' She was backing away – away from the stench in the larder, and away from the resentment she sensed in Rudd. 'Yes, I'll tell her.'

But not yet, she wouldn't. This was one piece of news that could wait, at least until after the ball.

—

Jess was allowed to watch the ball from the minstrel's gallery, where the five-piece orchestra was placed. It lay over one end of the great hall, reached by a flight of narrow stairs from a door hidden in the panelling of the staircase hall – a door which George the footman showed Jess. She sat on a stool in a corner, out of the musicians' way, half hidden behind pot plants and peering through a wrought-iron screen.

The ladies in the company below were decked in rainbow hues of silk and satin against which the gentlemen looked grand in their stark black and white. Lady Maud wore a nasty shade of green which went ill with her chestnut hair and pale skin, but Sir Richard looked noble. More people were arriving all the time, their carriages halting at the front door.

Guests were shown into the morning room, which had been prepared as a cloakroom – Sal Gooden was on duty there; they were then announced at the door of the great hall by Mr Longman.

The far end of the room, and the doors to further rooms where supper was laid out, were obscured from Jess's view by the glare of light from the chandelier. A hundred candles flickered, their flames reflecting from the facets of a thousand crystal drops strung like necklaces from the gilded frame. Still, she could see most of the great hall, its polished floor, chairs ranged round the walls, and the great ladies and gentlemen who had all come to help Bella celebrate her day.

'And the guest of honour...' the master of ceremonies sang out, 'Miss Bella Fyncham.'

As Jess craned to see, all eyes turned to the door beneath her perch, 'Oh's' and 'Ah's' mingling with 'How dear!' Sir Richard strode forward to greet his daughter with smiles, but Lady Maud stiffened and stared at someone behind Bella.

Now Jess, too, saw Lily. She walked demurely in her bright kingfisher gown, her head dipped and her gaze on the floor, following as Sir Richard led his daughter to greet her mother, amid a chorus of applause and cries of 'Happy Birthday, Bella!' Sadly, pale pink was as unsuited to Bella as that green was to her mother. Jess's heart went out to the child.

Lady Maud bent to offer her daughter a cheek to kiss, then glared at her husband, muttering something to which he replied by beckoning to Lily, who dipped an immaculate curtsey. She had decked her dark hair with green and blue feathers to shade with her gown. Its sleeves were mere caps, leaving a daring amount of upper arm showing above her long white gloves.

She looked wholly elegant and beautiful, Jess thought mistily, thrilled that she herself had helped to dress Lily and do her hair.

277

Oh, she did hope nothing would go wrong for Miss Lily tonight. She deserved better than she'd had so far. Jess asked nothing for herself – she'd come from nothing, turned out nothing and had nothing waiting for her. But Lily was different. Lily had high hopes and dreams. Please Lord, let Mr Ashton Haverleigh come, she prayed. Let him prove himself worthy of my young lady. If he do hurt her now, I don't know what she'll do.

She saw Lily move on to greet her adoptive father respectfully and Miss Peartree with more warmth. The old lady was obviously telling her how lovely she looked. Blushing, Lily leaned and kissed her cheek.

More guests arrived, filling the great hall and overflowing into adjoining rooms. The dancing began, led off by Sir Richard and his little daughter, much to everyone's amusement. Among the throng the kingfisher gown mingled, now with one group, now with another, with Miss Peartree acting as chaperone, and when the dancing began Lily was not short of partners. She even danced with her papa.

But Jess, who knew her so well and could almost read her thoughts, saw her constantly glancing at the clock or eagerly watching as new arrivals were announced. She was waiting for Ashton Haverleigh.

Jess had started to watch the clock, too. She'd been told to be down in the staircase hall at midnight, to take charge of Bella. The child was dancing again with her doting papa, her face solemn as she watched her feet and tried to follow his steps. Some guests smiled at the sight; others looked askance – in some circles the squire's affection for his daughter was considered excessive, if not downright unhealthy. Little he cared, Jess thought. Just look at him now, proud as a puffin. The fact that he'd lost his son made him all the more fond of his daughter. What was wrong with that?

As the music ended, Sir Richard lifted Bella into his arms, laughing. It wanted five minutes to midnight, Jess saw. She was searching the throng for a sight of Lily when George the footman gave a soft whistle from below, attracting her attention, beckoning her to come. It was time for Bella to be put to bed.

The orchestra members were setting up their next piece of music with a deal of paper-shuffling and muttered comments and laughter. Even so, Jess heard the loud voice below calling the names of yet more late guests. 'Mr and Mrs Oliver Clare…' Longman declaimed, and 'The Honourable Ashton Haverleigh…'

Jess sighed to herself as she closed the door and went on down the narrow enclosed stairs. Thank the Lord he'd come! Lily would be happy now, for a little while at least.

Unable to be still, anxious because Ash was so late, Lily had made her way to the morning room. The front half of it was reserved for gentlemen, with a footman on hand and coats and cloaks arranged on a rail. Huge lacquered screens, brilliant with peacocks, shielded the inner half of the room, where stood a few chairs and a table provided with trays of pins, extra flowers, scent sprays and carafes of water. Two or three large mirrors reflected the scene. Ignoring the hovering Sal Gooden, Lily checked her appearance while, outside, the crunch of wheels on gravel presaged the arrival of another carriage. Only by an effort of will did she prevent herself from flying to the window to peer between the long white drapes.

She heard the murmur of voices as the new arrivals came in – a small party, evidently. She heard the gentlemen being greeted by the footman as, behind her, the ladies appeared round the end of the screen, the older one in mustard and claret, the other a golden-haired vision in...

Lily jerked round, doubting the evidence of the reflection in the mirror. But it told true: the first lady was Cousin Oliver's plump wife, Letitia, and with her, golden hair piled in intricate curls, shoulders white against the outrageous frills and flounces of a gown made of tartan silk – scarlet quartered with greens, blues and yellow – was Clemency.

It was hard to tell who was most disconcerted, they to find her there or she to see them. Clemency's eyes looked icy blue against the sudden hectic colour that stained her face.

'Lily!' Letitia Clare looked her up and down in astonishment and not a little displeasure. 'Whatever... what are you doing here? And in such... We had heard you were employed as a governess.'

'I am.' Lily could hardly think. What on earth was Clemency doing here? Looking so stunning, too, her golden hair and the white skin displayed by an extreme décolletage being a perfect foil for the vibrant, ultrafashionable gown. She looked thin, her nostrils flaring like a nervous mare's, her eyes too wide and bright...

'Well, really,' Letitia was saying. 'I know the Fynchams enjoy cocking snooks at convention, but—'

'Don't be long, Letty!' came her husband's impatient voice from behind the screen. 'We're already late. It's almost midnight.'

'Mama, dear.' Clemency laid a gloved hand on her mother's arm. 'Why don't you go and join the gentlemen? I want to have a word with Lily. I shan't be long. Tell Ash I shall be there directly.'

'Very well, my love.' She cast another look at Lily. 'But don't keep him waiting.'

Lily was hardly aware of her leaving. What had Clemency said? *Ash?* Ash was here? Escorting Clemency? Oh, surely she had misheard. 'Did you say—'

'Fetch me a glass of water,' Clemency snapped at the waiting maid. 'Fresh water. From the kitchen.'

Sal had been about to pour from the carafe on the table, but she paused, looking from one to the other, bobbed a curtsey. 'Yes, miss,' she said, and departed. There was silence now from beyond the screens – the others had gone on into the lobby.

'Now.' Clemency's hand fastened on Lily's wrist, drawing her away to a corner by the draped window, where she stared into Lily's face with burning-cold eyes. 'Yes, I came with Ash Haverleigh. You may as well know that we shall be announcing our engagement very soon.' Her nails bit into Lily's arm, even through both of their gloves as she leaned closer, saying in an undertone full of threats: 'And listen to me, Lily – you're not to say anything – not *one single word* – about that silly fib I told you last June. It *was* a fib. I only said it to shock you.'

'No…' Lily managed.

'Yes!' Releasing Lily's aching wrist, she straightened her shoulders and tossed her head, adding, 'The fact is, Ash and I had a rendezvous by the river, where unfortunately we were discovered. But I swear to you that was the first time we had been entirely alone together. There was *never* any improper conduct between us. You must believe that. You won't be so hateful as to utter a word to the contrary, will you?'

Lily shook her head, though she didn't believe a word. This could not be happening. Ash loved her – *her*, not Clemency. Clemency was lying. Lily could sense how high-strung her cousin was, nervous, brittle, and so very thin. She had been through some bad experience and now she was frightened. Lily could almost smell the fear on her. But what was she afraid of?

'My parents thought the attachment was nothing more than infatuation,' Clemency went on hurriedly, as if she wanted to have it all said. 'They hoped that by taking me away for the summer they would put an end to it. They were wrong. Absence has only increased the bond between us. Our parents – mine *and* his – are now agreed that Ashton and I must be married very soon. Probably by Christmas. We are to live at Syderford for the present and he will work for Papa in some—'

'He *can't* marry you!' The frantic whisper burst out of Lily before she could stop it. 'He's going to marry *me*! He said so. He said...' The words trailed off as she saw her own horror and dawning comprehension mirrored in Clemency.

They had both been used, both lied to. Both of them had trusted Ashton Haverleigh.

'He's mine!' Clemency spat, her blue eyes bright with terror. Her gloved hand came up and struck Lily's cheek with the swiftness of a snake. 'He promised me!'

Lily stared at her, soothing her cheek. The blow hadn't been hard. What hurt most was that it had happened at all. Brokenly, she breathed, 'He promised me, too. Oh, Clemency...'

'Stay away from me!' Clemency recoiled from the hand held out in sympathy, spots of bright colour on her cheeks making her look like a painted doll, except that no doll ever had such pain in its eyes. 'Stay away from us both. I never want to see you again. Damn you, Lily, I knew you'd ruin everything for me if you could. You *knew* he was mine. You've always wanted everything I ever had. Well, you're not having Ash. If you ever say anything... If you ever come near us...'

Lily was blinded by her tears. She didn't see Clemency leave.

But she heard the latest arrivals announced: 'Mr and Mrs Oliver Clare... the Honourable Ashton Haverleigh and...'

–

Lily found herself outside, in a night still haunted by sea-fret. The world looked strange and ghostly, lit by silver moonlight that spread through the mist from above. The mist now lay only some eight or ten feet deep. It was ebbing, like a tide.

Guided by that strange unearthly light, Lily started to walk along the drive, not knowing where she was going until she realised her feet were taking her to the rectory, to old familiar hiding places where she could huddle and nurse her wounds.

She couldn't think clearly. She could only see Clemency's face, pale blue eyes and spots of colour on alabaster cheeks. *He's mine! Stay away!* Oh God. Oh, God!

She walked on, holding her rustling skirts clear of the ground, not even aware of the cool, damp cling of the mist that laid a fine dew on her clothes and hair. At last she came to the gate of the rectory garden and made round the house, towards the old shrubbery. No one would ever find her inside its tented branches. Perhaps Gyp would come and keep her company, as he had so often. It was their secret place. Theirs alone. Except... except that she had shared it with Ash! How could she ever feel the same about the hiding place now that—

As she came round the corner of the house she stopped, startled by a blur of bright lamplight behind the mist. Someone was at the side door – two male figures, in dark clothes and caps, one tall and thin, the other also tall, but broader – Lily thought she ought to know him but couldn't place him. Eliza was in the doorway, taking charge of the bundles the men were bringing.

Lily drew back, into the shadow cast by the wall, her slipper scraping on a stone. The small noise sounded loud in the night.

'Sssh!' The thinner man glanced behind him at the crowding darkness.

'You're jumpy tonight,' Eliza observed. 'There en't nothin' there. Won't be nobody back from the ball for hours yet – 'less Miss Peartree have one o' her turns.'

'Thought I heard something.'

'Like what?'

'I dunno.'

'Not a dog barkin'?' she enquired, and laughed. 'Don't say you're gettin' a conscience in your old age, Jim Potts.'

The bigger man said sourly, 'That en't funny, 'Liza.'

'En't it? Well, that make *me* laugh. I warned that primmickin' little diddicoy by-blow I'd do for her if she crossed me.'

'Don't you talk about her in that manner!' the big man warned. 'You're jealous is all.'

'Jealous? Just 'cause you've gone shanny over her? Oh... clear you off, both of you, 'fore Reuben Rudd do come after you. He's already suspicious. If he catch you here, he'll know what's to do, whatever story I tricolate for him.'

As she turned back into the house, the two men set off in opposite directions. One of them made away into the garden, heading for the far gate; the larger of the two headed straight for Lily, a big dark figure against a bloom of light in the second before Eliza shut the door.

Lily froze, backed up against the rough coldness of the wall, terrified as a cornered rabbit.

The man's heavy footsteps stopped. He was peering into the darkness, listening. Had he seen Lily in that moment before the light died? 'Who's that?' he muttered in an undertone, as if he didn't want his confederate to hear. 'Who's there?'

Cowering away, Lily stopped her mouth with her hands, hoping he might go by without seeing her.

The man took another step, his boots gritting on the path. 'Miss Lily? Is that you, Miss Lily?'

Lily couldn't bear it. She turned and ran.

The man came after her. He caught her before she reached the gate, his hands coming hard and heavy on her. Lily let out a shriek, but the man's horny hand clamped over her mouth as he held her back against him and the scent of dead pheasants and wet woods assailed her nostrils.

'Miss Lily!' the breathless mutter came in her ear. 'Miss Lily, don't be afeared. That's on'y me. It's Matty. Matty Henefer. Jess's brother. Be still now. Don't cry out. If them Pottses hear us—'

Lily stopped struggling and, slowly, Matty let her go. She threw herself round to face him, though she couldn't see him properly for the maze of shadows. What had he said? Jess's brother? The one who'd been in Hunstanton that day? Of course, *that* was where she'd seen the gardener Henefer before.

'What are you doing here?' she demanded, keeping her voice low.

'I was a-goin' to ax the same of you. Lor', Miss Lily, you hen't got no shawl nor nothin'. Whatever have happened? You're all a-shiver. Here, take my coat.'

'I don't want your coat!' But as he laid it round her shoulders she was glad of its warmth and drew it closer round her. The world seemed to have gone mad; she couldn't make sense of anything. 'You're always watching me, following me. I've seen you! What is it you want?'

'Right now, miss,' said Matty, 'I reckon what I want is to get you safely home.'

Home? Lily thought dully. Where was that? She had no home any more.

But having no energy to argue, she let Matty lay his arm around her shoulders and together they made for the big house...

Twenty-Two

After the night of the ball, when he'd learned what had happened to Gyp, and when he'd brought Lily home safely, Matty ended his association with the Pottses. He moved out of Mrs Kipps's cottage and took rooms with a fisher family in Martham, much to Jess's relief. It was one bright spot in a winter that stretched into one of the dreariest she had known. At times she thought spring might never come.

The life of the big house went on, but in the nursery disconsolation held sway: Bella wasn't well, suffering from coughs and colds, and Jess herself was sad, missing Reuben Rudd, listening for every word of gossip about him and grieving when someone said he'd been seen walking Eliza Potts home from chapel; but the main source of the darkness was in Lily. She was little more than a shadow, quietly going about her life.

Quietly – that was the disturbing thing. Lily had never been quiet for long; she was naturally exuberant, both in joy and in distress. Now she was like a mouse. She never sang, or laughed, or cried – not in front of Jess, anyway. It was because of Mr Haverleigh, Jess guessed.

Gossip had whispered many different tales about Clemency Clare's absence. Now it had as many opinions about her sudden return. Only Lily had nothing to say on the subject. Whatever the truth, the fact was that Miss Clare announced her engagement to Ashton Haverleigh only a day or two after the Belladay Ball. The wedding was to take place at Christmastide, the first service to be celebrated in the newly refurbished church at Syderford. And, though Lily wouldn't talk about it, Jess knew that the coming wedding was a prime cause of her melancholy.

Another cause was the loss of Gyp. Learning that her pet was dead seemed to have been the last straw for Lily. She had lost everything – home, family, lover, position in life, and now her pet. So she gave up fighting and accepted her fate. She devoted all her time and attention to Bella, organising lessons and pastimes to keep the sickly child occupied. But it was all done dutifully, without any of her usual ebullience. She didn't even complain when Lady Maud sent a bolt of grey cloth up to the nursery suite. Instead, she helped Jess to cut out and sew some plain dresses which she then took to wearing constantly – she who had sworn she would never wear grey.

Jess fretted about her, but Lily was shut in with her grief and wouldn't talk about it. She didn't even tell her secrets to her journal; during those months the only entries were sketchy notes and reminders, not the usual outpouring of all her deepest hopes and wishes and despairs.

The two young women did, however, have one conversation which stuck in Jess's memory. One evening, as they sat sewing by candlelight, Lily said, 'It takes nine months for a baby to come, doesn't it?'

Jess started, glancing covertly at her friend's slender figure. For a moment she feared... then she remembered that Lily's 'curse' had come last week, on schedule; Jess had found the bloody rags soaking in their usual bucket. 'That's what they reckon.'

'Is it always nine months? I mean... how long is it before you realise you're that way? When does it start to show?'

She questioned Jess closely on the time-scale of pregnancy and Jess realised she must be thinking of Clemency. In June, Clemency had declared herself pregnant; in September she returned as if nothing had happened, except that she was thinner, and high-strung, from all accounts. Whatever had happened, the three months had not been easy.

''Course,' Jess said slowly. 'Things do go wrong, 'times.'

Lily's head came up sharply, candleflame dancing in her narrowed eyes. 'For instance?'

'Could be the little 'un come too soon, afore that's ready. So that miscarry, or gets born dead – stillborn, they say. And... 'times when the baby en't wanted for some reason, well...'

'Well?'

'Well... there's ways.'

Catching her breath, Lily threw down her sewing. 'Tell me!'

Jess looked down at her work, pulling it to straighten the seam. 'You can get it cut out of you,' she said bluntly. 'There's women as'll do that, for a price. If you hen't got the price, then...' Her flesh turned cold as she remembered – her mother hadn't had the price. 'Then you can do it yourself.'

'How?'

'There's ways,' Jess said, her throat clogged with awful memories. 'That's dangerous, though. That don't alluss work. You can hurt yourself bad. Even kill yourself.' She was staring into the past, seeing again the blood glistening in the lamplight, and her mother so pale, trying to smile, whispering, '*Forgive me, Jess.*'

Because of Merrywest. Merrywest! God damn his evil soul.

Lily stared at her, inwardly squirming. She only half understood what Jess was saying, but it sickened her. Clemency would never have tried to kill her child. Would she?

Lily shook herself; she couldn't bear to think about it. Whatever had happened, Clemency was a ruined woman now, her reputation in tatters; no decent man would want a wife with such a history. So Ash was obliged to marry her, to 'make an honest woman of her', because he was the one who had debauched her. There was no doubt of it. It was the only explanation. Whether he loved Clemency or not, his family, and the Clares, had forced him to do the honourable thing.

Honourable! That was a fine word. The Honourable Ashton Haverleigh had proved himself nothing but a heartless, deceiving liar.

Though she sometimes wept at night her tears were more for her own stupidity than for love betrayed; she saw now what a fool she had been, enamoured of a dream, letting it blind her to the reality of the man. But she sorely missed the dream. And she sorely missed the comforts of loving.

–

After a while, when Nanny's room had been redecorated with sprigged wallpaper and brown paint, Lily moved in there, across the far side of the schoolroom. Jess missed the company; already out of favour in the servants' hall, she'd come to enjoy her closeness with Lily, but now she was alone again after she went to bed.

Lily felt lonely too, and nervous. At first she found it hard to sleep; she kept hearing noises, covert footsteps and breathing. Sometimes she thought she was being watched.

'Oh, that's just this old house,' Jess said. 'That do creak and groan and sigh to itself.'

'Yes,' Lily would say gravely, 'of course,' though she was convinced the noises had other causes. In the evenings, after the lamps were lit, any slight sound would make her start and peer into dark corners. She was haunted by the tale of the dead heir, young Harry Fyncham, and by thoughts of Nanny dying all alone in that same room where she herself now slept.

The room was fresh and clean now. Mrs Roberts had found some nice pieces of furniture for her to use; Lily's own belongings made it homely, and Jess's needle had added prettiness in new curtains and bedcovers. But Lily still felt it was Nanny's room, not hers. Though that awful smell had gone, at times Lily fancied a whiff of it lingered.

-

In November, Reverend Hugh Clare left Hewing for his new post in York. Though Lily affected not to care, that parting was another wrench. She went several times to the rectory to collect the rest of her belongings, packing them herself, refusing to allow Eliza anywhere near her. Eliza and her brother had killed Gyp – Lily knew it, but she was helpless to do anything about it. Every time she visited that sad little grave, in the place she thought of as 'the heart of the wood', where Rudd had erected a wooden cross carved with Gyp's name, Lily sat and numbly wondered what further wounds life could deal her.

As her adoptive father took his final leave of her, he presented her with twenty pounds, 'to tide you over. However, after this I expect you to stand on your own feet, as many young women of humble birth are obliged to do. You have been fortunate, Lily Victoria. I hope you will remember that, and not call further on me – or on my nephew and his family.'

He was disowning her, abandoning her, but that came as no surprise. She was a foundling brat who had proved herself a disloyal, ungrateful, recalcitrant daughter – and who, moreover, had become an embarrassment because of her open admiration for a man who was soon to become her cousin's husband. The Clares had closed ranks to exclude her.

She had thought she was beyond hurt. But the pain went on.

The Dunnocks, Peter and his mother, soon moved into the rectory and, since they brought with them the housemaid they had employed for years, they dispensed with Eliza's services. Jess and Lily thought this a fitting end for Eliza until, to their astonishment, she was taken on as head laundry maid at the big house. Reverend Clare had organised the move, it seemed, and written a glowing reference extolling the maid's virtues. Since she went home every night, the new job did keep her well away from the nursery, but it didn't stop her spreading her vitriol, repeating and enlarging on slanders against Lily and Jess and dropping hints about Matty, too. The Pottses didn't believe in forgiveness – once they found an enemy, he remained an enemy.

Jess couldn't believe that the rector had so highly recommended a maid whom he knew to be bone idle, disrespectful and unreliable. But when she mentioned it to Miss Peartree that lady refused to discuss it – indeed, she seemed embarrassed by the whole business – and Lily only shook her head and made a pale smile: when her whole world had gone awry, what did one more stupidity matter?

The departure of Reverend Clare did, however, bring one or two small blessings. When the squire heard that Miss Peartree had nowhere to go, he invited her to become his tenant in Park Lodge – the house he had intended for Nanny – and he kindly asked only a minimum rent in keeping with the small income Miss Peartree received from a legacy. Lily and Bella often walked to the lodge of an afternoon, when the weather allowed, and sometimes Miss Peartree came up to share a nursery tea. She employed little Dolly Upton as her maid-of-all-work and the two got along happily. Thanks to the squire, the old lady looked forward to ending her days in tolerable ease.

Another unexpected comfort for Lily was her rediscovery of the old, faded rush basket in which she had been found as a baby on the doorstep. She kept it by her, using it for her sewing, and though the gold bangle was too precious to wear often she did put on her string of amber beads now and then. They were a link with her real parents, especially the father she had so long looked for.

With so many dreams shattered, she knew that this one too might turn out a fantasy, but she couldn't let it go entirely. The amber beads were a symbol of that last, tiny, flickering hope. '*Your heart's desire*,' the gypsy had promised and, after all, her very oldest, dearest wish was to find her real father.

–

On the Monday before Christmas, Hewinghall held its Servants' Ball. The occasion followed the pattern of the Belladay Ball, being held in the great hall, with the same orchestra engaged. Everyone who worked for the estate, in whatever capacity, had been invited.

Although Lily had donated one of her own dresses to be made-over to fit Jess, when the day arrived Jess decided not to attend. She didn't feel comfortable with the other servants any more; since Eliza had joined the household the atmosphere below stairs had become even more chilly – Merrywest had started the decay and now Eliza was continuing it. 'No smoke without fire' seemed to be the general opinion, though there were a few who still supported Jess, including George the footman and Mrs Roberts, who had warmed again to Jess because she had soon seen through Eliza and wished she had never let the squire persuade her to find the girl a job. Eliza was good at bossing the others around, not so good at turning her own hands to useful work, and she was a disruptive influence. Mrs Roberts had remarked one day in Jess's hearing, 'I really can't understand what Mr Rudd sees in that girl. It's not like him to be so blind.'

That was another thing Jess preferred to avoid – the sight of Eliza Potts being squired by Reuben Rudd at the Servants' Ball. But her admitted excuse was that she couldn't leave Bella, whose latest cold had left her with a hacking cough.

'But I shall be here,' Lily said. 'I've neither energy nor heart for dancing. You go. Matty will be there. And Mr Rudd. You like Mr Rudd.'

'I 'spect he've put his name all over Eliza's card,' Jess replied tartly. 'They're walkin' out, so I hear.'

'Well, there's that handsome footman – George, isn't it? He always seems to stick out his chest when he sees you. You can't let Eliza win, you know. Please go to the party. One of us ought to be enjoying herself tonight. After the trouble we took to get that dress right...'

That dress... It had been one of Lily's least favourites, seldom worn because she didn't like the coffee-and-cream colours of the satin and old lace. But on Jess it brought out the fair lights in her hair and emphasised her tawny eyes and handspan waist. Looking at her reflection in the long cheval glass in Lily's room, Jess hardly knew the elegant creature who stared back at her, shoulders white against the froth of creamy lace, workworn hands disguised by a pair of Lily's evening gloves.

Perhaps half an hour wouldn't hurt.

She crept down the back stairs in a turmoil of nerves and made her way to the main staircase hall. Noise and laughter spilled from the great hall. The hidden door to the gallery was open, with the same orchestra up there merrily sawing away. Hearing someone coming, Jess slipped through the 'hidden' door and went slowly up the stairs. One or two of the musicians gave her a smiling glance as she hung back, trying to see what was going on below without herself being seen.

The chandelier was a blaze of candles, as it had been for the Belladay Ball, and at first glance the company below might have been the same too. The great hall whirled with couples executing a lively polka; others stood about gossiping and observing. Sir Richard was dancing with Mrs Roberts, while Lady Maud sat out, chatting with the oldest of her grooms. Other ladies and gentlemen must be the house guests who had arrived early for Christmas, all mingling merrily with servants decked in their best. Some of the maidservants' dresses had originated in Lady Maud's wardrobe; Mr Longman looked resplendent in his best white tie and tails, while the footmen had donned their livery of blue coats with gold braid, silk breeches and white stockings; the other men wore their Sunday-best suits.

Jess saw Matty dancing with Sal Gooden, though he wasn't paying her much attention; he was watching the door – watching for Lily, Jess guessed. Poor Matty was getting ever more besotted with Lily, ever since he'd 'rescued' her, as he called it.

But everything else faded as she saw Reuben Rudd, hardly recognisable in a dark cloth suit, candlelight bringing out red glints in his thick hair and his skin extra brown against the whiteness of his shirt. Her heart seemed to wrench in her breast at the sight of him. Just as she had feared, he had Eliza in his arms. Wearing scarlet satin, she was laughing, flirting in that way she had, tossing her head and flicking her green eyes. Rudd was smiling, aware of her ruses but still captivated by her. Seeing how close he held her, Jess leaned against the wall, fighting a wave of jealousy so bitter that it made her throat hurt. No, she wouldn't shed tears – if Reuben was such a fool as to let himself be misled by a woman's wiles, then he wasn't the man Jess had thought him to be. She refused to waste time sighing over him.

She turned away, making for the stairs, knowing it had been a mistake to come. Her legs felt like lead and she had to put a hand on the wall to steady herself. What she wanted to do was sit down right there where no one could see her and howl her eyes out.

Then the door at the foot of the stairs opened and George the footman was smiling up at her, all crooked teeth and blue velvet coat, his even-featured face flushed from ale. 'I thought I spied you. My, don't you look grand! Come on, Jess, you're missing all the dancing.'

'I en't in no mood for dancing,' said Jess. 'Get you out o' my way, George. I'm goin' back where I belong.'

'Not until you've danced one dance with me. Oh, come on, Jess. One twirl around the floor. It *is* Christmas! Don't you want to show off that dress? You look a real queen.'

Aware that if she argued he might try more physical persuasion, and in that confined space she couldn't escape him, Jess reluctantly agreed: 'All right. One dance. I told Miss Lily I'd only be half an hour.'

The orchestra had just struck up an eightsome reel. Jess didn't know the steps, but George dragged her into a set which, weaving and circling and briefly changing partners as the pattern wove on, included Reuben Rudd and Eliza. She'd seen the gratifying surprise in Reuben's eyes when he'd first spotted her; it had told her she looked her best, but somehow it only made her feel angry with him. Angry, and hurt, and hopelessly heart-sore. Though she tried to concentrate on the dance, all she could think of were the moments when his arm spanned her waist and whirled her round before passing her on.

When the music ended, Jess found herself being propelled by George towards a table where men were queuing for a turn at the barrel of ale while ladies accepted glasses of fruit punch.

'Jess.' Matty pushed his way among the throng and grasped her arm. 'Where's Miss Lily? I've been—'

'Hey now, Henefer,' George objected.

Matty drew himself up, glaring under a lick of rough brown hair. 'I'm speakin' to my sister. Mind you your own matters, you great fancy mawkin.'

Big as the footman was, he hadn't Matty's muscle; he stood and glowered as Jess was led away. Everybody knew by now that Matty was her brother and that, at least, was a relief.

The great hall was quieter now; the supper interval had been declared and the orchestra was taking a break. Where was Rudd? Jess hadn't seen him since the reel ended, but she was conscious that he couldn't be far away.

Steering her into a spot shaded by potted palms, Matty again demanded to know where Lily was. 'I've got somethin' for her. A Christmas present. I'd give it her Christmas Day, on'y I'm off tomorrow.'

Work in the gardens being slack, Matty had been laid off until the spring, so he was heading for Lynn, to see the family and maybe to find work on the boats, if he was lucky. Jess was going to miss him.

Concealing a surge of homesickness, she said, 'What sort of present can *you* give a lady like Miss Lily?'

'It's a bracelet. To match that necklace she's been a-wearin' lately.'

'What? Why... where'd you get the money for amber beads?'

'Never you mind where I got it.' Matty had that stubborn look on his face, and the telltale brick-red flush of guilt creeping up his neck and ears. He took a package out of his pocket, wrapped in red paper and done up with green ribbon. 'You give her that, come Christmas.' Another pocket yielded a package in blue paper, ribboned in pink. 'And that's for you.'

Jess eyed the packets dubiously. 'You hen't stole them, have you?'

'What d'you take me for?'

Shaking her head, she looked up at him, thinking that she took him for a great foolish lummox, but she loved him dearly. He meant well. He wasn't bad, just easily led. As to his infatuation with Miss Lily...

'Don't you know by now she en't never goin' to look twice at you?'

'Why not? What's wrong with me?'

'En't nothin' wrong with you, you great fool,' she sighed. 'Not for the right girl. Somebody like Sal, now...'

'It en't Sal I want. She's a good old girl, but she don't... well, you know. And you're wrong about Miss Lily.' Glancing around to make sure he wasn't overheard, he informed her in an undertone, 'She let me kiss her – and she kissed me back – that night I found her by the rectory.'

'Matty!' Jess was horrified.

'It's true!' he insisted. 'Oh, I know she was upset, and all confused, but she wouldn't a let me get so near if she'd no regard for me. See, Jess Know-it-all – you en't so sharp as you reckon.'

'You're askin' for a whole lot of heartache,' she said sadly. 'But thanks for the present, Matty.' She reached up on tip-toe, leaning on his arm to pull him down so she could kiss his cheek. 'Wish I was goin' home with you. Give them my love, won't you? Tell them I'll be over to see them some day, when I can. And you... you take care of your great daft self.' She'd always felt his coming to Hewinghall was a mistake but now she wondered if this might be the last time she would see him. If he went back to sea, in the winter storms… Besides, Merrywest was in Lynn.

'Mind you steer clear of Preacher Merrywest,' she begged. 'En't no point in makin' more trouble.'

'We'll see about that,' said Matty. 'I want to know what he mean by all these tales. Why'd he say such things about you?'

'I've told you…' Oh, how could she explain without risking the safety of her whole family? 'Matty, trust me. Please—'

'You're off then, Henefer.' Reuben Rudd strode up to them, holding out his hand, all bluff friendliness. 'I wish you a right Merry Christmas, and a Good New Year. You'll be back come the spring?'

'I thought I might. See how it go.'

'I could do with a good man on *my* team,' Rudd said blandly. 'Fancy a spot of keepering, do you?'

Matty goggled at him. 'Well, Mr Rudd…'

What was Rudd playing at? Jess wondered. Was the offer just a taunt, or a genuine flag of truce now that Matty had fallen out with Jim Potts?

'Think about it,' Rudd said. 'But remember it's long hours and hard work. I'm off just now to get changed before I relieve old Obi. It may be Christmas, but the poachers don't rest. Well… good night.'

For the first time he let his eyes meet Jess's, stunning her with the force of a grave glance that searched her soul, setting her skin afire and her lips tingling. Before she knew what he intended, he stepped forward, lifted her chin and kissed her full on those soft, waiting lips, murmured, 'Merry Christmas,' and strode away across the polished floor.

'Oh, now, that explain it,' said Matty in disgust. 'He're had too much of the squire's free ale!'

Every pore in Jess's body seemed to be steaming as she touched a gloved hand to her awakened mouth. Had she imagined it, or had she read regret in Rudd, perhaps an apology, perhaps a promise? All of those things remained with her, making her heartbeat unsteady and her breathing erratic. She became aware of other people, some in the doorway, little groups about the room, more returning in the hope of further dancing. How many of them had seen Rudd kiss her? Had he intended them to see? Across yards of space she encountered Eliza's glance, chilly green as Arctic seas. It made her pause, sobering in the

294

instant before a chirrup of sheer joy lightened her spirits and made her turn to Matty with a smile.

'I reckon he meant it, Matty – he want you to be a keeper. Maybe he hope that'll keep you out of mischief.'

Eliza was still glaring. Jess let her smile widen, seeing how it maddened the other girl. Well, well. If Eliza was so sadly jealous then the gossips must be wrong about her and Rudd. It had been worth coming to the party just to know that, and to have the memory of that brief, telling kiss. It would fuel her dreams for weeks to come.

–

Though Lily neither expected nor received an invitation to the wedding of her 'cousin' and the Honourable Ashton Haverleigh, which was to take place on Christmas Eve, as the date approached she could think of little else. Since the autumn, she had had little contact with the Clares, save for a letter or two from Aunt Jane Gittens, penned in Miss Wilks's copperplate, which told about Ching's doings and expressed understanding that Lily's new post kept her from visiting the Manor. Evidently the Clares had made excuses to explain Lily's absence; they had not told the old lady that Lily was no longer regarded as a member of the family.

On the night before the wedding, Lily took sick with nausea and a feverish headache; she languished in her bed for forty-eight hours, hardly even rallying for Christmas Day. She was pleased with Matty's gift of amber beads, though not curious about the reasons for their giving. She could think of nothing but the fact that Clemency Clare had become the Honourable Mrs Ashton Haverleigh.

The Sunday following, being a sudden mild day with all the promise of a false spring, Lily, Jess and Bella took an afternoon stroll. Guided by Lily, they came to the newly refurbished Syderford church, where a carved stone plaque recently set into the wall declared: 'This building was restored by Oliver Clare and his wife Letitia, of Syderford Manor, 1892'. Lily read it out, her face grey as the sky, making Jess worry that she'd come out too soon after her illness.

'You all right, miss?' she asked.

And Lily just looked at her, those strange eyes empty of all emotion, like gazing down into a pair of deep wells, one in brown shade, one blue with sunlight, both calm but for a tiny flicker at the bottom – a flicker of black pain. Jess sometimes thought that was Lily's soul she could glimpse down there. Lily's soul, trapped and screaming...

–

That impossible winter had one more dart to throw at Lily: in the early part of February, Aunt Jane Gittens died. Though deep snow lay on the ground, Lily walked to Syderford church for the service, determined to pay her last respects whatever the Clares thought.

She sat at the back of the church, where she was joined by a desolated Miss Wilks, who was now also displaced: she was intending to go and live with a married niece and her family, in the northern metropolis of Leeds, in a small terraced house which already had five people in it and another baby on the way. Lily felt sorry for her, but her main concern was Ash and Clemency. A part of her would have welcomed a confrontation with them, but neither of them was there.

'They're away,' Miss Wilks whispered. 'Visiting his great-uncle in Derbyshire – hoping to beg money off him, if you ask me. Our Miss Clemency is furious that her husband's not as wealthy as she thought. She expected him to draw on his inheritance once he was married, but it's tied up until his great-uncle dies, and his great-uncle's a healthy man. Turned seventy, but just married a young wife. If he gets a son of his own, that'll really put Mr Ashton's nose out of joint. Serve him right, too – and her.'

Now that Aunt Jane was dead, Miss Wilks's resentment was being given full rein. 'What will happen to Ching?' Lily asked. 'Will you take him?'

'That I will not! You know he hates me – and it's an entirely mutual antipathy, I assure you. No, Miss Gittens has left him to you.'

'To me?' Lily was astonished.

'Well, the Clares don't want him.'

And so Ching, the wayward, beautiful, spoiled feline, came to reside in the nursery suite at Hewinghall, because no one could bear to think of his being destroyed. The rooftops became his kingdom, where he lay in wait behind twisted chimney stacks and terrorised birds. When he prowled along the parapet with his tail high even Bella loved to watch him. His proud pacing robbed the roof of some of the horror it held for her.

Ching would never own a mistress, but he condescended to allow Bella to pet him, and he would often stay in her room, lying with her on her bed, until she was asleep. His presence comforted and calmed her and after he arrived she no longer suffered so badly with nightmares, nor did she walk in her sleep. Some said she was growing out of those afflictions, but Jess and Lily liked to think it was Ching who made the difference.

–

Shortly before Easter, the Fynchams – all three of them – went on a visit to Gillingherry Hall, in Kent, where Lady Maud's sister and her family lived. Gillingherry had a full nursery, four children under ten, with a nanny, a governess, and a complement of nurserymaids, so neither Lily nor Jess was required on the visit. Bella travelled under the charge of the lady's maid and the valet. In her absence, Lily was given leave to have a holiday: Jess used the time to spring-clean the nursery.

Lily would have gone walking but the cold, wet weather prevented her and boredom made her depression grow deeper. Occasionally she went to see Miss Peartree; at other times she stood at the attic window for hours, staring out in a grey reverie, or sat reading her *Young Ladies' Journal*. The serials in that paper were of a romantic nature; having them read aloud made Jess's floor-scrubbing and furniture-polishing that much lighter.

In the evenings, much to Jess's delight, Lily at last found time to listen to her efforts at reading. Slowly, the printed word was starting to convey meaning for her, though squinting by lamplight made her eyes ache after a while – all close work seemed to give her a headache.

'I think you need glasses,' Lily said, which horrified Jess. If she had to wear glasses Reuben Rudd would probably never look at her again.

'I'm plain enough already, Miss Lily.'

And Lily looked at her in vague surprise. 'Vanity, Jess? I thought you were above such things.'

They had talked about going to the Easter Monday Fair again, but when the day dawned in a steady downpour from a leaden sky Jess settled down to do some repairs on the winter curtains she had just brought back from the drying room, resigning herself to yet more eye-strain. Lily tried to read one of her library novels, but eventually threw it aside, crying, 'I shall go mad if I don't go out!' She went to her room and emerged wearing her galoshes and macintosh cape, an umbrella in her hand. 'I'm going for a walk. I'm going to see Cousin Oriana.'

The door slammed behind her and her galoshes fell heavy on the thin runner along the passageway, the sound growing fainter until the door at the top of the back stairs closed. Jess let the silence gather round her, enjoying it. She, too, would indulge in some free time today, once the curtains were mended.

Going down to the servants' hall for lunch, she found the talk all about the evangelical crusade which was taking place in the area. Meetings had been held in barns and farmyards as well as chapels, bringing the Good News to the country folk. That afternoon, a gathering was planned on the shore at Martham. Several of the Hewinghall staff were going.

'Why don't you come with us, Jess?' George the footman suggested.

'I've got work to do,' Jess said.

One of the under-laundrymaids, a follower of Eliza, remarked to herself, 'Thought she had a fancy for preachers.'

'That's enough!' Mrs Roberts snapped. 'I won't have backhouse gossip repeated at my table.'

'How about news from Syderford, then?' Sal Gooden put in, coming to Jess's aid. 'The Haverleighs are back – and suckin' sorrow by pailfuls, so it seem. She en't speakin' to him, and when she do, she do nothin' but mob and minify.'

While Jess appreciated the change of subject, the news only served to worry her. If the Haverleighs' marriage was in trouble, would that Mr Ashton come sniffing round Miss Lily again?

During the afternoon the weather cleared, clouds moving away to let the sun shine through. Jess went out on to the roof to savour it, leaning on the broad stone parapet and gazing out across the park as she wondered how the Martham evangelical meeting was going. Was Merrywest himself there that afternoon? Eliza had made sure that Jess heard about the posters and bills that were going up everywhere, announcing that the main preacher of the weekend was to be Nathanael Merrywest, of Lynn.

Matty, too, on his recent return, had confirmed that Merrywest planned to bring spiritual enlightenment to this benighted corner of Norfolk. 'It hen't got nothin' to do with you, though. Honest, Jess, he have forgiven you. He say that's now up to you to seek forgiveness from the Lord. He'll be glad to see you at one o' his meetings, and if you feel the call he'll welcome you.'

'I'm sure he would,' Jess had said, a taste like metal in her mouth.

Merrywest was a master of tactics, always careful to keep his public face clean. He was praised as one of the best preachers on the Lynn circuit, whose words could make the most hardened sinner fall on his knees and repent. He walked miles to spread the message; he taught Bible classes and Sunday school; he was a good landlord to those who were his tenants, a good husband to his quiet, nondescript wife and two quiet, well-behaved children. A fine, God-fearing, upstanding man was Preacher Merrywest. Everyone said so.

But little no-account Jess Henefer knew better. She knew the Sunday saint was a weekday devil, brutal, rapacious, unfeeling, with a conscience made of stretching leather. But how could she prove it – her word against his? Words were his weapons and his armour. She could never compete.

The thoughts broke off as she saw someone coming at a run along the drive. It looked like Matty, and evidently his mission was urgent. There hadn't been another accident, had there? Not Rudd…

She waved and called, but Matty didn't see her perched so high up on the roof. He went out of sight behind the west wing, making for the kitchen courtyard.

Jess climbed back through the window and went to find out what was amiss. In Little Africa, she encountered Sal Gooden, who was coming to find her with half a tale about some mishap, Lily falling into a pond and needing a change of clothes. They'd taken her to Rudd's cottage.

Having dashed upstairs to pack a basket with fresh clothes from Lily's room, Jess found that Matty had gone on, not waiting for her.

Though the sun was now out, the woods were dripping, branches springing droplets as she brushed by, undergrowth crackling, birds stirring and starting. It took her a good half hour to get to Rudd's cottage, by which time her boots and skirts were soaked. In the garden the broody hens were again sitting on pheasant eggs in their crates, safe behind wire enclosures.

Jess had no time to take it all in. First Dash came charging down the path to greet her, then Matty was there, near beside himself with worry, wanting to know what had kept her.

'I came as quick as I could!' Jess exclaimed. 'If you'd a waited, to tell me what this is all about—'

'It's Miss Lily!' He dragged a hand through his hair, leaving it standing up in greater disarray than usual. 'I had to get back to her. I was frit—'

Jess was stepping into the kitchen, meeting Reuben Rudd's steady gaze. It stopped her, telling her things that made her feel cold.

'She's all right,' he said, though the look on his face belied the words. 'There's an old wives' tale about that pond being bottomless, but it's nobbut four feet deep, even at the middle. Obi found her in time.'

'She just fell in!' Matty said.

Rudd afforded him a sympathetic look. 'Happen she did, lad. Happen she did. Any road up, she was soaked right through, and she's worn out, but she's sleeping now. I reckon she'll do. Thanks for coming, lass. She'll be glad to see thee.'

Jess stared at him, not wanting to understand. What was he implying – that Lily had tried to kill herself? 'Where is she?'

'I put her in my bed – it's the only one that's aired.'

Twenty-Three

Lily lay flat on her back, the covers pulled up to her chin and her hair swathed in a towel from which a few damp tendrils escaped to cluster round a face that was almost as white as the sheets. Hearing Jess's footsteps she opened her eyes and tried a wan smile. 'Jess.'

'Now, what's to do?' Concerned for the pain written clear on the beautiful face, Jess sat on the edge of the bed. 'You shouldn't've been out walkin' in this wet. No wonder you got soaked. Did you slip and fall?'

Lily blinked, a tear dripping down her temple. 'Is that what they told you? Oh, Jess… I thought I might as well walk into that bottomless pond and sink into oblivion. But it wasn't deep enough!' A bubble of painful laughter burst out of her. 'I couldn't even do that right.'

'Thank the Lord!' Jess said sternly. 'You didn't mean it.'

'I *did* mean it,' Lily wept. 'I can't bear it, Jess. Ash and Clemency are back. And she's having a child. Cousin Oriana told me. It's as if nothing had happened between him and me – as if I had never existed. Their life goes on, and mine…'

'Yours go on, too! 'Course it do. Forget them. You've got other friends. Me, and Miss Bella. And Miss Peartree, and Dolly. And Mr Rudd, and Mrs Roberts. Why, everybody at Hewinghall think the world of you. And some love you, if on'y you'd pay them mind. Take our Matty now…'

More tears swelled in Lily's eyes, blurring their colours as she turned aside, croaking, 'Oh, *Jess!*' and bit on the sheet to stifle her desolate laughter.

–

Leaving Lily sleeping, Jess crept downstairs and found Matty toying with a plate of rabbit stew. The savoury aroma from a pot over the fire filled the room, making Jess feel hungry.

'Where's Rudd?' she asked.

'Gone off on his rounds. How's Miss Lily?'

'Sadly. What're we goin' to do, Matty? I shall have to get back, else there'll be more talk, but I can't leave Miss Lily alone here.'

'Well, we'll see what Mr Rudd say when he get back. He say you're to eat, if you want. The stew's good.'

He was right about the stew. With a chunk of Mrs Obi's crusty bread it went down a treat and made Jess feel better. She'd almost forgotten how peaceful it was in Rudd's cottage, with the woods sighing beyond the door, the hens clucking as they brooded, the old clock tick-tocking steadily.

She had lit the kitchen lamps by the time Rudd came back for his own supper. He sat at the table eating while Jess and Matty remained either side of the fire.

'Best thing you can do, lad,' Rudd said to Matty, 'is go explain to Mrs Roberts that Miss Lily's had a fall and she's staying here tonight. Jess can stay with her – no, it's all right, I'll not be here. I shall be out all night, keeping watch. You can come back here yourself, to save leaving the ladies alone. Better get off now. The sooner you're back, the sooner I can be about my work.'

Matty left, taking a lantern to light his way. Finding herself alone with Reuben Rudd for the first time in months, Jess stared at the fire, feeling self-conscious, wishing she had something to do with her hands.

'Shall I make some more tea?' she asked.

'Aye, if you like.' He was cutting an uneven wedge of bread to mop up the remains of his stew.

Jess busied herself with the tea, trying to ignore Rudd, but his presence was a burning reality prickling all her nerves.

After a while, he said quietly, 'Like old times.'

Jess stopped, poised over the singing kettle with the tea pot in her hand. 'You reckon?'

'No.' He sounded rueful, and when she looked at him he gave her a wry smile. 'I'm making conversation, lass, that's what it is.'

'Then don't trouble. I en't here to be entertained.' She turned her back on him again, watching the steaming kettle.

Unexpectedly, he said, 'I've missed thee, lass.'

Jess stared at the fire, seeing the red heart of it shiver and go shapeless through tears as she cleared her throat. 'Is our Matty now workin' for you?'

Rudd hesitated, then sighed as he accepted the rebuff. 'Aye, when I need him. He's not a bad worker. He's willing to learn.'

That was true, Jess thought wryly. Trouble was, Matty didn't much care who he learned from: his mates down the 'Admiral Nelson', Jim Potts, or Reuben Rudd, it was all the same.

'At least he was bright enough to see through Jim Potts,' Rudd added.

'And Eliza.'

The silence seemed to stretch, then just as the kettle was coming to a full boil, bubbling and spitting, Jess heard him sigh, 'Aye. And Eliza.' Wondering if she dared believe her ears, she looked over her shoulder and encountered his sombre gaze. 'I think I knew, any road,' he said. 'I tried to give her the benefit of the doubt, but after Matty told me... Are you making that tea, lass, or letting the water boil away?'

Snatching up the pot-holder, Jess filled the teapot, rattled the lid into place and carried it to the table. 'What did Matty tell you?'

'About them using the rectory for hiding birds overnight. I knew they must have a place, but I didn't think they'd have the gall to use the rectory – well, not until what happened to Gyp. That set me wondering. But I still didn't believe Eliza had owt to do with it. I should have listened to you, lass. Happen I might have, if you'd said it more plainly.'

'You din't want to hear.'

'I was trying to keep an open mind.'

'Oh, hum? Is that why you walk her to chapel?'

Rudd sat up. 'Who says I do? That's a downright lie! Eliza doesn't go to chapel – you know that. Have you ever seen her there? You've been listening to idle gossip, Jess Henefer.'

'It wan't gossip when you squired her at the Christmas Ball!'

'I was just keeping in with her, to find out what she knew. She has a soft spot for me—'

'And you for her!'

After a moment, he said slowly, 'I'll not deny I've an eye for a pretty woman – the same way I've an eye for a good dog, or a cock pheasant in his mating feathers, or a tree in new leaf, or a sunset. I appreciate beautiful things. That's why I noticed *thee*, Jess.'

'Squit!' she flung at him.

A suspicion of a twinkle started deep in his eyes. 'You reckon?' he teased her, using her own words.

Jess felt as though hot water was being trickled all over her. 'Yes, I do so reckon, Reuben Rudd. Oh… you're a-tyin' me up in knots just cos I en't so clever as you. Do you now—' The words broke off as a hysterical cry stabbed through the cottage: 'Jess! *Jess!*' Forgetting everything but the fact that Lily needed her, Jess ran for the stairs.

Lily had woken out of bad dreams and, in the darkness, hadn't known where she was. 'I hate the dark. I hate it, Jess! Light the lamp for me.'

By the time Jess had settled her down, brought her tea and then some stew – because she was ravenously hungry all of a sudden – Matty had returned and Rudd had gone to keep his night vigil for egg thieves.

Sharing the double bed with Lily, Jess found it hard to sleep. She couldn't forget whose bed she was lying in, and the warmth of Lily beside her made her wonder what it might be like to lie here with Rudd: the closeness, the comforting cosiness of lying together and talking about their day; then kissing, and… Her eyes snapped open as cold sweat broke from every pore. Even trying to imagine it made her brain explode with panic and her body curl up to repel invasion. She could never be a real woman, never a wife like Rudd deserved and needed.

–

No one at Hewinghall questioned Lily's 'accident'. They were, anyway, more interested in what had happened at the evangelical meeting at Martham Staithe: Merrywest had preached up a storm, warning so strongly of the consequences of sin that two women had seen visions and fainted; a child had been sick and so terrified himself that Merrywest had had to cast out the devil in him; the landlord of the 'Admiral Nelson' had thrown himself into the tide-flooded creek seeking instant baptism, and half a hundred souls had gone forward claiming to have 'seen the light'.

Among those half hundred had been Eliza Potts.

'That came over me all at once,' she declared to anyone who would listen. 'All I hear was this voice, cryin' out, "Repent! Repent!" and that struck me to the heart. I fell on my knees. Seemed as how the clouds all rolled away and there was this brightness. Then I seen the preacher, and he lay his hand on me and a whole weight of sin fell off of me. *You* ought to be saved, too.'

It was hard to decide which was the least attractive – the old, malicious Eliza or this new saintly exhorter. Knowing she'd been Saved, she pitied and derided those less fortunate. She also became a regular at chapel – which made Jess wonder if the conversion was yet another attempt to impress Reuben Rudd.

In the week after Easter, the Fynchams returned from Kent. Jess was delighted to have young Bella back and Lily too seemed glad to resume the routine of lessons. Bella hadn't enjoyed the rough and tumble of her four cousins; she preferred her own quiet nursery, where she felt at ease with Lily and Jess, and where Ching was always willing to be petted.

The cat won his immortality when he came to be included in a portrait of Bella which Sir Richard commissioned. The artist, Mr Anstruther, felt inspired to portray the child with the cat on her lap and Ching, seeming aware of the honour, indulged his human friends by posing sedately – for an hour, or two minutes, as the mood took him.

On an afternoon when a few thin streaks of rain spotted the window, Lily sipped tea and watched the clock. Time seemed to move particularly slowly when she and Bella were in the private drawing room. Those times were trying for Bella, too; she desperately wanted to please her mother, but every day she managed to do something wrong.

That day, when the child stumbled for a tenth time over a passage of reading, Lady Maud snatched the book from her. 'She's not improving!'

'She's nervous,' Lily said.

'Nervous?' Lady Maud's eyes glittered dangerously.

'I think,' Sir Richard intervened, strolling across the room from his stance by the window, 'that Bella is tired. After all, she spent two hours this morning posing for Mr Anstruther. We know she can read much better than that. Can't you, my love?'

'I was trying very hard, Papa,' Bella said plaintively.

'Yes, of course you were. And you were doing very well.'

Her ladyship was still glaring at Lily, who felt sure that another tirade on her shortcomings as a teacher was about to ensue. Fortunately a maid interrupted with news that Lady Maud's favourite mare was about to foal. Lady Maud was on her feet and on her way to the door before the girl had finished speaking.

'I shall go and change. I must be there. Well, Bella – there's to be a new foal. Tomorrow I shall take you to see it. Perhaps I shall allow you to give it a name.' Not giving Bella time to reply, she swept out.

Bella was looking sickly: she was terrified of horses and hated visiting the stables, a fact which infuriated her mother.

'We shall all go,' Sir Richard said, touching her hair for comfort. 'Now, why don't you run back to the nursery? I wish to have a word with Miss Clare.' At this, Lily looked up, starting out of her seat, but his smile reassured her. 'Be still, Miss Clare. This will only take a moment.'

Having bestowed her usual kiss on his cheek, Bella hurried away. Her father lowered his long body to a settee opposite Lily's, watching her with steady grey eyes.

Unable to bear that clear, perceptive regard, Lily stared at her hands, twisting them in her lap, seeing the badly bitten nails and the snags of skin caught up by embroidery needles – needlework had never been a favourite occupation. Maybe she should try making lace, or pegs, or tying bunches of lucky heather...

'I'm sorry her ladyship is not pleased with Bella's progress,' she said into the silence. 'She does work very hard. It's just...'

'Just that my daughter is not the stuff of which great intellects are made,' Sir Richard completed the thought. 'Harry was the same.'

Surprised, Lily glanced under her lashes and saw him gazing at the portrait above the mantel – a picture of a copper-haired boy wearing a sailor suit, standing under trees with a dog beside him. He looked to be about the same age as Bella was now. When her portrait was finished it would make a pair with this one of her lost brother.

'But he was an active boy,' the squire added softly. 'He loved animals. Dogs, and horses – not cats.' He shared a glance with Lily that said much. Lady Maud had adored her son because he shared her interests. She wanted to love her daughter, but she did not find Bella lovable, or compatible.

'Is the portrait going well?' he asked.

'I'm afraid I haven't studied it.' He probably knew more about the picture than did she; he seemed to be for ever appearing in the morning room while Bella was sitting for Mr Anstruther – Lily often glanced up from her sewing or reading to find the squire standing quietly in a corner. Watching her. Or so she felt. The thought made her feel hot.

'Miss Clare...' he was saying. 'Excuse my asking, but are you unwell? You seem unlike yourself. You've grown thin and silent. I'm concerned for you.'

Looking again at her hands, Lily said, 'It's kind of you to enquire, Sir Richard, but—'

'It's not kindness!' he broke in. 'It's concern. I... I care for you, Miss Clare.'

Care? The word made her lift startled eyes, vivid blue and velvet brown, the only real colour about her, enchanting in her pale face against her dark hair and the plain grey gown.

'—as I try to care for everyone in my employ,' he amplified, though his glance softened as it caressed her face. 'I wish there was something I could do. May I ask... Has your unhappiness anything to do with Ashton Haverleigh?'

Lily stared at him, the flush in her cheeks making her eyes ever more bright with dismay and the threat of tears.

'Your attachment to him was no secret, I fear,' Sir Richard said. 'Your father and Miss Peartree were both aware that you harboured hopes of Mr Haverleigh. There's no shame in that, Miss Clare. Many of us have loved unwisely, in our time.'

Feeling the blood ebb and flow in her face, she stared at him, caught by the empathy in his eyes. Everyone knew he and his wife lived separate lives. Had he agreed to a loveless marriage after being disappointed by another lady? If so, then perhaps, in a way, he did understand. But, for her, losing Ash was only part of it. For her, along with the loss and the grief of betrayal, there was shame. She had thoughtlessly thrown away her virtue: what man would want her now? She had lost everything, including her dearest dreams. There was to be no happy ending. No fond lover. No kind father...

A sob escaped her. She leapt up, knocking into the small table that held the tea tray, watching in helpless horror as it fell, throwing hot tea, and milk and sugar and pieces of porcelain, across the carpet.

'Oh, no!' she wailed.

'It's all right.' He was on his feet, coming towards her. 'It's of no account. My dear Miss Clare, don't give it another thought.'

Lily turned her back on him, grief dredging up from the black depths of her despair. She tried to contain her tears with her hands but they kept falling, running through her fingers.

'Oh, my dear,' Sir Richard murmured, drawing her gently into his arms to hold her against him.

The storm of grief ran its course and left her exhausted, clinging to the tall, comforting presence which, as her sobs lessened, she realised was a living, feeling man. His arms still circled her, supporting and strengthening her, and beneath her cheek she felt the strong beat of a heart that was not insensible to her nearness. Her own pulse began to beat in answer, sending hot blood pounding through her veins, warming her face. Her body became aware of places where it was in contact with his, her breasts hardening against his ribs, her womb tingling in response to the light pressure of his thigh on hers. Her ready awareness horrified her. He was being kind, as he would to anyone in distress. If he knew that she was thinking of him in *that* way...

Something in the way he held her told her that he, too, could feel those strong currents running. Yet he was making no attempt to let her go.

Not daring to look at him, she flexed her hands against his chest and he instantly relaxed his hold. She turned away, murmuring, 'I must go. Excuse me, Sir Richard. I must go to Bella.'

Panicked and confused, she escaped to the nursery, where she hurried across the schoolroom ignoring Jess and Bella, and shut herself in her room.

–

After Bella was settled for the night, Lily asked Jess to bring in the hip bath. The filling took some time, entailing the hauling up, by Jess and the bootboy, of six large ewers, but eventually Lily declared it was enough. Mellow lamplight warmed her room as she luxuriated in warm water and scented soap applied with a big sponge to every inch of her pale skin.

Wrapped in a big towel, she stood before the cheval glass. It had misted over, making her face a pale blur amid a cloud of dark hair, marked by two dark pools for eyes. She wiped the mirror and stared at herself, really seeing herself for the first time in months. Her face was almost gaunt, with violet shadows under her eyes, her cheekbones standing out over hollows, her throat strained with sinews. No wonder Sir Richard had been concerned.

Sir Richard... The thought of him caused a painful upheaval inside her. 'I care for you,' he had said.

She had always thought him a kind man and since coming to Hewinghall she had grown to admire him more, but lately, as if emerging from a fog, she had sensed a deeper feeling growing between them. Each time they met there had been some word, some look, some small sign of increasing attachment. She had feigned not to notice – she had been grieving for Ash – but she had been grateful that someone cared.

Now, she wondered if what she felt was something more than gratitude. Down in the drawing room that afternoon, powerful new forces had stirred.

Slowly, inch by inch, she let the towel slip. Her skin looked like ivory in the lamplight, with the bloom of condensation still on the glass to veil the details. Last time she had looked, she had seen a girl's rounded contours; now her figure was a woman's, high-breasted, full-hipped. Too thin, but that could be remedied.

Tentatively, she began to touch her breasts, remembering Ash's hands on her, remembering Sir Richard's strong body pressed against her. Her own body leapt into instant response, every nerve alive, heat flowing in her loins. She had known the delights of love. Now the need consumed her.

A tapping on the door made her freeze. 'Miss Lily? You decent, Miss Lily?'

'Yes!' Lily drew the towel round her. 'You can empty the bath now.'

Jess came with her pail and dipper, taking half a bucket at a time to empty in the drains out on the roof. While she worked, Lily sat on her bed wearing the towel like a toga. She felt empty, like a hollow tree that looked strong from outside but was only waiting for the next storm to bring it down. Thank God for Jess! There was something steadying, calming, about the slight young woman who knew so much but said so little.

Taking a long breath, Lily said, 'Will you forgive me?'

'For what, miss?'

'For everything. Especially... especially for the wicked thing I tried to do at Eastertide. I'm grateful to you – and to Mr Rudd, and to your brother. I don't deserve your loyalty.'

Turning her great tawny-brown eyes on Lily's face, Jess said, 'That wan't no hardship, not for any of us. We all love you.'

'You make me feel very humble. I want you to know that... that I am happy for my cousin Clemency.'

'Yes, miss.'

'I am!' Lily avowed. 'I no longer care for Ashton Haverleigh. He is my cousin's husband and I wish them joy. Even if it's true that they quarrel all the time, it's no concern of mine. He made his choice. And I... I am not deceiving myself any more. I'm just a governess. That's all.'

Just a governess.

But even as she said it she knew she didn't believe it. She had always known she was born to *be* somebody. Not a rector's adopted daughter. Not a grey governess. She had dreamed that her real father would weave the transformation, but perhaps it was fated to happen in some other way. She dared not try to imagine how, but her dreams that night were full of Sir Richard Fyncham...

Days of wind and rain prevented Lady Maud from insisting that her daughter should visit the new foal, though she continued to speak about it, trying to rouse Bella's interest. Bella did try to respond; she asked questions – how big was the foal? what colour was it? might they name it Gyp?

'Gyp?!' Lady Maud screeched. 'That's no name for a thorough-bred!'

'It's short for Gypsy, milady,' Lily put in.

Bella's grey eyes opened wide as the thought came to her: 'Gypsy Lady! Mama, you said it was a girl foal. Gypsy Lady would be—'

'A filly!' Lady Maud snapped, and threw an unpleasant glance at Lily. 'I would have thought that you might have taught her that. I suppose you spend all your time talking about cats. Ugh! Horrible animals.'

Opening her mouth to reply, Bella paused, reconsidered, but decided that the risk was worth it: 'Ching's not horrible, Mama. He's *very* intelligent. Mr Anstruther says—'

'I really don't want to hear what that dauber has to say,' Lady Maud said irritably, rising from her seat to ring the bell. 'Come and give Mama a kiss before you go.'

Mr Anstruther needed only one or two more sittings to perfect Bella's face and hands and to finish his painting of Ching nestled in her lap. Then he proposed to fill in the background – the drapes against the window, with perhaps a clematis peeping outside to soften the severe lines of the window frame. His sense of artistic balance desired an extra touch – he wished to paint Lily in the corner, to hint that the child was well cared for. At least, that was what he said.

The revised portrait meant extra sittings for her, sittings to which Sir Richard invited himself, to stand at the artist's shoulder observing his method, or to sit on a corner of the desk by the far window, watching Lily. She tried to ignore him, but his presence made the air thrum.

On a morning when the inclement spring weather made the day drear, she presented herself in the morning room and found Sir Richard alone there. As she paused in surprise, he eased himself away from the desk where he had been perching and came to close the door behind her, saying:

'Anstruther sent word that he would not be coming today. He has business to attend elsewhere.'

'I see.' Her heart was beating fast, nearly suffocating her.

In the singing silence she felt him move closer and when he spoke his voice was low. 'I should have let you know.'

'Yes, perhaps—'

'You know why I did not.'

She couldn't speak for the net of apprehension and need that tangled about her vocal cords. How dearly she longed for him to hold her as he had before. He had made her feel safe, as Ash had never done. With Ash, it had been all taking, all wanting. With Richard Fyncham there was giving, and caring.

His hands came on her shoulders, caressing her, fingers stroking her neck. She felt his breath stir her hair as he hoarsely muttered, 'Lily...'

'Please...' she managed.

'I know.' He turned her to face him, watching her for signs of resistance as he slowly, tenderly, drew her into his arms. 'I know I should be strong. I have tried. I cannot resist any longer. Let me hold you. That's all I ask. Just to hold you, my lovely, lovely Lily...'

'We must not!' she breathed.

'I know,' he answered, drawing her closer, bending his cheek to her temple, surrounding her with a sensuous web of warmth and security.

'Richard!' With a sigh she gave in to the need and let her arms slip round him. Oh, such feeling could not be wrong! Never, never. This moment had been inevitable. Fated. For ever.

After endless moments of sweet, sweet rapture, she lifted her head, looking up into his face, seeing his equal awareness, and his desire, too strong to be denied, a love and longing that matched her own. Something jolted inside her, a physical twisting that terrified her. She wanted to break free but could not. The sight of his mouth, a whisper away, mesmerised her.

Which of them made the beginning? Did she lift her face, or did he bend over her? All she could remember was the sweetness of their lips' blending, and the rush of madness that pulled them tightly together and made them cling. Her arms wound about him, holding him down to her, her body willingly bonding with his. Even through their clothes she felt his response to her, knew he wanted her as she wanted him.

Frightened by the intensity of her feeling, she attempted to pull away, but he caught her hands, holding them together at his breast while he stared down at her with darkened eyes. 'Don't be afraid. I would never do anything to harm you. Lily... I love you. Only believe that. And then forgive me. Find it in your heart to understand...' He let her go, stepped away, shaking his head at his own folly. 'This will never happen again. I swear. Forgive me...'

And he was gone, leaving her shaking so much she was obliged to move to the nearest chair and sit down until her nerves had steadied. But her body was on fire, her senses all aroused and screaming. Never again? Oh, he couldn't mean it!

–

That afternoon the weather cleared and the promised visit to the foal took place. Lily was asked to go along, though she walked a discreet distance behind. Lady Maud strode ahead wearing her split riding skirt over a pair of tweed bloomers, saying, 'Oh, do hurry up, Richard!' as her husband loped behind. He was carrying Bella secure in his arms, so that she should feel safe – Lily tried not to envy the child.

The mare and her foal had been let out to a paddock behind the walled garden, where the mare was grazing and the foal was kicking up its heels. Safe outside the fence, Bella admired the little animal, but when Lady Maud insisted they go into the field Bella fell silent, clinging round her father's neck.

Lily remained where she was, feeling for both the child and the squire as Lady Maud tried to force him to put Bella down and have her greet the foal. He did so, remaining crouched with his arm round Bella. Then the mare moved closer to protect her offspring, and the approach of that huge animal made Bella scream and leap for the safety of her father's embrace.

'Put her down, Richard!' Lady Maud's voice carried to Lily.

'No, Papa!' Bella clung more closely round her father's neck, while her mother clucked her tongue irritably.

'Don't you want to meet her properly? She's yours. Your Gypsy Lady. When she's bigger, you shall learn to ride her.'

'I don't want to!'

The outing ended in disarray, with Lady Maud stalking off towards the stables and Bella in tears against her father's shoulder. Over her coppery head his eyes met Lily's, full of concern.

'Let us walk a while. There are primroses in the wood. Have you seen the primroses, Bella?'

The woods were springing with fresh growth, alive with the song of birds, and in a sheltered glade the ground was thick with pale primroses. Bella ran among them in delight, picking posies to take back for Jess, while Lily stood watching her, aware of the squire only three feet away. Under the music of the birdsong unspoken agonies united them. Lily felt herself trembling and clenched her hands trying to control it. She slid a glance towards him – and met undisguised desire burning in a pair of desolate grey eyes.

She felt as if she were being showered with rain, now cold, now hot, its drops raising every hair on her skin with unbearable awareness.

'We must go in,' she said.

'Yes,' he answered, and called Bella and kissed her, and told her to go back into the house with Miss Clare before she caught another chill.

Just before the trees hid them from each other's sight, Lily glanced back and saw him still standing there, reluctant to miss one second of the sight of her. Oh, Richard... For endless aeons they stared at each other, silently affirming their mutual affinity.

For the rest of the day Lily thought of nothing but Richard Fyncham, reliving every moment of their acquaintance – the way he had kissed her, the way he had looked at her with longing written eloquently on his face... The memory drenched her in shivers, tormented her with hope and despair. It was wrong. It was wrong in so many ways. And yet, and yet...

313

That night she couldn't sleep for wondering how it would end. One moment she was deciding to leave Hewinghall; then she was sure she would die if she never saw him again; then she remembered his nearness, longed for his kisses, knew that only the reality of him beside her could quench her need...

Having tossed restlessly for an age, she got up and lit her lamp, taking her journal from its drawer to read over the passage she had written describing the visit to the foal and those moments of awful awareness in the primrose glade. Underneath, she now wrote, *I am in love with him*, and underlined it twice, and sat staring at the words in disbelief. Her emotions were so confused that she felt sick. How could feeling so strong burgeon so swiftly?

Faintly, she heard the stableyard clock strike midnight. The wind was rising, blustering round the eaves, finding its way round her windowframe and making the old timbers of the attics stretch and shift. Was that a step? Lily stared at her door, picturing young Harry Fyncham teetering on the parapet. She could almost hear the ghostly echo of his scream. She jumped to her feet as a floorboard creaked, close at hand. Was someone in the schoolroom? Harry's ghost, come to tempt her to leap with him?

Summoning all her courage, she picked up her lamp, unlatched her door and snatched it open. Light washed out into the schoolroom, a wide circle beyond which she could see the windows outlined by faint starlight. There was nothing there. Only the wind, blustering round slated roofs and whistling down barley-sugar chimney stacks. Consciously defying her own fear, slender in her linen nightgown with her hair loosely knotted behind her, she walked barefoot across the darkened schoolroom, skirted the rocking horse, and looked out at the balcony. It was empty, of course. Harry Fyncham was not prancing there.

'*Prrrp?*' With a little interrogatory purr, Ching sprang from his basket and came running to leap up the steps to the window.

'Do you want to go out?' Lily asked him. 'At this hour?'

But the cat evidently misliked the look of the windy night. He jumped soundlessly down to the floor and, with tail high, made for the open door of Lily's room.

'Oh, I see,' she sighed. 'You intend to honour me...' The sentence trailed into silence as the light from her lamp reached her doorway and discovered the tall figure leaning there. He was no ghost.

Suddenly her pulse was leaping wildly. He looked as if he had been undergoing similar tortures to those she had experienced that night; his shirt was rumpled, his waistcoat hanging open, his hair dishevelled, agony in his eyes. A different kind of terror assailed Lily. Now was the moment when she must choose.

His voice a strained rasp, he said, 'If you tell me to go, I shall do so, and never bother you again. For weeks I've been telling myself I must not do this. But I have to, Lily. I have to know if what my heart tells me is true – that you feel as I do. Tell me, must I go?'

Lily hung there, on the edge of an abyss whose depths she both feared and craved. Here was no longer her employer, the kindly squire, fond father of her charge; here was a strong, hot-blooded man whose embraces she needed as a flower needs sunlight. Looking at him, crumpled and disarrayed in the lamplight, she knew that she loved him as she had never loved before. How could one deny fate? *Your heart's desire…* perhaps this was what the gypsy had meant.

Her lips said, 'Yes,' but she was shaking her head, moving towards him as in a dream. 'Yes, you should go. But I want you to stay, too. Oh, Richard… I knew you would come. I believe I was waiting for you. My heart said—'

'It was answering mine!' the anguished whisper came as he threw up his hands to capture her face and bent to kiss her in a way that swept aside all her doubts. She only knew that he set her body alight with a desire that equalled his need of her. Beyond that, nothing mattered.

Beyond that, nothing even existed.

Twenty-Four

To Jess's relief, as the spring advanced so Lily's spirits lifted, too. It was the old Lily who now went about smiling and singing. Of course, she'd always loved walking in the woods and with the warmer weather she was free to roam again. She took Bella with her, teaching her about the wonderful things that nature had to show. Sometimes Jess went with them, and on Sundays they often had tea at Park Lodge with Miss Peartree and Dolly.

'Miss Bella have fairly taken to Miss Lily,' Dolly declared as she and Jess washed dishes to the accompaniment of laughter from the next room, where Lily was playing the harmonium and singing a silly song about a cat. 'Why, you can see her fairly bloomin'.'

'You too,' Jess said, smiling at Dolly's rosy face. 'You like bein' here with Miss Peartree.'

'That I do. She're a dear old soul.'

The lodge stood by Hewinghall's west gate, a spacious cottage with a garden which Matty tended in his spare time, out of fondness for Miss Peartree and, Jess guessed, because it was a way of seeing Lily.

'Even Lady Maud seem to approve,' said Jess, watching her brother out in the garden, on his knees tying up faded daffodils. 'Bella sleep better, and eat better. That's been ages since she had one o' her bad nightmares.'

She spoke too soon. Only a few days later she was shocked out of sleep by terrified screams. The little girl lay on the floor, having apparently fallen out of bed; she was giving agitated, incoherent cries, pointing at the window where the curtains were pulled back to show a starry sky.

'Mama! Mama!' she kept whimpering.

'That's all right, my darlin',' Jess crooned. 'You've been havin' one o' them bad old dreams again. There en't nobody out there. Nobody at all. Your mama's safe, fast asleep in her own room.'

'She's not! She was out there. Harry called her! Harry wants her!'

Crooning comfort, Jess picked her up, reflecting that she was getting heavy, growing fast. Then, as she put the child in bed, she heard the schoolroom latch give a soft *snick* and a moment later the telltale floorboard creaked as someone crept towards the family stairs.

Lily came to see what was happening and after they had settled Bella down they went back to the schoolroom and lit a candle.

'When I looked out of my door,' Lily said, 'I saw the schoolroom window open – and Lady Maud climbing back in. Do you suppose she was drunk again? They do say she turns to gin when she's unhappy.'

Jess recalled, 'That must be a year ago that I last saw her out there. She was walkin' on the parapet.'

'Gracious goodness! Do you think she's mad? Oh… how dreadful, Jess! There might be madness in her family. Perhaps poor Harry was infected with it. You don't think that dear little Bella might—'

'What I think, miss,' said Jess, getting wearily to her feet, 'is that the middle o' the night en't no time for thinkin'. Let's go to bed and see what that look like in daylight.'

By morning the incident seemed less disturbing. Lady Maud just had these spells, that was all. She was, as Jess had always thought, a very sad lady.

‾

Lily, though, was happy. Gloriously happy. Oh, she felt sorry for Lady Maud, but Lady Maud had only herself to blame. She was a frigid wife. She had endured Richard's lovemaking until she became pregnant and then she had banned him from her room. Their sexual relationship had never been other than perfunctory.

Richard told Lily so, lying with her in her narrow bed, warm and close in the afterglow of love. The lovemaking was only a part of the joy they took in each other; beyond that physical conjunction lay a calmer, even more precious companionship.

'I have never been able to talk to anyone as I can talk to you,' he told her. 'You're infinitely precious to me. You always have been, ever since I saw you growing up. Did you know that? I've watched you becoming a beautiful woman, and I've loved you. Even so, my love…' He lifted himself to look down at her, stroking the tumbled hair from her face with a hand that trembled. 'I did not intend to seduce you. I swear I did not.'

'I know that, Richard.' She caught his hand to her, kissing it with tender passion. 'But we were meant to be together.'

'Yes,' he said, and there was pain in his eyes as he looked at her. 'I feel that, too. It may be wrong in the eyes of blinkered men, and in the eyes of the great, unforgiving God they invented. But the old gods know what it is to love unwisely. They make allowances for human frailty. They will be smiling on us. You're my soulmate, Lily, my sweet other-half.'

At moments like this she didn't think of the future, or the past, only this present time, when being with Richard meant everything. He found her beautiful – he even loved her odd eyes and would kiss them tenderly. He liked to kiss her, every inch of her, taking his time, touching and rousing her until she was trembling for him. She had never dreamed how sweet and right love could be.

How could she ever have thought she loved that arrogant youth Ash Haverleigh? She had been naive to mistake infatuation for love. Ash had always left her vaguely unsatisfied; she had never been sure of him, never really trusted him. If only she had waited for Richard!

He'd known, of course. The first time they made love, he had known he was not the first man for her. He'd been angry and had vowed to kill the vile seducer. But she had begged him to forgive her, to understand how young and foolish she had been, seeking love blindly.

'It was not like this with him, Richard. It was never like this. I was a child, and he left me still a child. Unawakened. You… You have made me a woman complete. All woman.' And it was true. Every time he came to her their mutual pleasure increased. Richard showed her delights that Ash had never known – Ash was too selfish to give so much joy to any woman.

Poor Clemency. Oh, poor, poor Clemency.

And poor, sad Maud, detesting the sexual act, more comfortable with horses than with people… She continued to mourn her son, blaming herself for his death. Nor was time healing that wound. Every year on the anniversary of that tragic day she locked herself in her room and drank herself into a stupor.

Richard was horrified to learn that, as a final act of remembrance, she walked the parapet where Harry had danced like a wild Indian.

'Maud saw him fall,' he recalled. 'She was in her room and heard him scream as he fell past her window. And then… she ran *up* to the nursery to find him, not *down* to the courtyard below. I'll never understand why.'

Lily didn't understand it, either, unless Lady Maud ran *up* in the hope that she'd find Harry still alive. Perhaps that was why she felt driven to come to the attic. Perhaps she believed he was still there, somewhere. If so, was she mad? And if she was mad, might Richard divorce her? Divorce was scandalous, of course, but no longer the stigma it had once been – not among people of Richard's class.

But mention of it made him draw her even closer and cradle her against him, her head pressed to the smooth hollow of his shoulder.

'I could never divorce her,' he said quietly, his arms tightening when she tried to move, to protest. 'No, listen, my darling. Think of what it would mean. Not for Maud, or for me, not even for you, but – for my little, innocent Bella. I could not let my love for you harm Bella.'

'You love her more than me,' Lily muttered, and again tried to escape his tender captivity.

'I love you both,' he breathed into her hair. 'That's the cross I have to bear. Would you prefer me to lie to you? I love you too much to be other than honest, however brutal the facts. We must go on as we are, loving each other in secret. And we shall go on – for as long as we are both alive. I shall always love you. Whatever happens, Lily, I shall look after you. Can you be content with that?'

No, she thought. I can never be content with less than all. And yet... Oh, he was right. The scandal of a divorce would destroy everything. She knew who would be blamed for it – *she* would, the gypsy brat, the scarlet woman, the seducing governess... Tears seeped out between her tight-closed eyelids and fell like a libation on his skin. She tasted the salt as she let her lips move against him, adoring him, her arms winding round him as she begged, 'So long as you love me! Never stop loving me, Richard. Please, don't ever stop loving me.'

Writing her journal later, she reminded herself that she would not be alone in her role as mistress. Mistresses were fashionable, even accepted and tolerated, so long as they were discreet – one had only to look at the Prince of Wales to see the most illustrious example. Love affairs went on for years, sometimes for a lifetime. The partners might be married to others, have children by others, lead an outwardly respectable life, while all the time they continued to meet with and enjoy each other.

But... Oh, surely it could not go on like that for ever, not for her and Richard! They would surely, one day, find a way to be together, legally and unashamedly. They *must*. One day... oh, one day soon...

–

At first, Jess simply thanked the Lord that the worst was over, that Miss Lily had come back to herself, but she soon began to wonder if there was more to it than a simple lightening of depression. Lily was as gay and careless as she had been last year, during those weeks when she was seeing Ashton Haverleigh.

Once started on that course, Jess began to garner a collection of hints and observations which became like pieces of a jigsaw puzzle, all helping to complete the same picture. Nor was she the only one. Too many people knew of Lily's former attachment to Ash Haverleigh; too many people now saw how merry she was, after being in the pit of despair all winter.

'Betty say as how that Mr Haverleigh have been seen shootin' pigeon, all by hisself in Bennet's Wood,' Sal Gooden remarked one day as Jess was passing. 'Don't Miss Clare like wanderin' that way?' Someone else said Mr Haverleigh had been seen walking his horse along the coast road, very slowly, and a third tale recounted him sitting on a stile one evening, as if he was waiting for someone.

The Haverleighs did not get on, it was said, nor was Mr Ashton a favourite with his in-laws. Oliver Clare had offered to train him to the law, but he didn't take work seriously; he preferred to be out hunting or shooting, or driving too fast in a fancy sporting gig, or dining out with fashionable friends.

Jess's suspicions finally congealed into certainty when Matty told her he'd actually been approached by Ashton Haverleigh, who had offered him a shilling if he'd deliver a message to Lily.

'Blast, but I'd a liked to give him a troshin'!' Matty said angrily. '"What d'you now take me for?" I say. "I hen't your messenger-boy. Nor don't Miss Lily want no doin's wi' the likes o' you no more. Clear you off and don't come back," I say. So off he go, cursin' me up hill and down dale as if that was me as was the wrong 'un.'

'You done right,' Jess assured him.

Matty looked down at his battered boot-toes, then slid a look at her from the corner of his eye. 'She wouldn't... I mean, if he tried... You don't think she'd...'

'No, 'course she wouldn't!'

'Ah. That's what Mr Rudd now say, too. But Miss Lily en't worldly-wise. He bruck her heart, but if he come a-sniffin' round her again she might still believe his sweet-talk. Lor', Jess, I reckon I could kill that man do he do more hurt to her.'

'He 'on't! She've now learned her lesson.'

But even as she denied it, she was remembering the outings Lily took after supper, going to see Miss Peartree and take a stroll with her, in the woods or down to the sea as the evenings lengthened to midsummer – so she said. When Jess mentioned it to Dolly, the maid usually confirmed that Lily had been at the lodge. But there were times enough when she could also have met with Ashton Haverleigh.

She'd learned discretion, though, Jess thought. She didn't chatter about him as she had last year, except to mention the rumours about his marriage and say how sorry she was for Clemency. Otherwise, she talked about everybody in the friendliest way, finding all her acquaintances splendid, forgiving them all their faults, praising Bella until the child glowed under such open approval. Lily's world was bright.

Until she heard the gossip about herself and came hurrying, ashen-faced, to find Jess.

'I just saw Eliza! She said… she hinted… Oh, you know how she makes remarks so slyly… Jess, have *you* heard these rumours? Why didn't you tell me? Oh, it's not true. It's not! I haven't seen Ashton since… since before the ball last year. Well, not to speak to. Once, I saw him in the distance. But I went another way to avoid him! I did, Jess! Oh… why do people make up these tales?'

Jess tried to believe her, but she knew how Lily could lie even to herself when it suited her.

After that, she began to see a change in her friend. Lily tried to keep up a face, as she always had in the past, but behind her brittle smiles now lay fresh heartache and uncertainty. She no longer went out quite so readily but stayed in the nursery suite – using it as a hiding place: Lily had always needed hiding places. Whether she could hide away for ever from the gossip she'd now invited was another matter.

The Fynchams went to London for the season as usual. Lady Maud loved mingling with royalty at Ascot and Goodwood, but Sir Richard wasn't so fond of the social round. That year he came home twice during July and August to keep an eye on the estate. The weather wasn't good: the hay came in damp, the corn was long in ripening, and the pheasant poults were prey to gapes – Matty said Rudd was wearing himself out working all hours. So the squire came home to share the worries of his staff. Bella was always glad to see him, and that cheered Lily up, too, temporarily. But Jess knew there was something wrong, something giving her that wild, worried look again.

It was late August, when her own menstrual cycle caused her the usual day of cramps and discomfort, that Jess realised there'd been no bloody rags soaking in Lily's slop-pail lately. She hadn't had her 'curse' for six or seven weeks.

–

Lily had told herself that the delay in her cycle was one of the minor changes that occurred now and then. But as the days stretched into weeks she knew it was something else. The second time Richard came home she'd intended to share her fears with him, but he'd been so happy to see her, so ardent in his lovemaking, and so tired... he'd fallen asleep in her arms and, for the first time, stayed with her until morning. He had had to creep out when Jess went down for the hot water; and there had been no opportunity for Lily to tell him anything. Besides, she kept hoping that it might be a mistake.

Then one morning when she got out of bed she felt faint and had to grab for the slop-pail as her stomach erupted with bitter bile. While she was still huddled there shivering, Jess came in and found her.

'You all right, miss?' she asked.

Lily looked up, knowing she looked a fright and seeing from the expression on her face that Jess knew her secret. Neither of them could pretend any longer. 'No, Jess, I'm not. And don't look like that. *Please* don't look like that! Don't desert me now. I need you to help me.'

The look on Jess's face only froze harder. 'Help you do what? If you think I'm a-goin' to—'

'No! Oh...' A shudder of revulsion shook through Lily. 'No, I'd never ask you to... I couldn't do that. I *couldn't*.'

'Well, I'm glad o' that,' said Jess flatly. 'So what is it you reckon I can now do?'

'Just...' The lovely, mismatched eyes drowned behind tears. 'Just help me. Be my friend. I'm so afraid... But I'm not sorry. That's the strangest thing – I'm not a bit sorry. I'm glad! I want to have this child. But I didn't do it intentionally. I never meant...'

Jess sighed to herself. No, Lily never meant any harm or any wrong, she simply went along her merry way, with her head so full of dreams she didn't see the pitfalls waiting in her path.

'Here, get you back into bed. I'll bring you some tea and a biscuit – that'll help to settle your stomach.'

Lily allowed herself to be put back into her warm bed and have the covers pulled up and tucked round her. It was like being a child again. Jess would look after her. Jess wouldn't let anything bad happen. But through a dazzle of tears she saw that Jess wouldn't look at her: Jess's brown eyes were sombre, her face set. 'Please!' Lily threw out a hand and grasped the thin wrist. 'Please, Jess! Don't be angry with me. Don't you… Don't you want to know who—'

'I reckon I already know,' Jess said.

Letting her hand relax, Lily murmured, 'You always know everything. Maybe there's some gypsy blood in you.' The look Jess flashed her from those tawny eyes made her wince and she tried again: 'Please try to understand. We couldn't help ourselves, Jess. I love him! And he loves me. And I need to be loved, I can't do without it. Oh… you've never been in love, how could you know?' She threw herself over on to her side, away from Jess, fighting hard against her tears.

Watching her, Jess felt the hardness inside her begin to crack. How could she know, indeed? How could she ever hope to understand the intimate pleasures that might be between a man and a woman when they loved? She would never know it the way Lily did; for her the joy had been destroyed, long ago. Inside her now there was only a cold shrinking, a fear of hurt. No, she didn't understand. But, knowing and loving Lily, she could sympathise.

'Do he know?' she asked.

Lily shook her head, her voice muffled in her pillow. 'No, not yet.'

'Are you a-goin' to tell him?'

'Of course!' She flung herself on to her back, displaying her blotched face, her dark hair strewn around it in tangled curls.

'He 'on't marry you, you know. He already have a wife.'

'I know.' The words were choked. She cleared her throat, saying again, 'I know that. But… he said he'd take care of me. Always.'

'And you believed him?'

'He meant it! Don't you dare say otherwise! He *will* take care of me.' Frightened by the look on Jess's face, she shrank deeper into the bed, adding in a small, desperate voice, 'He must.' She had to believe that. If Richard deserted her now...

—

The Fynchams were due home a few days before Bella's seventh birthday, which that year fell on a Sunday. Celebrations were to be held on the Saturday, as usual, even more lavish than in previous years, but Lily couldn't dredge up any enthusiasm for the event; her only interest was in seeing Richard. The more time went by, the more urgent became her need.

In the event, Sir Richard's homecoming was delayed by matters of business. Lady Maud arrived, and with her a flurry of guests to fill the house, to play tennis, go boating and shooting and walking, but the squire himself did not appear until the Friday evening. Then, as Lily paced up and down the schoolroom, she suddenly heard his voice – he was in the dressing room where Jess was washing Bella before putting her to bed. Lily heard the child cry, 'Papa! Oh, Papa!' and her own heart lurched and began to race. She started across the schoolroom at a run, only to collect herself, so that she appeared calm and sedate as she paused in the doorway of the dressing room. A night-gowned Bella was wrapped in her father's arms, hugging him tightly. Jess was busy, as ever, tidying up.

'Why...' Lily said in a breathy voice. 'Sir Richard! Good evening.'

Across his daughter's copper head, the grey eyes met hers and she saw the swift, fierce gladness in them; it made her want to fly to him and hug him, much as Bella was doing.

'Miss Clare,' he answered, and bent to set Bella down. 'Be good and let Jess put you to bed, my love. I shall be there directly to kiss you good night. But first I must find out from Miss Clare whether you have been a good girl, and whether you deserve the birthday surprises I've brought you.'

'I do, I do!' Bella cried, and, 'What surprises? What have you brought me, Papa?'

'You must wait and see.'

Lily preceded him into the schoolroom, heard him close the door. As she turned he took one long stride and pulled her into his arms, his mouth capturing hers, silently assuring her of how much he had missed her. She linked her arms round his neck, feverishly returning his kisses, weeping with both joy and fear. Then she glanced apprehensively at the door.

'Richard—'

'They're occupied,' he murmured, nuzzling her temple, holding her achingly tight. 'We have a few precious minutes. Oh, my love... I couldn't wait to see you. I had to know – will you be waiting for me tonight?'

'Richard—'

'It might be late. With guests in the house I might not get away until gone midnight. They like to sit and talk. Especially Jenkins. He can—'

'Richard, please!' She grasped him by the shoulders and leaned away, staring up at him with anxious eyes. 'I need to talk to you.'

'So you shall, love. Later.'

'Now, Richard! Richard... I'm sorry, but...' Not knowing how to phrase it, she heard herself announce portentously: 'I am with child.'

She felt the shock that rocked him – saw that he had not anticipated such an event, or if he had then he had put it to the back of his mind, as she had until it happened. He said, 'Are you sure?'

'Two months.'

'Dear God—'

'Forgive me!'

The sight of her tears made him fold her again in his arms. 'There's nothing to forgive,' he said savagely. 'The fault is mine, not yours, my love. Don't weep. It will be all right. But there's no time to lose. Two months... Let me think about it. Wait for me, later. And don't worry. I shall stand by you. I shall find a solution.'

He was so distracted that he left without going in to Bella, which upset the child and had Jess racking her brains to invent excuses for him.

Looking back, long afterwards, Jess supposed that that was when she first began to suspect the truth. But it was only a tiny suspicion, easily argued away. She was convinced the man in the case was Ashton Haverleigh; she didn't care to examine the clues that might lead to an even more shocking conclusion.

–

It was not so very late when Richard Fyncham came to the attic suite that night; he had encouraged his guests to seek their beds early, to prepare for the morning regatta he had planned. Then he had made his way to the library and up the secret staircase which came out in the schoolroom – his private way, which only he knew. Now, he paced Lily's room like a caged beast, while she sat white-faced and trembling on her bed.

'You should not have left it so late, Lily. You should have warned me as soon as you suspected.' Then, regretting his irritation, he sat down beside her and gathered her into his arms. 'No, forgive me. This is not your fault. But something must be done, and soon. I could arrange for—'

'I won't have it killed!' Lily whispered desperately. 'I won't!'

He was horrified. 'How could you think such a thing? But we must find some way of concealing it. You must go away, until it's born. We'll find a good home for it and—'

She turned her huge, hurting eyes on him. 'Abandon it – as I was abandoned? No, Richard. Never! This child is mine, and yours. I want to keep it. I shall love it, if I have to walk the streets to raise it.' The notion terrified her, but she couldn't bear to think of her child left, as she had been, unloved and unwanted, never sure of its parentage.

'Then there's only one solution – we must find you a husband.'

Lily almost choked on a burst of wild laughter. 'A husband? Who would have me?'

'We shall find someone.'

–

When morning came, Lily felt unable to face the Belladay celebrations. She begged Jess to go in her stead. Assuming she was simply afflicted with morning sickness, Jess agreed, put on her best print dress and straw bonnet, and accompanied Bella to the regatta at Martham Staithe.

If she hadn't been so worried about Lily, she might have enjoyed the day. It was hot and fine, the sky and sea both a brilliant blue, with a brisk wind that sent the boats scudding. Matty and a couple of his Martham fisher mates were in the race to the point and back, and while they were doing that Reuben Rudd appeared and stood near Jess, passing the time of day – testing the water, she fancied, and finding it lukewarm. She exchanged a few verbal sideswipes with him, fending him off in a lighthearted way that disguised the turmoil inside her.

'Well,' he said eventually. 'I'd better get back to my birds.'

'Don't you never take a holiday?' Jess asked.

'Happen I might – given the right reason.' His look was bright and bland, challenging and charming. 'You fancy a walk tonight?'

Oh, if only she could!

Then beyond his shoulder she saw a bearded face topped by a black hat, with shadowed eyes that pierced her. Merrywest here again. Merrywest still haunting her. He always seemed to be about, encouraging his converts in the area; he'd recently started a temperance campaign, so she'd heard, and here he was again, standing with a little group of chapel-goers. Amongst them was Eliza Potts, wearing a fashionable dress and hat that made her look as if she was somebody.

'I have to work tonight,' Jess said, more sharply than she intended.

'Aye, all right,' Rudd grudged. But he glanced over his shoulder to see what had made her start and stop like a frightened pheasant, and what he saw made him give her an odd, speculative look. 'The preacher?'

Jess tossed her head. 'I was just thinkin' how ridiculous Eliza Potts do look in that there hat!'

'Well, *I* think she looks right bonny,' said Rudd, and went away.

That was when the boats came scudding in, with Matty in the lead, and what with her pride in him, and the wind in her face, it fair made her eyes smart and her nose run. Weeping over Reuben Rudd? Huh, would she be such a fool?

Back at Hewinghall, games and sports for the children took place, and a cricket match had been organised between the men of Hewing and the men of Syderford. Jess took Bella for a stroll to watch a bit of the match, and just after they arrived the batsman sent the ball at a cracking pace across the grass, to end up only a few feet from where Jess was standing. The shirt-sleeved fielder who came dashing after it was Ash Haverleigh.

Seeing Bella, he jerked a look at the woman with her, but when she wasn't Lily he only nodded and went back to his place.

Later on, when Jess was by the dais watching Bella and her father dole out prizes, she glimpsed Lily's grey-clad figure near the shrubbery walk. She also saw Ashton Haverleigh, covertly moving from tree to tree, making his way across the park. Lily saw him coming and vanished in among the shrubs. But was she avoiding him, or had she been waiting to meet him?

Jess was not the only one to have noticed that small incident. Whispers began to spread, noting further proof of 'goings-on' between Lily and her cousin's husband.

The whispers reached Matty, who came seeking Jess in a rage against Ashton Haverleigh. 'I went lookin' for him, but he've gone. Let me catch him and I'll knock his solin' head off!'

'Hush, Matty!' she begged him. 'Don't talk that way, bor.'

But he wasn't listening.

By the time Jess took Bella up to the nursery for her nap, Lily was back. In fact, much to Bella's alarm, she was out on the roof.

'Come in!' the child begged, backing away from the open window. 'Oh, do come in, before you fall.'

Lily climbed back in and closed the window. 'There's nothing to fear,' she told Bella for the hundredth time. 'You can't fall if you're sensible.'

'Harry fell,' said Bella.

'Yes, but Harry wasn't being sensible. He was being disobedient and very, very silly. Oh… go and have your rest, my dear. You want to be fresh for the ball. By the way, Jess… I shan't go to the ball. I don't feel well enough. You must go. I expect you could wait on the gallery, as you did last year.'

A Fancy Dress Ball had been planned. Bella was to be a fairy, so Jess had been busy, sewing a costume and making wings out of cheesecloth, with a wire frame that Matty had brought: 'Mr Rudd made it,' he'd announced. Rudd kept reminding her of his existence in ways like this, either sending her small objects of interest, or getting Matty to pass on a message about nothing, or perhaps turning up unexpectedly, the way he had today. He wasn't pushing, just letting her know he was there.

Jess often wished he'd give up and let her be; then times like today, when she suddenly found him near and realised how much she missed him, her heart wept for what might have been.

–

Ready for the ball, Bella was a vision in winged white, a tall and awkward seven-year-old with a diamond tiara on her ginger hair, her nose sprinkled with freckles and a front tooth missing.

After Jess and Bella had gone down, Lily roamed the attics wishing she could breathe. All day she had felt half suffocated by the heat, which was why she'd gone out for a walk, just to see what was happening. She had never imagined that Ash Haverleigh would have the gall to show himself so openly. But she had no wish to see him. No, never again. To avoid him, she had fled back to the safety of the nursery suite. It was Richard she loved, Richard whose child she was carrying – Richard who wanted her to marry in order to conceal her shame. Oh, if only she could think!

Her quest for fresh air took her out on to the roof again, beneath a sky thick with stars and a waning moon riding low over the woods. Even there, Lily felt stifled. The mild air and the starry sky seemed to press down on the old house. Music floated up from the great hall far below as she gazed into the distance, beyond the church tower that was just visible in the night, to the rise that hid the rectory. How she wished she could turn time back to when she was younger. She had not appreciated what her papa had done for her. If she'd been more winning, less of a rebel, might things have been different?

Oh, if only her *real* father would come! He would know what to do. He would sweep her away from Hewinghall and make everything right. She pictured him arriving to rescue her, his carriage careering down the drive with its lamps agleam, four plumed horses tossing their manes as the whip cracked over them and the liveried coachman hauled on the reins to bring them round, into the courtyard with a shower of gravel and dust, the door swinging wide—

'There you are!' Richard's voice, low and vibrant, made her start, the fantasy fading. He was climbing out of the window, stepping down with agile ease, a tall figure in hose and doublet, with a feathered bonnet, a short cloak, a sword… Romeo, if she was not mistaken. 'I had to come. I've been worried about you. My dear darling…' He gathered her into his arms, holding her hurtingly tight. 'How anxious you must have been all day. But I haven't been idle. I've been racking my brains and… I believe I've found the solution.' Through a thickness in her throat, she managed, 'You have?'

'Yes. The perfect answer – it came to me as I heard his name being announced this evening. He's dressed as Young Lochinvar – appropriate, don't you think? I've been chatting with him and he evidently thinks warmly of you, Lily.'

'Who?' she croaked.

'The rector. Peter Dunnock.'

Lily stood quite still, her mind blank and her body draining cold with shock, while his voice went on: 'Your father did moot the possibility before, I believe, and Mr Dunnock was not unwilling. He would not be the first man to agree to such a marriage, nor would he lose by it. I shall offer him some financial inducement. It will be ideal, Lily! You can remain as Bella's governess, perhaps start a small school – that would be good for Bella, better than remaining cooped up here with no companions of her own age.'

Was it Bella he was thinking of? She wrenched away from him, crying, 'But what of *me*, Richard? To marry Peter Dunnock… To have him know my shame… To have his dreadful mother know—'

'Then who do you suggest?' Richard exclaimed, capturing her flailing hands. 'I'll speak to Dunnock – not tonight, but tomorrow, after church. This must be decided at once.'

Sounds which had been no more than a faint disturbance began to resolve themselves into a raucous chorus of shouts and scufflings. On the still air the noise carried clearly, floating up from the park, where a band of people were approaching, some carrying lanterns on bean-poles. The leader was wearing a broad-brimmed hat, but the group centred around a man who was being forced along by four others. He was struggling and wrenching to be free, swearing at his captors.

'We'll see what Sir Richard have to say!' the voice came clear. 'He's the magistrate. We'll ax *him* what he think.'

Richard had pulled back against the slope of the roof, not wanting to be seen. He said, 'Forgive me, love. We'll talk more of this later,' and clambered back through the window.

Twenty-Five

Jess was up in the minstrels' gallery when guests began to crowd at the windows, peering out, while others made for the main door. As the music faltered, Jess could hear the shouting outside, people bawling for Sir Richard to come out. Another voice, booming above the cacophony, sent trickles of alarm over her flesh: that resonant, commanding voice belonged to Preacher Merrywest; it was the voice he used to call down hellfire on the heads of sinners, a voice that turned her blood to wash-water.

She slipped down the 'hidden' stairs and pushed open the door at the bottom in time to see the costumed squire come running down the main stairs, holding his sword out of the way, his cloak billowing behind him. He made through the door to the great hall and thence to the lobby and the front door, with Jess not far behind.

Half the party had spilled out into the gravel courtyard by that time, out of curiosity and the need of air. Cavaliers and roundheads, warlocks and warriors, medieval princesses and fairytale ladies mingled oddly, exclaiming at the rude disturbance.

'What the devil is going on?' Sir Richard demanded, making his way to the front of the group. 'How dare you invade my property in this manner!'

Jess edged through until she could see the jostling rabble, including a few women amongst whom was Eliza Potts. They were spreading in a semicircle against the railing, lanterns swinging, fingers pointing, raised voices arguing. Four men were struggling to contain a raging, cursing figure whose drunken strength was nearly a match for them. He was raving, kicking out, striving to break free of the hands that held him, his fury directed at Preacher Merrywest.

The preacher, though not a big man, stood out because of his black hat and his ferocious beard. He was thundering, 'Hold him!' as the captive got an arm free and swung a punch at the air. The effort unbalanced him and he fell to the gravel. His captors leapt on him immediately, one wrenching his arm behind him, another sitting on his legs.

'Blast and damn you!' the man raged, refusing to own defeat.

Jess felt as though her heart had stopped her throat: she knew that voice. The drunken, cursing captive was her brother Matty!

'What is the meaning of this flagrant intrusion?' Sir Richard demanded. 'You're trespassing on my property and disturbing my guests. Who are all these people? Who's your spokesman?'

'I am,' Merrywest said, and raised his voice to command, '*Enough!*'

Immediately the noise diminished, though Matty continued to struggle vainly, spitting obscenities. Even lying face down, pinned on the gravel, he exuded hatred at everyone around him.

'My name, sir, is Merrywest,' the preacher informed the squire. 'I have the honour to be a lay-preacher of the Methodist church, attached to the Lynn circuit.'

'What of it?' Sir Richard was impatient.

'My friends and me have been conducting a crusade hereabouts, sir. A Christian temperance crusade, to foil the demon drink. Sore needed, you'll agree, sir. Drink, that's one of the evils of our time. That leaves women destitute and children hungry. That turns men into wild beasts and—'

'You're not here to deliver a sermon,' Sir Richard said shortly. 'Get on with it, man. You're wasting my time.'

Allowing himself a thin smile, Merrywest explained, 'Tonight we were gathered in Martham Staithe, outside the "Admiral Nelson" inn, to reason with lost souls and offer them a chance to repent and sign the pledge – I've copies here if any of your guests would care to—' The look on the squire's face interrupted that line of argument and Merrywest, knowing when to hold his tongue, went on, 'I was conducting a peaceful campaign, sir, when this here man,' with a dramatic gesture at the prone Matty, 'this man – who just so happen to be an employee of yours, sir, name of Matthew Henefer – he run mad. He start a-swearing and a-cursing. He disrupt our prayer meeting, and attack my congregation.'

Exclamations came from the assembled partygoers, men muttering, 'Tut-tut, disgraceful,' ladies gasping, 'Save us!' A young Britannia giggled behind her fan as her partner, wearing a cloak and domino mask, whispered in her ear.

'When we tried to stop him,' Merrywest went on, 'he pick up a shovel and threaten further violence, to me and to others.'

'He've broke my nose!' a man by the railing snuffled, holding a bloody kerchief to his face, the sight of which made the guests exclaim anew.

'Whiles I don't like to have to speak ill of any man,' Merrywest added, enjoying the reaction of his distinguished audience, 'this en't the first time he've done something of the kind. I know this man of old. The drink let the devil into him, that's fact – when drink go down the throat, sense and reason go out the head. If we han't stopped him, sir, I reckon there'd a been murder done tonight.' He paused again while that dramatic claim ran its course, then concluded, 'So we brung him to you, sir. You're the squire hereabouts. You're a magistrate, too. And he's *your* man. Let you now decide what's to do. Have you got a place where he can be put?'

'Yes, yes,' the squire said irritably, anxious to have it done with. 'We can hold him here overnight.' He glanced around and, seeing his butler and two of his footmen waiting, summoned them to help take Matty away, saying to Merrywest, 'Do you intend to bring charges?'

'Aye!' voices cried from behind him. 'Assault and battery,' and, 'He want lockin' up,' from Eliza Potts, but also, 'He were provoked!' with, 'It warn't his doin'.' Arguments broke out among the crowd, until Merrywest turned and roared, '*Hold you hard!*'

'It appears to me that I ought to arrest the whole lot of you!' Sir Richard shouted. 'Well, Merryweather, or whatever your name is… what about it? Are you accusing him of some specific crime?'

The preacher's glance slid to where Jess was standing, a diminutive figure in her maid's black and white. He said, 'I en't a vindictive man, Sir Richard. Forgive and forget, that's my motto. Do you strongly warn him, when he's sober. That'll suffice. Lock him up. Let him cool his head. He'll be sorry enough, come morning.'

Was he being cautious because of her? Jess wondered. If this came to court, she might be called as a witness for her brother: she might be angry enough to tell the whole truth about his accuser. That she might! she thought fiercely, and with a final flash of eyes at her enemy she went after the men who were dragging her brother off.

Knowing where they were taking him, she hurried round the end of the east wing. The window of the lock-up looked out into a north-facing side-yard floored with uneven cobbles. The window was barred with iron behind four panes of glass, one of which was broken, half the glass missing at the bottom. Near it, a drainpipe from the roof had become misaligned, so it missed the drain and poured water into a corner that was damp with moss. In darkness dimly lit by stars, it smelled dank and unwholesome. Not that Jess noticed; she was too worried about Matty.

Someone was bringing a lantern that shed uneven light through an open doorway, from a passageway into the lock-up. Several men bundled Matty into the rough room, pushing him towards what looked like a butcher's block set low against the back wall. He staggered and fell to his knees on the uneven floor, cursing as the men and the light went away, the door clanged shut and a key grated in the lock.

'Blast you!' Matty yelled after them, but his curses faded into incoherence as he realised his helplessness.

Jess could have wept for him. 'Matty?' she ventured, close to the broken pane. 'Matty, that's me – Jess. You all right, bor? What happened?'

'Go away!' he answered hoarsely, and, 'What're you doin' here, Jess? You shun't be here.'

Slowly, with many outbursts of temper and outrage and bitterness, he told her how he had been at the 'Nelson', downing ale and thinking about Lily, building up a head of rage in which he decided to go and find Ashton Haverleigh and kill him. In the yard that fronted the inn, Merrywest had been standing on a barrel declaring the evils of alcohol to a knot of villagers and amused inn-goers. Some were from Syderford, some from Hewing, others from Martham. There was already argument, Syderford having won the cricket while Martham claimed victory in the regatta and Hewing felt cheated of both.

Seeing Matty reeling from the inn, the preacher had made pointed remarks about 'goings-on' among the gentry, both at Hewinghall and Syderford. Many men had been affronted by his slanders. Then someone in the crowd had mentioned Lily's name, someone else had laughed, and that had set Matty off. He didn't wholly remember what else had happened, except that there'd been a general to-do with men on all sides trading punches. He'd been picked out, by Merrywest, as the instigator.

Just as Jess had thought – Merrywest would do anything to harm her and her family. Yet there'd been fear in him tonight. He wasn't as secure as he pretended. Perhaps he was afraid that she could harm *him*, if she tried.

In the small hours of that night, a wretched, sleepless Lily confided in her journal all that had happened. The page was spotted with her tears. In a jagged, ill-formed writing, the passage concluded: *'Dear God! Peter Dunnock! I would sooner wed Matty Henefer!'*

She was still fully dressed, pacing up and down the schoolroom, when Jess finally returned with her face set and her apron stained with green lichen and brick dust.

'Where have you been?' Lily demanded. 'Lady Maud was not best pleased to find you missing. Sally had to bring Bella up and I had to put her to bed myself. She was over-excited. I left Ching in there with her – you'll have to remember to put him out before you go to sleep. Well? Answer me, Jess. Explain yourself. If you've been dallying with that George—'

'I've been with our Matty. He got in a fight and they slung him in the lock-up.'

'It was *Matty*? Oh… Jess, I'm sorry. I didn't realise… Is he all right?'

'No, he en't,' Jess said flatly. 'He's hurt and bleedin', he're drunk, and he're got the miseries. All on *your* account. He was stickin' up for you because folk were talkin' about you. He was defendin' your good name. Like the blame fool he be.'

'Why…' The attack bewildered Lily. 'That was kind of him. But I don't see that I can be held responsible for—'

'No, miss,' Jess said wearily, turning away. 'No, I don't reckon you would see, at that. Sorry, miss. Will that be all?'

Long into the night Lily lay wakeful, feeling as if there was no help left. Richard wanted to be rid of her; Cousin Oriana would never understand; even Jess had started being snappish.

Matty… How awful to think of him lying alone in the dank, dark, rat-infested lock-up – all because of her. He'd actually fought for her. Shed his blood. That was more than any other man had ever done. How sweet of him to care. And he *did* care – she knew that. He'd proved it in a dozen ways. Lily remembered how Matty had found her in the rectory garden, exactly a year ago. He'd been kind and surprisingly gentle for such a big, uncouth man. He'd laid his coat around her to keep her warm and, as they parted, she had allowed him to steal a kiss.

She was really quite fond of him, she realised. Certainly fonder than she was of Peter Dunnock.

When dawn came, Lily got up and dressed and, by the first grey light, stole down the back stairs and through the house, along the long, flagged west corridor to the store rooms. She didn't know what she would find, she only remembered someone describing where the lock-up lay.

Tentatively, she patted at the door with the flat of her hand. The metal felt cold, gritty with incipient rust. She wiped her hand on her skirt, said, 'Matthew? Matthew Henefer?' No response made her slap the door again, harder this time. 'Matthew Henefer, are you there?'

'Who's that?' the sleepy mumble came.

'It's I – Lily Clare.'

After a moment of utter silence she heard his boots scrape on the floor. When he spoke again his voice was closer, incredulous: 'Miss Lily?'

'Yes.' She was scanning the door, thinking how huge and solid it was. If only… And then she saw the ornate head of the big old key still sitting in the lock. She put her hand on it, tested it, heard it scrape and grind, turning the mechanism. As the door swung inwards, she saw Matty staring at her, regarding her with awe, as if she were a vision.

Nausea churned in her stomach, morning sickness, apprehension, pity, guilt… What a sight he looked – his clothes torn and thick with dust, dried blood crusting one corner of his mouth, the flesh around his eye swollen, his eye half shut.

'Oh…' she managed faintly, tears coming all too easily. 'I can't bear it! You did this for me, Matthew. How am I ever going to thank you?'

'Why… En't no need for thanks, Miss Lily. I done what I had to do. What any man would have done.'

'No, that's not true. Only *you* would do this for me. Only you, Matthew. You're fated to be my champion. My good, gentle knight. But… You ought to know – I'm not worthy. I don't deserve your loyalty. I am such a fool. Such a terrible, wicked, hopeless fool. And a sinner, too.'

'No, you en't!'

'Yes, I am. I am! When I tell you… Oh, you'll never forgive me. You'll hate me.'

'Miss Lily…' He moved nearer, stirred by the sight of her distress. She was pale in the early light, her hair disarrayed, her eyes huge and desolate. 'I could never hate you, Miss Lily. Whatever you've done.'

'Couldn't you?' She peered tearfully up at him, her heart twisting inside her as she saw that he was sincere. 'Oh, Matthew… If I could believe that to be true I should be so happy. You see, I… I'm in the most terrible trouble – the most terrible trouble that a stupid woman can be in. I need someone to help me. I shall be ruined unless someone, some kindly, unselfish, perfect gentle knight comes to my rescue and…'

'Blast!' His voice was low, thick with sick rage as he caught her pleading hands and held them against his dusty coat. 'I knew he was a wrong 'un, fust time I seen him. Blast him, that he'd do this to you…'

–

Having done her early cleaning and hauled up the hot water, Jess knocked on Lily's door and went in. The room was empty. Where had Lily gone so early? Her journal lay on the night table, open with the pen lying across a page scrawled with black ink. Then, as Jess set down the ewer of water, a step outside made her glance round.

'Jess.' Lily was in the doorway, crumpled and tear-stained but with a new glow of serenity about her. 'Oh, Jess…' She came drifting across the room with her arms open to embrace Jess. 'How I thank God that you came into my life. You – and your brother. We've always said it was fated, haven't we? So it was. I'm sure of that now.'

Jess said nothing. She couldn't. She had a feeling that something dreadful had happened.

'Your brother…' Lily said. 'He's a fine man. A fine, good man, Jess. I've been to see him. I went to thank him for being my champion. And… as we were talking, I found myself confiding in him. And he… he has been good enough to understand. Jess… your brother and I are to be married. Very soon. He has offered to stand by me, to claim the child as his own.'

No!

Jess's mind wouldn't seem to work beyond that flat denial.

'Be happy for us,' Lily pleaded. 'Oh… it's not ideal, for either of us. But he's a good man. He's strong, he's kind. He loves me, and I am very fond of him. I could do worse – much worse! I'll be good to him, I promise you. I shall never forget what he's done for me. I'll always be grateful.'

'And faithful?' It was out before Jess could stop it. 'Or will you go runnin' back to that Mr Haverleigh the minute he crook his little finger?'

'Ash?' Lily blinked at her. 'But surely you know... I never want to see Ash again. I promise you, Jess.'

–

Later that day, Lily was summoned to the library, where Richard Fyncham was standing by a terrestrial globe, twirling it round at a pace that had days passing in seconds.

'Close the door,' he bade her, and when she had done so he came striding across the room to take her by the shoulders and demand, 'Why? *Why*, Lily?'

'Because he loves me! Because he won't ask questions!'

'But a gardener...'

'I'd rather have him than Peter Dunnock!'

Releasing her, he stared at her for a long moment, as if trying to read her mind. 'Very well. It may be best, at that. I've spoken with him and he's loyal to you. Very loyal. Did you tell him...'

'He thinks it's Ashton Haverleigh's,' Lily said dully. 'Everyone will think so. Such a reputation I have.'

'Oh, my love...'

'Don't touch me.' She shuddered away as he reached again for her. 'I know I've become an embarrassment. You want to get rid of me, in any way you can. You used me, just as Ash—'

'No, Lily.'

'Yes, Richard!'

Again he was silent, watching her with those clear grey eyes full of sad reproach. Unable to bear it, Lily turned her back on him, folding her arms around herself for comfort.

'We won't argue about it, not now,' he said. 'But you're wrong, Lily. You – we – are in this predicament because I was careless, because I love you, "not wisely, but too well". Believe me, love, if it were humanly possible I would claim you as my own and stand proudly beside you for the rest of my days. As it is, I shall do all I can to help you and Henefer – and the child, when it's born.' He moved closer, his hands on her arms turning her to face him. 'Lily, my love... Forgive me. Please.'

Needing reassurance, she lifted her arms round his neck and felt him fold her to him, safe and secure. It would be all right, she told herself. So long as Richard loved her, everything would be all right...

—

Letters were sent to York, seeking Reverend Hugh Clare's permission for the match; his affirmative answer came by return.

There was talk, of course, when the news got out. Gossips went on and on, like pigs in a harvest field. The official tale was that Lily and Matty had been in love for months, despite the difference in their station. Frustration, and the desire to protect Lily from wicked tongues, had driven Matty to drink and fisticuffs; so the squire had agreed that, to calm the young man down, it was best for them to marry. They would be setting up home in Park Lodge, with Miss Peartree, and Lily would continue to give Bella lessons until a new governess could be found.

Lady Maud was angry: she called Lily to her room and demanded to know what had been going on. But she wasn't really interested one way or the other, so long as her own life wasn't disrupted. The squire had persuaded her that a fuss would only draw more attention: the matter was being resolved. Let it rest.

Matty and Lily were married on the twenty-first of September in a quiet, early-morning ceremony conducted by Reverend Peter Dunnock. Jess was at the church that golden morning, and Miss Peartree and Dolly, and Reuben Rudd stood as best man. He and Jess both signed the register as witnesses. At the churchyard gate, the newly wedded pair climbed into one of Sir Richard's carriages and were whisked off to the station in Hunstanton, bound for a few days in King's Lynn, where Lily would meet her new in-laws for the first time.

'Well, well,' Miss Peartree said heartily, smiling through her tears as the carriage lurched away. 'Let us pray they will be happy. Come, Dolly.' Leaning on the little maid's arm, she moved away, not wishing to discuss the event. There wasn't much to be said, except lies...

Jess remained where she was, standing in the church gateway with the morning breeze teasing a tendril of hair across her cheek as she watched the carriage turn on to the main driveway.

Beside her, Rudd said, 'Matty seems happy, any road.'

He would, daft great lummox, she thought tiredly.

'He knows what he's doing, Jess.'

'Do he?' She threw a shadowed look at him.

'We had a long talk about it, him and me. Happen he's grown up. He's a different man from the one I first knew, when he was letting Jim Potts lead him by the nose.'

Jess wished she could believe that. It seemed to her Matty was still being led by the nose, this time by Lily and his own blind worship of her. She had bad misgivings about it all, her earlier unease about Matty now settled into a dark shadow across the future. 'You've helped him a lot,' she said. 'I… I'm grateful for you takin' him under your wing. He could easy have gone wholly wrong.'

'The lad only needs a bit of encouragement. If he keeps in the right company, he'll do all right. Now he's got Miss Lily to consider…'

'Maybe you're right,' Jess sighed. 'Well, howsomever, "What can't be cured must be endured," as Granny Henefer used to say. That's done now. For better or worse.' She still didn't believe it, though. Standing there with the early sunlight slanting across the park, she did not believe that her brother had married Lily Clare, knowing her to be pregnant by Ashton Haverleigh. They'd claim the child was early, of course – they wouldn't be the first to use that old excuse. Folk would wink and nod, and that would be another nine-day wonder.

But after the child was born, when the novelty and the excitement were all over, would Lily Victoria Clare be content as Mrs Matthew Henefer?

'What about you?' Rudd asked.

'Me?' Surprise made her look fully at him. 'How d'you mean?'

'Well, you don't plan to spend the rest of your life in that nursery, do you?'

Feeling as though a spear had torn into her vitals, she turned away, blinking against the bright, low sunlight. 'Why not?'

'Because you're worth a sight more than that, that's why.' His hand fell on her arm, pulling her back to face him. 'Jess… Jessie, lass… It's probably not the right time, but I hardly get to see you lately and I want you to know… I've talked with your Matty about a lot of things. I know I was wrong to doubt you. Forgive me, lass. Let me have another chance. Will you? I'll not pretend I understand about this preacher chap, but I know there's got to be another side to it. I know you've been hurt. Was it through him? If only you'd talk to me, Jess!'

The passion in him stunned her. She'd never expected to hear him talk that way.

'Don't you know how it hurts me, the way you keep cutting me out?' he asked her. 'You make me feel you don't trust me. What is it you're afraid of, lass? I'd never hurt thee. Never in a million years. Tha knows how I feel about thee, surely? So how about it? I have to see the squire today about the shooting. I could ask for his say-so, and then see the rector. We could be wed by the end of October.'

Jess stared at him, a hand to her head partly to keep the sun out of her eyes and partly to hold her whirling thoughts. Wasn't this what she'd wanted, to be swept off her feet by Reuben Rudd? 'Wed?' she managed.

'That's what I want, Jess.'

'Reuben...' she got out. 'Oh, Reuben, bor! I don't deserve it. To hear you say things like that... I'm wholly humbled. On'y...'

She could feel the stillness in him. 'Only?'

'Only there's things I have to do, and think about. There's Miss Bella, and... and I reckon Miss Lily's goin' to need me for a while yet.'

Frowning, he searched her eyes for answers, knowing there was more to it than she would say. 'Miss Lily's got herself a husband now. She's not your concern any more, if ever she was. What makes you think...'

'I just feel it, Reuben. 'Sides... you've a real busy time comin' up, what with the shootin' season, and watchin' for poachers, and all those other things you have to do. You hen't got time to be thinkin' about your own concerns, and nor have I.'

'That's just excuses, Jess. What are you trying to tell me? Am I wrong? Don't you feel the same?'

She stared at him, seeing his dear face behind a dazzle of hot tears. Feel the same? Of course she did! She loved him with a love that was an echoing, aching emptiness inside her. She couldn't imagine anything sweeter than being his wife, living in that cottage with him, cooking and cleaning for him, helping him with his birds, walking with him through his woods, learning from him, sharing joys and sorrows, supporting and being supported; waking up beside him every morning... lying beside him at night – dear heaven, not that!

'I can't,' she whispered. 'Reuben... I'm sorry, but... I just can't.'

Slowly, carefully, Rudd removed his hands from her and stepped back. She couldn't see him clearly, but she knew she'd cut him deep.

'Then I'll get back to my birds,' was all he said, and whistled to Dash who was waiting nearby. 'So long, lass.'

—

Lily could hardly believe how tiny the Fyshers' cottage was, crammed in with seven similar cottages around a narrow yard where animals roamed, babies crawled and washing hung to dry. 'Sprat' Fysher was away at sea, fortunately, so his wife Fanny and her new baby slept downstairs, leaving the front bedroom for the newlyweds. To Fanny Fysher, her brother Matty's bride was like a being from another world.

The youngest Henefer – Joe, who was eight – asked silly questions and made idiot remarks that maddened Matty. Joe, and the quieter Sam, who at fourteen was working at the coconut matting factory, had the back bedroom, behind a partition wall so thin you could hear every breath. Under those circumstances, Matty did not try to consummate his marriage. That suited Lily. She needed time to think.

All the time she was in Lynn, she felt as if she were in a play whose run would end once they returned to Hewinghall and normality. She would go back to being Bella's governess; she would meet with Richard, somehow; Matty would provide the screen she needed to preserve appearances. But beyond that everything would fall back into place.

Unhappily, it wasn't that simple.

For one thing, she was expected to live with her new husband at Park Lodge, attending the big house every morning to give formal lessons while the afternoons were reserved for more informal pursuits. She saw little of Richard, who was usually absent when she took Bella down to the private drawing room for her half hour with her mama. However, he did contrive to leave a note for her in the book she was reading. It read,

> *Forgive me, oh my dearest love. I have not forgotten, but discretion is vital at this time. I long for you. When the time is right we shall be together. We shall find a way. Until then, forgive me if I seem aloof. If I were to spend more than a few moments in your company I fear I might not be able to be strong. I find*

myself envying Henefer with a passion so strong it consumes me.
Does he hold you as I did? Does he make you sigh? Do you
kiss him so tenderly as you kissed me? Ah, Lily… Lily, I love
you more than life. You are mine. For ever mine. Soul and mind
and flesh. Bone and nerve and sinew. Do not forget me. But
forgive.

Lily wept over the note, kissed it a hundred times and, remembering, vividly imagining, found herself needing Richard's nearness.

Perhaps Matty sensed the softening in her. When he decided that evening to assert his husbandly rights, he found her not unwilling. She closed her eyes and imagined he was Richard, with Richard's lips, Richard's hands, Richard's body. He hadn't Richard's finesse, but his enthusiasm made up for it and she found herself shuddering with wondrous release as he groaned aloud in his own ecstasy.

From then on they made love whenever they could. Matty was astounded by his young wife's eagerness, and for her part she had found sexual release to be a sure means of comfort. But, '*Oh, Richard,*' she commented to her journal, '*how long must it be like this?*'

Twenty-Six

As autumn turned to winter, the keepers were busy. Rudd's campaign against the poachers kept him and his men out most nights and resulted in a flurry of encounters, some violent. Several poachers – including a Potts cousin – were brought to court and sent down for varying terms at Norwich gaol. Jess worried about Rudd. He'd thrown himself into his work regardless of his own safety.

Soon, though, she had cause for other concern – this time over Matty. When not on duty he began to spend all his evenings at the 'Nelson', as Eliza Potts was only too happy to inform anyone who would listen.

'He soon got disappointed in his new wife,' she was heard to remark one day as Jess went to the drying room to fetch the nursery linen. 'She think herself too good for him. Well, what sort of a life do he have, out all hours and all that's waitin' for him that fussy Miss Peartree and a wife a-mournin' her lost love?'

Furious, Jess showed herself at the laundry door, where Eliza and the other laundrymaids were busy amid clouds of steam and a scent of grated soap. 'Hen't you never finished your mischief-makin', Eliza Potts?'

Eliza merely tossed her handsome head. 'I'm on'y repeatin' what Dolly Upton say. You're a sorry lot, you Henefers – Matty gone gartless over a woman and you so hoddy-doddy you can't catch a man at all. Still, blood will tell, as Preacher Merrywest alluss say. "Some folk are born to grief," he say. "And some do fetch it home by the pailful."'

'Merrywest say anythin' but his prayers!' Jess retorted. 'And them he shout for fear the Lord have turned his back.'

'Hah! There speak a woman scorned! First by a preacher, then by a gamekeeper. Who'll you try next, Jess Henefer – the lavender-cart man?'

She wasn't worth arguing with. Jess turned on her heel and walked away, mortified by the sound of laughter in the steam behind her.

Matty never talked about personal things, but when she saw him he seemed content. Lily was still outwardly the same, light and smiling, sometimes singing, but the face she wore might cover all manner of hidden emotions. Jess no longer understood her. She was especially puzzled when news came that Clemency Haverleigh had given birth to a daughter whom she named Jane Mercy; and Lily's only reaction was to say, 'Jane Lassiter was her best friend at school,' for all the world as if she didn't care.

When Bella fell ill, with a chill that turned to whooping cough, Lily volunteered to move back to the big house, to help Jess nurse the child. Jess was grateful of a respite during the day, though she sat with Bella through the nights while Lily slept in her old room. Sir Richard and Lady Maud were frequent visitors, too – the squire quietly worrying himself to death, Jess thought, while her ladyship was more showy, disturbing Bella more than comforting her.

Lady Maud chose to blame Ching for her daughter's illness.

'Keep that horrible cat out of here!' she screamed on one occasion when Bella had just drifted into sleep. Bella woke with a start, and began coughing again. Ching made himself scarce.

However, after a terrible day or two when Bella's life was feared for, the crisis passed and she began to recover.

'You should go home to your husband now,' the doctor advised Lily. 'You must rest. You're looking a little peaked.'

'I'm quite well,' she assured him. 'Don't concern yourself about me, Doctor Michaels.'

He fastened his bag, threw his coat across his shoulders. 'I'm concerned for all my patients, Mrs Henefer. But I do have a special soft spot for you. I was called in when you were found, you know. The Clares were anxious to know that you were healthy. And you were – a very healthy girl-child indeed.'

'Strong gypsy blood,' Lily said, her tone deceptively light.

'You may be right.' His velvet-brown eyes surveyed her narrowly. 'Even so, you must take care. If you need any help, I am there.'

Jess gathered that he was telling Lily he knew she was pregnant, but Lily elected merely to smile and say, 'You're too kind, doctor.'

–

After that, Lily found many reasons to spend a night now and then in her old room at Hewinghall. If Bella was even a little off-colour, Lily

345

would insist on staying. Or perhaps the wind was too cold, or the frost too hard, or the snow too deep. Even to herself she didn't fully admit that she was avoiding her husband: the novelty of marriage had lost its first bright allure. Matty was not Richard; he hadn't Richard's finesse, and as the child inside her grew she found lovemaking increasingly uncomfortable. Besides which, his conversation was so limited – he didn't understand about books, or music, or theatre, and when she and Cousin Oriana discussed the finer things of life Matty made it clear he was bored. As often as not, he took himself off to the inn at Martham, where he spent most of his evenings. He often came in quarrelsome with drink.

'I see no point in struggling to get home when my husband won't be there!' she said crossly to Jess. 'He never comes in until late, if he appears at all. He knows I'm concerned about Bella. Besides, I have never liked being out in the dark, Jess, you know that. And in my state of health I must take care when the weather's bad.'

Her 'state of health' remained rosy, but as Christmas approached Jess saw that the pregnancy was beginning to show. Nor was it long before other eyes noted the clues – they'd been expecting something of the kind. Now they began to count the months. 'That wouldn't surprise me if that little 'un come in time for a slice o' the weddin' cake,' was the general feeling.

Lily knew what they were saying. But she had had long practice at wearing a smile while dying inside. Behind hands, everyone knew her marriage had been rushed through for a purpose, but to her face they'd never dare mention it. She told herself she didn't care. She was carrying Richard's child – perhaps Richard's son – and Richard loved her. She closed her eyes to the rest.

When she was at Hewinghall, she was happy, knowing Richard was close by, finding reasons to stay so that he could come to her and love her. Then, the world beyond her room ceased to exist. There were only he and she, together in the night, safe in their nest. Nothing else mattered to her, not Jess's worried looks, not Cousin Oriana's remonstrances, and certainly not Matty's increasingly bitter nagging. None of them knew the real, wonderful, miraculous truth, that Richard Fyncham was the father of her child. Her lover, her soulmate, her dearest darling...

On Christmas Eve, though, she was at home at the lodge, alone with Miss Peartree enjoying the fire and a glass of mulled wine, when the happy sound of carol-singing, accompanied by an accordion, reached them. Lily went to the window and pulled the curtain aside, seeing several lanterns shedding light over the little knot of singers well wrapped against the cold. Trodden snow lay on the ground, a few flakes slicing across the light on a bitter wind, but the song was sweet and stirring: 'It came upon the midnight clear...'

'They must have walked a long way,' Lily said. 'We must invite them in. We'll offer them some spiced wine.'

'How many are there?'

'Half a dozen or so, as far as...' She stopped as she saw that one of the men was wearing a broad-brimmed black hat. 'Perhaps they won't want wine. They're Methodists – that trouble-making preacher is with them.'

Miss Peartree blinked worriedly through her spectacles. 'You're not going to invite *him* in, I hope?'

Remembering the trouble Merrywest had brought, both to Jess and to Matty, Lily let the curtain drop. 'Perhaps not. But I ought to give them something. They've been good enough to come all this way to bring us Christmas cheer.'

Going into the hall, she opened the door, huddling into her shawl against the icy wind. As she appeared, the carol stopped. The accordion-player struck up a new chord and the voices rang out, singing stridently, 'Sinner, turn: why will ye die? God, your Maker, asks you why...'

As the hymn of exhortation went on behind him Merrywest stepped out, crying aloud in that terrible, carrying voice, words that struck at Lily like blows: 'Woman! Confess your sins! Harlot! Admit your wrong! Down on your knees before your Lord, woman of scarlet, steeped in lust and shame! Begotten in sin, cursed with the mark of Satan! Miserable sinner! Vilest offender. Turn now to Him who is your only salvation. Or will you burn in everlasting hellfire? – yes, and your misbegotten child with you!'

'Amen!' a voice cried, the woman lifting her face so that lantern light swung under her bonnet and identified her as Eliza Potts.

Sick bile rose in Lily's throat. She threw a hand to her mouth to stem it, and slammed the door. But she could still hear that awful voice: 'For the sins of the fathers shall be visited upon the children, to the tenth generation! Cursed be she who hears and will not listen! Cursed...'

'Lily!' Miss Peartree was there, taking her arm. 'Come away. Come away! Don't listen to him. You're not wicked. You're just… just young, and misguided, and foolish, and…' She was in tears of such distress that she blurted, 'I blame your papa for this! He never guided you rightly. If anyone was the sinner, then *he* was. That wicked, wicked man!'

Lily wasn't really listening. She felt detached from it all, both from the singing and ranting that was continuing outside and from Oriana's loving concern. None of it had any meaning. As she had known for a long time, there was no God. Or, if there was, he had long ago abandoned her.

She was not the only sinner the ranters had visited that night: Merrywest's newest crusade was the talk of the district.

'Why din't you tell me he'd been here?' Matty demanded of his wife when he heard what had occurred. 'Blast, if I'd a known…'

'What would you have done, Matthew? Got yourself thrown in the lock-up again?'

'You din't seem to mind that last time,' he reminded her bitterly. 'You called me your champion. En't I now allowed to stick up for you?'

Lily sighed. 'I'm too weary to care what anyone says about me. Maybe it's true – maybe I am a lost soul. A gypsy bastard, bearing the mark of Satan. Cursed from the cradle to the tomb.'

It made him uncomfortable when she used language like that. Sometimes he didn't understand her at all. 'Don't talk that way, Lily.'

'Why not?' she asked, and turned the full force of her strange eyes on him. 'It's true, isn't it?'

She had begun to wonder if her child, too, would be cursed as she was, born never to know who it really was, born to unhappiness. Except that she would make it believe it belonged to her and Matty. Its name would be Henefer. It would never know the truth. It, he, she… the thought of the child, stirring now inside her, filled her mind. A daughter for her, a son for Richard… which would it be?

–

On a bitterly cold night in January, Lily stayed late at the big house, anxious about Bella, who was sick again. The doctor had them move her bed into the schoolroom by the fire, and told them to keep Ching out of the sick room in case his fur was an added irritant to the child's weak chest.

348

Lily would gladly have stayed overnight, but lately Matty had been growing ever more resentful of her absences and she was aware that Lady Maud regarded her now-evident pregnancy with distaste. Lady Maud had begun to query how much longer Lily could continue in her role as governess and, indeed, Lily wondered the same. The trek back and forth in winter weather, though scarcely more than a mile, was becoming increasingly difficult.

That evening she set off bundled up against the cold and carrying a lantern to guide her way. Tracks of carts formed two frozen lines along the drive between swathes of snow indented by marks of hooves, fox-pads and tracks of birds. Lily kept to the side, where crisp snow gave her feet some purchase as she hurried along, anxious for the warmth of home, head down against the biting wind. She felt particularly bloated; her chest ached with heartburn – a sign that the child had lots of hair, so Cousin Oriana said – and her back was stiff after long hours of sitting reading to Bella.

She didn't even see Matty until he was on her, erupting out of the night to grab hold of her and shout, 'Where have you been 'til this hour?'

Wincing away from the sour stench of brandy on his breath, Lily tore her wrist free. 'You know where I've been, Matthew – at the big house. If you don't believe me, ask Jess.'

'Ask Jess. Ask Jess,' he mimicked. 'Our Jess'd swear black was white if you axed her to. Don't lie to me, Lily Henefer. I know where you've now been – off with that fancy man of yours. That Haverleigh!' As she tried to protest he grabbed her arm again, twisting it behind her.

'Matthew, stop it!' He'd been angry before, but never quite this angry, or quite this drunk. The violence in him frightened her. 'Please, stop it!'

'Why don't you admit it? Everybody know about you and him. I *seen* you sneaking off and meetin' him that first summer. That's why you were so upset at that ball when he turned up with Miss Clare. But soon's he crook his little finger, back you go for more, and when he put you up the stick you latch on to poor fool Matty Henefer to hide your sin and shame. I could've forgiven what you did afore we was wed, but I 'on't be made a laughin'-stock by my own wife. I'm off to see Haverleigh. Now. Tonight.'

'Matthew—'

'I'm a-goin'!' In the light of the lantern his face was dark, eyes bulging from his head as he took hold of her and swung her round,

349

shouting at her, 'I'll kill him! That's what I'm a-goin' to do. I'll kill him!'

'You can't! Matthew, no, you mustn't. I swear to you, I... I haven't seen Ashton for over a year.'

'You're a liar!'

'It's the truth!' Lily cried, knowing only that she had to stop him somehow. 'He's not the one...'

He became utterly still, his eyes demonic, his teeth gritted. His fingers bit into her arms, making her cry out, but squirm as she would he refused to release her. Instead, the pressure increased.

'Then who? *Who?!*'

'Please!' Instinctively, hoping for help, Lily glanced towards the big house, where light showed from one or two of the windows.

'Blast!' Matty swore obscenely and pushed her away from him with such force that she stumbled and fell to her hands and knees on the frozen grass. She dropped the lantern. Its glass smashed and the flame flickered out. The smell of paraffin came strong on the bitter wind as, for the briefest second, the moon showed behind scudding cloud. White flakes drifted out of the sky, tiny pieces of ice that fell on Lily's clothes, thickening all the time. Within moments, snow was swirling down.

Lily picked herself up, holding her stomach, frightened in case she had harmed the child. She felt sick and dizzy, and so very cold. Already the snow was caking on her cape. 'Matthew, please... Matthew...'

But Matty had gone.

Was he making for the big house? To do what? Had she inadvertently revealed the truth? Had he guessed about Richard? Oh, God...

Somehow, she stumbled and groped her way home to the lodge, where Cousin Oriana came anxiously to greet her: 'Lily, my dear. Oh, what's happened? Is it snowing? Did you see Matthew? He came in looking for you. He was in such a rage... He hasn't hurt you, has he?'

Lily shook her head. 'No. No, I'm perfectly all right, Cousin Oriana. Just shaken. And tired.'

Sleepless, wretched, she lay chewing her sheet, staring into the darkness, imagining what must be taking place at the big house. Richard and Matty...

–

Waking before dawn, Jess heard the silence and knew the snowfall had been deep. She got up stiffly from the pallet where she had lain, fully dressed and wrapped in a blanket, on the schoolroom floor to be near Bella. The fire was a glowing mound, the lamp burning low beside the bed. The child's breath came hoarse in her lungs and sweat dewed her brow and upper lip. Sweat! The fever had broken, thank the Lord.

Ching was scratching at the passage door. Jess let him in to the schoolroom, though she caught him and carried him, keeping him well away from Bella as she went to open the window. It was blocked with snow. The casement, opening outward, dislodged a wedge of whiteness and, in the faint light, Jess saw that the roof balcony was full of snow. Snow lay two feet deep on the parapet and on the roofs all around; the whole park was one vast, soft whiteness with blobs to show where the trees were.

Such snow! Jess had never seen anything like it. Suddenly everything was altered, the house isolated, cut off from the outside world. It gave her the strangest feeling of unease. Something awry, something amiss…

Though the cat wasn't keen on going out, she made sure he did what he had to do before she let him back in and then she took him and put him in Lily's room while she tidied round and did her early chores.

Soon she was going down to fetch hot water from the boiler in the big range in the kitchen, where two maids were already kneading dough and speculating whether the staff who lived out would be able to get to work.

'Morning, ladies!' George the footman came yawning into the kitchen in shirt-sleeves and braces. 'Oh – morning, Jess. Been snowing, I see. Well, *that* won't help the constables find our burglar, will it?'

'What burglar's that, then, George?' one of the maids enquired.

'The one that broke in last night – through the garden door.'

Tilly laughed. 'Oh, you and your tales! Pull you the other one.'

'No, it's true, sure as I'm standing here gasping for a cup of tea. He broke the glass and unfastened the bolt. Got all the way to the library. Sir Richard heard him and called us to help put him out, but by the time we got there he'd gone. Fetched a lot of books off their shelves, he had, and rifled the desk – it was a proper mess in there.'

He was subjected to an excited cross-examination. Jess would have liked to stay and listen, but she was anxious about Bella so she took her hot water and returned to the nursery.

She found Sir Richard gazing down at his sleeping daughter, haggard and unshaven, wearing a dressing gown over an open shirt and loose trousers.

'How is she, Jess?' he asked anxiously, turning haunted eyes on her.

'The fever's now broke, sir,' she said. 'That mean the worst is over. We must keep her warm, and build her strength back. Poor little 'un. Every time she get well somethin' else pull her down.'

'She wasn't...' he began, and licked his lips as if he was nervous. 'I mean, there wasn't any disturbance in the night, was there? That you heard? Nothing... unusual?'

'You mean the burglar, sir? Oh – George now mention it when I was below stairs. No, he din't come up here, if that's what you mean. That's a terrible thing, sir. Did he steal anything?'

'No. No, not that I can see. There was no money or anything...' He clawed a hand through his hair distractedly. 'Well, I'll leave you to it. I'll be back later to see how Bella is. I only hope she doesn't need the doctor. He'll never get through.'

Bella was doing all right. She started to eat a little, and take interest again; she would recover. So why did Jess still feel vaguely uneasy?

It was several days before the men got round to clearing the drive as far as the lodge, and then they brought back word that Lily was indisposed. It was several days more before Jess decided to ask Sal Gooden to sit with Bella for an hour while she walked down to see how Lily was. And Matty – for some reason she was anxious about Matty.

It was like walking down an ice tunnel, hard-packed snow underfoot and either side great walls of shovelled snow, higher than her head, with the sky blue above and the air so cold it made her head hurt and her breath turn to steam. The tunnel ran all the way to the door of the lodge, where Miss Peartree came beaming to greet Jess.

'Come in, come in. Well! This is a treat. *Two* visitors come toiling through the snow. I've got the kettle on. Tea won't be long. You go in.' She gestured to the parlour, calling, 'Look who's here, Mr Rudd.'

Rudd. Jess hesitated, then squared herself and went into the cosy parlour.

Rudd was rising from his chair, but Dash came wagging to greet her and she bent to pet him to avoid having to face his master.

'How'd you get here through all this snow?' she asked.

'It's patchy,' Rudd said. 'Drifted. Some spots in the wood there's hardly any at all. Any road, I've had to get out, to see to my birds. Nobody else to do it. Obi's hurt his back and the boy's ailing.'

She did look at him then, asking, 'En't Matty been at work?'

'That's what brought me here,' he said. 'I haven't seen him since yesterday week.'

Dear Lord! Eight days. Now she knew why she'd had a feeling something was wrong.

Miss Peartree came in, smiling and hospitable with a laden tray. As she poured tea, she chatted about Lily – 'I think she must have caught Bella's cold. She had a terrible throat two days ago and now she's streaming, poor child. I told her to stay in bed for a few days. I can manage, though Dolly isn't here. She was at home with her mother the night the snow came, so I don't expect her until it clears a bit. Matthew too – as I was saying to Mr Rudd when you arrived, Jess, we haven't seen Matthew since that night, either. I think...' she glanced at the door, lowering her voice as she confided, 'they had a little argument and he went off in a temper, the way he does. Oh, it was nothing. A tiff, no more. Matthew generally heads for the inn when he's had words with Lily, so I expect that's where he is – snowbound in Martham Staithe.'

Jess shared a look with Rudd. Aloud, they agreed that Miss Peartree was probably quite right – Matty would turn up soon. But he didn't entirely believe it, any more than she did.

She took a cup of tea up to Lily, but Lily was feeling sorry for herself, full of cold and didn't want to talk. She, too, said that Matty must be trapped in Martham, but her eyes said otherwise – she was worried.

Leaving the lodge together, Jess and Rudd, with the dog trotting ahead, went out into the ice tunnel and paused by a side branch running into clearer territory under trees.

'I'll try and get through to Martham,' he said.

'What about your birds?'

'They'll fend for themselves if they have to.'

Jess wanted to protest, but she understood he was offering to do it for her sake, to set her mind at rest. And if truth were told she *was* wholly anxious for Matty. He'd been gone eight days. In that time, had he been at Martham, he could surely have got back if he'd tried.

So she said, simply, 'Thank you, Reuben. But... take you care. We don't want to be sendin' out search parties for you, too.'

A smile flickered in his eyes, quirking a corner of his mouth. 'I'll let thee know, soon as there's news,' he promised, and set off into the wood with Dash at his heels.

I love you, Reuben Rudd, Jess thought fiercely as she watched him go. Oh, if only...

–

Matty was not in Martham Staithe. No one there had seen him since before the snowstorm. With the snow so deep the postal services were suspended; it was ages before Lily could write and ask Fanny Fysher if she'd seen Matty. His friends said he'd been restless lately, talking about wanting to go back to Lynn, back to the sea. Maybe he'd decided to leave.

Maybe he had, but if so he'd gone empty-handed, without any of his clothes or other possessions.

Worried about her brother, Jess questioned Lily closely, but Lily couldn't imagine where he'd gone, either. She was distressed, her face puffy, her body ungainly, tears coming easily.

'We quarrelled, Jess. We're always quarrelling. I haven't liked to say too much about it – I mean, he is your brother, but... Well, he will keep going to the inn and getting drunk, and then losing his temper. I'm not *used* to that kind of behaviour. When I married Matthew, I... I didn't expect it to be like this. I thought... well, I thought he was kind, and understanding. I didn't think he'd ever be angry with me. But he *is* angry. More and more. He regrets his bargain. It wouldn't surprise me if he'd gone off back to Lynn. Washed his hands of me. Oh, Jess... you don't think anything bad has happened, do you?'

More snow fell, enough to cause the men constant work keeping the paths clear. Slowly, connections were made with the nearby villages and, at the beginning of March, Mr Witt the carter got through from Hunstanton.

During those weeks, Jess kept Bella company. Lily was getting near her time, not so able to walk up from the lodge every day.

'I wish I could be at the big house with you,' she said one day when Jess called to see her. 'I feel safe there. What shall I do if the baby comes and I'm all alone with Cousin Oriana? Oh, Jess... you will be with me, won't you? Say you'll come and help me.'

Matty's absence was a continuing sorrow for Jess. Where had he gone that night in the snow? Had he gone off to Huns'ton and taken the train to Lynn? Had he run away to sea, maybe Lowestoft or Yarmouth? Fanny hadn't replied to Lily's letter yet, but Fanny wasn't much more of a writer than Jess was; she'd have to get young Sam to do it for her – he was the scholar of the family. Oh... Jess didn't know what to think. She only knew she had a horrible, empty feeling about Matty. It wasn't like him to have gone away without a word, without taking any of his belongings. She wished she could know what had happened that night.

She blamed herself for letting Lily use her brother, but when she said as much to Rudd he shook his head and told her Matty was a grown man: he'd known what he was doing.

'And try not to blame Miss Lily, either,' he advised. 'She's been badly hurt, tha knows. She's not strong like you. You once told me you had a feeling she needed thee. Well, happen you were right, lass. She needs thee more than ever now. You won't desert her, will you?'

No, she wouldn't. She couldn't. The bond that had sprung between her and Lily when first they met was still there. Slightly battered, maybe, but it remained a strong force in Jess's life and would be so, she felt, as long as she lived.

–

Alone with her thoughts, awaiting the birth of her child, Lily spent hours at her window. She was unable to do anything – not read, not sew, not even write in her journal beyond a few sketchy thoughts. Where was Matty? What had happened to him?

Richard seemed to have no time for her. He seemed to be avoiding her, afraid that their liaison might be discovered.

'Yes, Henefer was here,' he had said during one of their few, brief meetings. 'He was here, then he left – and no one any the wiser, thank God. That's all I know of it, except that he was drunk and in no fit state to do anything sensible. I don't know where he is.'

Sometimes Lily caught herself wondering with horror if he had killed Matty. And if he had, to her shame she knew her main concern would be for Richard.

It was a Friday in mid-March when Dolly Upton came running to the big house to fetch Jess. Longman sent one of the boys to go for the doctor, while permission was sought from Lady Maud for Jess to absent herself. Lady Maud grudged it, but she consented and Jess and Dolly returned to the lodge where Lily was in the grip of both contractions and terror.

Jess sat by her, cooling her brow and trying to calm her, but Lily was prey to wild fears. 'What if it's deformed? What if it's marked with the devil's mark? What if it dies... Oh, Jess, Jess! I'm so afraid. I wish Matthew was here.'

'Aye, me too,' Jess said softly, freshening the cloth in some lavender water before replacing it on Lily's forehead.

The wide, frightened eyes stared up at her, bright blue and velvet brown. 'Jess... I never meant to hurt him. I really thought he would be happy. I never meant...'

'I know, miss.'

The doctor arrived and went away again – Lily had called for help much too soon. Jess pitied her, felt angry with her, wanted to scold and hug her all at the same time. Lily was a child, not yet twenty, not wise in any way. For all her mistakes, she remained an innocent, trusting in dreams and happy endings.

Her labour went on through the night. Dr Michaels returned in the early hours and saw her through the last stages, but it was Jess she clung to, Jess who was so close she could smell the fear on her as the contractions grew stronger and sweat poured from her, her face and body contorted with effort. And then suddenly the child was delivered, sliding out on to the soiled sheet, yelling lustily.

'Is it all right?' Lily asked anxiously. 'Is it all right?'

'It's a boy,' the doctor declared as he quickly checked it over. 'Ten fingers, ten toes, good lungs on him too... a fine strong boy. What else do you want?'

Jess had the pleasure of washing the baby and wrapping it in a flannel sheet with just its red, wrinkled face showing, while Miss Peartree and Dolly tended Lily, getting her washed and into a fresh nightgown. She was quiet now, allowing them to settle her back into bed where she lay exhausted and pale, her eyes closed. Her two attendants came to have a good look at the baby, exclaiming over him.

356

Slowly, smiling down at the tiny boy-child in her arms, Jess walked to the bedside. He had a mass of dark curls, just like Lily's, but he was long – he was going to be tall. He appeared to be gazing up at her with quiet trust and curiosity, one tiny hand pushing out of the enwrapping blanket. When she put her finger there he grasped it, holding it tightly – laying claim to her heart, she always thought in later years.

'Don't you want to have a look at your son?'

Only Lily's pink lips moved, saying again, 'Is he all right? Tell me the truth, Jess! His eyes…'

'He have a beautiful pair of eyes,' Jess said. 'Dark blue.'

Lily did look at her then. 'Both of them?'

'Both of them, Miss Lily.'

'Oh…' Tears starting, Lily sat up. 'Let me have him. Let me see him. Oh… Oh, isn't he a darling!'

Robbed of the sweet weight that had briefly filled her arms, Jess said, 'He're a beautiful boy. You should be proud.' She felt compelled to add, defying the fates, 'Our Matty will be, when he know he have a son.'

The words fell hollow. No one in that room believed this was Matty's son, born only six months after a hurried wedding that had followed on the heels of scandal whispered about Lily and a certain Mr Haverleigh. More than that – no one in that room believed that Matty would ever return to claim or disclaim the child.

Jess felt the knowledge crawl across her skin: Matty was never coming back. With every day that passed she was more sure of it.

–

The thaw came slowly, melting the mounds of ice, turning the ground to mud. Snowdrops nodded in the woods and, as April came, the birds were busy. So was Ching, out on the rooftops watching for unwary nest-builders.

Since Lily was occupied with her baby, Jess had full charge of the nursery, where Bella was gradually returning to full health. That winter's ailments had depleted her strength, but when she wasn't resting she liked making jigsaws and drawing, or playing with her many dolls. She and Jess got along famously, but she missed Lily.

'When can I see the baby?' she kept asking. 'What is he called? I can't remember the name.'

'Jabez,' Jess replied. 'It's a name out of the Bible. Jabez Matthew Hugh Henefer – there's a mouthful for a titty-totty bor.' Lily had chosen the names with care – Matthew for her husband, Hugh for her adoptive father, and Jabez because it had a strange, exotic sound to it – like Lilith. Jess had a feeling that Lily thought Jabez might be a gypsy name.

They'd brought a low day-bed couch into the schoolroom and placed it where Nanny's chair had been, near the fire. Bella took her afternoon rest there, often with Ching curled in her lap, though the cat had to be shut elsewhere when Lady Maud came up.

Her ladyship had taken to visiting the schoolroom for tea since Bella had been so ill. She brought with her a whiff of the outdoors, talk of horses and dogs. Was it enforced idleness, because of the snow, that had caused the new tension that showed in jerky flicks of her auburn head, in restless eyes and an inability to settle more than a few minutes? Her visits left Bella exhausted, as though the mother's nervous tension drained her child's energy, but as far as Jess could tell Lady Maud did not visit the nursery at night any more. Perhaps she had realised that her visits frightened Bella, or perhaps it was Ching's presence that deterred her. Lady Maud detested the cat and the cat knew it – he would torment his enemies, if he had the chance, as he had tormented poor Miss Wilks.

Sir Richard's visits were more welcome. He came smiling, bringing kindness and love to his daughter.

One afternoon his stay was curtailed when George arrived with an urgent message – 'Mr Rudd is most anxious to see you, sir.'

The squire left at once.

Having settled Bella down to rest, Jess went to stand at the window, looking over the balcony parapet to the wide acres of the park, green now with spring. Different from the way it had looked that winter morning, blanketed with snow. The day Matty disappeared. She wished she could go down and see Rudd, if only for a minute. She hadn't seen him to speak to since they met at the lodge. Oh... it was best not to see him. Thinking about him was bad enough.

'Jess!' Sal Gooden hissed from the doorway. 'You're wanted. In the library. Quick sharp.'

'In the—' Jess had never been inside the library, not in all the time she'd been at Hewinghall.

'That's what I was told. I reckon Lady Maud want to see you about somethin'. Maybe they're hirin' a new governess.'

If they were, Lily would be disappointed: she'd set her heart on coming back to the big house before long.

Quickly tidying herself, Jess ran down to the library and knocked on the big, carved door.

'Come in,' bade the squire's voice.

She saw him outlined against one of the windows, then a movement drew her attention to the far side of a grand marble hearth where a fire was crackling. Reuben Rudd stood there. He looked as if he'd come straight from the woods, wearing his tweeds and leather cape. Mud and leaves caked his boots and buskins and there were further traces of mud on his hands, even a streak down one cheek which might have looked comical had it not been for the sombre light in his eyes.

Something bad had happened. The atmosphere in the room fairly screamed disaster. Why else had she been summoned here? Why else was Rudd looking like that? And the squire... Though the fire sent out a deal of heat, something cold touched her soul.

'I'll leave you to talk,' Sir Richard said quietly, making for the door. 'I'll see you're not disturbed.'

As the door closed behind him, Jess forced herself to look at Rudd. He came and took her arm, saying, 'Sit down, lass. I've some news to tell thee. Bad news, I'm afraid.'

Jess sank to the edge of one of the big leather chairs, feeling the fire's heat all down her right side. As Rudd dropped on one knee beside her, she said, 'It's Matty, en't it?'

Twenty-Seven

It seemed a long time before Rudd spoke. He knelt there, watching her with heavy eyes, then took her hand between his own, rubbing it gently. 'Aye, lass. I'm sorry, but... Obi found him, early this morning.'

'Found him?' She didn't understand.

'In the woods, not far from the ice-house. Among a bank of thorn. A tree had come down on top of him. Quite a few trees came down under that weight of snow.'

She knew what he was saying, but... 'He's dead?'

'Since the night of the big snowfall, I'd say.'

Only half aware of the comforting pressure of his hands around hers, she stared at the fire, watching the flames dance. She'd known, hadn't she? She'd known Matty must be dead. He wouldn't just have gone away. Not Matty.

Even so, she didn't believe it.

'You reckon the tree fell on him?'

'That's what we thought, at first. Then later, after we got the tree away... then...'

She stared at him, not even breathing. In his eyes she read the sick horror of what he'd seen; she didn't need telling what a state Matty's body had been in, lying under the snow all that time, then the thaw, the animals all waking, hungry...

'I'm sorry, lass,' Rudd said, pressing her hand harder. 'There's no easy way to tell thee. He was shot. Through the head.'

Shot?

'One single shot. Not a shotgun. A pistol of some kind. We thought at first he must have shot himself, but we couldn't find any gun nearby. The police are searching, but—'

'The police?'

'It's for them to investigate now, Jess.'

She didn't comprehend him. What was he saying – that Matty had been murdered? How could that be? Who would do such a thing?

Her mind provided the name: Merrywest.

'Look...' From his pocket Rudd produced a bedraggled shred of cloth with something attached to it – a button: a silver button with a wavy edge and a trellis pattern, a button from 'Hardlines' Henefer's waistcoat, that his oldest son had worn. 'I brought you this, so's you'd know for sure.'

She took the button, and as her fingers played over the shape of it the first tug of grief came, like something far distant that had no real connection with her. 'One of these buttons was in your cottage,' she said. 'Do you remember?'

'Aye,' Rudd replied gravely, and when she looked at him he added, 'He told me about it, Jess. It's not important.'

She stood up, staring across the room at the windows, holding the silver button tightly in her fist. The light seemed dazzling and the grief was inside her now, deep inside her, ripping up through her vitals, into her chest, rushing up her throat... Beside her, Rudd straightened too and she looked up at him, saying, 'That foolish great lummox!' And then the tears came, roaring up to fill her head and burst out in a cry of bottomless pain. Rudd put his arms around her and drew her to rest against him, and stood there, holding her, letting the grief rage.

-

When the news reached Park Lodge, the truth that Lily had feared for weeks came rearing up to stun her: Richard had killed Matty – she was sure of it. Richard had killed him, hidden him and then called in his footmen as a means of explaining the mess in the library. Then he'd got Matty out to the wood and left him in the snow. Richard had been madly jealous of Matty – he'd said so in the note she kept tucked inside her journal. He'd turned murderer out of love for her – and that meant she was to blame for Matty's death.

She came flying to the big house, scarlet flags on pallid cheeks, eyes abrim and bonnet askew. She paused on the threshold of the nursery, where Jess was folding linen and Bella played on the hearthrug with the cat.

'Jess! Oh, Jess... I just heard. About Matthew. Oh... I don't know what to say. It's *my* fault. It was because of me.'

Jess felt hard and cold, her heart dead, but beneath it resentment stirred. How typical of Lily to take the blame, drawing attention to herself. She couldn't bear not to be at the centre of everything.

'No, Miss Lily,' she said flatly.

'But it was. It *was* my fault! If he hadn't married me, he would be alive now. Oh… I never meant to hurt him, Jess. How did it go so wrong? Poor Matthew—'

'His name was Matty!' Jess cried, pressing her fists to her head for fear it might explode. 'Nobody never called him Matthew, 'cept you and Miss Peartree. He was Matty, just Matty. But *you* had to change it. Even his name wasn't good enough for you. Because *he* wasn't good enough!'

Lily was shaking visibly, her pink lips trembling, her eyes wide and wet. 'That's not true, Jess. I *did* care about him. He was good, and kind. It was *I* who changed him. I hurt him, disappointed him. Oh… Jess, I'm sorry. I'm so, so sorry!'

That she meant it sincerely was obvious.

Unable to hold on to her resentment, knowing that Lily needed someone to share her grief, Jess held out her arms and together they wept for Matty.

–

'Murder, by person or persons unknown,' was the verdict of the inquest.

For Jess, the arrival of her family was a comfort. Fanny and her husband 'Sprat' Fysher, and Tom, who had been Matty's best mate, came to Hewing for the funeral, bringing with them Sam – how he'd grown! – and young Joe. Jess embraced them all, glad of their support.

After the service they returned to Park Lodge for refreshment.

Rudd was at the lodge. Every day that passed gave Jess more reasons for admiring the gamekeeper – his steady strength, his supportiveness, his patience… Maybe one day soon, now that Matty was gone, she'd be able to tell him the whole truth. For now, too much else weighed on her mind.

The Fyshers had brought momentous news – Preacher Merrywest had been arrested, charged with Matty's murder.

'Merrywest?' Lily queried. 'Who…?'

'The preacher – the Methodist preacher.'

Lily couldn't take it in. Guilt gnawed like blight inside her and she felt desperately alone despite the people around her. They held her responsible, she felt sure, and so she kept her baby out of their way and soon made excuses to go up to him, to feed him.

'She think herself too good for us,' Fanny said. 'Well, I shall see that little 'un afore I go, whatever she say. If he's Matty's son then he's my nephew, part of our family, and she 'on't keep him from us.'

'She don't mean to,' Jess excused her friend. 'She're in a bad way over losing Matty. Now, what's all this about Merrywest?'

Police enquiries had revealed that Merrywest had been in the area on the night Matty vanished. The preacher had become a frequent visitor to Martham Staithe, leading Bible classes and prayer meetings with his recent converts, and he had been lodging in Hewing with the Pottses' relative, Mrs Kipps. On the night of the storm he had not come in – got snowbound on his way back from a meeting and had to spend the night in a barn, so he'd claimed when he turned up next day. As soon as the snow had allowed, he had trekked to Hunstanton and taken the train back home.

And now he had been arrested on suspicion of murder.

Jess pitied his wife and children. Perhaps now, at last, Merrywest's real self would be revealed. If she was called to give witness, she'd tell everything she knew. There was nothing to stop her now.

However, after only a few days, below-stairs gossip reported that Merrywest had been released.

Jess went down to the lodge, taking Bella with her to have a reading lesson, but while Bella cooed over the baby in his pram, outside in the spring sunshine, Jess relayed the news to Lily and Miss Peartree.

'Eliza Potts have given Merrywest an alibi.'

Lily shook her head, her mouth curving bitterly though her eyes remained dead. 'Then that is that.' She had known, anyway, that Merrywest wasn't the culprit. She knew that Richard Fyncham had killed Matty.

But, 'Eliza?' said Miss Peartree worriedly. 'Why, what does she know about it?'

'She say she was at that meeting, and walked home with him. She got trapped in the same barn, and stayed there the whole night with him. Didn't say so afore for fear of scandal, but now she're had to confess, to save his skin.'

'Do you doubt her word, Jess?' Miss Peartree asked.

'I dunno, miss. All I know is that Merrywest have an eye for the ladies, and Eliza is a handsome woman. 'Course, that was wholly innocent, so she say. He din't lay a finger on her. She're just one of his faithful followers...'

As the baby gave a faint wail from his perambulator outside, Lily leapt up and hurried out to see to him, not sorry to escape.

Behind her, into the silence, Miss Peartree said, as if to herself, 'Eliza Potts is no novice in the ways of the flesh. And… she does appear to have a particular taste for men of the cloth.'

'Miss?' Jess's expression must have been eloquent.

The old lady's face was troubled. 'I've never told anyone else, but… I have reason to believe that Eliza was Reverend Clare's mistress.'

What? 'Why, Miss Peartree, ma'am!'

'Didn't you ever think she took liberties?' Miss Peartree asked. 'I certainly did. But he wouldn't hear a word against her, would he? I thought it was because he didn't want to trouble himself with domestic matters, but, just before Reverend Clare left, Mr Rudd asked me if I'd ever suspected anything untoward might be going on with Eliza and her brother. Poaching, that kind of thing. Well, I hadn't, but I'd never felt comfortable with her, ever since she accused Dolly of stealing, so one day, when she was out, I made it my business to look in her room. I found some pheasant feathers under her bed, and then…' Pale eyes behind her spectacles blinked unhappily. 'I discovered some poems. They were… love poems. Passionate love poems, Jess. Written in the Reverend Clare's hand. And as I looked further… I found some of my dear cousin's jewellery – he'd given her things belonging to his own dead wife!

'Oh, we were fools not to see! Those Tuesday afternoons when he liked us all to go out, when she was there alone with him… the power she had over him. I mean… why else would he have recommended her so fulsomely to Lady Maud? He felt guilty, and he was trying to compensate her. Oh, Jess, my dear, I have felt so badly about it. So helpless. I can never tell poor dear Lily. But I fear Eliza is trying to hurt Lily as a means of punishing Reverend Clare. All the gossip, and then this terrible preacher, and… and Matthew…'

Matty, yes.

Jess was sure now: Eliza had lied, to save Merrywest's skin. But what did she hope to gain from it?

–

'*Dear God, thank you, thank you, thank you.*' The writing was jagged, splattered with tears, but Lily didn't care. She'd been out for a walk in the soft April evening and Richard had come riding along one of the woodland paths – quite, quite by chance. Now, she was happy for the first time in weeks, because she knew he hadn't harmed Matty.

Leaping down from his horse, he had tried to take her in his arms, but she had backed away, saying something incoherent about the blood on his hands: 'It will always be between us – his blood crying out. "All the perfumes of Arabia will not sweeten this—"'

'Lily!' He had taken hold of her, shaking her. 'You surely don't think that I... Oh, my sweetest dear, what have you been thinking? Yes, he came to the hall; he came and found me in the library. He was drunk. Raving. He didn't know what he was doing or saying. He swung a punch at me – and landed on the floor in a heap. I went for help, and by the time I returned he was gone. He'd stormed about the library, knocking books down, opening drawers and cupboards. I don't know why. Maybe he hoped to find money, maybe just as an outlet of rage. But I thought it more discreet not to mention names, to say simply there was an intruder. Darling love, I swear to you that when I last saw him he was alive.'

Relief sent her into his arms, to share passionate, drowning kisses, rediscovering each other, reconfirming their love.

'But who could have done it?' she said then. 'Who, Richard?'

He held her tightly. 'I don't know. Oh, my love, forget about Henefer! He's too much on your mind.'

'How can I help it?' she protested. 'I feel responsible. If I had not married him—'

'Hush! God knows I wish it had been different, but his death was not our doing. Believe that, Lily. Believe it.' His arms pressed her tight until he felt her begin to relax. He surveyed her with ardent eyes, clear and grey. 'Oh, my darling love, how I've missed you. We *must* find a way for you to return to the big house. Not yet, perhaps, but in a little while. I'll speak to Maud. I'll see if she will agree to your returning – with the child, too. Bella will like that. It will be good for her to have another child in the nursery. Besides...' He gazed passionately into her eyes, stroking her face. 'He is her brother, after all. He is my son. He should be at Hewinghall.'

–

The mystery of Matty's death remained unresolved: it looked as though neither the weapon nor the culprit would ever be found. For

Jess it was a continuing wound. If only she had killed Merrywest when she had the chance! Now, because of Eliza, the villain went free.

As the anniversary of young Harry Fyncham's death approached again, in May, Jess sensed the rising tension in Lady Maud. She had been upset for months – because of Bella's long illness, Jess assumed – but now she often came to the nursery in a talkative, high-strung state, her breath strong with scented cashews chewed to cover the odour of gin.

When the fateful date arrived, Jess lay awake far into the night, watching and listening until a fitful sleep overcame her. She woke at once when the banister on the family stairs cracked as if someone was leaning on it. A faint gleam of lamplight passed her door, the telltale board creaked and then, because her ears were tuned for it, she heard the bolt on Bella's door being drawn back.

Jess threw her covers aside and reached for her wrap, shivering in the dawn chill. The first streaks of light showed beyond her high window, touching pink on the underside of wind-stretched cloud as she crept barefoot to her door and waited there, her ear pressed against it.

The silence went on so long that Jess unlatched her door and edged it open. As she looked out, Lady Maud came out of Bella's room, her wrap flowing behind her, the flame in her lamp dancing as she strode for the schoolroom, leaving its door open, too. An added draught told Jess that Lady Maud had opened a window. She was going out on to the roof.

Fearing that the rush of cold air might disturb Bella, Jess hurried to the child's room and found her peacefully sleeping. On the night table beside her there lay an envelope with the name 'JESS' written on it. A note? From Lady Maud? Jess picked it up, slit it open with fumbling fingers, peered at the words in grey dawn light…

She was doing her best to learn to read. She'd listened hard when Bella was studying, and she'd pored over books by herself in spare moments – she was proud of her prowess with print. But she still had trouble making sense of hand-written words, especially when they were scrawled all over the page like a spider's tracks. She deciphered: '*If you came about my d…*' Jess guessed the word was 'daughter', and it must be 'care' not 'came'; so, 'If you care about my daughter…' but she couldn't make out any more.

366

The light was growing, seeping through the curtains. Across them a shadow moved – Lady Maud walking on the roof balcony. Jess withdrew, closing Bella's door gently behind her.

The draught still blew from the schoolroom and the shrill cries of soaring house martins came loud. Jess stole across the bare boards and worn rugs to the open window, going cautiously for fear of being seen. Outside, the sun waited to rise from a dark bank, throwing angry red light on to the underside of higher cloud. Against that sky, pale and dark blue streaked with scarlet, with martins darting around her, Lady Maud stood on the balcony, her hair and clothes blowing on the morning breeze, her hands knotted into fists as they rested on the stone parapet. Though Jess couldn't see her face, every line of her body expressed misery. She was speaking to herself, muttering softly, something about 'Harry,' and 'Why? Why?' Then, as if making a decision, she threw one knee on to the parapet and hoisted herself up, poised on all fours, breathing, 'Yes, like this. Brave boy! Like this, Harry,' and with her arms outstretched she slowly straightened to her full height.

Jess drew back, as if by doing so she could wrench her mistress away from danger. But Lady Maud had perfect balance. Despite the wind that wrapped her clothes close about her body and blew her hair round her face, she walked steadily along the parapet, treading like a dancer in her bare feet, going briefly out of Jess's sight behind the edge of the dormer. Jess heard her laugh, and say, 'Oh, Harry! Yes!' as she came back. The light of the rising sun glittered in the tears that wet her face as she let her wrap loose and stood there with it flying behind her, her head up, staring into the brightness of the sun.

Then Ching appeared, jumping lithely down from the roof slates to the leaded balcony and up on to the parapet, two feet away from her ladyship. Tail sinuously stroking the air, he gave a little '*Prrp?*'

Lady Maud glanced down and saw him. She uttered a cry and began to teeter, her arms flailing wildly.

'Milady!' Jess's cry mingled with her lady's scream as she fell.

Ever afterwards Jess retained the impression that Lady Maud could have saved herself – could have jumped the other way, down on to the balcony. Instead, she let herself go over the edge. As if, all along, part of her had wanted to fall. To follow Harry…

Lady Maud was dead! Lily could hardly believe it. First Matty and now… Fate was opening the way for her and Richard to be together. *This* was how it would happen, her heart's desire, at last. Oh… she grieved for Matty – she had shed many tears for him – and she was sorry for Maud, dreadfully sorry, but the way Jess told it Maud had been growing ever more deranged over Harry's death. She was happier dead, off in heaven with the son she had adored. Her daughter she could safely leave in Lily's hands; Lily would love Bella, be a real mother to her. That was how it would all end. Happily. As in all good fairy tales.

That Richard too saw the same eventual ending was proved by the way he had immediately sent Bella to stay with Lily, to keep her away from the scandal and upheaval that were inevitable. He and Lily would have to be discreet, perhaps for several months, but in the end they would be together. Happiness would flower from this dreadful, dreadful accident.

It *was* an accident. Of that Lily was convinced. Maud had, perhaps, courted the danger, but she hadn't *intended* to kill herself.

'Then why'd she leave a note?' Jess blurted, and immediately wished she had bitten her tongue.

Lily became still, her eyes bright and hard. 'Note? What note? What did it say?'

Now Jess felt badly. She'd promised the squire never to mention that note. 'I en't sure. I couldn't make out her writing, not clearly.'

'Well, where is it now?'

'Thrown away.' She didn't add that Sir Richard had destroyed it.

'I see. Well… gracious goodness, Jess, perhaps she was asking you to… to take Bella to see her later. Or just to see that she ate her porridge. It could have been a million things.'

'Then why'd she never write down her instructions afore? She alluss sent word by Mrs Roberts, or one of the maids – or told me herself when she came up.' Jess had an uneasy feeling about that note.

She'd left it on the table in the schoolroom and forgotten about it until later, when Sir Richard was there. He'd seen the note and asked what it was and when she'd told him she wasn't sure, because she couldn't read it clearly, he'd read it himself. Then he'd gone very quiet, and crumpled the paper up and thrown it into the cold hearth and put a match to it, watching until it was all burned.

'It's nothing,' he'd said. 'Ravings. I'd be obliged if you would forget it ever existed, Jess. My wife's memory needs no further soiling. There will be talk enough without this.'

–

With Bella staying at the lodge, Jess divided her time between there and the big house; she went early to wash and dress Bella, and again in the evening to get her to bed, but unless she was specifically needed at the lodge she took her meals in the servants' hall and did extra jobs that Mrs Roberts found for her. Below stairs there was much fresh gossip about Master Harry. Those who had been at Hewinghall when the young heir died now found many parallels in his mother's death, not to mention new cause for superstition and legend-building.

Crossing the yard one breezy morning, Jess heard Eliza Potts's voice behind a bank of billowing sheets: '...and didn't Kate Hewitt – Kate Lester as was, the last nurserymaid – alluss say that attic was haunted? Well, now we know. Harry Fyncham lured his mother after him.'

The other maids twittered nervously in response.

'And who'll he call next, heh?' Eliza went on. 'He 'on't be satisfied with one. These things alluss run in threes. Maybe Miss Bella'll run mad. Maybe grief'll send the squire shanny. Maybe the Fynchams'll die out.'

'That's enough!' Jess swept aside the damp sheet and confronted the gossips. 'Miss Bella's frit enough already without you spreadin' more wicked gossip. Call yourself a Christian, Eliza Potts... you oughta be ashamed of your evil tongue. Lady Maud *fell*. The cat scared her and she fell. There wan't no ghost. There never have been no ghost.'

'Tell that to Miss Lily,' Eliza retorted. 'Or should I say the Widow Henefer? Sal Gooden heard her say to Mrs Roberts as how she was alluss a-hearin' things in the night and reckoned she was bein' watched.'

'You're alluss tryin' to blame Miss Lily,' said Jess, stung by that reference to Matty. 'She han't never done anythin' to you. Or is that a case of "the sins of the father"? Is it *him* you're gettin' back at?'

For the first time that Jess could remember, Eliza blanched and looked confused. So Miss Peartree had been right! Contenting herself

369

With a look of total disgust, Jess walked away, making for the back door. She was surprised to find herself trembling.

Behind her, Eliza's wooden pattens clopped on the cobbles as she came hurrying. 'What'd you now mean by that remark?' she demanded in an undertone that wouldn't carry beyond the two of them.

'I reckon you know what I mean,' Jess replied, equally low. 'Reckon *I* shoulda known, too – long ago. I remember you sayin' you had your sights set higher than a gamekeeper, on'y I thought that was just talk.'

'You en't got no proof o' nothin'!'

'No more'n you've had proof of things you've said about me and Miss Lily – and a dozen others. But mud sticks, Eliza. I'm now warnin' you – do you imitate to do any more harm to Miss Lily, and I might have to mention a word about Reverend Clare somewhere.'

As she turned away, Eliza's hand on her arm stopped her. 'Hold you hard, Jess Henefer. We en't been friends, but I don't reckon you're the sort as'd talk out o' turn. 'Specially... that'd be wholly bad for me right now. I'm goin' to be wed soon. If he found out...'

'Wed?' That was news. 'Who to?'

Eliza's green eyes narrowed, as if she had not planned to tell, but pride made her toss her head and straighten her shoulders as she said, 'The preacher. Merrywest.'

'What?' Was this a sour joke?

'I reckon he owe it to me, after I ruined my reputation for him by tellin' how we was together in that barn, the night your Matty got hisself killed. I made my choice then. I knew my family wouldn't be best pleased, but I had to tell the truth. And it *was* the truth.'

The high colour in her cheeks, the flash of her eyes, said much more – she and Merrywest were lovers.

'You in love with him, Eliza?'

'I reckon.'

'And him?'

'He feel the same.'

Jess could hardly believe it but she actually pitied the girl. 'Do he? Well, that's prob'ly what some o' his other women thought, too – them as came willing. Not them as he forced, or blackmailed. Like my mother. And me, and other young girls from his Sunday school.' Funny, but it was easy to say it to Eliza, not to hurt her but to warn her. Jess felt entirely calm about it.

'You're a liar!'

'No, I en't,' Jess denied quietly. 'And you know it. In your heart you surely know that man han't got an honest bone in his whole body. He've used you, just like he uses all women. And when he've got tired of it he'll go back home to his quiet little wife and his two quiet little 'uns, safe behind that mask of holy—'

Eliza stiffened and jerked as if she'd been hit. 'He're married?'

'Din't you know that?'

'I don't believe you!'

'Then don't. All you have to do is go to Lynn and call at number seven, Port Street. Mrs Merrywest'll soon tell you who to believe. Funny, I wonder why he never mentioned her? And him such a fine, upstanding, preachifyin' man, so hot after sinners!' She watched as a flurry of emotions chased across Eliza's even features – disbelief, bafflement, dawning realisation... a recipe whose end-product was righteous anger.

'Blast him! He can't do this to me! Blast! My family'll kill him. Wait till I tell our Jim, and my dad. No man crosses the Pottses and gets away with it. No man! Not even a high-talking, lying, snaky-tongued preacher!'

'You still say you were with him in that barn?' It was important for her to know for sure.

Eliza's eyes narrowed, turned crafty. 'Mebbe I wan't, after all. I can deny it, can't I? I can say I was lyin', to protect him. Blast, so I can!'

'But were you there?' Jess cried. 'Were you with him that night?'

Eliza stared at her, a slow smirk spreading. 'Wun't you like to know, Jess Henefer? Wun't you just like to know?'

—

They gave Maud Fyncham a fine funeral, on a beautiful day in May. A glass-sided carriage filled with flowers bore the shining coffin, drawn by six black horses. Half the county came, including the Clares and the Haverleighs, but Lily stayed discreetly at home.

The coroner's verdict had been: accidental death.

Bella was dressed all in white, walking beside her father with Jess not far away. Watching the child bravely throw a handful of earth down on to the coffin, Jess held back her tears with an effort. Perhaps the little 'un didn't fully understand. Or was she relieved that her mother was gone? At least she didn't know *how* Lady Maud had died. Everyone had agreed that, given her horror of the roof, the details should be kept from her, if possible.

Despite the brightness of the day, Jess felt a heaviness on her spirit. Eliza had said something about tragedies running in threes; Jess believed that, too – if a second death followed a first, you could look for a third before the end of the year. Matty, Lady Maud… When she glanced at the faces about her it seemed as though she was seeing them through a veil of black muslin such as many of the ladies wore. But Jess wasn't veiled. She had on a simple black bonnet, tied down with long crape streamers. The dark veil was in her mind.

Trying to blink it away, she looked further, and there, at the back of the crowd, one face shone clear, like a beckoning, guiding light: Reuben Rudd's face, wearing the steady look that always gave her new heart. Reuben – the one bright hope in her life.

As the interment ended and the party moved away, Rudd contrived to come close, to say a cheerful word to Bella and make her smile; then he straightened and looked at Jess in that direct, disturbing way he had, saying, 'If you need to talk, lass, you know where to find me.' And he was gone, before she had time to reply.

The invitation remained in her mind, the lure growing stronger. On that day, what she needed most in all the world was to be with someone who cared. And so, while the adult company gathered for the funeral repast, Jess took Bella for a walk, making slowly in the direction of the gamekeeper's cottage.

In May there was plenty to see, wildflowers to pick and identify, nestlings learning to fly, young rabbits bobbing away across sandy banks. Jess hadn't Lily's depth of knowledge, but she had learned a lot and so had Bella – if Jess hesitated, the child often supplied the answer. She soon forgot the mournful occasion they had left behind.

'Look, Jess!' Bella pointed along the grassy lane they were following. Near the stile a black retriever stood, gazing into the field hidden behind a flowering whitethorn hedge. 'It's Dash. Mr Rudd's dog.'

'Looks like him.' Jess's heart gave a little chirrup of pleasure at the thought of Rudd waiting for her, expecting her. But then the dog turned and saw them and started to bark so ferociously that Bella drew back, reaching for Jess's hand.

It couldn't be Dash, Jess thought, placing herself in front of Bella. Was it Bracken? Was Jim Potts somewhere nearby?

The answer came with a low whistle that took the dog wriggling under the stile, out of sight. And away across the field with his master, Jess hoped.

'That's all right, he've gone,' she said. 'Let's hurry. That path to Mr Rudd's cottage en't far away.'

But as she led Bella past the gap where the dog had gone, Jim Potts stepped out from behind the hedge to lounge with arms akimbo on the top rail of the stile, bowler hat on the back of his head, the gap in his teeth showing under the dark curve of his waxed moustache. 'Afternoon, Miss Bella,' he greeted. 'Afternoon, Miss Jess. Lovely day.'

Jess looked at him askance, hurrying on. 'Come along, Miss Bella.'

'Wait! I want a word with you.' As he started to climb the stile, the dog barked. 'Quiet, dog!' Potts snarled, and slapped it with the end of a rough lead he had attached to its collar. He quickly tied the string round the stile, and himself leapt over.

'I hen't got nothin' to say to you,' Jess said, backing off, keeping between him and Bella. 'D'you now leave us alone, or...'

'I on'y want a word,' he assured her. 'That 'on't take a minute. Here, Miss Bella, see what I got here?' He tipped off his hat in the manner of a conjuror, carefully cradling the contents as he displayed them to Bella – six olive-green partridge eggs. Laying the hat in the grass, he grinned at Bella, 'Do you look after them for me whiles I talk to Miss Jessie. We 'on't be long. And don't worry about old Bracken. He 'on't hurt you. His bark's wholly worse'n his bite. Now...' He laid hold of Jess's arm, pulling her away.

Jess resisted, warning, 'I'm now on my way to see Mr Rudd. He're expectin' me. He might come lookin' for me.'

'Then be a good mawther and listen!' He dragged her with him until, several yards from Bella, he released her arm and spitted her on a hard green glance. 'Is that right, what you told 'Liza about that blasted preacher? He're married?'

'Yes, he is.'

'And she en't the first woman he've led astray?'

'Not by a long chalk!'

'I see. Well... he'll be sorry, then. We'll see to him, don't you fret. On'y, I en't about to stand by and see him sent down for murder. A gaol sentence is one thing. Hangin's altogether another. So you ought to know... our 'Liza *was* with him that night. He wan't nowhere near your Matty. Look, Jess... Your Matty was all right. I know he talked to Rudd, but he could a said a lot more'n he did. He could a got us in a lot o' trouble. So, whatever you might think, I wouldn't a seen him harmed. It was him comin' at us with a gun that done it. You start usin' firearms, things get serious – folk get killed.'

What was he saying – that Matty had gone after him and his poacher mates that night? 'Matty never had no gun! Where'd *he* get a gun?'

'Search me. But he had one. He damn near done for Mr Haverleigh – the bullet went through his coat.'

Shock held Jess pinned where she was, like a butterfly on a board. 'Mr Ashton Haverleigh? He was with you… poaching?'

His face darkened as he grabbed hold of her again and pushed her against a tree. 'You repeat this and I'll deny it. You hear? I'm on'y sayin' it because you've a right to know. Yes, it was Ashton Haverleigh. He wrestled with Matty. Got the gun off him. Shot him – before we could stop him. It was all confused, in the dark and the snow… We scattered and I saw Matty fall and that's all I know. I hen't seen Haverleigh since. Nor don't I want to see him ever again, blasted madman. And that's all I'm sayin', now or any time.'

Twenty-Eight

Having tossed his news into Jess's startled face, Jim Potts strode back to where Bella was sitting on the grass. He scooped up his hat and vanished over the stile. Him, and his dog, and the partridge eggs.

'It's all right,' Jess soothed Bella, stroking her dishevelled hair and brushing grass from her white skirts. 'He din't hurt me. Nothin' to fret about. Let's go see Mr Rudd.'

She had to keep calm, for the child's sake, but inside her sickness broiled. Could she believe Jim Potts? Was Ash Haverleigh the guilty one? It had sounded like the truth, but... how could it be true? Matty had used a shotgun, 'times, when he worked with Rudd. But this had been a pistol. Where would Matty have got a pistol?

Only the 'grinning boy', Bob Gooden, was at the cottage, sitting on the front path scrubbing out hen coops in the company of a lively terrier. In the pens, broody hens sat contentedly in their coops, incubating pheasant eggs. Rudd and Obi had gone down to the rearing field, the boy said; they had taken the most recently hatched poults with them on the donkey-cart.

The rearing field lay half a mile away in an open, gladed area of the wood. Shrubs and rough grass, providing cover for the young birds, were enclosed by a wire fence. 'High enough so the poults don't fly over it too soon,' Jess explained to Bella. 'They don't fly very high, or very far, 'til they're a bit older, and then they're put in the woods to roam free.' She hadn't forgotten the lessons Rudd had taught her that first magical summer, before Merrywest turned up and spoiled everything. It all seemed so long ago, like another life. Now she came back with new burdens on her mind, a feeling of wretched helplessness.

When she saw Rudd, behind the wire fence, busy about his work, only willpower prevented her from crying out and running to him.

Dash was waiting patiently outside the gate, though he got up, wagging his tail in pleasure as they appeared. Inside the pen, chicken coops faced all directions, with foster-hens poking their heads out between the slats while their broodlings scampered about the grass, or chased back to Mother at the first sign of danger. By a rough hut where one keeper always spent the night during the raising season, Rudd and Obi were busy sieving hard-boiled eggs and chopping cooked rabbit meat for the poults. The aroma of the food hung appetisingly on warm air thick with midges.

Just as Jess and Bella arrived, a flurry of young poults all took flight, tiny wings whirring madly as they lifted a few feet, sailed a few yards, and landed exhausted, test flight over for that day. The sight made Bella laugh and clap her hands, drawing Rudd's attention, and Jess saw his swift smile of pleasure.

'Come on in,' he bade them. 'Don't let Dash in, though.'

Jess obeyed, and watched as Rudd showed Bella how the food was prepared then let the child help him scatter it. She made a quaint sight in her pure-white mourning dress with her bright hair flowing down her back and tiny birds pecking about her feet.

But to Jess the sunlit day was overlaid by a picture of a dark night, snow falling fast, Matty and Lily parting in anger. Had Matty, patrolling the woods only a short while later, come across a gang of poachers, one of whom had proved to be his hated rival Ashton Haverleigh?

Obi, off back to his cottage to fetch a fresh bag of biscuit and his evening snap – he being on duty that night – wondered if Bella would like to take a ride in the cart with him and say hello to his wife. Bella would, and since it was a means of keeping the child's mind off the horrors of the day, Jess agreed she might go.

'On'y, sit you still and do what Mr Obi say,' she added as Bella ran off beside the dour, loping man.

Rudd breathed a soft laugh, his eyes merry as he lounged against a trestle.

'Somethin' funny?' Jess asked, ready to bridle. This was not the first time someone had laughed when she spoke Obi's name.

'No, lass. Nothing at all. Except… it always makes me smile to hear you call him "Mr Obi". Happen I should have said before – his name's Joybell. Peter Joybell.'

'Then why do you call him…'

'They called him that long before I came here. It's because he's always so solemn and mournful, and with a name like Joybell… "Oh, be joyful" Joybell. Oh, be – Obi.'

At any other time, Jess might have laughed. Now, the joke struck her as meaningless. 'I see.'

The amusement in him died as he scanned her face and noted her tension. 'You know we'll be alone now, till Obi gets back? Don't you want to run after Miss Bella?'

'She'll be all right.'

'Aye, *she* will. But will you, alone with me?'

Wrapping her arms around herself, Jess moved a little away, watching the feeding poults. 'Don't laugh at me, Reuben.'

'I'd never do that,' he assured her softly. 'Happen I'm just happy to see thee. Whatever the reason that brought thee.'

'I en't sure why I came. I wanted to talk to you, but...' It was no good, she couldn't keep it to herself: 'We met Jim Potts on the way. He now say that was Mr Haverleigh as killed Matty.'

Rudd came off the trestle as if stung. '*Haverleigh?*'

'So he say.'

She told him what had happened, in detail, leaving nothing out, ending with a tear trickling down her blotched face and her eyes huge and sad: 'On'y, we can never prove it, can we? Jim Potts'll deny it all, and who'd believe Mr Haverleigh was out with a lot of poachers? And... where'd the gun come from, Reuben?' Shaking herself, she looked away again, tightening the hold she had on herself.

'Here, come and sit down, lass.' Laying his arm around her, he led her into the hut.

The hut was a rough affair with a single door, a small window, a table, two chairs, and a truckle bed where Rudd made Jess sit down. A pot-bellied stove gave off a fair heat and the kettle hanging over it soon began to sing when Rudd placed it on the hob.

Jess took off her bonnet and fiddled with her hair, saying distractedly, 'I was sure Merrywest done it. That would've made sense.'

'Doesn't this make even better sense?' Rudd asked. 'Haverleigh was jealous. Lost his head when he ran up against Matty. Happen the gun was his, too. In the dark, Jim Potts could have mistaken what he saw.'

'Aye, happen,' she wearily echoed his phrase. Her head seemed to be going round in circles.

'We ought to tell the police,' Rudd said. 'Potts might deny what he told you, but we ought to find out. Don't you think so?'

'Oh... I dunno, Reuben. I don't know nothin' no more.'

'Then leave it to me. I'll go and tell the constable what Potts said. If it's not true, Mr Haverleigh ought to be given the chance to deny it, I reckon.'

'Mebbe so,' Jess sighed, too tired to think.

Rudd poured some of the kettle's contents into two tin mugs – it was tea, boiled up with milk and sugar and left to stew all day. Still, it helped, somehow.

Holding the hot mug, Jess stared down into the trembling liquid, saying, 'Eliza must've told her brother I was anxious to know who... I mean, about Matty.' She shrugged, twisting her mouth awry. 'Poor Eliza.'

'Why?'

'She'd got it into her head the preacher'd marry her – until I told her he already have a wife.'

Under his breath, Rudd whistled to himself.

'I en't proud o' myself for that,' she added, her voice thick. 'I was glad to hurt her. Wickedly glad. But then...' She held the mug tighter, feeling its heat start to burn her palms, welcoming the pain as she closed her eyes tightly and said through her teeth, 'I *am* wicked, Reuben.'

She felt him sit down beside her, making the truckle bed sway and creak. 'I don't believe that, lass.'

'That's funny,' she said with a choked laugh, 'I can regret wantin' to hurt Eliza's feelin's, but some things I en't sorry for at all. When I think about Merrywest... Lord, I wish I'd killed him. I *still* wish I'd done it! I know that's wrong and wicked and sinful, but blast! if I'd managed it a lot of this grief wouldn't never have happened!'

With the door wide open they could clearly hear the poults chirping, the hens clucking, the songbirds singing. Rudd's silence strummed louder than the sounds of nature as he leaned across and took the hot mug from her, reaching to set it on the table. He said, 'It's true, then. You did...'

'Oh, yes.' Her voice was hoarse but calm, belying the turmoil inside her. 'Yes, I tried to kill him. I wished him dead. Then, and now. I still wish him dead, Reuben. Because of him...' Taking a long breath, she lifted sore eyes to look out of the window at the moving trees and the bright clear sky. 'He killed my mother,' she said, and heard him catch his breath. 'Oh, not with a knife, or a gun, or anything as sure as that. Nothing you could prove. But he was the cause of it, all the same.'

Once she had begun, the rest just flowed out.

After 'Hardlines' Henefer drowned, Jess's pregnant mother had struggled to bring up a family of five – soon to be six – on her own. Still a young and handsome woman, Sarah Henefer had taken in washing and sewing, working all hours for pennies, determined to manage. Young Matty's earnings from fishing had helped, little as it was, and Fanny had found work in a shop, and then Jess, at the age of twelve, had gone as daily maid-of-all-work to Butcher Bone and his wife. But there had been Sam and Joe to feed and clothe, too, and the latest baby, Sarah-May, until she died of diphtheria.

Merrywest had been their landlord. He owned several properties around the North End of Lynn and he was a strong voice at the chapel the Henefers attended. He took particular interest in the widowed Sarah and her family, often calling round to make sure they had all they needed, and urging the younger ones, especially Fanny and Jess, to attend Sunday school and Bible classes and hymn-singing nights. Jess became a Sunday school helper, telling Bible stories and teaching the youngest ones simple, happy songs. Merrywest made her feel as if she was of real use. She admired him, looked up to him as a kind of second father.

Her sister Fanny had been planning to marry 'Sprat' Fysher when she turned twenty-one. However, with Fanny's twentieth birthday only just past, Mother decided it was time the pair were wed; the ceremony took place without delay. Everyone, including Jess, assumed that Fanny had got herself into trouble – a common enough reason for a rushed marriage.

But Jess, and the rest, were wrong: it wasn't Fanny who was pregnant.

Jess shared her mother's bed and one night, soon after the joy of Fanny's wedding, she woke up to find herself wallowing in warm stickiness. Black stickiness, so it seemed until she crawled out of bed and with shaking fingers lit a candle. Then, the thick wetness, coating her and the bed, footmarked on the floor, showed itself to be blood-red. Her mother was lying in a pool of it. It was pulsing out of her.

Jess remembered her mother's face, blue-shadowed and deathly white as she clutched her stomach, writhing in pain, gasping, 'Forgive me, Jess. Forgive me. Take care of yourself, girl. Don't trust nobody. Not nobody! Understand me?' Jess's arms had borne the marks of her mother's dying grip for weeks.

She'd been old enough to guess what had happened, but if she had any doubts the gossips had soon told her – Sarah Henefer, the respectable widow, had been in sin with a man and had tried to rid herself of the unwanted bastard that would bring shame and disgrace on her name. She must have been to one of the backstreet quacks who did the service, or perhaps she'd used a knitting needle. Whichever it was, she'd paid the price. The Fyshers were among the worst of the critics: no wonder Sarah had wanted her Fanny safely married before the scandal broke, they said; they were respectable folk – they might not have wanted the daughter of a whore in their family. Well, Fanny was now a Fysher, and she must behave like a Fysher and have nothing more to do with 'that woman's' family.

Rudd had listened this far in silence. Now he said, 'They surely didn't blame *you* for it? You and the boys?'

'They did,' Jess answered thickly. 'For a time, they did. There wan't many folk stuck by us, except...' The memories had been dark, but now they grew darker, clouded with hate and self-disgust.

Jess and Matty had decided to bring up the young 'uns between them. He'd found work anywhere he could, while Jess scrubbed, cleaned, cooked, sewed, scrimped and saved. Fanny was too scared of her in-laws to help openly, though she did keep in touch, on the sly. The only adult Jess felt able to turn to was her Sunday school superintendent, the kindly, caring, sweet-promising Preacher Merry-west. He comforted her, and cajoled her to stay and talk after Bible classes, alone with him in the upper room they used for meetings.

'He used to do that,' she recalled. 'Kept his favourites behind – the girls, anyhow. I envied them. I wanted to be one of them. On'y then I found out what he used to make them do, in the little back room where they kept the song-sheets and the banners.'

Rudd looked sick, his freckles standing out and his eyes darting with anger. 'Bloody hell!'

She didn't need to go into detail, thankfully – there was much she could never say, even to him. How Merrywest had persuaded her to allow him deeper and deeper intimacies, assuring her that Lord Jesus himself wanted her to do it, and after he ravished her he silenced her with threats, and forced her to go on meeting him and 'serving the Lord' as he called it; it was a penance she had to pay for tempting him. On Sundays his sermons had held further threats, his thundering voice blasting down at her, his black eyes searing her soul.

One night, after a huge rally when success made him feel all-powerful, he boasted about his conquest of Sarah; he told Jess how he'd threatened to put up the rent beyond her means unless the comely widow allowed him sexual favours. Jess fought him off then and screamed that she'd never let him touch her again. So he forced her, made her do unspeakable things, raped her with more violence than he'd ever used, and left her bloodied and sobbing.

Unbelievably, it was his wife who had come to help her, to wash her clean and soothe her hurts. His wife knew about his depravities. She was just too afraid to go against him. Jess had pleaded with her to tell, but Mrs Merrywest only shook her head and wept.

Then had come the night of the fire – the sudden conflagration in the corn warehouse on the docks, when half the people of Lynn had turned out to watch. That was when Jess had seen Merrywest standing by the edge of the dock, with the ship rearing above him, swinging in the wind. The flare of the fire had joined the scarlet rage in her head and all she had thought was that she wished Merrywest dead. So she pushed him, saw him fall, heard him scream. And then she ran for her life, not caring where she went…

–

At some point during her tale, Jess drank her tea, welcoming its warmth and milky sweetness. Now she stared down into the empty mug, clutching it so hard her knuckles were white. Her head felt blocked with tears that wouldn't come. She only felt numb, and dirty, and ashamed. She wanted to get away from there; she couldn't bear having Rudd look at her, knowing.

'I wish you'd told me before,' he said.

'I couldn't. I couldn't tell nobody. I could hardly even bear to *think* about it. Most of all I was scared Matty might find out. If he'd known, he might've…' But her silence hadn't saved Matty, had it?

That thought brought tears brimming. Aware that Rudd was about to take hold of her, she thrust the empty mug at him and leapt up, rushing out of the hut. The sun's brightness hurt her eyes, made her pause, and when Rudd's hand came on her arm she flinched away, not daring to look at him and see the revulsion she was sure would be on his face. 'No, don't. Don't touch me, Reuben. How can you touch me when you know—'

'How can I not?' he asked, taking hold of her more firmly. 'I love you, Jessie. If I'd known—'

She braced her hands against him to keep him away, her head averted. 'You don't understand! Maybe I *did* lead him on. Maybe I *did* give him reason to think I was willin'. I can't remember. All I know is, ever since that happened I don't feel clean. However hard I scrub, the dirt's still there. He turned me into a whore, Reuben. He turned me into a murderess! I en't worth nothin' no more. I'll never be a proper woman because I can't never let a man touch me. I can't, Reuben. Every time I even think about it, I see him – I feel the pain inside me, and my head feel as if that's goin' to burst wide open with fear and shame and hate and—'

'Jessie!' Throwing his arms round her, he held her tightly to him, held her despite her resistance. She had curled up, her hands in fists, her arms wrapped up across her chest, her head down, her whole small body rigid.

'You can fight me all you like,' Rudd said hoarsely. 'I'll not give in, lass. I'm a patient man, tha knows. And if tha doesn't know, then I'll prove it to thee a dozen times over, however long it takes.'

'No,' she muttered.

'Yes!' he answered, his arms tightening even more as he bent his head to mutter in her ear. 'Dust tha not know I've been waitin' on thee, bidin' my time, for over two years? Ever since I picked thee up out of the brambles and carried thee back to the rectory, a little bit of a thing, all hurt and frightened. All prickles, like a hedgepig. You puzzled me, lass. Intrigued me. I've not understood thee, until now. But now I know, I can fight it. And I will. By God I will! We'll not let that blighter win.'

Slowly, as he talked, Jess found her weary muscles relaxing. Oh, she was so tired – tired of bearing the burden all alone, tired of trying to make sense of it all.

'I love thee, lass,' he said against her temple.

Reuben... She was too full up to speak, but her heart cried his name as she let her arms creep round him, feeling his sturdy warmth begin to seep into her, loosening the frost that had held her soul in bondage for so long. The healing would take a long time, but she might, one day, feel worthy of the love of this man.

Rudd escorted Jess and Bella back to Park Lodge, where they were to pick up Bella's belongings and transfer them back to the big house. Bella had enjoyed her stay at the cottage, being cosseted by Miss Peartree, mothered by Lily and with baby Jabez for company. By contrast the nursery must have seemed a dreary place, especially when it contained old fears and half-understood new griefs.

'Never mind,' Lily smiled. 'You shall come to me every day for lessons and, who knows? In time I may be able to be with you. I – and Jabez too.'

'Oh, my dear,' Miss Peartree fretted. 'You mustn't promise such things. It wouldn't do. It really wouldn't.'

Lily turned her strange, bright eyes on the old lady. Of course she would be going back to the big house – she, and the baby: Richard had said so. 'Why not, Cousin Oriana?'

Since all of them knew why not and none of them understood her smile, an awkward silence fell. Into it, Rudd said, 'You might have to find a new nurserymaid, though, Miss Lily.'

'Oh?' Startled, Lily turned to Jess. 'Why, where are you going?'

'Not far,' Rudd said.

'Reuben!' Jess's protest was a breath. 'I en't yet said—'

'No, but you will. The fact is, Miss Lily, Jess and I are going to be married before long. I won't say she's set the date, but she's thinking about it.'

'Well, that *is* good news!' Miss Peartree cried, impulsively hugging Jess. 'At last, some good news in all this—' She stopped herself, remembering Bella.

The child was looking bewildered, her grey eyes searching one face and then another until Jess bent and hugged her. 'That's all right, Miss Bella, my darlin'. I 'on't be desertin' you yet a while. Come on, let's go see how old Ching's doin'. Mr Rudd'll carry your things.'

'You see?' Rudd sighed, hazel eyes twinkling. 'She's already got me right where she wants me.'

Their news cheered the atmosphere at the cottage and was instrumental in urging Lily to act. Jess was happy: now Lily, too, needed to be sure of her future. For her, one final step remained before her happiness was complete: she had to see Richard again. Most of all she needed to hear him confirm that he shared her dream of their being together openly, in the face of all the world, man and wife before God and under the law. The strength of their love demanded it. Oh, there would be talk. There would probably be scandal. But others had weathered much worse.

'*I have contained my soul, though not in patience,*' she wrote with wry humour in her journal only a few days after Maud Fyncham was buried.

> *How much longer can I wait? I must see him, must hear it from his own dear lips, even if he chides me. He knows I cannot bear to be uncertain. Once I am reassured that he feels as I do, once I know that I shall one day be his wife, then I shall be content to wait, for as long as he wishes. Oh, Richard, my dearest love. Just to see you. To be held in your arms, however fleeting the moment...*

She had no doubt as to when she would go: the calendar gave her the exact date – her chosen birthday, May the twenty-ninth, the day she would officially be twenty years old. Since Richard had not yet seen his son, she would take Jabez with her.

Having lain awake all the previous night, feverish with longing, tormented by doubts and uncertainties, she rose early and took her time over preparing. She donned her costume of turquoise and white – two years outmoded but the best she had; she dressed her son too in his best gown and bonnet, and wrapped him in a shawl, singing to him, kissing his little hands, watching him laugh. How she loved him! Indulging her sense of the dramatic, she placed him in the rush basket in which she herself had been left on the doorstep of the rectory. She had never known her real parents, but Jabez would know his. In time, the world would know.

'I'm taking him for a walk in the woods,' she explained to Miss Peartree. 'It's too rough for the perambulator. Oh... I feel so happy today, Cousin Oriana. The gypsy wasn't wrong – she just didn't tell me the bad things that had to happen before I finally found my *real* heart's desire. Perhaps, even now, my real father will come and find me and then... oh, then, for sure *everything* will be well. *Dear* Cousin Oriana!' She leaned to kiss the startled old cheek. 'Bless you for standing by me. You won't be sorry. I shall never forget how kind you've been.' And she picked up the basket, making little tutting noises at the baby to make him smile before she set off, heading along the drive.

That lovely, smiling morning, Jess and Bella were enjoying the sunshine in the garden – Bella running after a hoop while Jess sat with a basket of mending until, with a thump and a cry, Bella fell headlong on the gravel path, taking the skin off one knee and sorely scratching her face. Jess hurried her back to the kitchen to tend the wounds; all the maids gathered round clucking and fussing and Mrs Roberts soothed the patient with a gingerbread man fresh from the oven. Eventually, Jess led the bandaged child back to the nursery and put her in bed to rest a while, with Ching for company.

She had hardly settled down with her mending, beside the window in the schoolroom, when a disturbance sounded in the passageway, someone stamping up the 'family' stairs, knocking into furniture and walls, sobbing... As Jess ran and flung the door open, Lily appeared, her turquoise bonnet half off, her hair disordered, her face red and her odd eyes wild with tears. She was carrying a basket which, to Jess's surprise, contained the baby.

'Miss Lily—'

'Don't ask!' Lily cried, placing the basket on the table, bending to kiss a tiny hand with hurried anguish. 'Oh, my little love... Take him for me, Jess. Keep him safe. And whatever you do, don't let his father have him! Don't ever, *ever* let Richard Fyncham have him!'

Then she was gone, gay skirts flying as she ran across the schoolroom to the far door, heading for the back stairs. Jess might have gone after her, but Bella was calling her, upset by the commotion; Jess hesitated, pulled three ways – Lily, the little girl, the baby... She picked up the basket and set it on the floor, for fear the baby might roll, then went in to Bella and assured her that everything was all right.

She was lying. Everything was very much wrong.

'*Don't let his father have him...*' The words echoed again and again in her head. Was Jabez, then, Richard Fyncham's child? Dear Lord...

Afterwards, Jess was to remember a time when Lily had said how easy it would be '*just to walk out into the water and keep going. Let it take you up in its arms and sweep you into its depths. Where it's all calm, and quiet. Where there's no more noise and strife.*' The water had always fascinated her, called to her.

This time, she hadn't risked failing in her purpose. This time, she had gone down to the sea, into the fast-flowing channels where the tide was swirling, where the undertow surged with a force that no human could resist. The mermaid princess had gone back to her own.

By a piece of irony, her body was found by a gypsy. The diddicoys had camped a few miles further down the coast that year and it was a few miles down the coast that Lily came to rest, washed up on the beach with her hair wreathed in seaweed. It was said in the villages that when the woman Bathsheba heard the news she wept and stormed and laid a bitter curse on Richard Fyncham's head. Jess wondered at it when she heard.

She herself went about her duties in a state of shock. She'd always liked and respected the squire, but now she despised him. She wondered how she could have missed the signs. Had Lady Maud guessed? Was that why she had been so distraught those last few months? Was that why she had thrown herself off the roof?

She couldn't stay on at the big house, not even for Bella's sake. Sal Gooden took over in the nursery and Jess moved to Park Lodge with baby Jabez. Sir Richard made no objections.

Lily was laid to rest beside Matty, though there was some argument about it, her having taken her own life, but Sir Richard set his stall out and objectors were silenced. So she and Matty were united for ever, in death. It seemed wrong to Jess, but what else could be done?

Amid all the other trials that summer, police investigations into Matty's death continued. Rudd had reported Jim Potts's allegations about Ashton Haverleigh and the detectives came to interview Jess, to hear her version of the tale. But when later they approached Jim Potts he denied having spoken to Jess, denied being out that night, denied poaching... Ashton Haverleigh himself had, it seemed, gone abroad somewhat hastily, but he wrote sending evidence that 'proved' he had been elsewhere that evening. His involvement did seem a bit unlikely, anyway, as the police inspector remarked to Jess. After all, Mr Haverleigh was a gentleman. There'd been enough slander against his name with all the talk about him and Lily Clare. Jim Potts had probably used his name to muddy the waters. Most likely one of the poachers had shot Matty, but the inspector doubted they'd ever find out which man, or why, or how.

Another problem was the pistol that had been used. The bullet had come from a derringer – a small handgun, not common in England. Where had it come from? Who had been carrying it? No one knew.

Most probably, the policeman intimated, no one would ever know.

—

Sir Richard took his daughter away to the Continent. He appointed, and took with him on his travels, a new nurserymaid and a new, older governess who, coming from London, knew nothing of the scandals at Hewinghall. By the time they returned, Bella's head was so full of new things that she had almost forgotten the traumas of the past.

That August, Jess and Rudd were married: it was convenient, and it suited them both, even if it was a little sooner than Jess had expected. She was rigid with fear the first night, but Rudd didn't rush her, only lay holding her hand, talking to her. A night or two later she was able to let him hold her as they went to sleep, and by stages, sweetly and lovingly, he broke down her barriers. In after years Jess often thanked the good Lord for putting Reuben Rudd in her way; he was everything she could have wished for in a husband.

They took Jabez with them to the cottage in the wood. Sir Richard had intimated that he would be happy with this arrangement and would not interfere – in obeying Lily's last wish he was also shrugging off any responsibility, in Jess's opinion, but Jess was happy to have the baby. Officially he was her nephew, Matty's son, but she loved him for himself.

One satisfaction was that in choosing Eliza Potts to join his band of 'handmaidens', Nathanael Merrywest met his match. Eliza was no naive girl to be terrorised by his threats, and with her formidable family behind her she exposed the preacher's sins. Jess, too, spoke up. With her husband's support and encouragement she was a vital witness in the case that sent Merrywest to prison for twenty years, the main charges being several cases of aggravated rape and sexual assault on children in his care. The church and the law demanded a heavy price of a man who would so misuse a position of trust. Even his timid wife took heart and divorced him, and in time remarried happily.

Standing in the dock, flanked by burly policemen, Merrywest was a diminished man, robbed of his glamour, his thunderous voice reduced to a surly mutter. Jess could find no pity for him – he deserved every day of his sentence – but she no longer wished him dead, so at least one sin was removed from her conscience.

Another day in court saw Jim Potts and one of his cousins sent to gaol for six months for poaching and assault, after a fracas when 'Obi'

Joybell was knocked senseless by a bludgeon. He recovered, but after that Rudd became more disillusioned with his job – working all hours, against such odds, raising fine birds only to see them slaughtered; he and Jess decided to leave the bad memories of Hewinghall behind. In the summer of the Queen's Diamond Jubilee, Rudd got his licence to deal in game and they moved, with three-year-old Jabez, to a fine house in the middle of Lynn. In time, Jess even had her own maid-of-all-work, and later a parlour maid too. Sometimes she had to pinch herself to be sure it was true.

She also, at last, swallowed her vanity and acquired a pair of spectacles, which made close work and reading suddenly so much easier, and she joined the library, where she was astonished to discover what new horizons waited to be explored through the printed word. It had taken her a long time, but now she made up for the delay, delighting in educating herself. It made her, she felt, a better wife for Reuben.

Her one continuing sorrow was her failure to bear a child of her own. Reuben said it didn't matter – he said she was enough for him and what with Jabez, and the Fysher brood always in and out, he didn't want for youthful company. But Jess brooded on it for years. She was barren and for both her and Reuben, whatever he said to cheer her, that was a sadness.

Still, they had Jabez, whom they both loved like a son. He grew into a fine young man, with dark curly hair like Lily's, and vivid blue eyes, and an easy charming way that was part Lily and part Richard Fyncham. His tall, rangy frame was all Fyncham. But his name was Henefer and as far as he knew Matty Henefer had been his father. No one in Lynn, other than Jess and Reuben, knew the truth.

Nor did it seem that Sir Richard Fyncham cared. Never in all that time did he enquire after his motherless natural son, though he continued to devote himself to spoiling his daughter.

News of Hewinghall came from Miss Peartree, with whom they kept in touch. The old lady remained at Park Lodge, with Dolly Upton to look after her even after Dolly married Bob Gooden, Rudd's apprentice; he moved into the lodge, too, and continued keepering.

Miss Peartree wrote that Sir Richard was so anxious to protect Bella he had attempted to prevent her marrying, but when Bella turned twenty-one she defied him and became Mrs Gerald Stroud. But she was never strong. The following year, just as war broke out, she died giving birth to her son, Hammond Fyncham Stroud. Sir Richard was desolated.

When the Great War began, Jabez Henefer was twenty. He volunteered at once, much to the despair of his adoptive parents. Jess and Rudd spent three years in daily terror of hearing black news and finally it came, in December 1917: Jabez had been wounded and was gravely ill with septicaemia. The generals sent home a thin, sickly skeleton over whom Jess wept many tears, but Jabez was strong; he fought back to health and while he was on leave, he married his cousin, Fanny Fysher's daughter Bessy. Then, in April 1918, newly promoted to Corporal, he went back to the front, proud and laughing, telling his family that he'd faced his fate and beaten it – the war wouldn't get him.

His young bride Bessy made her home with her aunt and uncle Rudd and they were the first to learn that she was pregnant with Jabez's child – Lily's grandchild, Jess thought. It didn't seem possible.

That summer, while the bloody war still raged, an unexpected reminder of Lily came in a parcel from a firm of solicitors who were dealing with Miss Peartree's estate. The old lady had lived well into her nineties and left most of her belongings to the faithful Dolly Gooden. To Jess, though, Oriana Peartree bequeathed what were probably her most precious, private keepsakes – Lily Clare's journals and papers. Whether Miss Peartree had read them, Jess never knew. In many ways, once she had read them herself, she hoped she had not.

It took her several weeks to get through the journals – some of the scribbled writing was hard to decipher. At times she felt she was prying, so raw and honest were the emotions expressed, but at last she began to understand Lily a little better. The puzzle remained, though, right at the end: the last entry had been written the night before Lily set off for the big house, when she had still been entirely confident of her welcome.

So what had happened between her and Richard? Why had she said that he must never, *ever* be allowed to have his son?

The enigma fled from her mind on a bleak day in November, 1918, with the arrival of a telegram which told them Jabez had lost his wager with fate. He had been killed in the trenches during the final week of that long and bloody war. The shock sent Bessy into labour, and Jess was there with her when her child was born, as she had been with Lily when Jabez was born. Now she held Jabez's son in her arms – Matthew Henefer, the third to bear that name.

What would become of this dear little scrap? she asked herself. No father, no real grandparents...

Subconscious angers and memories must have been working in her. That was why, when she saw in the newspaper that Sir Richard had lost his only legitimate grandson, she felt compelled to write to him, for Little Matty's sake. And he eventually replied, inviting her to come…

Twenty-Nine

So here she was, returning to Hewinghall after twenty-two long years, bringing Lily Clare's grandson to the place where he belonged. She'd never have done it if Bella had lived, or her child, but they were gone; there was no one left but the old man himself.

Maybe old Bathsheba's curse had found its mark.

Unable to stop herself, she bent and tweaked a weed from the crack in the front step, tossing it down by the pram. Little Matty was still sleeping, bless his heart, and the sight of him made her smile, feeling fierce and soft all at the same time. She wanted him to understand, to know that his grandmother had been, not a bad woman, but a driven woman. Driven by hopes and dreams and desires, always searching for something she was destined never to find – a 'real' father, a true love, a place to belong...

Reading those journals had made Jess see that what Lily had been searching for were roots to hold her secure, an identity of her own. Jess didn't want that uncertainty to plague Little Matty. She wanted him to know the truth.

When the door of the big house creaked open again her heart stepped up its pace and she knew she was nervous. 'Sir Richard will see you,' Longman grunted. 'Follow me.'

'Hold you hard.'

She made him wait while she took the sleeping baby from the pram and wrapped him in his blanket. His dark hair lifted slightly on the breeze as he stirred, but he settled again when she nestled him in the crook of her arm. He was going to be tall, as his father Jabez had been – as all the Fynchams were. At seven months old he was a boy any man ought to be proud to own as his kin. Surely Sir Richard would see that.

Following Longman into the gloomy lobby, Jess peered around, curious to see how much had changed. She remembered those wonderful balls, all the glitter of diamonds and silks and candlelight. Now, the big house was dark, with most of the shutters closed. Even in the June heat the place felt cold and smelled vaguely musty, its furniture shrouded in dust sheets that loomed pale amid shadows. Stray gleams of light showed up dust on wooden floors, and drapes of gossamer cobwebs in corners. Mrs Roberts would have grieved to see it.

She wondered what had become of Mrs Roberts and the rest. Some of them she'd had word of, over the years: Eliza Potts had married a Martham man and gone off to Yarmouth to work with the seamen's mission – something of her 'conversion' must have stuck; Jim Potts had made his fortune out of black-market dealing during the war; Sal Gooden was now married to one of the Pratts and had half a dozen grandchildren; and old 'Obi' Joybell was still working at Hewinghall – keepering had gone by the board during the war, but Sir Richard had kept the old boy on as his woodsman. Bob Gooden had joined the Flying Corps, become a pilot and come home covered in glory. He and Obi reckoned there'd be a fine lot of game birds ready, 'time things got back to normal.

If they ever did. Somehow Jess felt sure that nothing would ever be quite the same. The war had destroyed too much.

As she followed Longman up the broad sweep of the main stairs, she marvelled at finding herself there, where she'd never dared tread before. She'd always used the back stairs, occasionally the family stairs, but never the grand main stairs. They curled up through a hallway that lifted to the full height of the house, lit by a great ornate skylight way above. Down the centre of the well hung a long chandelier, its crystal dulled by dust and decked with cobwebs. And there in the corner was the panel which hid the door to the gallery where she'd sat to watch the 'Belladay' ball, when Lily's hopes of Ash had been dashed. Memories caused a catch in her throat as she gained the upper landing and was ushered into the library.

It faced south, bright with sunlight on that day. Before her eyes could adjust, she heard a quiet voice say, 'Thank you, Longman. Now go down and wait for Mr Sanders.'

He was standing against the backdrop of a press full of leather-bound books: Sir Richard Baines Fyncham, in his sixties now, still tall, but thinner than she remembered, his shoulders more stooped. His once-receding hair had lost its battle and given way to a shining pate with a fringe of white hair hanging unkempt over his ears, but fine bones ensured that he was still a good-looking man despite the wear and tear of the years, the fine lines, the deep hollows. As she walked towards him she saw that his eyes were just as clear and compelling, pure light grey with a darker rim to the iris. Perceptive eyes, that saw much but gave little away.

Those eyes regarded her with calm interest, perhaps even with respect. 'Jess Sharp,' he said softly. 'Or should I say Jessamy Henefer? Isn't that the name you threw at Longman? As a reprimand for me?'

Jess almost smiled. He'd read her right: she had meant to remind him of her brother Matty. 'It's Jessie Rudd,' she replied. 'Mrs Reuben Rudd. And this,' pulling back the blanket to let him see the baby's face more clearly, 'is my great-nephew, Matthew Henry Henefer.'

'Henry?' His interest quickened and he stepped forward to look at the baby, staring down at the small sleeping form, his own face working with emotion. When he spoke again his voice was hoarse. 'My first son was named Henry.'

'So was this little 'un's maternal grandfather. Henry Fysher. They called him "Sprat". He was my sister Fanny's husband.'

'Was?'

'He's dead, and so is my sister. Little Matty have no one, except his mother – and me, and Reuben. Like I told you in my letter, Jabez – the boy Lily had – the boy Reuben and me brought up as our own – he... he was killed, last November, before his son here was even born.'

'Yes.' He was staring at the child. The light glinted on a trickle of wetness under his eye that he didn't try to hide – that, or the crack in his voice. 'Yes, you said. You also said he was a fine young man. I wish I could have known him. Did you ever tell him—'

'No, we didn't,' Jess interrupted. 'There wasn't any point in that. As far as Jabez knew, my brother Matty was his father. He was happy enough in Fisher's End. That's where he believed he belonged, where Henefers have been for years. If we'd told him he wasn't a Henefer it would only have made him restless. He might have wanted to come here, to Hewinghall. You wouldn't have wanted that.'

'No.' His mouth made a wry curve. 'No, that would not have helped anything. Certainly not while Bella was alive. Now... even her son is gone. I am left with no one.' He was talking mostly to himself, watching the baby. Little Matty was waking, stretching his arms and hands, wanting to sit up. As Jess propped him on her arm, Sir Richard offered a bony finger and smiled as the small fist closed round it.

Jess saw the baby looking up at the old man with his great blue eyes, and smiling, smiling. Blessed, friendly, placid little man. How she loved him! All at once she wanted to hug him to her and run away; she didn't want to lose him. But she and Reuben had talked through all that. They had agreed – and so had his mother, young Bessy – that Little Matty deserved a chance to reach for the inheritance which had been denied to his father.

For a moment more the squire continued to watch the child, then he looked at Jess, saying, 'I suppose you hate me.'

Hate him? She thought about it. No, she didn't hate him. Not any more. If anything, she felt sorry for him. He was an old man with nothing left but a mouldering old house and no one to leave it to. She could see that he hadn't escaped the suffering – he'd been through his own kind of hell. Well, maybe he deserved it. She was in no position to judge. But the fact remained that he *had* abandoned Lily, and Jabez her son – his son. Whatever his reasons, that had been wholly wrong.

'Your brother found out the truth, you know,' he said. 'He knew the child was mine.'

Jess narrowed her eyes, trying to read his inscrutable face. 'How?'

'Lily told him – yes!' he added swiftly as she drew breath to protest. 'She did, though unintentionally. Matty thought she was still seeing Ash Haverleigh and that Ash was the father of her child. He threatened to go and see him, to do him harm, and Lily panicked and let slip that he had the wrong man. Somehow he guessed that *I* was her lover, and so he came here and… he tried to blackmail me.' Seeing how this news dismayed her, he said gently, 'I'm sorry, Jess. This is hard for me, too. Yes, sit down. There's much more to tell.'

Sinking into the nearest seat, a low armchair in green leather, Jess fumbled one-handed with the fastening of her fox stole and threw it off, suddenly stifled. This felt like a dream. It was here she had sat when Rudd told her how he'd found Matty. In this same chair. Now she sat here holding Little Matty on her knee, and all at once she wondered if she had done wrong to bring him. Maybe it was best for him *not* to know who he was.

Sir Richard had moved across to the window, gazing out across his park, back into the past, to a bitter winter's night. 'You remember there was talk of a burglar breaking in?'

'Yes. George the footman said...' She stopped, realising with cold ants on her scalp: 'That was Matty?'

He nodded. 'He broke in through the garden door. I was in here, in the library, working on some papers, when he burst in. He was drunk, I'm sorry to say. I think he expected me to deny what he accused me of, but I was so taken by surprise I didn't think of it. He demanded a thousand pounds as recompense and payment for his silence. Naturally, I refused. I only pointed out what harm he would do – to my wife, my daughter, to Lily and the child, and to himself – by repeating such a story. He came at me, but he was incapable. He fell across the desk and ended up on his knees on the floor, weeping. I went to look for one of the men to put him out, but by the time I returned he'd gone. He'd ransacked my desk, swept a shelf of books on to the floor, emptied cupboards...'

'I see.' Jess was staring at nothing, imagining Matty drunk and desperate in this room, tearing open drawers in the hope of finding something – anything – to help him get back at the man he hated.

'I didn't know he'd taken the gun,' Sir Richard said.

Jess looked up sharply. 'The gun?' She felt her eyes widen with horror. 'Is that where it came from – from here?'

'It belonged to my wife.' Moving slowly, as if his joints ached, he walked to the desk and picked up an object which had been hidden under a piece of paper. It was a small double-barrelled pistol, a beautiful thing inlaid with mother-of-pearl. 'This gun.'

The sight of the gun raised all manner of dreadful doubts in her mind. She couldn't find words.

'I didn't even know Maud had left it in the desk until she informed me it was missing,' Sir Richard said. 'We couldn't tell the police about it, of course – that would have led to too many embarrassing questions. Maud, you know, thought that *I* had shot Matty.' Shaking his head, he weighed the gun thoughtfully in his hand. 'Strange. Lily thought so too, at first.' His clear eyes met Jess's frankly across the room. 'My wife had suspected I was having an affair with Lily. She was convinced of it after they found Matty – that was why she killed herself. That note she left... it told about my involvement with Lily, and about the gun. I couldn't let the police see it, could I? She knew I had been unfaithful and she believed me to be a murderer because of it. Poor Maud.'

What was he saying? Had he, after all, been the one who shot Matty? Feeling as if she had walked into a trap, she glanced at the door, wondering if she should run.

Sir Richard's mouth twisted into a travesty of a smile. 'No, Jess. God knows I am, and have been, many things that I now regret and despise, but, whatever else I may be, I am not a murderer. Matty must have found the gun, but then he vanished into the night. I never saw him again. Believe me, if I had known he had taken this pistol with him I'd have organised a search for him. I'd have sent for the police.'

'Why?' Her bitterness showed, but she didn't stop. 'You never cared about Matty.'

'He might have used the gun on Lily.'

Of course. Lily. 'Then who did shoot my brother?'

Wearily, Richard Fyncham sat down behind his desk, still examining the gun as if it might provide answers. 'I don't know. I suspect that it was probably as Jim Potts said – that it was Ashton Haverleigh who actually fired the shot. We found the pistol when we cleaned out the ice-house, the year the old king died. Nineteen ten, wasn't it? That's right. Bella turned eighteen, I remember. I gave her a phaeton.' Realising that he was digressing, he sent a rueful glance at Jess. 'Forgive me. Rambling is a sign of old age. You know, of course, that Ashton Haverleigh is dead? Influenza. His widow, Clemency, married Lord Wycherley's son. He's a diplomat. Went out to India. And Dickon Clare died a hero, at Verdun. All of them gone. So many of them...' His face was bleak, suddenly old, lined, tired. 'What were we talking about?'

'You were saying about the gun. They found it in the ice-house.'

'Where it had been thrown, after the murder. Yes.' He opened a drawer in the desk and laid the pistol there, shutting it away; then he sat rubbing his eyes as if they ached. 'It's all so very long ago, Jess. And yet, sometimes...'

'It en't finished yet,' Jess said. 'There was Jabez. And now there's this little 'un, his son – your grandson. You can't put them away in a drawer and forget about them.'

He regarded her with infinite sadness. 'Is that what you think I want to do? Good God...' Wrenching himself to his feet, still lanky and tall despite his bent shoulders, he turned his back on her. 'Good God, if I'd had my way I'd have claimed that boy as my own. Proudly. It was what I intended doing. I had made up my mind. But when it came to it... I couldn't do it without telling Lily the truth. She had to know, too. She had to accept, as I did. I couldn't mislead her. Oh, fool. Fool!' His fist slammed down on the window board.

The sound made the baby jump and Jess held him closer, reassuring him, getting to her feet as she instinctively prepared to leave. She was sure now that she ought not to have come.

But she wanted to know the final answers. What had made Lily abandon her baby and run into the sea?

'*That* was my mistake,' Sir Richard said hoarsely. 'I should not have told her...'

'Told her what?'

He looked over his shoulder, frowning as if he had forgotten she was there; then, 'Come,' he said with a sigh. 'I have something to show you.' He walked unhurriedly over to a corner of the room, pressed a catch and swung part of the bookshelves back into a cavity in the wall, beyond which lay another door. Looking back at Jess with hooded eyes, he said, 'There's nothing to fear, Jess. Now that you're here, before we finally settle this matter, you might as well know it all. Come...'

The further door gave into a big bedroom – his room, by the look of it, cluttered and untidy, shoes scattered on the floor, clothes on the bed, brushes haphazard on the dresser. Ignoring the mess, Sir Richard drew Jess's attention to two portraits which flanked the chimney breast – his children: Harry with the dogs; Bella with the cat, and in the background, demure and yet strikingly beautiful in her governess grey, was Lily.

'I had them put in here,' Sir Richard said. 'I wanted them with me, the ones I loved best in all the world. The children, and Lily. Here, give me the boy.'

Before Jess could prevent him, he had scooped Matty away from her and was taking him to show him the portrait of Bella: 'Look at the cat. See the cat there? And this pretty lady in the corner? She was your grandmother. Your... most dear and beautiful...' Overcome, he held the baby tighter, pressing the little head to his shoulder.

Jess glanced away, her eye lighting on another portrait on the nearer wall, this one a dazzling picture of Lily posing in flamboyant gypsy costume, dripping with gold beads, bangles, earrings. Lily as Jess had never seen her, confident and arrogant, her raven hair flowing in wild curls about bare shoulders, her red mouth smiling and provocative, her eyes challenging. Brown eyes – had the artist corrected that little error of nature? The picture was Lily... and yet not Lily. A strange, alien Lily. Striking though the picture was, Jess found it somehow repulsive.

'When did she sit for this?'

He was taking something from the mantelpiece, something that he secreted in his hand as he looked round, looked at the picture and back at Jess with inscrutable eyes.

'Before I knew her,' he said.

Before... what did he mean? Hadn't he known Lily all her life?

Still carrying the baby in capable, loving hands, he came closer, his eyes on the portrait. 'It was painted by a friend of mine. He fell in love with her, too. When I saw the picture I was captivated. I had to meet her. She was even more desirable in the flesh. Such darkness. Such fire. I believe I would have married her. I was mad enough to do anything for her. But she laughed. She didn't want to be tied down by the sort of life I had to lead. At the end of the summer she vanished, and left me desolate.'

He was not talking about Lily.

Something with the chill of the grave touched Jess's spine and turned her flesh clammy.

'I gave her this,' he said, and held out his hand. On the palm lay the gold bangle which had been left with the baby Lilith – the bracelet with the word MIZPAH inscribed on it, and the initials 'R' and 'S'. 'Her name,' he said, 'was Sheba – Bathsheba.'

'No!' Denying the terrible thing he was saying, she lashed out and caught his hand, sending the bracelet spinning through the air to fall on the rumpled bed. 'No!'

'I'm sorry, Jess, but it's so. The gypsy Bathsheba and I were lovers, one idyllic summer. I was nineteen years old and insane with desire. And then she disappeared. Totally. I was so distraught that my parents sent me abroad and there I stayed for three years, until my older brother's death forced me back to marry my cousin Maud and try to carry on the Fyncham name here. I heard, of course, about the child left on the rectory doorstep, but I thought little of it, I certainly never dreamed she might be *my* child. But there was something about her. That dark loveliness... those flawed, beautiful eyes... that sweet vulnerability... I watched her grow, and I fell in love with her, Jess. I couldn't help myself.'

Jess was backing away, not wanting to hear any more but unable to escape, not when he had Little Matty in his arms, holding him securely, almost hostage, forcing Jess to listen though her head shook from side to side.

'I swear to you I didn't know she was my daughter until the year she finished school. Then Sheba came back.' Remembering it, his eyes clouded. 'A changed Sheba. Changed by being mangled under a cart and mistreated by her various menfolk. She'd suffered a great deal – not least because she'd given birth to a Gorgio's child afflicted with the devil's mark – her own people would have killed the baby, that's why she left her here... It was only then, when Sheba returned, when Lily was eighteen, that I knew she was my child. You must believe that, Jess. Sheba came back and asked me to take care of our daughter. And I tried to. I tried!'

His face was bleak. He looked older than his years, a haunted man. 'By then it was too late. By then, I had grown to love Lily as a man loves a woman, not as a father his child. I tried to resist, but... I loved her. I wanted her. And she loved me, too! Jess, have you never known what it can be like to want someone so badly you can think of nothing else... To lie awake at night... to spend your days in a haze... I had to be with her! Don't you understand that?'

Jess shivered, feeling sickness swell inside her. 'You... you were her father! All her life she'd longed for her real father. She dreamed that when he came everything would be all right. He'd sweep her away somewhere wonderful, take care of her, make everything good...'

That was what had happened at the end! Lily had come running home to be with the man she loved, only to learn this final, unspeakable secret – that her lover was her longed-for 'real' father. That knowledge had been too much for her to bear. Her one last dream, her dearest dream, had been destroyed. Oh, Lily... dear, bruised, damaged Lily...

'I'll take the baby,' Jess got out. 'I'll take him and we'll—'

'No, you won't.'

He pushed her aside as he passed her, heading for the door. Jess stepped on one of the shoes he'd left on the floor and it turned under her heel, sending her sprawling. By the time she righted herself, Richard Fyncham and Matty had gone. What did the old man plan to do with that child? Dear Lord...

Frightened now, her ankle hurting, she wrenched open the door, only to be confronted by the back of the outer door, whose catch was cunningly contrived and defeated her for what seemed minutes. She had to get Matty! If some harm came to him... At last her anxious fingers solved the mechanism. The heavy door, with books stacked on its shelves, swung inward, letting her back into the library. It was empty, but another corner door, diagonally opposite this one, stood ajar.

Jess hobbled across to it and found herself in an empty cupboard with a side panel swinging open, revealing a narrow flight of stairs like the ones on the ground floor that ran up to the gallery. These stairs, though, as she discovered when she opened the panel at the top, came out in the attics, in a corner of the schoolroom right next to the door of what had once been Lily's room. Was that how the squire had come to Lily's bed without anyone knowing? Creeping up these stairs... Oh, shameful. Sinful!

But in Lily's mind, she knew, that love had been something wonderful. Her journals had been full of joy when she wrote about Richard. They had loved each other, right or wrong, and now Jess tried not to judge. She herself had been so lucky, to have Reuben.

The schoolroom remained much as she remembered, except that it was dusty and cobwebbed. Had Hammond Fyncham Stroud, Bella's boy, ever played here? But there was no time to wonder, not with the dormer window wide open and Sir Richard just finishing climbing through on to the roof balcony, taking her precious little man with him. The roof! Oh, dear Lord, please...

In her haste, Jess barked her shin on the sill and stumbled down the last step outside, lurching to grab at the stone parapet to save herself from falling full length. 'Please!' she gasped. 'Sir Richard...'

He was standing peacefully holding the baby, pointing out things in the park – the trees, the grazing cattle, the tower of the church...

'Give him to me!' Jess cried.

He looked at her, and she saw that his eyes were wet, filled with deep sadness. 'Do you think I could harm him, Jess? Blood of my blood, flesh of my flesh. My grandson and my great-grandson all in one. You haven't been listening! You can't see beyond your petty, moralising, little Methodist mind. I *loved* Lily. I loved her in all the ways a man can love a woman. I loved her long before I knew she was my daughter, and I couldn't stop loving her. Yes, it was wrong. You may think it was a sin, but it didn't seem that way to me. Not when I was with her. My stupidity...' He pressed his lips to the baby's head in tender agony. 'My stupidity was in telling her, in expecting her to understand. She was so young, so trusting. I should have married her and let her go on trusting me.'

'Don't say that! That's… wicked!'

'Why is it?' he asked savagely. 'She would have stayed with me, then. She would still be here, where she belonged – here in the home she always dreamed of finding one day. Instead of which… she died, all too soon, and I have spent my life alone, knowing that I killed her. They've all gone – all the ones I loved best. And what do I have left, Jess – what? Nothing except the knowledge of eternal damnation waiting for me because I loved the wrong woman. My daughter. My beautiful, beloved Lily.' Over the child's fluffy dark head, he stared at Jess in anguish. 'Do you believe I could harm all that is left of her – this precious scrap of humanity who is as dear to me as he is to you? I want to acknowledge him as my grandson. I want to name him as my heir. It will be no surprise – after Lily died many people suspected the truth. She *was* my mistress. She was my love and she bore my child. Let the world know that. The rest… The rest only you and I know, Jess. *I* shall never tell. Will you?'

Along the main drive a car was coming, making heavy way over the ruts, its engine sounding louder as it wound between the twin elms.

'This will be my solicitor,' Sir Richard said. 'I asked him to come, to bring the draft of a new will. I hoped you might witness it for me. I intend to name Matthew Henry Henefer, my grandson, as my heir, through Jabez, my natural son by Lily Henefer. He can live here at Hewinghall, if that seems right – he, and his mother, will be welcome. And you, and Rudd, may visit all you please. Or take him back to Lynn, if you will. I shall provide for his education, to be sure he's fitted for the life he was born to.' Fixing her with those clear, compelling eyes, he added, 'I shall do this, Jess, whether you will it or no. One day, he will own Hewinghall. That is his right and due.'

Jess leaned on the parapet, feeling dizzy, trying to think.

'So…' he said as the car drew nearer, 'what will you do? Will you keep my dark secret for me? Will you forget, for Matty's sake? Or will you tell him the truth and damn him for the rest of his life – as Lily was damned?'

Looking at the bright-eyed child as he grabbed for Sir Richard's collar, trying to chew it, she knew she couldn't condemn Matty to knowing the whole, shameful truth. Illegitimacy was bad enough; incest was… unspeakable. So she wouldn't speak of it. What would be the point, except to inflict yet more hurt? Enough damage had been done. Enough lives destroyed.

The car was near now, coming up the last hundred yards. In the courtyard below, Longman was opening the gate to let the vehicle in. And, from the opposite direction, from the west lodge, a man and a woman came walking – she slenderly curved, with long brown hair blowing under a little hat, clinging to the arm of her escort, an older man, sturdy, supportive… Jess's heart leapt at the sight.

'Who's that?' Sir Richard asked.

'It's Reuben. And Bessy, my niece – Matty's mother. They walked round by the coast road because Reuben wanted to look at the woods and call in at Park Lodge to see Dolly Gooden. They said they'd meet me here.'

'Then we'd better go down and join them,' Sir Richard said.